A SUNLIT WEAPON

KU-750-678

By Jacqueline Winspear

Pardonable Lies

Messenger of Truth

An Incomplete Revenge

Among the Mad

The Mapping of Love and Death

A Lesson in Secrets

Elegy for Eddie

Leaving Everything Most Loved

A Dangerous Place

Journey to Munich

In This Grave Hour

To Die But Once

The American Agent

The Consequences of Fear

A Sunlit Weapon

The Care and Management of Lies

a&b

A Sunlit Weapon

A Maisie Dobbs Novel

Jacqueline Winspear

Allison & Busby Limited
11 Wardour Mews
London W1F 8AN
allisonandbusby.com

First published in Great Britain by Allison & Busby in 2022.
This paperback edition published by Allison & Busby in 2022.

Copyright © 2022 by JACQUELINE WINSPEAR

Excerpt from *A Spitfire Girl* © 2019 by Mary Ellis (née Wilkins) and Melody
Foreman reprinted with permission of Frontline Books/Pen & Sword Books
Ltd and the author's estate.

Eleanor Roosevelt quotation by permission of the estate of Eleanor Roosevelt.

All characters and events in this publication,
other than those clearly in the public domain,
are fictitious and any resemblance to actual persons,
living or dead, is purely coincidental.

All rights reserved. No part of this publication may be reproduced,
stored in a retrieval system, or transmitted, in any form or by
any means without the prior written permission of the publisher,
nor be otherwise circulated in any form of binding or cover
other than that in which it is published and without a similar
condition being imposed on the subsequent buyer.

A CIP catalogue record for this book is available from
the British Library.

10 9 8 7 6 5 4 3 2 1

ISBN 978-0-7490-2832-9

Typeset in 10.5/15.5 pt Sabon LT Pro by
Allison & Busby Ltd.

The paper used for this Allison & Busby publication
has been produced from trees that have been legally sourced
from well-managed and credibly certified forests.

Printed and bound by
CPI Group (UK) Ltd, Croydon, CR0 4YY

In memory of Margaret Elizabeth Morell, née Callahan
1918–2012

Margaret, a first lieutenant with the American Army Nursing Corps, volunteered for overseas duty following the Japanese attack on Pearl Harbour in December 1941, and soon after shipped out to England on the RMS *Queen Mary*. Margaret was about to be deployed to the Pacific theatre when VJ Day was announced, and did not return home to the United States until 1946. She was my mother-in-law. Of her service to her country, Margaret told me, 'They were the best days of my life.'

We are in a war and we need to fight it with all our ability and every weapon possible. Women pilots, in this particular case, are a weapon waiting to be used.

– ELEANOR ROOSEVELT

(Eleanor Roosevelt wrote to the US aviation authorities after hearing about the service of women ferry pilots with the British Air Transport Auxiliary. They were among the women working in wartime roles she made a point of meeting during her 1942 visit to the UK.)

Oh! I have slipped the surly bonds of Earth
And danced the skies on laughter-silvered wings;
Sunward I've climbed, and joined the tumbling mirth
of sun-split clouds, – and done a hundred things
You have not dreamed of – wheeled and soared and swung
High in the sunlit silence. Hov'ring there,
I've chased the shouting wind along, and flung
My eager craft through footless halls of air . . .

– FROM 'HIGH FLIGHT,' BY JOHN GILLESPIE MAGEE

(John Gillespie Magee was an Anglo-American pilot with the Royal Canadian Air Force. He was killed in a mid-air collision while flying a Supermarine Spitfire over England in 1941. He was nineteen years of age.)

PROLOGUE

Nick had told her about this feeling; a wild rush, a sensation of utter freedom that seemed to course through the veins with every twist and turn at the controls of a Spitfire. He'd described the way the Merlin engine would rumble away as he swooped down over harvests sunlit in summer and mist-drenched in the grip of autumn. Now Jo Hardy loved the Spit as much as Nick had – hardly surprising, as he'd always said the aircraft was a lady in the air. 'It's a woman's kite, if ever there was one,' he'd told her: compact in the cockpit, easy for a petite feminine frame to get in and get out. But Nick – her tall, wonderful Nick, the RAF officer who had swept her off her feet with his silly jokes and impish impressions of fellow officers – never got out. Nick never had a chance to push back the aircraft's hood with scorched hands and escape the flames as his Spitfire crashed to earth.

So much had come to pass since that day – since she

received the confirming message of his death from her commanding officer. Jo had no more tears to shed now. She had been a WAAF – a member of the Women's Auxiliary Air Force – on duty in the ops room on her shift. Nick knew she was there, headphones clamped to her ears as she scanned the screen in front of her. She was tracking the exact position of the squadron when Nick seemed to lag behind; when, for no apparent reason, he began falling from the sky. She was staring at her radar screen as the other WAAFs turned to her, stunned. Then Nick's voice came in loud and clear. 'I've copped something. Don't worry, I'll land this thing.' There was an easy laugh that calmed her, a few seconds' worth of assurance that all would be well. 'See you later, Josie.' And then he was gone. The dot had vanished. Another pilot down – and there had not been a Messerschmitt in sight.

Jo had not wasted time. Grief was something to be indulged for just a brief moment, because for every tear that ran down her cheeks, there were thousands of bereaved souls shedding more, their hearts broken for dead husbands and lovers, for dead fathers and mothers, and for children killed during three years of war. Her mother had offered fleeting sympathy, and then counselled, 'Well, you've just got to get on with it now, darling. Just get on with it.' Ellen Hardy had considered her daughter's fiancé 'flighty' – and wasn't that an irony? thought Jo, that night as she pressed her face into her pillow and keened her loss. Now the man whose ring she kept in a pocket close to her heart was gone, and her mother was complaining about the means by which Jo had decided to just get on with it – by transferring to the

Air Transport Auxiliary. She'd already learned to fly before the war, indulged by a father anxious to annoy his estranged wife by any means possible, and now Jo was in the air, ferrying fighters, bombers, and training aircraft from one air station to another. She had amassed more hours in the cockpit than Nick had under his belt on the day he died. Yesterday she was at the controls of a Blenheim, tomorrow it could be a Beaufighter or perhaps even a Lancaster, those four massive engines daring her to make a mess of her landing while a gaggle of engineers formed an audience on the ground. Those same men had been shocked when Diana, all five feet two of her, had climbed down from the cockpit of the Lanc she'd ferried to its destination, a bomber station in Northamptonshire. Just Diana, no seven-man crew. That bomber had been lined up for an expert landing by a woman on her own – a woman who had to put pillows on the seat to drive a motor car.

But today – today there had been a Spitfire on Jo's chit. It was the second time she would be ferrying a kite she could take to four hundred miles per hour with ease – if only she were allowed such leeway. But really, who was to know? That first time it took only the usual half an hour with the instruction book, and she'd been up in the air determined to put the Spit through its paces before she landed – with no one around to catch her having some fun. Everyone wanted to fly the Supermarine Spitfire – that's why the American aviatrices came over and joined the ATA even before Pearl Harbour brought thousands of GIs to British soil. Now there was an Argentinian among their number, a Czech, a few Canadians and a Polish girl too, the latter as fearless as her country's fighter pilots who had taken off when the Nazis invaded their country. Those Poles had flown to Britain determined to have their revenge on the Luftwaffe.

Should she risk swooping under a bridge? She had the measure of the Spitfire now and felt like an old hand . . . so, well, why not? Last week when Jenny was delivering a Spit to Biggin Hill, she thought she'd execute a couple of barrel rolls before landing her charge – only to shock the RAF officer waiting on the tarmac, red with temper and at the ready to tear the pilot off a strip for indulging in risky airborne high jinks. There was no love lost between the RAF brass and the ATA. According to a story that had already become legend, the crusty officer was stunned into silence when he saw the aviator pull off 'his' helmet as Jenny clambered down to the ground, revealing long blond hair and a winning smile as she approached him, saluted, and said, 'Good morning, sir. Apparently I've got to shift a Hurricane down to Hawkinge. Mind if I have a quick cuppa before I leave?'

Jo had ferried this route before, and though captivated by the fields and farms below as she crossed into Kent bound for Biggin Hill, she kept a keen eye around and above her. Ferry pilots had no ammunition on board, so if a lone-wolf Luftwaffe pilot came out of the clouds in his Messerschmitt, she'd have to move fast – evasive action was the only option to save her own life and a valuable aircraft. And that was her job, her remit – to deliver an aircraft in one piece, because God knows they couldn't lose any more aeroplanes or pilots.

At last she saw the bridge – they all knew where it was,

a railway bridge high enough and wide enough for a thrill. Ease up on the throttle, bring down the nose, level flight under the span and then open her up and climb fast on the other side. Jo felt the rush of adrenaline hammer through her body as she pulled up the Spitfire, the carburettor flooding the engine with fuel for sudden acceleration. She began to laugh. She hadn't laughed in so long, it was as if shackles were beginning to fall away from her heart. Turning the Spitfire, Jo swooped in low over the fields. That's when she heard it – a crack aft of the Spit, as if something had snapped, or she'd hit something – or something had blown or flown into the aircraft. She reduced speed, turned and swooped low again, just to make sure she could climb, relieved when she realised she wasn't losing fuel nor was she on fire. Perhaps it was a bird, or just one of those sounds that seem to come out of nowhere to keep you on your toes – the gods of flight making sure you were paying attention.

Then she saw him. A man standing by the open door of a barn in the middle of a field, his firearm pointed skyward. She pulled up again and then came in low – but not too low – for another look. And he was firing once more, as if a mere bullet could bring her down, though she knew as well as anyone that a bullet could bring you down if it caught an aircraft in the wrong place.

Jo Hardy manoeuvred her ship once more to loop around the barn, just as another man ran from the open doors to grab the man with the weapon, still pointed skyward. Losing not a second, she identified her landmarks. There was the bridge, and there was a farmhouse. There was the road – and the railway line running close by. The corner of the field was at a fork in the road. Yes, she could find this place again, her mind a map and the coordinates memorised as if she'd pressed pins into paper. Someone had tried to shoot her down, and for once it wasn't a German – and it wasn't a crusty old RAF officer who thought women had no business flying aeroplanes and who used words and official reports as the weapon of choice. Someone had it in for the pilot of an aircraft flying low across the skies over the Garden of England.

Consulting the map spread across her lap, Jo Hardy sat alongside her friend Diana 'Dizzy' Marshall, who was perched on the pillow that allowed her to see over the steering wheel from the driver's seat of her mother's Riley Nine motor car.

'I hope this isn't too far, Jo, I've barely enough petrol to get home, and I'd like to have a bit in the tank so we can drive down to the White Hart later. There's that dishy pilot officer I have my eye on. Thank goodness we've another day off tomorrow. We can languish at the house before driving back to Hamble for our next duty. I've been flying for three weeks straight, so I need a long lie-in.'

'Hmm, yes,' said Jo, staring out of the passenger window. 'Look! Here we are, Dizzy! Yes, turn here. This is the fork in the road. You can park over there, on the verge.'

'Righty-o,' said Diana, turning the steering wheel.

Jo folded the map as Diana pulled onto the grass verge and turned off the engine. 'It's across that field.'

'And how do we know there's not a nutter in there ready to hold a gun to your head?'

Jo rested her hand on the door handle, then stopped. 'You're right, Dizzy. Though seeing as it was a few days ago that a joker started taking potshots at my Spit, I'm sure whoever it was is likely to have moved on. Anyway, you stay here, and if I'm not back in about twenty minutes, then raise the alarm.' She looked at her wristwatch. 'Five minutes to get over there, five minutes back, and ten minutes in the barn, at the most.'

'All right. I'll stay here. Twenty minutes, at the outside. I'll read the newspaper to keep my mind off you and also work out how I am supposed to raise an alarm in an emergency when we're in the middle of nowhere.'

Jo laughed, picked up her knapsack and stepped out of the motor car, turning to her friend before she slammed the passenger door. 'I think you should lock the doors, old girl, just in case.'

'Good idea. And when I see you running across the field again, I'll have the engine purring, ready for a quick getaway!'

'Very funny!'

Except I wasn't actually joking, thought Diana, as she watched Jo Hardy cross the narrow country road, clamber over a five-bar gate and set off across the field.

Jo could see the barn in the distance. She'd circle round, she thought, to make sure there was no motor car outside, or anything indicating danger inside. Approaching the barn, she slowed her pace and tried not to make squelching sounds in the mud as she lifted each booted foot and put it in front of the other. She stopped to survey the landscape; a blue-grey afternoon mist hung listless over autumn fields left barren after the harvest. The sun was just a circular outline in the sky, as if a penny were being held aloft behind gauzy cloud cover. She lingered at the rear of the barn and put her ear to the wood. Nothing. Creeping along towards the corner, she held her breath and peered around. Again, nothing. No sounds, no sign of human presence.

She exhaled. 'Right, Jo Hardy – galvanise yourself,' she whispered. 'Someone tried to take you down, so it's time to see if you can find out who and why.'

Jo shimmied along the side of the barn towards double doors that were old, heavy and moss-covered, with rusty hinges. She took a quick glance at the bolt, which appeared to have been left open, though when she tried to pull back the left door and then the right, they refused to budge. An overnight storm and the shuffling of cattle coming close to a food source had kicked up mud against the base of the doors, rendering them almost impossible to move.

'Didn't think I'd need a shovel,' Jo whispered to herself. She shivered, an unaccustomed feeling of vulnerability leaching into her bones. She gave the left door one last pull. 'Blast!' The word came out louder than she intended. The last thing she wanted was someone with a cosh to come up behind her.

She was about to turn around and run as fast as her legs would carry her towards the five-bar gate and Diana in the motor car when she heard a whimper. She stopped, listened again. Another whimper, though now it seemed more like a moan. Was it a trap? She made her way along the rear of the barn until she was sure that what she had heard wasn't just a breeze skimming across the roof. She swallowed hard. Diana would be waiting, watching the minutes pass.

'Is anyone in there?'

This time the sound was more akin to a wail – the wail of someone who could not scream.

'Oh God. Oh dear—' Jo looked down at the base of the barn, at the worn and rotting wooden boards, soaked through and coated with a good century's worth of mould.

'Right—' She began tearing at the planks, surprised when the first came away with ease. Then the second. She glanced towards the heavens. 'Nick, if you're up there, help me or tell me I've lost my marbles and I should run like mad.'

No voice came out of the ether with a ghostly warning for Jo Hardy, so she pulled the next board and the next, the sodden wood giving way to a strength she always knew was inside her, but she'd never had to use. Soon there was enough of a hole at the back of the barn to crawl through.

Light from a fallen roof beam illuminated bales of hay and the remains of a fire on the ground. As she knelt down by the ash and blackened wood, Jo wondered what kind of fool would light a fire in an old barn. Then the moaning started again. She felt sick as she came to her feet. The sound was coming from behind the bales. Now she could hear her own heartbeat, as if it were swishing through her ears. She continued to approach the source of the noise with caution, craning her neck without entering the space behind the bales – she had to be ready to get out, and fast.

'Good Lord!'

The man on the floor was bound hand and foot, with a scarf tied tight around his mouth and a blindfold across his eyes. He whimpered, appearing at once terrified and grateful.

'All right, don't worry, I'll get you out of here.' Jo fell to her knees, and began to work the knots on the blindfold. 'Blast!' She reached into her knapsack and pulled out a penknife, which made a snapping sound as she opened the

18

blade. The man flinched. 'I'm not going to kill you, just hold on, and I'll get you out, and then we have to move like lightning, because whoever did this to you might be back soon.'

Diana fidgeted and checked her watch again. Fifteen minutes gone and five remaining – and they were ticking away fast. She drew down the window to clear condensation forming against the glass, and looked across the field, her brow furrowed. That was when she heard another motor car approaching. She closed the window and ducked down, only to hear the vehicle slow, but not quite stop, before continuing on. She sat up as the motor car turned the corner ahead.

'Bloody hell – he's going to the barn. Oh for heaven's sake hurry up, Jo! Hurry-hurry-hurry, you lunatic woman!'

Diana fought the urge to leave the Riley, ready to yell out a warning across the field, when she saw two figures running towards the gate, one holding onto the other. She started the engine, feeling her stomach lurch as her hands began to shake. She would rather be taking off in a new aircraft than sitting here in the driver's seat of her mother's motor car. She revved the engine, watching as Jo climbed over the gate – but the man faltered, slipping back, before trying to gain purchase again.

Holding her hand to her mouth she watched, Diana saw Jo lean over the gate in an effort to help the man by taking his arm. Then, as if frustrated by the loss of momentum, Jo grabbed the man by his collar and half dragged him over the gate. Pulling his left arm around her shoulder and with her right arm around his waist, she supported him as they staggered across the road. It was clear he had lost all strength in his legs. Diana leapt from her seat to open the rear passenger door.

'Let's get out of here, Dizzy, and fast,' said Jo, bundling the man into the Riley and slamming the door.

'Right,' replied Diana, taking the driver's seat once again and glancing at their passenger in her rear-view mirror while Jo took her place and slammed the door. 'And then when I've been as sick as a dog all over mother's pride and joy, you can tell me where that poor man came from – and what we should do with an American soldier. I wonder if he's a deserter.'

'I ain't no deserter, ma'am. And I saw them take my friend Charlie and I heard them say they were going to kill him, and I reckon they meant to do it.' He gasped back tears. 'Charlie ain't like me. No, ma'am – he's a white soldier. I pray they don't think it was me who did wrong.'

Diana's fingers became blue on the steering wheel, so tight was her grip. She leaned forward as if to make the Riley go even faster, and was about to speak when Jo turned back to the man.

'Whoever "they" are, I'm pretty sure they tried to kill me too – so I will vouch for you.'

'Won't do no good, ma'am. Won't do no good at all.' He began to weep. 'And he was my friend.'

The tears running down the man's face persuaded Diana that the American Jo had just dragged weak with fear from a barn in Kent probably had a better idea of the fate awaiting him, despite any vouching on her friend's part.

CHAPTER ONE

'So, what happened to the poor man after you handed him over?'

The young woman, First Officer Erica Langley, was wearing the navy-blue-and-gold uniform of the Air Transport Auxiliary, as were her three companions. They were awaiting their instruction chits for the day, surrounded by their fellow service pilots chatting in clusters. Some might be flying three or four different aircraft, one after the other, from a bomber to a fighter or a training aircraft, perhaps direct from the factory, or returning the aeroplane to an engineering unit for repair.

Jo Hardy sipped from her mug of hot, strong tea and winced. 'Ugh.' She shuddered before continuing her story.

'Well, the MPs at Biggin Hill got onto the Yanks, and that was it – it wasn't long before a Jeep came whizzing along and picked him up.'

'He'll be lucky to get away with his life, make no

mistake,' said Elaine Otterburn, a Canadian aviatrix who had ferried a bomber into Britain, another workhorse for the RAF. Otterburn and her co-pilot had flown via Gander in Newfoundland and Shannon in Ireland.

Jo and the two British pilots looked across at the Canadian, who had an air of assured maturity, and was known to harbour a certain disregard for the rules. They all knew Elaine Otterburn, who would remain in Britain until she and her Canadian co-pilot had orders to join a return flight across the Atlantic because there was another bomber to fly to Britain following manufacture at a Canadian factory. The aviatrices were a little in awe of Otterburn, not least because she was an excellent pilot, well versed in what they called 'airmanship.' Not everyone would want to bring a bomber across the Atlantic, or put up with the indignity of having to wear – of all things – a nappy! Elaine had once suggested that it was all very well having a bomb bay, but why hadn't some bright spark aircraft engineer thought of a lavatory?

'What do you mean?' asked Jo, taking up the conversation. 'We know the Yanks have an attitude towards the colours mixing, but surely—'

'They still go in for lynching, down there in America,' said Otterburn. 'Didn't you know the Americans asked Churchill to institute segregation in Britain before they sent over troops? Old Winnie isn't without his prejudices – we all know that – but there's regiments from across the bloody Empire here, to say nothing of civilians, so how could the old boy have agreed to dividing the country by colour?' She shook her head and drew from a cigarette. 'Bloody stupid, if you ask me. All the same, remember this – what the Yanks do on their bases is their business. It's pretty much seen as US soil on British land.'

'Blimey,' said Diana. 'So the man Jo found in that barn will get sent back to the USA? He said his pal might be dead, yet as far as we know, no one has found a body.'

'*As far as we know*,' said Jo. 'That pretty much sums it up. But let's face it, no one's going to let us in on the outcome just because we found the soldier.' She looked at the clock and came to her feet. 'Better not drink any more of this, otherwise I'll be the one needing a nappy for a short run across England!' She set her mug on the table and turned to the Canadian. 'Elaine, I'm fairly determined to find out what happened to that man, not only because I'm pretty sure I saved his life – you should have seen the state he was in when I found him – but I saw his fear too. And remember why I was lurking around that barn in the first place – a man on the ground outside the barn had taken a potshot at my Spit, and at the time I was low enough for it to cause a bit of damage. Not that I can admit my fun and games, because I shouldn't have been skylarking around in the first place.'

'We've all done it,' said Erica Langley.

'Jo, don't be stupid – this is a job for the police,' said Diana. 'Just let them look into it. Drop the whole thing.'

'Dizzy, my problem is that having looked into his eyes, I don't think I can just drop the whole thing. I felt awful for that poor soldier. I've thought about going back to the barn and poking around a bit more; see if I can find anything to support his story. Perhaps even talk to the farmer. I heard from Gillian, who took a Spit to Biggin Hill yesterday, that the word over there is that some American military police had a look around the barn, and it was decided the man – his name is Private Matthias Crittenden – could have done everything himself. Apparently, there's a sort of knot that goes from loose to tight with just the flick of a wrist. If you've got everything else in place, it's the last thing you do if you want it to look as if someone else tied you up. Magicians do it all the time, apparently. Frankly, he didn't look the sort to have a go at something like that, and with that cotton shoved in his mouth, every time he tried to speak it made him choke. Anyway, from what I saw of the military police when they came to collect the soldier from Biggin Hill – they turned up driving one of those upholstered roller skates they call a Jeep as if they were in a chariot – it struck me they might be fast to make a judgment about the missing soldier and who was responsible. But that's just my opinion.'

'I couldn't believe they asked us if Private Crittenden had attacked us. I mean, the poor man could hardly stay on his feet, let alone get the better of anyone!' Diana shrugged.

'Hello – look who's on her way.' Elaine Otterburn pointed to a woman in uniform making her way towards the mess. The officer seemed tired, circles under her eyes testament to the constant pressure of scheduling ATA pilots to deliver multiple aircraft, and to getting those pilots into position to do their job. 'Here come our marching orders,' she added.

'Ladies, it's a nice day for flying!' exclaimed the officer as she crossed the room, handing out the chits informing each pilot of their instructions for the hours ahead.

'Righty-o, First Officers Otterburn and Hardy, here you go. You're taking a couple of Hurricanes to Hawkinge – the Anson air taxi is outside now to fly you over to collect them from maintenance, so jump to it because the pilot wants to get in the air and back here again for another lot. Marshall, lovely job for you – a Wellington to Hendon and a rare chance to impress the lads on the ground – the Anson taking you is coming up behind number fifteen hundred. And last but never least, Langley, it's your lucky day – a Spit from the factory to Biggin Hill. There's a motor car ready to take you over to Trowbridge to pick up your kite – you'll probably be back before anyone else, but remember, no trying to see just how fast you can take her, no victory rolls, and don't go under that bloody bridge, whatever you do. Make sure you bring her in for a nice, smooth landing, and don't show us all up in front of the RAF.'

'Ha! I've got the winning ticket, ladies!' said Erica, slipping the chit into the pocket of her Sidcot suit. 'Nice day for flying indeed.'

'Billy, sit down, please. You're only getting yourself into a lather.'

Maisie Dobbs, psychologist and investigator, looked across the room towards her assistant, Billy Beale, who was pacing in front of the floor-to-ceiling window looking out over Fitzroy Square. 'I know MacFarlane said he would be here by half past ten, and he's rarely late, but perhaps he's just been held up.' She glanced sideways at her secretary, Sandra, who shook her head. Maisie nodded and pressed on, taking a deep breath to remain settled on behalf of the less than calm Billy Beale. 'Well, until he gets here, I'm going to my desk to clear a few things that came in from last week.'

Billy Beale said nothing as he continued pacing, pausing only to stare out the window towards the square. His features were drawn, his once wheaten-blond hair now grey. His jacket seemed to hang on a frame that had always been slender, but now revealed a weight loss that could only have come from one quarter – a profound state of worry.

Sandra raised an eyebrow. 'Here you are, miss – the ledger from last month. There's a couple of overdue bills in there. I think I should send a second letter.'

'Right you are, Sandra,' said Maisie. 'I'll have a quick look first, just to make sure we're not nagging people who have lost their homes, or who are grieving.'

'He's here!' Billy shouted, turning from the window and all but sprinting to the door.

'Billy—'

'Miss, I've got to go down and let him in.'

'I know . . . but I want you to remember this, Billy. Although Robbie MacFarlane has a lot of information at his fingertips, he doesn't know everything, and anything he knows is always subject to an element of doubt.'

Maisie saw Billy's face crease as he left the room, his footfall heavy while descending the staircase to the building entrance, ready to let in the man who might give his family hope, who might tell him his son – the soldier they still called 'young Billy' – was alive.

'I hate to say it, but not having any news at all is worse than getting a telegram with bad news,' said Sandra, placing a sheet of paper in her typewriter. 'Billy's limp is more evident than it's been in a long while, and I'm amazed Mrs Beale is holding up, especially with the other one an engineer on bombers.'

Maisie nodded, moving closer to Sandra's desk. She kept her voice low. 'Doreen's had a lot on her plate over the years, and though I feared for her when news of the fall of Singapore came through, I have seen her resolve become stronger – plus she has Margaret Rose to consider. Billy's love of his family will keep him on his feet. And so will we.' She looked up, turning to greet their guest as he appeared in the doorway.

'Maisie – good morning.' Robert MacFarlane held out his hand to Maisie, the slight shake of his head signalling a warning. He nodded towards Sandra, who had come to her feet.

'I was just about to make a pot of coffee,' Sandra said. 'We still have some from Miss Dobbs' stash. Would you like a cup?'

MacFarlane turned to Maisie. 'Is it the good stuff old Blanche liked, from that place in Tunbridge Wells?'

'Ground Santos beans – Maurice's favourite,' said Maisie. 'I managed to buy some a little while ago, but it's remained fairly good in the tin. We only use it when our most esteemed associates visit.'

'Count me in, then. If I'm not esteemed, who is?' He pointed to Maisie's office. 'Let's get on with it, shall we?'

With Billy and MacFarlane in her private office, Maisie

closed the accordion doors, taking a seat alongside Billy to face MacFarlane, who clasped his hands atop the long table set perpendicular to Maisie's oak desk. It was the table upon which a length of paper would be pinned in the midst of an investigation, where Maisie would begin to draw her 'case map,' a record of everything discovered in the course of their work.

'Tell me, Mac. Just tell me straight,' said Billy.

Maisie registered their guest's barely raised eyebrow – Billy had only ever referred to Robert MacFarlane respectfully as 'Mr MacFarlane' or 'Sir.'

'Here's what we have, Billy – it's precious little, I'm afraid. And let me tell you, it's more than most in your position would be privy to and must be received with care. The Japs are being . . . are being . . . *obstructive* with regard to the Red Cross obtaining information on our boys caught in Singapore, but we have some intelligence coming in, and of course we've matched it to any scraps discovered by the Red Cross.'

'What about our son?'

'As far as we know, the news is fair. We know he is still alive, but he was transferred from Changi Prison – which was where many British, Australians and Canadians have been held – and now he's on his way to Burma.'

'What?'

'The Japs don't just let the men sit there starving in prisoner-of war-camps – they put them to work. I'll be honest with you, there have been tremendous losses – torture, starvation, dysentery, malaria – but your Billy is still alive.'

Billy leaned across the table towards MacFarlane. 'Can

you get him – and the others – out?'

'No. No, we can't.'

Billy placed his hands on either side of his head, as if the information imparted by MacFarlane was too much for his imagination to bear.

'What will happen to him? What will happen to my boy?'

'Billy, your boy is a man now, and a very strong man into the bargain. He came through Dunkirk, and there's others who were with him then and who are with him now. There's strength in those connections among the men.' MacFarlane pressed his lips together and looked down at his hands before bringing his attention back to Billy Beale. 'I'll wager your son will come through. As long as he understands the best thing to do with the enemy in this situation is to keep your head down, look after yourself and your mates, and do what you're told.'

Billy shook his head. 'My boy has always had a quick tongue. I told him when he was a nipper that he'd have to wind his neck in or someone would chop it off for him.'

Maisie had been silent throughout the exchange, but turned to her assistant and rested her hand on his arm. 'Billy, you understand your son better than anyone, but Robbie is right – he's a man now. He's not stupid, he learned his lessons, and as Robbie said, he's come through Dunkirk, so he will come through this. Now you have to do your bit. Keep your family strong, because he's going to need you all.'

Billy scraped back his chair and walked to the window, hands in his pockets. Then he turned to MacFarlane.

'Thank you, Mr MacFarlane. Thank you, sir, for finding out about my son and for coming here. I'm grateful. Now if we could only get Bobby out of that bloody Lancaster bomber without him having to go down in it, then we'll all be there for Billy when he comes home.'

MacFarlane took a deep breath. 'There's thousands out there with the same bone to gnaw away at, Bill – thousands of mums and dads, sweethearts and boys and girls. Anyway – I've to get on.' He glanced at Maisie and motioned towards the door, stopping to shake hands with Billy and once again nod towards Sandra, who had only just returned with four cups of coffee.

'Any chance of taking it with me, hen?'

'Hold on, I'll pour it into a mug,' said Sandra. 'That might be easier for you.'

Maisie followed MacFarlane – now holding a mug of steaming, aromatic coffee – down the stairs to the front entrance. A black motor car was parked on the flagstones outside, waiting for MacFarlane.

'I'm sorry there wasn't better news, Maisie,' MacFarlane said, before taking a sip of coffee. 'Oh, that's lovely.' He took another sip. 'Lass, I don't need to tell you that it's been a bloody disaster since the Japanese moved into Singapore.'

Maisie nodded. 'It wouldn't be so bad if Billy hadn't clung to the idea that his son was safe in a jammy posting, doing a bit of square bashing and drinking fruity cocktails.'

MacFarlane shook his head. 'No one's having fun in this war, Maisie – well, perhaps a few flyboys when they're on the ground, and then they're lucky if they come back again after they've taken off. Pity his other lad was determined to get into bloody bombers, though I understand he's a clever engineer.' He raised his forefinger to his driver as he held the mug to his lips with the other hand. *One more minute.* 'Something else we found out. Young William Beale put his name on his attestation papers as "Will". I wondered about that, so I did a bit of nosing around, found an old mate of his who was medically unfit after Dunkirk, and he said it was the son's way of being his own man – he was fed up with being "young Billy" or being called "a chip off the old block." Mind you, you'd know more about that sort of thing than me, wouldn't you?'

Maisie opened her mouth to speak, but MacFarlane went on. 'Anyway, from everything we know, it will be a bloody miracle if the lad comes home again.' He passed her the mug. 'Mind taking this for me, hen? Lovely drop of coffee.'

Jo Hardy maintained level flight on the port side aft of Elaine Otterburn. If she were honest, she had always kept the Canadian at arm's length in the mess and she found it difficult to converse with her, their exchanges lacking the ease and banter she enjoyed with her fellow pilots. Yes, she'd heard the Otterburn name; Elaine clearly came from privileged stock, but so did most of the women in the ATA – how else could you afford to fly before the war, unless you had money to throw into thin air? But there was talk that Elaine had already made her mark as an aviatrix, before the war evacuating an important person out of Munich. It was all a bit hush- hush, so Jo thought it might be best not to know any more than that. Elaine had a son too, a boy now in Canada with her mother, sent over there for his own safety.

Jo kept her thoughts under control as she approached Hawkinge, landing seconds after witnessing the Canadian demonstrate a perfect wheels-down. She brought the Hurricane to a halt alongside Elaine, who gave her a thumbs-up from the cockpit, and as if her hand were clutching a mug, she made the time-honoured sign that it could be time for a cuppa, if not quite the hour for something stronger.

Elaine and Jo walked towards the office where they would present their chits for signature by an officer, proof that the aircraft had been delivered and at what time. They talked about the cloud coming in, the fact that they both quite liked a Hurricane and how long it might be before each had another short leave. Running their fingers through hair flattened by their leather flying helmets, they were laughing as they entered the office – straight into a wall of silence. No jocular banter greeted them, no 'all-in-good-heart' critical commentary on their landings from RAF men. Just a poker-faced squadron leader and a pale WAAF clerk.

'What is it?' asked Jo.

'You two look like you've just seen Goebbels landing with the Führer,' added Elaine.

'Hardy, Otterburn. I've had your superiors on the blower, and I have some terribly bad news, I'm afraid. Bad for you and for us. I believe you were both with First Officer Erica Langley this morning.'

'Erica? What about her?' demanded Jo.

'What's the matter?' asked Elaine, whose pallor now resembled that of the WAAF clerk.

The squadron leader turned to the clerk, not bothering to hide his disdain. 'I cannot abide bloody emotional women – shouldn't be allowed up in an aeroplane in the first place. You can deal with it.' Having delivered his opinion, he marched to the door, slamming it on the way out.

The WAAF clerk cleared her throat. 'First Officer Langley came down in farmland not terribly far from Biggin Hill. Perfect weather, no enemy aircraft in the area. It's been speculated that she was—'

'Being reckless?' snapped Elaine Otterburn. 'Is that it? So what if she was? For God's sake, we've all done it. But we're not bloody amateurs. We know what we're doing, and most of us have far more hours in different kinds of aircraft than your flyboys. She's come down on a good day in the air – is she all right? In hospital?'

'Look, we weren't born yesterday,' said Jo, her temper salted by Elaine's. 'You can tell us what's what, and you don't see either of us bawling because one of our number had to land in a field, do you? I mean, it wouldn't be the first time – there's not a failsafe aircraft in the sky.' Despite her indignation, she was already feeling a sense of dread in her gut.

'Don't have a go at me, for heaven's sake! I'm only the bearer of bad news,' said the clerk. 'We only just heard it anyway, and we're being good enough to let you know. Biggin Hill has jurisdiction, and according to the report, there's nothing to indicate anything but pilot error. Langley was killed in an instant, and the Spit is – well, that's another one off the books. Another one we needed up there instead of in bits across a field.' She picked up a folder, clutched it to her chest and left the room, her eyes reddened by unshed tears.

'I don't believe it!' said Jo Hardy, on the train to London. The women were back in their distinctive navy-blue-and-gold uniforms of tailored jacket, trousers and caps, their warm Sidcot suits rolled up and stashed in canvas kit bags. 'I wish I knew what to do, because I can't help feeling Erica could have been brought down by the same bloke on the ground with a gun. And then there's the poor man I rescued from the barn. He seemed absolutely sure he'd be under suspicion for having something to do with his friend's disappearance. I reckon he must know something about the man with the gun – even if he was blindfolded, he must have heard something.'

'Jo, we have no idea what happened to Erica. And it's a long shot that your man in the barn knows anything.' Elaine paused. 'Sorry, I didn't mean that to come out like a bad pun,' she added, lighting a cigarette. They sat in silence for a couple of minutes before she spoke again. 'But I do have an idea for you – because, frankly, you're a pilot, not some sort of sleuth.'

'Go on,' said Jo, her voice becoming testy. 'I'm all ears.'

'You should talk to a woman named Maisie Dobbs.'

'Oh dear, she sounds like a parlourmaid.'

'Don't be so bloody stuck-up, Hardy – you Brits are all the bloody same.' Elaine blew smoke out the open window, and shook her head. 'I learned "bloody" at boarding school in Sussex. No wonder I was kicked out.'

Jo sighed. 'Sorry – we're both a bit wound up. Go on, Elaine, please continue. Clearly I'm out of my depth, and all I have is a hunch.'

'Just as well, because Maisie Dobbs is the only person I can think of who might trust your hunch.'

'I said I'm sorry! Now then, tell me who she is.'

'She's a psychologist and a sort of investigator. She's worked with Scotland Yard – they ask for her assistance, not the other way around – and I have it on authority, though I am not supposed to know this, that she is also . . . also *associated* with the secret service.'

'And how do you know her?'

'It's a long story, but – oh, Lord, here goes.' Elaine drew from her cigarette again. 'It was my fault that her first husband was killed. Then to add to the deficit in my moral account, a few years later she kindly saved my life in Munich, before the war. It was an act of extreme forgiveness and resulted in me taking responsibility for my son, which was long overdue. I ended up meeting my husband through her. He's British, an engineer back home in Canada now – war work – though when we met he was assisting one of the men I brought out of Munich, one of those clever boffins. That's all I can say about it.' She came to her feet, threw the remains of her cigarette out of the window and closed it before taking her seat again. 'Maisie Dobbs should have been the second passenger, but gave up her seat for someone else, a man she claimed needed it more than her – he was a Jew, and she said he wouldn't stand a chance if he remained in Germany. Anyway, I suppose you could say she forgave me my trespasses – even invited me to Sunday dinner a few times, along with a motley assortment of other people. Someone told me that hosting Sunday dinner was her way of getting out of her own shell.' She sighed. 'If you ask me, she was trying to get out of her own private hell.'

'What happened to her?'

'The short of it is that she ended up marrying the American who saved her life after she'd packed me off in a Messerschmitt with those very important people on board – by that time the Nazis were after her. I told you it was a bit of a long story. The new husband works at the embassy, some sort of high-up political attaché. They've been married about ten months, I think, and I have it on authority – all right, from my father, who has his own connections – that she now spends most of her time at her home in Kent with her daughter. Otherwise she's up in town at her office working, probably only a couple of days a week though.'

'Oh – a daughter?'

'Adopted.' Otterburn shrugged. 'Actually, it's a wonder she even speaks to me at all, because if it hadn't been for my stupidity, she might not have suffered a stillbirth when her first husband – Viscount James Compton – was killed. It was the shock of witnessing the aeroplane come down that did it for her. James was testing a new kite in Ontario and was killed instantly. They were living in Canada at the time. I should have been flying that day but was nursing a terrible hangover.'

'Good Lord, Elaine, I'm surprised you ever flew again.'

'It's a debt I'll be paying for a long time, Jo, not least the reason for my wild night of drinking.' She looked out of the window, then back at Jo Hardy. 'You see, I had a terrible girlish crush on James Compton, and seeing his beloved wife heavy with child just about did me in.' She paused. 'Anyway, when this job came along, I knew I was in the right place with the right skills at the right time. Flying is all I know, and it's my way to do my bit. The last thing I want is for anyone thinking I'm a snotty daddy's girl.' She opened her canvas shoulder bag, took out a notepad and pencil and began to write. 'Here's Maisie's office address in Fitzroy Square, plus her telephone number. Look – you might even catch her today. And if you're up for it later, we can get a drink in the bar at The Savoy, and you can stay at the house with me tonight, sleep it off before we make a dash for Hamble on the dawn train! It's a big house, and it'll just be us and a few servants – I suspect my father will be at his club. Or you can get a train down to Hampshire later today.'

Jo Hardy took the proffered sheet of paper. 'Thanks, Elaine. Shall I say you sent me?'

'I wouldn't, if I were you.'

'Sandra, it's been a busy day. You should get on and catch your train home to Chelstone. I am more than ready to go back to the flat and a nice comfy armchair too.' Maisie Dobbs glanced at the clock on the mantelpiece as she took a clutch of papers from her secretary and pushed them into her document case. 'Come on, I'll lock up and walk to the tube with you.'

'At least I managed to get through the paperwork backlog.' Sandra stood up and reached for her hat.

'For which I am very grateful! And I wish I were coming down to Chelstone too, but I'll be home tomorrow,' said Maisie. 'However, Mark said he's cooking my favourite meal tonight, which means he's cooking *his* favourite meal.'

'Not spaghetti again.'

'I hate to say this, Sandra, but I sometimes wish he wasn't able to get hold of the exact ingredients, but being an American, there's all sorts of things he's able to acquire for us.'

'Chocolates come to mind!'

Maisie laughed. 'I can take a hint. I'll "acquire" some for you.' At that moment, the doorbell rang.

'I bet that's Billy forgotten his keys again,' said Sandra.

Maisie shook her head. 'He's going straight back to Kent today – he wants to tell Doreen about the meeting with MacFarlane this morning.' The doorbell sounded again. 'You go on without me, Sandra, and I'll deal with whoever it is – and thank you for sorting us out. We would suffocate under the mound of unfiled papers if it weren't for you coming in once a week.'

As Maisie opened the door, the young woman outside had already turned to walk away.

'Excuse me!' Maisie called out, while waving goodbye to Sandra, who waved back before running towards Warren Street tube station.

'Are you Miss Maisie Dobbs?' asked the woman as she approached Maisie. 'I'm terribly sorry to call upon you so late in the day, but I don't have much time in London, and – well, you seem to be leaving.'

'It's something I try to do – get home before it's too late

so I can run down to the cellar if there's an air raid. You're lucky to catch me.'

'My name is Josephine Hardy – Jo, actually. A friend said you could help me.'

Maisie looked at the woman, identifying her uniform. 'And would that friend be Elaine Otterburn?' She didn't wait for an answer. 'Come along, Jo Hardy – you'd better come up to my office and tell me what this is all about.'

CHAPTER TWO

I t was dark when Maisie left the office. She wished she had a motor car at her disposal, though even if she had, she would have to face driving home with headlights covered so only a pinprick of light illuminated the road ahead. Instead, she was in time to use the tube; it would be another three hours before the trains stopped running and stations became the domain of exhausted Londoners seeking shelter from the German bombers that would surely sweep across the capital before morning. Women and children were already making their way down to the platform, seeking safe harbour for the night. Maisie walked with care lest she trip over a foot or step on someone's leg, though most of those who came had not yet laid out their bedrolls and blankets, and were instead just getting settled, setting out flasks of tea and tins of sandwiches.

Once on the train, Maisie leaned back in her seat and closed her eyes. As the train rumbled underneath London, she thought about her meeting with Jo Hardy, who had spent over an hour at the office telling a story that all but beggared belief.

Maisie knew that as a first officer in the ATA, Hardy was among the most accomplished civilian pilots and that she earned nearly as much as a man for doing the same job – a rarity indeed. It had been reported that within another year, female ferry pilots would be the only government employees who could boast the same pay as their male counterparts. But what to make of the young woman's story? And how could Maisie possibly help her? Jo Hardy had come to her for two reasons. One, because she was determined to find a way to clear the name of an American soldier. Having found him in dreadful circumstances, the young woman had taken responsibility for the life of Private Matthias Crittenden. Maisie turned the name around in her mind. If it weren't for his colour, with a name like that the man could have come from Kent – it was, after all, a typical Kentish name, ending in *den*, the Anglo-Saxon word for a clearing in the woods. Hadn't so many towns and villages throughout the county once begun as a clearing in the woods? It was an irony that, translated into Old English, the surname meant Matthias was 'a man living in woodland.' And his Christian name? She was no expert on the origin of names, but she knew this – Matthias was akin to Matthew, and hadn't the apostle Matthew been an honourable man chosen to replace Judas Iscariot? Maurice Blanche, her former mentor, would have said there was a connection in those names, an association worthy of attention. However, she suspected the American's forebears might well have been shipped to the United States as slaves and subsequently given the name of a colonial landowner whose own ancestors hailed from Kent or a close neighbouring county. Now Crittenden was in custody in Britain, and the woman who had come to his rescue had no means of knowing what might be in store for the young American – but she wanted Maisie to find out.

Maisie pictured Jo Hardy in her mind's eye. Though not as tall as Maisie – Hardy was about five feet, five inches – she exuded a certain physical presence. It was the demeanour of one who had never known want, who assumed there would be opportunities in life because anything she wanted had always been available to her – though Maisie wondered to what extent the young woman might be oblivious to the trials and tribulations of those less fortunate. And yet there was something in the way Hardy had described Crittenden – how she recounted releasing the binding on his feet and wrists, how she had to calm him when she realised that he was as terrified of being reunited with his fellow Americans as he was of remaining a hostage in the barn – that suggested a woman of compassion. She had an immediate understanding that Crittenden was also fearful of being alone with a white woman.

Then there was the second remit, that of finding out who had aimed a weapon at Jo Hardy and who may also have caused the death of her fellow aviatrix, Erica Langley. Hardy hoped that Crittenden might have some information to assist in the enquiry; that even though she had found the poor man bound and gagged, something he had seen or heard might identify the gunman. Maisie wondered how on earth she would gain an interview with an American

42

who could well be under suspicion of committing a crime against another soldier.

Hardy had concluded their meeting with a question: 'I want you to work for me, and I know you can't do it for nothing. What's your fee?' She had not blinked an eye as Maisie wrote down an estimate on a sheet of paper, and pushed it towards her. Maisie realised later that she had deliberately overestimated her charges in the hope that Hardy would withdraw interest in the enquiry. Instead the woman nodded, pulled a chequebook from her kit bag and paid the required retainer in full.

Now Maisie had to earn every penny.

'Hi hon,' a voice called out from the kitchen as Maisie closed the front door of her Holland Park garden flat and slipped her keys onto one of the coat stand hooks.

'Sorry I'm a bit late, darling – a late case came in.' She removed her black woollen coat and a paisley scarf and unpinned her black, Robin Hood–style hat with a brown band, then hung both on another hook alongside a mirror. 'And of course the tube took ages – we were stuck in a tunnel for a long time,' she added, leaning forward to see if she could detect any more threads of grey in her jet-black hair.

Her husband of ten months, Mark Scott, was chopping vegetables in the kitchen, and as she entered he turned towards her, leaning in with a smile and a kiss.

'That's better,' said Scott. 'Wine's in the icebox. And I'm doing something else with the pasta tonight.'

'Tuesday is always pasta night,' said Maisie. 'But you

know, I can cook too, Mark. I promise my skills run to more than soup with bread and cheese.' She uncorked a bottle of white wine and took two glasses from a cupboard.

'It's my way of relaxing, of mulling over things, and it's the one night I can escape work early. You can get a lot out of your system, chopping with a good knife.'

'Hmm . . . I prefer to walk. Maurice always said that to move the body is to move the mind, and he also said it opens up a door into the sixth sense.'

'Oh no, here we go!' Scott laughed. 'You go and sit down with your glass of wine and relax with that sixth sense of yours – I'll be there in a minute. The fire's lit.'

Maisie kissed her husband again and walked into the sitting room, where a table had been set for two. While there was a formal dining room in the flat, the couple preferred this room. In summer they had opened the French doors and taken supper outside in the garden on warm nights, the wicker chairs creaking as they sat back and watched searchlights moving back and forth across the sky. Despite having a cellar, they rarely used it as a shelter, though if they heard Luftwaffe bombers flying over in their direction, they would scramble down the stairs and sit covered in blankets, waiting for the wail of the 'all clear' siren.

Maisie set one glass of wine on the mantelpiece for her husband, and settled into a chair next to the fireplace, took a sip of her wine and felt the tension of the day begin to dissipate. Sighing, she reached down to the document case at her feet and pulled out the notes she had taken while Jo Hardy was recounting the story of finding Matthias

Crittenden, expressing her fears for the man who had seemed so filled with terror.

'Dinner is now simmering away, a fine dish for my bride,' said Scott, picking up the glass Maisie had set on the mantelpiece. He leaned over and kissed her on the forehead. 'Now, how's my lady love? Tell me about your day – I've missed you.'

Maisie was about to answer when Scott interjected.

'Jeez, sorry, sweetie – I meant to tell you – a girl called for you. The 'phone was ringing just as I came in the door. Took me by surprise – she's from my part of the world, an American.'

'Really? Who was she? I don't know any Americans here – well, only the ones you've introduced me to.'

'Oh yes you do, but it's been a while – I got the whole story.'

'Well, who is she, Mark?'

'Name of Patty Hayden – she said she knows you from when you came to stay with her folks in Boston, you know—'

'Charles Hayden's daughter! Oh, my goodness, I haven't seen her since she was – well, perhaps fifteen, something of that order! What's she doing here?'

'Turns out that little Patty Hayden is now First Lieutenant Patricia Hayden of the American Army Nursing Corps. She shipped out on the *Queen Mary* and is based at a US Army hospital here.'

'Where?'

'I asked her that, and she says she isn't quite sure, as all the signs are down on the stations, but somewhere north of

London. She's in town for a couple of weeks, some sort of training she's required to do, and she said she cannot wait to see you. Number's by the 'phone. Sorry, went completely out of my head.'

'She's a lovely girl. Very fair hair, almost white it's so blond, just like her mother, Pauline,' said Maisie, coming to her feet. 'Her father is an eminent brain surgeon and neurologist in Boston – I knew him in France, in the last war.'

'The guy who was a friend of your old beau?'

Maisie nodded. 'That's him. And he was my friend too. Seems a lifetime ago, but I stayed with them for a while in Boston – you know, after . . . after what happened in Canada. They were so good to me, so . . . understanding.'

'Call her now, my love – call her now and see if she can come down to Chelstone. We'll give her a good old Anglo-American welcome.'

Maisie put her arms around her husband. 'I love you, Mark.'

'Me too, you too,' said Scott, smiling as he returned to the kitchen.

Maisie placed a call to the hotel where Patty Hayden was billeted, and was delighted when she accepted an invitation to visit Chelstone, arriving on Saturday morning. She would stay until the following Monday, returning to London on the early train.

While Maisie and Mark Scott had forged a golden rule never to divulge aspects of their work with one another, the plight of Private Matthias Crittenden was nagging at her. Over supper she decided it was as good a time as any to break their pledge.

'Mark – this new case; it concerns an American soldier.'

Scott put down his fork, drew his table napkin to his lips and sat back. He reached for his glass of wine. 'Oh, I see. Need some advice?' He did not wait for her to respond. 'Drop it, Maisie. Don't get involved. That's my advice.'

Though surprised at her husband's response, she pressed on. 'I've taken on the case, so I am already involved – I've even received payment in respect of my estimated charges.' Aware that Scott was about to speak, she continued, choosing her words with care. 'Let me just say that the soldier is likely the descendent of slaves in your country, and my client fears for his safety and that he may not get fair treatment, given the . . . the way people are divided in America.'

Scott pushed away his plate. 'Now I'm off my dinner.' He leaned forward. 'Maisie, do you know what a can of worms this one could be for you? It's not my department, but I have a finger in a lot of pies and we've had problems already. A lot of the white soldiers can't understand why British women don't have any notion of segregation when it comes to dating a guy, that they don't seem to mind the colour of his skin as long as he can cut the rug. The military police are causing trouble by pulling soldiers out of lines at the movie theatres – yep, it's wrong that they do it here, but we can't just train it out of them. Anyway, seems British old ladies with umbrellas don't like to see our military police throwing their weight around, so our MPs have been sent on their way with bruises more than once.'

'You could tell them we're not America, that this is Britain – we just do things differently here. And look what

47

happened to that soldier who was originally from the West Indies – he was minding his own business, having a cup of tea in Lyons' Corner House, and your military police charged in and dragged him out. He was a British serviceman, and they didn't even think to look at his uniform or take note of the fact they were arresting not only a man they had no jurisdiction over but one of His Majesty's subjects. If that can happen in the middle of London, what fate might befall Private Matthias Crittenden?'

Scott shook his head. 'Maisie, I get it – really I do. I'm as troubled by it as you, believe me. But the military has its rules, and they're trying to keep them in place while dealing with a situation many of our men have never encountered – no matter their colour or creed. Most of them have never left their towns, never mind their country.' He paused, sipped his wine and pulled his plate back towards him. 'I'm too hungry to leave this. Now – tell me about Crittenden. In confidence – I won't let anything out, and it's important I know what's going on.'

Maisie summarised the story as Jo Hardy had relayed it to her, adding, 'The reason I wanted to talk about it is because I thought you might be able to help arrange a meeting with Crittenden. I hate to press, but I'm sure there are strings you could pull. I'd like to ask him some questions, because I believe he may be able to throw light on the possible identity of who was taking potshots at our pilots.'

'Be truthful, Maisie, you also want to see if you can find this other soldier, the angelic friend. What did your ferry pilot say his name was? Private Charles Stone? The one

48

who has mysteriously vanished. And who knows if that is true.' He sighed. 'Anyway, that's not your business, Maisie – really, I don't want you involved in any way. You're out of your depth – and treading on some very important toes.'

'Mark, I'm aware of what I'm asking. If I find out anything of interest to the American military authorities as a result of my enquiries, believe me, you will be the first to know.'

'Unaccustomed as I am to making house calls first thing in the morning, being treated to a cup of decent coffee is certainly good enough reason to answer the telephone before I've even put the kettle on. And the words "advisory capacity" coming from you, Maisie, sealed the day's fate. I haven't a bloody clue what an advisory capacity is, but it piqued my curiosity.' Robert MacFarlane settled himself in an armchair and looked at Maisie and Mark Scott. 'So, here I am, ready to advise. Ladies first, Maisie – what's going on?'

Maisie cleared her throat and recounted Jo Hardy's story, from the incident when she saw a man pointing a gun at the Spitfire, to Erica's death. Glancing at Mark, she described Hardy's discovery of Private Matthias Crittenden and the fear that consumed the man as he confided his suspicion that he would take the blame for his friend's disappearance.

'Hardy. Hmm. Hardy. Parents are divorced and she comes from just outside Salisbury? Father wouldn't be Alexander Hardy, would he?'

'I have no idea,' said Maisie. 'I know they're well-heeled, because he paid for her to get her licence to fly before the war, and when she first joined the WAAF she was already a top aviatrix, doing stunts and the like. She was in the control room when her fiancé was killed. Jo told me she just had to get out and get up in the air, so she joined the ATA.'

'Or she's another debutante thrill-seeker trying not to settle down to a life of country pursuits and London parties,' MacFarlane interjected. 'I'll look into it.'

'Does it make any difference what her motives were?' asked Maisie, again glancing across at her husband, who was unusually quiet.

'Money always makes a difference, Maisie.' MacFarlane raised an eyebrow and turned to Mark Scott. 'Anything from your end?'

'I was on the 'phone to our people bright and early. Private Crittenden is being held at a base west of London. In the meantime, another serviceman, Private Charles Stone, has been confirmed missing.'

'They served together?' asked MacFarlane. 'I thought you people were divided up by the colour of your skin.'

'True, but it turns out they knew each other. Both from the same town in Virginia where Stone's father is the local pastor, so he's a – well, what can I say? Stone Senior is known for supporting a move towards desegregation. By all accounts, he's a good boy, not a "good old boy".'

MacFarlane and Maisie exchanged confused glances.

'Divided by the same language again,' said Scott. 'Let's just say the missing soldier would not be averse to a friendship with Crittenden.'

MacFarlane shifted in his chair. 'How did they meet – what does the Crittenden man say?'

As the dialogue continued, Maisie observed how MacFarlane continued to fidget with each question, and Mark Scott alternated between leaning forward and pulling back, as if the movement helped him to recalibrate his answers to retain discretion.

'The bottom line is that Crittenden's story doesn't hold water,' said Scott, turning to Maisie. 'I didn't have a chance to tell you this before Mac arrived, but it seems our military investigators are still questioning Crittenden regarding the missing Private Charles Stone, and his story has changed several times. When that happens, it tends to suggest guilt.'

Maisie took a deep breath and exhaled before answering. 'I beg to differ, Mark. Such behaviour may also be caused by tension and by fear of not being believed, so the person being questioned tends to veer towards a variation on the chain of events that would render them more solid. In addition, a level of nervousness, of heightened adrenaline in the body, can cause errors of recollection.' She turned to MacFarlane, who nodded agreement.

Looking to Scott, then back to MacFarlane, she continued. 'Robbie, we called you because this is a very sensitive situation, so obviously the British authorities must be apprised of my work on the case – which I assure you will continue. I also know I must respect the American military legal system, so to speak.' Allowing a beat of silence, she went on. 'First things first. I wish to speak to Private Crittenden. He may recount all the same variations on the story, but he may also decide to tell me a bit more – which will help with my case. And Robbie, I believe the ATA and aviation authorities have deemed Erica Langley's crash "death by misadventure", and any enquiry is now closed. I wonder if you could procure the report for me. Oh, and I'd also like a report on the death of RAF Pilot Officer Nicholas Gordon – happened about eighteen months ago. Same area, not far from Biggin Hill. Crashed on a clear day and no enemy in sight.'

'Maisie—' MacFarlane sighed. 'It's no good – I know that whatever I say, you will still go about your business. So I'll see what I can do, but I can't say I will be successful with every item on that shopping list.' He looked across at Scott. 'Can you get her in to see this Crittenden fellow?'

'Long shot, Mac. Our military is a closed book, and I have to be careful because Maisie is my wife. Look – you make the request and I'll push it through. I don't want my fingers in that part of the pie any more than they are already – I've got enough on my hands right now with Mrs Roosevelt's visit, and believe me, she's a machine! She was invited here by your queen to observe the contribution British women are making with their war work, but now it seems our First Lady is set on talking to just about every GI in Britain so she can report back to his mom, and along the way wants to meet women workers – from antiaircraft gunners to the Wrens, the RAF radar plotters, meteorologists, you name it. And of course the ferry pilots. The First Lady has been making the case for more American female involvement in the war; setting up places where their children are cared for while they work, that kind of thing – observing what goes on over here is part of her plan. But if she hears about Crittenden in the brig, that will be it – I'll have the president in my ear before I've even lifted the receiver on the scrambler 'phone. I wouldn't put it past her to write about it in her newspaper column.' He shook his head. 'Intelligence troubleshooting is my job, and it became a whole lot harder when our guys came to Britain in droves.'

'When does she arrive?'

'Weather has affected her arrival, so not sure yet. And when she gets here, she'll be on the move nonstop until she leaves in November. She's doing everything from dinner at Buckingham Palace to walking around your East End to witness the bomb damage, plus she'll be heading out across Britain meeting, well, as many people as she can – and as I said, especially women. And with German agents crawling all over the British Isles trying to figure out how they can mount an assassination attempt, you could say it's become a bit of a headache.'

MacFarlane turned to Maisie. 'Compared to his job, yours looks like making jam to me.' He drew his attention back to Scott. 'By the way, wasn't your Mrs Roosevelt educated over here? According to some reports I've heard, she didn't want to go back.'

Maisie felt Scott bristle, but kept her expression neutral. MacFarlane grinned, while Scott just rolled his eyes.

'There's not much time to play with, hen,' said MacFarlane, looking to Maisie, then to Scott, who nodded. 'I'll see what I can do for you, and hubby can work some magic at his end.'

CHAPTER THREE

Maisie spent the afternoon reviewing a couple of enquiries that had come in and decided they were more Billy's bailiwick than hers – he had become more than proficient in dealing with investigations regarding home security, which was uppermost in the minds of many people, especially those of some means, given the increase in looting across London. She also continued with what she called 'desk work' on the enquiry instigated by Jo Hardy, knowing she would have to be patient while waiting to hear from MacFarlane and for the interview with Private Matthias Crittenden to come to fruition. Her fear was that the request would in all likelihood be considered without merit to the American military authorities. It was, as her husband observed after their meeting with MacFarlane, 'a very long shot'.

She left for Kent on Thursday morning, though she would have preferred to spend only two nights in London. It was a rhythm of her week agreed with Mark Scott, following his proposal of marriage. The union had to accommodate her family and their individual working responsibilities along with their hopes for a life together. Her husband would follow on Friday afternoon, all being well, and they would settle into family life at the Dower House at Chelstone Manor until Monday morning. Yet sometimes the settling part of the plan proved elusive for a couple engaged in work requiring the utmost secrecy – to the extent that the simple question 'And how was your day?' was rarely asked.

As the locomotive rumbled along the line towards Tonbridge station, where Maisie would change trains for the Chelstone branch line, she looked out at the landscape beyond, at trees displaying the burnished palette of a Kentish autumn, and thought about her daughter, Anna, the evacuee she had adopted. Mark had taken to Anna as if she were his own much-wanted daughter, and from the time he arrived at Chelstone on Friday until he left on a Monday morning, the child wanted nothing more than to know what she, Mummy and Daddy would be doing next.

At some point each day during the Friday to Monday sojourn, Anna would take Mark's hand and walk with Frankie Dobbs – Maisie's father – down to the stables. Frankie was always ever-watchful while Anna tacked up her pony, a task she insisted upon completing 'all by myself.' Then, with his new son-in-law, he would accompany his granddaughter to the paddock to watch her ride. Maisie loved to see the three of them together: the child in the centre, hands held tight by the two men she trusted most in the world.

Yet of late, Maisie had cause for concern. The previous week she noticed that Anna had started sucking her two forefingers again, as if she were a toddler seeking comfort, though she was now seven years of age. Maisie had already discussed the matter with her stepmother, Brenda, and they decided it was best to just keep an eye on Anna for the time being – after all, children tended to grow out of these things. Frankie Dobbs and Brenda, who looked after Anna when Maisie was away from home, lived at the Dower House, having given up their bungalow for the duration so that Billy Beale's wife and daughter could live there in safety away from the London bombings.

Brenda had expressed another concern about the child. 'She's becoming a little limpet. She's started to hang on to me while I'm cooking or going into the garden to peg out the washing. And you know how she used to run across to the manor to have tea with Lady Rowan as soon as she came home from school? Well, now I have to take her over there, and Lady Rowan brings her back later.'

Maisie knew that if the behaviours escalated, she would no longer be able to simply observe.

Arriving at Chelstone late morning, Maisie had several hours to dedicate to her work before it was time to collect Anna from school, so following a quick cup of tea with Frankie and Brenda, she made her way to the manor's garage. George, the Comptons' chauffeur, was peering into the engine of Lord Julian's old Lanchester when she joined him.

'Hello, George – still keeping that one going?'

The chauffeur looked up, wiped his oily hands on a cloth and stepped towards Maisie. 'Morning, ma'am.' Maisie understood that staff at the manor didn't quite know how to address her. Although she had married again and might under ordinary circumstances be known as Mrs Scott, she was still the widow of the heir to Chelstone Manor, and the matter of her title had led to some confusion. For her part, Maisie had never taken to adding what she considered an unwieldy prefix to her name.

'His Lordship prefers this old girl to the Rolls,' continued George. 'And to tell you the truth, she has my heart too. Lovely piece of engineering – they don't make them like that any more. Coach-built, a work of art all around.'

'Any chance of me taking out my own work of art today? I need the motor car just for the afternoon.'

'How far are you going? Ten miles? Twenty?'

'Hmm, probably closer to thirty, all told.'

'She's got enough in the tank for that, but don't push it. And I can give you a petrol coupon.' He turned towards another motor car, an Alvis, polished and shining. 'Give me a minute to check the oil and get her started and you can be off on your way.'

'Thank you, George.'

Maisie stood to one side and watched as the chauffeur readied her motor car, giving the engine and the tyres a onceover, then finally opening the double doors that led to a driveway that was still known as the carriage sweep. While Maisie waited, he hopped into the driver's seat, started the Alvis and manoeuvred it outside – she knew that only one person would drive a vehicle into or out of the garage, and that was George. It was his domain, and he ruled over it.

Stepping from the motor car, George reached in and removed a white sheet covering the leather seat. 'She's all yours, ma'am – and think of your petrol, no putting your foot down today.'

'Promise I won't,' said Maisie, placing a carrier bag containing her rubber Wellingtons into the boot. She settled into the driver's seat, waving as she drove towards the gate and the main road. Glancing in the rear-view mirror, she saw George wipe his hands on the cloth while watching her depart, then turn back to the garage and the care of motor cars that had seldom been used since war was declared.

With Jo Hardy's directions laid out on the seat beside her, Maisie monitored her speed with care. According to the map, it was fourteen miles to the farm where Hardy had found Private Matthias Crittenden in the old barn. The roads were, for the most part, narrow and winding, so she calculated at least half an hour's drive to reach her destination. She also had to take account of the fact that there were no road signs and that she was in a sensitive area, close to an important air station. She reduced speed as she approached a fork in the road, pulled across to the verge and brought the Alvis to a halt. Picking up Jo Hardy's map, she checked the reference against her own Ordnance Survey map of West Kent, then looked across the field to her left.

Stashing the two maps into the pocket of her grey Mackintosh, she changed into her Wellington boots and locked the Alvis, then stood for a moment before crossing the road and climbing over the five-bar gate, described by

Hardy as 'slippery with mould – so watch your step.'

Though there was a chill in the air and the field was muddy, Maisie found herself smiling. She thought it was the sort of day that might bring out an artist determined to capture the very best of the season. The sky was blue, yet with cumulus clouds beginning to gather, filled with rain, lumbering across the horizon in a way that reminded her of cows coming in at the end of the day, udders full as they moved: a line of ungainly pilgrims on their way to the milking shed.

It took just five minutes to reach the barn, which was exactly as described by Jo Hardy. It must have been over a century old. The roof's main beam was concave, with old peg tiles slipping and missing in places, exposing the structure to the elements. The wooden planks that formed each of the four sides were green with moss and mould, and she could see where Hardy had pulled away at the sodden wood to gain access to the barn and save Crittenden's life.

The barn door was ajar, and though the bolt seemed to have been shot across to secure the opening, it had not met the box on the other side. She had to exert all her strength to open the door, which she could see had been moved of late, by someone shovelling mud away from the opening. Jo reported that the doors had not been locked when she came to the barn, but were stuck. Maisie imagined how military police might conclude that the man inside could have set up a scene where he appeared bound and gagged – she conceded it could be done, though not with ease. The fact that cattle had kicked up mud and further incarcerated the man would be viewed as a natural occurrence in Crittenden's favour.

'Sounds like a horror film,' she said to herself when the door creaked and moaned as she stepped into the shadowy barn.

The fragrance of a past summer's hay seemed to assault her from each side and from floor to ceiling. She suspected there were now other barns in use by the farmer, perhaps newer structures with rounded roofs made of corrugated iron, not peg tiles that were expensive to replace and vulnerable to the elements. Yet hay was stored here, ready to put out in spring, perhaps for cows nursing newborn calves. She could see where a fire had been lit – no countryman or woman would have started a fire in a barn, so whoever had captured and tied Matthias Crittenden was someone who knew nothing of the land – and, she thought, also suffered a deficit of common sense.

Walking behind the bales, she came to the place where she could see a man had lain. There was a definite indentation in the hay strewn across the floor and signs of a scuffle, or perhaps the marks were left by feet sliding through the dust as a result of Jo Hardy's desperate efforts to drag the man from the barn. She wondered why the scene still seemed untouched; surely at the very least the American military authorities would have searched the barn, or the local police had been through with a fine-tooth comb. Kneeling down, Maisie prodded the ground where brownish-red marks were visible on the dirt floor, lifting her fingers to identify the tell-tale stain of old blood. There had not been a flood, but enough to suggest that Crittenden had bled as he tried to free his wrists from their bindings. She entertained the possibility that if indeed Crittenden had been attacked, a beating might have caused him to lose consciousness.

She came to her feet and stepped around the stacked bales of hay. Looking up, she took account of the state of the loft: slats missing, hay falling through the gaps and a ladder with only half its risers. Perhaps her assumption that the local constabulary and even Scotland Yard had visited the barn was misplaced; it was possible they would have been happy to sidestep a delicate situation concerning an American serviceman. Or if a search had taken place, had it been superficial, intended only to confirm a foregone conclusion?

'Here we go,' said Maisie aloud, taking off her Mackintosh. She folded the coat and placed it on a bale of hay before climbing onto another bale, then, using both the remaining steps and the stacked bales alongside, grappled her way up onto the floor of the loft. Mindful of the missing boards, she chose not to stand but instead began to crawl between the mounds of hay. She suspected the barn offered a fair place to camp out for local children in search of adventure, or itinerant workers looking for shelter to bed down for the night. Yet more than anything, she felt it was a refuge, for around her she sensed a powerful aura of – what was that feeling? She sat down, surrounded by hay, and closed her eyes.

'There's something here for me, something I'm missing,' said Maisie.

As she uttered the words she heard a sound from the rafters above, and looked up.

'Oh,' she said, and smiled. 'I had an idea I wasn't alone.'

A barn owl looked down at her, closing and opening her eyes as she rotated her head from side to side.

'Show-off,' said Maisie. 'Mind you, I bet you've seen a few things,' she continued in a whisper. 'Pity I don't understand owl – I'd ask you some questions.'

Maisie began her examination of the hayloft floor, clearing the hay in batches and sending dust into the air. She sneezed and began searching again. Not for the first time in an enquiry, she had no idea what she was searching for, but was giving in to a feeling – perhaps it was a manifestation of hope – that there was something to be found. She was moving another batch of hay when a screech filled the air.

'Good Lord, what on earth is it?' She looked up at the owl and crawled back to a spot under the beam where the creature held court. It settled again, keeping its gaze upon her.

'I wonder—' Maisie came to her feet and took a step away, causing the owl to screech once more. 'You're an interesting study, Mrs Owl.'

Stepping back so she could stare straight into the creature's eyes, Maisie looked up again. 'That's strange – you give your barn owl screech when I'm moving away, not when I'm coming closer. Perhaps your nest is over there. I daresay you'll be laying a clutch of eggs soon enough.'

As Maisie stooped down once more and began to crawl farther into the eaves, she felt the owl continuing to watch. That was when she heard a different sound, a metallic sound, as if her hand had disturbed coins. She groped around the space in front of her until her fingers came upon something cold and tinny. Clearing back blades of hay, she gripped her find, lifting up a slender ball-bearing chain with two rectangular pieces of metal attached – what soldiers called 'dog tags'. At the sound of the jangling, the owl screeched again and took flight to a beam on the other side of the loft.

'Private Charles Stone.' She read the name on the tags and looked across at the owl. 'No one will ever believe me, but I have a funny feeling you wanted me to find this and take it out of your barn. You don't like it at all, do you? I'll do that now and leave you in peace – but I would give a mint to know what you've seen here.'

Slipping the tags into a pocket, Maisie crawled to the ladder and made her way down to the lower floor, where she claimed her Mackintosh, dusted off her clothing and sneezed again. Had she found all there was to find? But she knew that wherever the other young soldier was, he had no identification on him, and someone preferred it that way. And was he dead or alive? Now she wanted nothing more than to leave the barn, and she suspected the owl in the rafters above would be seeking somewhere new to raise a family of owlets. A place where suffering had occurred held no welcome for any living creature. Yet Maisie did not move and instead began retracing her steps towards the back of the barn, feeling a breeze blow through the gaps created when Jo Hardy had torn away wooden slats to free a terrified man.

As she passed the bales to her right, something caught her eye. It was the merest hint of white. She turned and studied the baled hay at length, until her gaze finally settled on the tiny triangular corner of a piece of paper poking out between two bales. A second later she was holding two pages of creased vellum bearing handwritten notes. She had no time to study her discovery, so she stashed the papers in her pocket, where they rattled the tags belonging to a pastor's son, the young man Private Matthias Crittenden considered to be his friend from home.

'Oh no, that's all I need!' uttered Maisie as she approached the five-bar gate. A police constable was walking around the Alvis with his notebook open, having rested his black bicycle against the adjacent hedge.

'Good afternoon, Constable,' said Maisie, as she approached the policeman. 'I'm just going to move my motor car now. Sorry – I didn't know I couldn't park there.'

The constable turned to her. 'I'd like to see your identification, madam, and your registration book.'

'Of course. I understand, Constable – sorry, I should have asked your name.'

'Eames. Police Constable Eames. And this is a silly place to park, madam, if you don't mind my saying so. Biggin Hill isn't far away as the crow flies – you could have come across anyone here. You never know if a German is going to sail down in his parachute with a gun in his hand.' The man's eyes widened as if to warn her. 'And if your papers aren't up to snuff, I might have to take you down to the station – we're keeping an eye out for spies, you know. And fifth columnists.'

'Yes, I appreciate your point, Constable. We all have to be vigilant. Just a moment.' Maisie unlocked the motor car and removed the vehicle's registration documents from the glove compartment, which she handed to the police constable along with her identity card.

'Is this your motor car?' asked the constable.

'It is indeed, though I rarely use it now – it's been mothballed since war was declared, but I had to bring it out today.'

'And why might you be driving around – what makes today different? Doesn't look like you've been doing any shopping.'

'Actually, I was going into Tonbridge to see if I could find a birthday present for my daughter. I have some clothing coupons saved and wanted to buy her a new party frock. I missed the train, and I don't have much time.'

'What are you doing parking here, then?'

'This is very delicate, Constable,' said Maisie. 'You see, I . . . well, I needed to use the—'

'Oh, right you are, madam.' The young man blushed as he handed the documents back to Maisie and looked across at the barn. 'Old Barney Love should've kept up that barn. His cows will come down with something if he goes on giving them the hay he keeps in there, what with the state of the roof.'

'Barney Love? Is that the farmer?' asked Maisie.

The constable nodded. 'My dad used to work for him until he . . . well, until he retired. Then Mr Love wanted the tied cottage back, so my mum and dad had to get a place in Tonbridge, and ended up in one of the new council houses. It's not like being on the farm though.' He put away his notebook, but continued his complaint about the farmer. 'My dad always said Barney Love was a tight old sod – oh, sorry, madam, I forgot who I was talking to.'

'I've heard worse, Constable. And to be fair, I think all

farmers are probably a bit like Mr Love. It's a hard life – as your father would know – and money is always short. It takes just one failed harvest due to the weather, or a pack of dogs in with the sheep, and a farmer is crushed.'

The constable nodded. 'But Mr Love has three land girls working for him, and he's not shelling out anything for them. The government pays their wages. They also paid for him to plough in a fair bit of woodland, and then he had the Americans working there for nothing over the harvest – you know, doing their bit for England and all that.'

'Really, Constable? I've not heard about that – what do you mean?'

'I'm not sure how it started. As far as I know, it's all part of their . . . I don't know what you would call it, but it's what they did to get to know the locals, you know, put themselves on the right side of things with us and, well, I suppose it was also to stop us all getting worried about them being here, because they're different, aren't they?'

Maisie smiled. 'Oh yes, those Americans are definitely different. But let me get this right – there were American soldiers working on the farm, bringing in the harvest?'

The constable nodded. 'That's it. And you know what, according to Wally Walton, landlord down the Eight Bells, well, he said it was all very interesting because they had the colours working together there, and we know they're not supposed to do that, where they come from. He said there were military police coming to check on them, making sure they didn't work too close and mix.' He looked at his watch, then back at Maisie, smiling. 'It was a laugh one night. The pub darts team was in there, and some of them American lads – the dark ones and one white soldier – had joined in, formed a team, and when them military police came in to split them up, our darts team sent them on their way so they could get on with the game. Made everyone laugh. Wally said playing darts together did more for us getting to know their boys than them working on the farms, but old Barney appreciated the help. Like I said – he won't turn away free anything.'

'Very interesting, Constable. I'm surprised I've not read about it in the papers – you know, the American soldiers, working on our farms during the harvest.'

The policeman shrugged and moved towards his bicycle. 'Tell you what you won't read about, madam – the Yanks visiting that barn a few days ago. Something about one of them lads gone missing. I reckon he deserted. Mind you, it's not as if he can get home in a hurry, is it? I had word not to come out this way on my round when they were over there in the barn, though according to what I've heard, the Yanks didn't stay long. In and out and on their way in one of them funny old motors they cart themselves around in, you know, with nothing but a bit of cloth on the roof. Anyway, I'd better be off. Nice to have a chat, madam, but I would advise you to be on your way and don't stop in these places because you don't know who might be along this lane. I only come round here once every day and, well, it's best to be careful.'

'I will, Constable. I'm getting in my motor car now. Good day.'

The constable touched his helmet, stepped onto his bicycle and made his way along the road. Maisie watched for a few seconds before climbing into the Alvis, whereupon she pulled the two sheets of paper from her pocket, unfolded them and began to read.

'Oh dear – code or nonsense?' She could make neither head nor tail of handwritten notes that amounted to a series of notations alongside what she thought were dates, though not written as she might expect. It seemed like gibberish. And what did Rover stand for? A motor car? She sighed, folded the sheets of paper and slipped them into her shoulder bag along with the dog tags.

The tags troubled her. If there had been a search of the barn, even a cursory one, how could those tags have been missed? Unless, of course, the resident owl objected to the visitors, flying at them to make it clear that they were far from welcome. Yes, she could imagine someone reaching the loft and then having second thoughts about venturing farther upon seeing those talons. But there was another possibility, one she could not ignore given Crittenden's situation. Could the tags have been planted? Questions about her discoveries would have to wait, because for now she had more to do before returning to Chelstone. Opening the Ordnance Survey map, Maisie pinpointed the farmhouse where she believed she would find a tight old sod named Barney Love.

CHAPTER FOUR

Maisie had visited quite a few farms over the years. There were the familiar farms forming part of the Chelstone estate, run by tenant farmers who worked fields their fathers and grandfathers had tended before them, and though she had been London born and bred, she loved the land. Indeed, the Comptons' estate manager was coming up for retirement in a year or so, and Mark Scott had surprised Maisie while they were walking with Anna and Little Emma one Sunday afternoon, taking a route through one of the farms. 'I think I could do that job, you know, Maisie.' She had laughed at the comment, reminding him that it might be just the right move for a man who wanted to leave the world of political intrigue behind – there was always intrigue on a farm. 'You may laugh, Maisie,' Mark had continued. 'But this is my kind of land. And if I can wrangle you away from trying to outsmart the Nazis, I'm sure I could get along with the farmers around here.'

The Love farm seemed well kept, though she thought the farmhouse roof could do with some attention. There was no answer when she knocked at the door, which did not surprise her – there was a lot to accomplish in a day on a farm. With not an hour unaccounted for, even the farmer's wife could well be toiling in a field. She turned and began to walk towards the milking shed, from which voices and a good deal of feminine laughter could be heard. Entering, she saw three Land Army women, one grasping a hose shooting water across the concrete floor, and the others sweeping detritus towards a ditch outside. All three were wearing standard-issue khaki overalls atop green pullovers and khaki blouses with green ties, their black rubber boots turned over at the top for ease of movement.

'Hello!' Maisie called out.

The women wielding brooms stopped laughing and looked up, as the one holding the hose ran to the tap and turned off the flow of water.

'Sorry to bother you,' added Maisie. 'I wondered where I could find Mr Love.'

'He's gone to market today, with Mrs Love.' The woman who answered had her hair tied with a scarf topknotted into a turban.

'Oh, that's a shame.' Maisie approached the trio. 'But perhaps you can help me in the meantime.'

'Are you from the ministry? We could do with a bit more money in the way of wages, and it wouldn't hurt to have a tractor around here.'

'Mr Love doesn't have a tractor?'

There was a snort of laughter from the women. A woman

wearing a flat cap answered. 'Yes, we have a tractor, but it's dead – needs a part, and it's an American tractor, so the exact part cannot be found, apparently. We hoped one of the Yanks could help out, but they couldn't. So now we're back to Ethel and Sadie.'

'Ethel and Sadie?' queried Maisie.

'The most recalcitrant pair of draught horses you've ever come across. Give me geldings any day. Take those girls out early on a frosty morning and they hold a grudge for weeks.' The third young woman, her hair braided to keep it back from her face, gave a good-natured chuckle. 'A bit of sugar helps – and I'd go without it in my tea, if it humours that pair of mares.' She leaned on her broom handle. 'Anyway, how can we help you? We've got a lot to get done here, so we can't chat all day.'

'Sorry – won't keep you long. I'd like to know about the Americans who came to help out during the harvest – do you remember them?'

'There were a number of those Yank boys,' said the turbaned woman. 'Nice lads, always a laugh, though old Love made sure we didn't mix with them. "Overpaid, oversexed and over here", he said – he got that from the papers. We thought they were very polite, didn't we, girls?'

'And they had chocolate and ciggies!' The girl wearing the cap blushed, causing the others to giggle.

'Did you witness any discord, anything untoward that you're not used to seeing?'

The women looked at one another, shrugging.

'Not really,' said the woman with the turban. 'By the

way, I'm Madge; this is Helen.' She pointed to the girl with the cap. 'And that's Gwen.'

The land girl with braided hair nodded. 'And who are you?'

'Sorry, I should have introduced myself. My name is Maisie Dobbs. I'm asking questions on behalf of a young man who worked here, an American soldier, Private Matthias Crittenden.'

'Mattie!' the women answered in unison.

'Ah, so you had an opportunity to get to know the soldiers.'

'Oh, you know, we'd stop and pour ourselves a cup of tea from our flasks in the afternoon, and they couldn't resist coming over to chat.' Helen nodded towards her friends to continue the story.

'I felt sorry for them,' said Gwen. 'I mean, it's different here for them, and they're a long way from home. They come over expecting it all to be like something out of the history books – you know, as if we all go and have tea with the king and queen every afternoon – yet half of every town worth visiting is gone, there are bomb sites even in the country here, and we're rationed, fed up and half of us jump out of our skins every time we hear an aeroplane go over.'

'I don't think they were all like that,' offered Madge. 'Take Mattie and his mate, Charlie, who reckoned he was going to follow his father into the ministry – they said they felt at home here, working on a farm. Mattie said his people would fit right in.'

'Really? Did he say anything else about his people?'

Helen turned to Maisie. 'He called them his "folks",

and he said that they had once been slaves, and then they were sharecroppers. Mind you, we had to ask what a sharecropper was, and to be honest, it sounded just like Mr Love – you know, a tenant farmer.' She laughed. 'I told him, "Mattie, we know all about being serfs here in England. All our ancestors were blimmin' servants, at the beck and call of the masters and working all hours, getting flogged if we didn't pull our weight".'

The women laughed again. Maisie stole a look at her watch – the repartee with the land girls was proving valuable, but she wanted to ask a couple more questions before it was time to leave.

'Was there ever any discord between the white GIs and the coloured chaps? I thought they were separated in terms of their battalions.'

'I reckon that's right,' said Gwen. 'And the MPs – the American military police – came around every now and again to keep an eye on them. Really, they seemed to get on all right when they mixed.'

'Let's be fair, though, mostly they kept their distance, you know,' added Madge. 'And besides, there was a lot of hard work to do. I reckon they were all too tired to have a go at one other.'

'But Mattie and Charlie, when they got talking, they found out they came from the same place,' said Helen. 'They said it was very countrified, like this. And green. They said they felt as if they were "right at home".' She mimicked an American accent, which led to more laughter. Then she grew serious. 'Mind you, Mattie told us, "I'm from one side of the tracks and Charlie's from the other."

Never heard it put like that, but we all know what he meant. I reckon that finding each other helped them not be so homesick. They'd sit and have a drink together in the afternoon. The other blokes called Charlie Stone 'Padre' on account of him wanting to be a vicar, or whatever they call them over there, and no one had a go at him making friends with Mattie. Tell you the truth, I reckon all them boys were a bit sad when the harvest was in. They'd done a fair job of work for us, but then they had to go back to being soldiers.'

Madge and Gwen nodded agreement, then Madge sighed and turned to Maisie. 'Ever so sorry, Miss Dobbs, but we really must get back to work. This milking shed has to be as clean as we can make it before the cows come in. Mr Love is a stickler for it.'

'Is he a fair man to work for?'

'A little tight with his money, but he runs a good farm. The animals come first – looks after them very well, compared to another farm I was sent to. He works us hard, but that's what we're here for. They keep very busy, the Loves. Both their boys are in the army, and what with one of them being in North Africa, working hard takes their mind off it all. Us too!'

'I appreciate your time. Do tell Mr Love that I called to see him.' Maisie reached into her pocket for a card and a pen, scribbling the Dower House number on the back before handing it to Madge, who appeared to be a leader among the women. 'I'm not in London for the rest of the week, so if he finds a way to give me a ring at that number on the other side of the card, I'd appreciate it. I

74

might be able to come out here tomorrow in any case.'

'Right you are, Miss Dobbs. They had a telephone installed last year. Mrs Love said they had to have it in case their sons came back to England and could put in a call from a barracks somewhere.'

Maisie thanked the women, and as she walked away from the milking shed, she heard Madge exclaim. 'She's an investigator! Blimey, you don't think I put my foot in it, do you?'

Maisie was about to unlock the Alvis, parked in front of the farmhouse, when she heard footsteps behind her. 'Miss Dobbs! Miss Dobbs! Just a minute.'

'Madge – is everything all right?'

The young woman flapped Maisie's calling card, as if to emphasise what she was about to say. 'Miss Dobbs, as long as you're looking into something to do with Mattie, I reckon you should know that he and his mate – the padre – they came to the farm again a few times after the harvest, just to walk around the fields, talking, or they'd come along with their fishing rods. We saw them. They'd sit around the back of that barn with a couple bottles of pop and chat for a while.' She caught her breath. 'Miss Dobbs, is Mattie in trouble? He was a nice bloke. We all liked him.'

Maisie rubbed her forehead. 'He's in some difficulty, Madge.' She waited a few seconds before continuing. 'Look – in absolute confidence, I want you, Gwen and Helen to rack your brains; try to remember if and when you saw any strangers on the farm, and in particular near the old barn. I know harvest time brings in a lot of new workers, but I think it's easy enough to pinpoint anyone who's not really supposed to be here. And any motor vehicles you weren't used to seeing, that sort of thing.'

Madge nodded. 'I know what you mean, Miss Dobbs. But that old barn is in the far field – seems you've seen it. It's not used much these days, though we moved some hay in there for the livestock, because the ministry didn't hold with that field being left fallow. There is a rough track that veers off to the left as you come through the gate, and to tell you the truth, anyone could drive down that in the middle of the day, and if you weren't over there, you wouldn't see them. They could be in and out without anyone the wiser.'

'I thought as much,' said Maisie.

'But we'll put some thought to it, and I'll get in touch if we remember anything.' She paused. 'Trouble is, by the end of the day we're so tired, all we want to do is flop on our beds. It's all very well having a night out at the village pub, but I'm half asleep before I've even walked in the door.'

Maisie nodded. 'Where are you from, Madge?'

'Stepney. Born and bred.'

'Do you like the country?'

'Love it.' The woman turned to look across the fields, holding her hand to her forehead to shield her eyes from the low autumn sun. 'If I had my way, I'd never go back to the Smoke. Never. I'd just stay here on the farm – it's made a strong woman of me.' She laughed. 'I s'pose you could say it's the war that's made strong women of all of us.'

Maisie thanked her for her help, opening the motor car door as she watched the land girl walk away towards the milking shed. It was time to drive back to

76

Chelstone. She smiled. Time to pick up Anna from school and perhaps pretend that life was normal, though she sometimes struggled to remember what normal had ever felt like.

'Mummy, Mummy, Mummy! You're here!'

The child with jet-black hair and olive skin ran towards Maisie as she stood at the school gate. As was often the case, one of her daughter's plaits was almost undone, the other still with a green ribbon holding the braided hair in place. An unbuckled brown leather satchel bumped against her hip as she ran, stopping only once to pick up a book that had fallen out.

'And you've brought Little Emma!' Anna launched herself into Maisie's arms, then slid to the ground to cuddle her dog.

'Someone's had a good day!' said Maisie. 'Come along – let's get home before it rains.' She pointed to the darkening sky. 'Those clouds look like water balloons to me.'

'Just like Blossom the barrage balloon!' said Anna, who had taken the dog's leash and was now skipping along beside Maisie. *Blossom the Brave Balloon* was a book Maisie had bought for Anna, who was afraid when she first saw the giant antiaircraft balloons floating in the sky.

Maisie laughed, happy to be with her daughter. Happy to be home at Chelstone.

Heavy raindrops began to fall just as they reached the door leading into the Dower House kitchen, where Brenda had set out cups and saucers and slices of bread, thinly buttered and with a scrape of honey.

'I'm starving!' said Anna.

'Keep your fingers off until you're out of that school uniform, young lady!' said Brenda, pouring boiling water into the teapot. 'Run upstairs and change – it'll still be on the plate when you come down.'

'Yes, Grandma.' Anna held out her hand to Maisie. 'Come with me, Mummy. And Little Emma.'

Brenda raised an eyebrow as Maisie allowed her daughter to take her hand and lead her towards the staircase and up to her room.

'That's right. Fold your uniform so it's nice for tomorrow. And put your shoes in the wardrobe – Little Em hasn't chewed a shoe for a while, but we don't want to take any chances, do we?'

Anna nodded, and began to take off her green woollen school pullover and white blouse. Maisie asked questions about school as Anna undressed, leaving her clothing in a neat pile on the top of the dressing table. It was as Anna turned towards Maisie, still chatting away while putting on her play clothes, that Maisie's attention was drawn to her daughter's arm.

'Anna – how did you get that bruise?' Maisie reached forward and took her daughter's hand, inspecting a bruise just above her delicate wrist.

Anna shrugged. 'I don't remember.' She pulled back her arm. 'Probably playing with Emma.'

Maisie nodded. 'Yes, of course. She's a boisterous one, to be sure.' She looked out of the window. 'There should be just enough time to put on our Mackintoshes and take her for a nice walk across the fields before it gets dark. We'll use up a bit more of that energy.'

Just as Anna was lifting a clean pair of socks from a drawer, the telephone began to ring downstairs.

'I'd better answer that, darling. You put those on, then go on down to the kitchen for tea. I'll be there in a minute.'

'Don't leave me!' squealed Anna, taking Maisie's hand. 'Wait for me!'

'Anna, what is it, my love?'

The child's cheeks reddened and tears filled her eyes. 'Nothing . . . but please wait for me, Mummy.'

Maisie heard Brenda entering the library, and the telephone stopped ringing. Soon Brenda's voice echoed up the stairs. 'For you, Maisie. It's your Mr Beale. Says it's urgent – he'll hold on for you.'

'Coming!' Maisie called, then turned to Anna and knelt at her feet, taking the socks from her hand. 'Let's put these on, shall we? Hop on the bed now, there's a good girl.' She pulled the socks onto her daughter's feet one by one, then tickled her soles. 'Ha! That's got you! Right – tea, young lady!'

'Little Emma, time for tea!' Anna ran to the door, the Alsatian at heel, though the child looked back to make sure Maisie was with her.

'Oh dear . . .' Maisie whispered to herself. 'Oh dear me.'

'Billy – you're back at the office?'

'Yes, miss – we're like ships passing in the night, aren't we?'

'I'll be there in London soon enough. But what's the matter? What's wrong?'

79

'A woman named Jo Hardy telephoned for you.' He cleared his throat. 'Or perhaps I should say, "First Officer Jo Hardy".'

'She's a new client – I was going to brief you in case she called while I was away. What did she say?'

'Could you call her soonest. "Soonest", miss? How is it all these toffs use words that aren't even in the dictionary? Can't it just be "soon" or "as soon as possible"?' He gave a half-laugh. 'Anyway, she was hoping to find out about your "progress" on the case, and sounded upset that you weren't here.'

'That's strange, I could have sworn I gave her a card with the Dower House number on the back – she must be so busy she forgot. I'll place a call to her now and leave a message with someone if necessary – though I do hope she's not one of those clients who calls several times a day.'

'Well, she's more than that – she's visiting her friend's people in Westerham, just until tomorrow late morning, when she has to go off on duty again. So she wondered if you could visit her there to talk, and to give her all the details. She gave me the address and the time. I thought it was a bit of a cheek. Anyway, what sort of officer is she, miss? Wrens?'

'No, she's a ferry pilot.'

Billy laughed. 'Oh, she's an "Atta girl"! That's what they called them ATA women – you know, "Atta girl, you can do it!"' The laughter stopped. 'Mind you, whether they're men or women, them ferry pilots are blimmin' brave, if you ask me. Up there where any old German can have a go at them, and them with no ammo other than their wits.'

'She had a lot of flying experience even before the war – and she was an instructor, I understand. Anyway, Billy, I don't have a lot to report at the moment, though it might be a good idea for me to go to see her, as I've more to do in the area.'

'Right you are, miss. I'm off to see that man who wrote to us about his wife's missing jewellery.'

'Good luck with that one!'

Maisie ended the call and leaned back in her chair. The door was closed and she could not hear voices from the kitchen, so all must be well.

Why did everything have to come at once? Why a new case just when something was clearly amiss with Anna? Should she continue to monitor her daughter's behaviour and see if the situation improved – or, as Brenda suggested, wait until 'it all blows over'? Or should she seek advice? If she chose the latter, at least she knew who to talk to – a year before, she was dealing with a case concerning a boy suffering what amounted to the kind of shell shock she'd seen in patients during the last war. So, yes, she knew who to talk to if Anna's behaviour escalated. And what about that bruise on her arm? She knew what had caused it, because she had seen that sort of mark before, when she was a child. It was on her own arm, inflicted by a boy at school who had called her names because the colour of her skin was not Anglo-Saxon peaches and cream. He had followed the shouting by giving her what children referred to as a 'Chinese burn' – gripping the victim just above the wrist, the bully turned his hands in opposite directions, pulling the flesh, breaking capillaries, the friction causing a livid scarlet and purple bracelet of pain. It was a torment named for villains in children's books, villains who all seemed to hail from China. It was a distinctive wound – if you had one around your wrist, every other child in the school knew how it happened, and did their best to keep on the right side of the perpetrator.

'You were a nasty, spiteful little boy, Arthur Hicks!' Maisie said aloud. And she wondered which child was an Arthur Hicks at Anna's school.

She stood up and was about to leave the library when the telephone rang. She made a guess at the caller's identity.

'Robbie?'

'You've done it again, hen – taken all surprise out of this telephone call.'

'I'm just getting good at knowing when it's you, Robbie. The telephone shudders with every ring. What's the matter?'

'The matter is, Maisie, that I have managed to arrange a meeting for you with one Private Matthias Crittenden. It will be here in London, and it will be at the American Embassy. Almost neutral ground.'

'How on earth did you manage that?' Maisie wound the telephone cord around her fingers. 'I was beginning to think I didn't have a chance.'

'It's what we call "international diplomacy" – and having a hubby in the colonial embassy didn't hurt, though I will add your spouse had to box clever on this one.'

'When?'

'Next week – on Wednesday.'

'But—'

'Maisie, in this instance, beggars cannot be choosers.

There's nothing sooner, so it's that day or nothing. Come to my office at eleven, and we'll go over there together – and that's a stipulation. They are allowing this because I've made it clear – as has your hubby – that Crittenden may well have crucial information regarding a case you are involved with, and which also concerns the police. That last bit is a lie, of course, because I'm still wondering what the bloody case is supposed to be. It won't be a long meeting, by the way.'

'I'll take any crumbs that fall off the table. And thank you.'

'I wish I could say "any time", like one of those blokes in the American pictures that seem to be everywhere these days. But it won't be any time, because every time you ask me for a favour, I have to wonder what sort of trouble we're both getting into.'

CHAPTER FIVE

Clutching a leaf of paper bearing the address given to Billy by Jo Hardy, Maisie walked from Westerham Station to Dovecot House, home of the Marshall family. A well-pruned wisteria vine stretched up above the first floor of the four-storey white Georgian mansion house, surrounding the windows and flanking the front door. Maisie imagined the intense fragrance greeting people on warm summer days, days when the family would likely sit outside in the garden on wicker chairs while enjoying afternoon tea or tall glasses of fresh lemonade. She stood looking at the house for a few moments, wondering about Diana Marshall's childhood years. This was a happy house, a home where the children who grew up here had laughed and played, and where want was something rarely, if ever, experienced.

As she walked to the front door, Maisie composed her thoughts, hoping that Jo Hardy would allow her to conduct her investigation at her own pace. Yet she was familiar with clients who expected an enquiry to proceed at the speed of a detective story seen at the cinema, complete with clues that seemed to pop up out of nowhere and endings that were neat and all but tied with ribbon until 'The End' was emblazoned across the screen. Taking a deep breath, she reached for the bellpull.

'Bang on time,' said Jo, opening the door. She turned away from Maisie. 'It's all right, Mrs Hawkins – the caller is for me.'

Jo stepped back for Maisie to enter, straight into a reception room. Maisie glanced up and guessed that at some point a hall had been reconfigured to provide a more welcoming, spacious entrance for callers. The walls were painted in a pale yellow wash, offering just enough colour to avoid the stark brightness of white and to bring a hint of warmth to the room. A generously upholstered sofa covered in a cabbage-rose fabric was situated perpendicular to the fireplace, facing two armchairs in a deep burgundy velvet. Occasional tables complemented the room, and above the fireplace an oil portrait of a young woman held pride of place. Blond hair cascaded onto peach-cream shoulders, revealed by a gown of purest white.

'Is that Diana?' asked Maisie.

Jo Hardy nodded. 'Yes. Diana the debutante. What that picture does not tell you is that Dizzy made it to the ball by the skin of her teeth, because she was looping the loop in a flying circus earlier in the day.' She shook her head, smiling. 'I thought Pamela – Mrs Marshall – would absolutely throttle her when she finally arrived home. The gown was ready, the hairdresser was here and even another woman to do her face. Dizzy rolled up looking as if she'd been dragged through a hedge backwards. Cleaned up bloody well for the artist though, didn't she? Anyway, Dizzy's on duty and I've had some leave due, so I came here when I was allowed a paltry few hours to catch my breath. This house is more a home to me than either of my parents' – they're divorced now, and I don't get on with them terribly well. Now, enough about me – let's sit down and get on with it.'

Once seated, Maisie allowed the young woman to take the lead; she would pull ahead when she felt the moment right.

'Look, I've been thinking about this business with the American soldier and the connection with what happened to me. First I was shot at, then I found that poor man in the barn, and after that Erica came down . . . and then there's Nick too.'

'Yes, tell me about Nick again – is there more I should know?'

'He was in the RAF. Spitfire pilot. His kite went down about eighteen months ago, and not too far from where Erica was killed. And he wasn't in a dogfight either. I was in the Women's Auxiliary Air Force at the time, in the ops room. I saw it – heard him tell us that something had hit his Spit. Then he was gone. Pretty much what I told you when I came to your office.'

'And you joined the ATA after that?'

Hardy shrugged. 'Hate to say it, but I was the more experienced pilot, Maisie, and I knew I had to fly in the war effort. I had to do my bit. I've been flying from the day I turned sixteen, and Nick had only been up there since he joined the RAF when war broke out.'

'Sixteen?'

'I was old enough.'

Maisie raised an eyebrow. 'Jo, I want you to go over what you told me before – everything that has happened bringing you to this moment and your belief that these events are linked, and—'

'Don't you believe me? Do you think I'm losing my mind or something?'

Maisie shook her head. 'No, Jo, far from it. But to do my job, I have to reconsider the details time and again. Something you had not noticed might come to the fore in the second or third telling. Perhaps another man or woman you encountered could inspire an important reflection that becomes pertinent to the investigation. I may well ask you to tell me your stories repeatedly.'

'All right. Yes, I suppose I understand that.'

'And there's another reason,' said Maisie.

Jo Hardy held Maisie's gaze for a moment, then slowly nodded her head, as if considering a completely alien process and seeing its value.

'In telling me your stories multiple times, you're getting the pictures out of your head and into the open. In your job you need to cleanse the bad memories as much as you can, for your own safety. Only then will the good thoughts have enough room, enough breathing space to bring you joy. Now then, let's start with Nick, shall we?'

Jo Hardy shed tears as she recounted the story of her

dead fiancé once more, and rubbed her hands together while voicing her doubts regarding the official enquiry, which suggested mechanical malfunction as the cause of the accident. When Hardy had offered up everything she could remember regarding the man with the gun, Maisie turned the conversation to Matthias Crittenden.

'Private Crittenden is in a lot of trouble, isn't he?' said Jo. 'I wish I could do something more for him.'

'Have you been contacted by an American military lawyer to answer questions? They're called judge advocates general, just as they are here for the RAF and army.'

Jo shook her head. 'No, I've not heard from anyone – but I thought I would have by now. The people we left him with – as you know, we took him to Biggin Hill – they told me someone would be in touch. But nothing yet, not even another peep out of their military police.' She ran her fingers through her thick, shoulder-length hair. 'The thing is, I cannot see him killing anyone – and I know he feared being accused of something pretty serious if this Private Charles Stone isn't located. You see, Crittenden is a religious man.'

'Playing devil's advocate, there are a good many cases of suspects becoming God-fearing when accused of a crime. That said, how do you know he's religious?'

'It was as we were on our way to Biggin Hill. We were driving past a small church, and he asked us to stop. We were scared out of our wits – I mean, we never knew if someone with a gun would come after us all! But Crittenden asked if he could go into the church, and he seemed so intent that Dizzy stopped the motor car and we went in.'

'What happened?'

'The poor man began walking towards the altar – he half stumbled, but when I went to help him, Dizzy took my arm and said, "No, Jo – I think he needs to do this on his own." And she was right, because he suddenly stood upright, then bowed his head in front of the cross before going down on his knees to pray.' She paused. 'You know, we're not big on the church in my family and Dizzy's people are the same – you go in when you're christened, when you're married and at the end. But that dear man was pleading with God to help him, to walk with him. I think he even spoke some words from the Bible, something like that.'

'Do you remember the words?' asked Maisie.

'I heard it at a funeral once, for one of the girls,' said Hardy. 'There was a bit about the valley of the shadow of death. Sorry I can't be more help – I can memorise an aircraft manual in about twenty minutes, but I'm not very good with anything else. I suppose that says a lot about me.'

Maisie nodded. 'It's all right. Private Crittenden was reciting the Twenty-third Psalm. It's one I've whispered to myself many a time.' She looked at Jo Hardy. 'Did he say anything else, while you were in the motor car on the way to Biggin Hill?'

'He was pretty quiet, even though we asked him to tell us what had happened – I mean, Maisie, he was in shock. But as we passed a pub – the Eight Bells – he looked out the window and said something about having a last drink in there with Charlie, and that was where everything started to go wrong.'

'Go on – this is important, Jo.'

'He said he could hardly remember anything after Charlie told him they had to leave. It was all a blur. I hadn't mentioned it, I suppose because it might have reflected badly on him – I mean, the Americans might complain about our beer being a bit warm for their liking, but it's stronger than they're used to and goes to their heads a bit. I didn't want the American military police thinking he did something untoward while drunk – not that I think he was, but I had to be careful what I said on his behalf.'

'I'd like to know how to get to that pub, Jo. But in the meantime, tell me about Erica. The whole story, from the beginning. And one more time, about what happened when you thought you saw someone shooting at you.'

It was three-quarters of an hour later when Maisie left Dovecot House. The road to the station was flanked by grass verges and the dead fronds of spring cow parsley, now reduced to brown stems and dropping seeds. The leaves were changing colour as if, war or no war, trees were determined to honour the season with vibrant shades of red, gold and brown. A shower had left the road wet and puddled in places, but the sun was breaking through, and fortunately Maisie had worn sensible shoes for the outing. It was at that point a motor car drew up alongside and a man stepped out of the passenger seat. He was no taller than Maisie and wore an ill- fitting grey suit, topped with a raincoat. He put on his hat as he approached, not bothering to sidestep puddles; his shoes were already dirty.

'Miss Dobbs – why did it never occur to me that I might see you here?'

'Detective Chief Superintendent Caldwell – my goodness,

what a surprise!' She smiled, and looked at her watch. 'I'm sorry, but I must dash to the station, as I've to get back to Chelstone soon to collect my daughter from school.'

Caldwell shook his head. 'Normally, Miss Dobbs, I'd think you might have something up your sleeve that I should know about. I've been dodging around these parts to show we're working with the Yanks on a case. As if I don't have better things to do.'

'Oh dear, that must be difficult for you.'

Caldwell's eyes appeared to narrow as he smiled. 'I'd lay money on a bet that you know something about it, what with you being married to one of them. I suppose you can't help me out.'

'I wish I could, Superintendent – sorry.'

'Never mind – I just had to show willing by coming out here. You know, so the brass can say "Scotland Yard is also on the job with the Allies" – that sort of thing. Truth be told, the Yanks don't want us involved any more than we want to be, so the less said, the better. Now I can get back to London and all the joys it has to offer. Give you a lift to the station?' Caldwell stepped towards the motor car, then turned back to Maisie. 'Am I supposed to call you by another name now? Mrs Scott or something like that?'

'Miss Dobbs is best for us – I don't confuse my working life and private life.'

'So you are at work. Thought as much. Anyway, hop in, and we'll get you to the station in time for your train.'

'Oh good – I would hate to be late.'

'How's she coming along, your little girl?' Caldwell

turned from the passenger seat to speak to Maisie. It struck her that he was unusually chatty.

'She's a joy.' Maisie was thoughtful. 'But I'm a bit worried about her, to tell you the truth.'

'What's wrong – not liking school? My boy went through that – hated Mondays, and skived off on Fridays, the little so-and-so.'

'No, she's always loved school. But she came home with bruising on her arm, and said the puppy did it. The dog is still young and can be strong, but she doesn't leave a bruise like a bracelet around the wrist.'

'That's a Chinese burn, that is,' said Caldwell. 'Some nasty nipper had it in for her.'

'Exactly what I thought. I'm going to keep an eye on the situation. If it happens again, I'll have to talk to the teacher, but it's hard when it's a one-off – the children get so upset if they know you've gone to the school.'

Caldwell nodded. 'Oh, don't they! They reckon they'll get it again for being snitches.' He was quiet for a moment. 'The sad thing is, we both know that there's the odd bully at school who ends up being a tyrant when they grow up, and nasty with it.'

CHAPTER SIX

'I just couldn't wait for the end of the week – thank heavens it's finally Saturday! I just loved the train, Maisie. Once you get away from the city, the country down here is just gorgeous – now here I am! Reminds me of New England!' Patty Hayden sipped her tea, then looked at Brenda. 'Mrs Dobbs, these pastries are heavenly! What do you call them? Hmm, I could eat a horse!'

'Have another, my dear. They're Eccles cakes, Maisie's favourite, so I thought I'd bake some today.'

'I'm glad you did!' Using her fingers, the young woman wiped a crumb away from the side of her mouth. 'Thank you so much!'

Maisie watched as the American army nurse reached for another cake. Brenda, who might have expected their guest to offer a respectful 'Oh no, I couldn't,' cast an almost imperceptible glance towards Maisie, who shook her head as if to say, 'Let her eat as many as she wants – forget the rationing.' Patty Hayden had an ease about her that reminded Maisie of her father, Charles Hayden, who had been a physician with the American army in the last war. He had befriended Simon, her first love, who was also an army doctor. But now thoughts of Simon were blurred by time, and here she was in the company of Charles Hayden's daughter, a tall, fair-haired young woman who seemed on top of the world and who inhabited every inch of the space around her with expressive movements and a wide smile.

'Dad told me all about London, and even though I expected to see some damage to buildings, it was a real shock. I couldn't imagine what it was like to have those bombs falling down around you, but now I know.' She turned to Maisie. 'I'm doing more training at the moment – I'm an operating room nurse, and what we are likely to see in there is not what we're trained for in a regular hospital.' She sipped her tea, addressing her conversation to both Maisie and Brenda, focusing on each woman in turn with her pale-blue eyes. 'But we know a bit more now, because we've been helping people who've been hurt when the bombs drop.' She picked a flake of pastry from her plate. 'You know, we read about it back home and we see news at the movie theatre, but nothing prepares you for it – for seeing what happens when bombs fall on houses with ordinary people in them.'

'We've all had to get used to seeing things we never thought we'd see, Patty.' Maisie noticed the young woman's eyes redden with tears. 'I remember my first time assisting a surgeon in the last war – and we didn't have a lot of the advantages in nursing that you have today. It was such a shock. I wanted to just fall to my knees and weep, but you can't do that, because your attention helps save a life, just as your smile keeps a patient's chin up when you're on the wards. So we all just get on with it, don't we? Your father is a gifted surgeon, and I have every confidence that you are your father's daughter.' Maisie paused, looking up at the kitchen clock. 'Mark and my father will be back with Anna soon. It's not often she drags her feet when it comes to going down to ride her pony, but I think she's quite entranced by you.'

'It was bringing the toy that did it! I just loved going into Hamleys – that's the sort of toy store I would have begged to get into when I was a kid. And it was busy too – I guess life goes on, even in a war.'

'It was very kind of you,' said Brenda. 'She's keeping a little collection of toy horses and ponies, so that one was a real treat for her. Patty, now you've had a cup of tea and something to keep you going, let me take you up to your room and show you the bathroom. I'm sure you'd like to . . . to "freshen up", as you would say.'

'And get out of this uniform!'

Maisie laughed. 'Oh, I remember that feeling!'

'Patty seems to have settled in – nice kid.' Mark came into the bedroom as Maisie was brushing her hair and kissed her on the neck. 'And Anna has really taken to her – fascinated by her, I would say.'

'She's a little girl intrigued by a woman who's younger than her mother and grandmother – it's a way of looking up to someone, seeing the possibility of womanhood.'

She laughed. 'The attractive part, that is.'

'Oh, and what's not attractive about having me for a husband?'

'Everything's attractive, my love.' She smiled as she turned to him. 'I wonder if you'd help me with something, though.'

'Uh oh – haven't you had enough help this week? I had to pull out the stops and walk the plank to get you in to see Crittenden. Can't do any more for a while – my tab on that one is pretty long.'

She shook her head. 'It's not that kind of favour, darling.' She turned away, opened a drawer, took out a cardigan and began slipping her arms into the sleeves. 'Anna is happy at home on her own today – Brenda and Dad are here, and as we know she loves Patty already.' She looked down to secure the buttons on the cardigan before turning to her husband. 'There's a pub called the Eight Bells – Jo Hardy gave me the directions. We've time to get there for a quick drink before coming back for supper.'

'Long way to go for a beer – we could head down to the Chequers in the village instead. And aren't Priscilla and Douglas coming over with Tom and Tarquin?'

'That's tomorrow – Sunday lunch. Half past one-ish. Plus Lady Rowan and Lord Julian,' Maisie reminded him. 'Mark – this is to do with Privates Crittenden and Stone. Apparently, Crittenden told Jo they'd stopped at the Eight Bells for a drink – it was there that something happened, but he could only remember snippets of what came next, from the time they left until the day she found him. So I want to talk to the landlord, ask some questions, and it might be better if we pop in, just like any other couple.'

Scott opened his mouth as if to raise an objection, then sighed. 'Reckon we can take the Alvis?'

'I checked with George – he said he's put in enough petrol for us to take a run over there.'

Scott nodded. 'OK. I've as much of a stake in getting to the bottom of this as you.' He pulled her into his arms. They stood in silence for a moment, before Scott changed the subject. 'I wanted to ask – what's going on with Anna? The clinging isn't going away, is it?'

Maisie shook her head and leaned into her husband's embrace. 'No, it isn't. And there's something else – I think another child is picking on her, and—'

'What?' Scott looked at Maisie. 'What kid? What are they doing to her?'

Maisie recounted finding a bruise on Anna's arm, and another just yesterday.

'Well, let's get over there on Monday and talk to the teacher, to the principal – headmistress or whatever you call that woman with the glasses. I don't want anyone bullying my daughter.'

'Mark, it's not that straightforward. Children can be very sensitive about parents just running in and trying to sort things out. I have to find out if it's real bullying or an isolated playground dust-up. Anna won't thank me if I draw even more attention to her.'

'What do you mean, "more attention"?'

Maisie sighed. 'There could be something going on because she doesn't have what you would call a very English complexion – her father was a Maltese sailor, as you know.

97

And I've heard from Billy that Margaret Rose has come home from school miserable about being teased because she has a pronounced London accent. I would have hoped the local children are used to that by now, as there are a good number of evacuees around. But if Anna has seen her friend – who's older and better able to take care of herself – being teased, it'll make her feel even more alienated.'

Scott shook his head. 'It might not start with kids, but they hear things at home, don't they? They pick up on what's said by their folks. I'm worried. I think we should do something.'

Maisie nodded. 'I'll pop in and see the headmistress on Monday morning. Anna doesn't have to know.'

'Want me to come? Could be a good idea if we're both there. I can let my secretary know I'll be in late.'

She shook her head. 'It might be best if just one of us goes.'

They were silent for a while. 'Maisie, there's something I want to talk to you about, and now is as good a time as any.'

Maisie looked into her husband's eyes, and though she felt a frisson of concern, she saw only love. 'What is it?'

'I think it's time to talk to your lawyer guy. I want to adopt Anna, to be her father on paper. Legally.'

Maisie put her hand on her heart as if to still the conflicting feelings that seemed to assail her. 'Well – yes, of course. It's only right. Yes. I'll telephone him on Monday. Yes.'

'You're not sure, are you?'

'No – it's not that, it's just that—'

'Just that what?'

'It's ridiculous really, just thoughtless, but—' Scott waited for her to continue.

'I suppose . . . I suppose . . .'

'It was you and Anna in your mother and daughter bubble, and then I came along. But it's not quite you, me and Anna, a family trio, is it?' He paused. 'I get that, Maisie. I understand. But it's time now. It's time to let go a little – she's my daughter by marriage, and I want to see my name on a legal document that says I'm her father. Not just the guy you married who happens to love and care for her.' He sighed. 'I'm the guy who would do anything for her. Her protector until another guy comes along when she's . . . well, when she's maybe around thirty-five. I'll think about letting her go then.' He smiled at Maisie.

Maisie returned the smile, and nodded. 'I'll talk to Mr Klein. I'm sure it's a formality.'

'It is.'

'What?'

'It is just a formality, Maisie. I've checked. Call Klein, let's go see him – and let's be a legal and proper family.'

'You're right. Absolutely. Yes.'

'Then I can deal with whoever started the ball rolling that's hurting my little girl.'

'I'm not sure I like the sound of "deal with".'

'Neither will whoever started this. They'll find out that "Careless Talk Costs Lives" has another meaning altogether.'

A clutch of RAF pilots were standing near the fireplace when Maisie and Mark entered the Eight Bells public house. Maisie knew their favoured watering hole was the White Hart in Brasted, where they would sign their names in chalk on a blackboard, and raise their glasses to those who hadn't come home.

Maisie glanced at her husband and pointed towards two seats at an empty table to the right of the landlord's domain. 'I'll get us a drink,' offered Scott. 'Sherry?'

'A small one.'

Maisie looked around the pub as Scott gained the landlord's attention. Some farmworkers stood at the bar, raising half- pints of bitter and talking about the price of beer, which had escalated since the outset of war.

Scott returned with the drinks, setting them on the table. 'Now what are you going to do – call everyone to attention and ask them who the hell tied up Crittenden and shoved him in an old barn?'

Maisie shook her head. 'No one would believe you'd been the president's favourite field agent before landing a cushy job at the embassy.'

'Cushy? If only you knew.'

'I can guess.' She studied the airmen, laughing, teasing one another. Then a seriousness enveloped the group. They raised their glasses and as one chanted the name of a fallen comrade.

Maisie turned away and took a sip of her sherry. 'I think I need some crisps.' Seeing her husband begin to push back his chair to go to the bar again, she rested a hand on his arm. 'No – I'll go.'

She stood up and approached the landlord, who was drying glasses.

'Mr Walton, isn't it?'

'That's me. Name seems to get around.'

Maisie smiled. 'My friend lives not far from your pub – she told me I should pop in for a drink with my husband.' She leaned closer, lowering her voice. 'He's an American, you know. Likes what he says is all the quaintness of an English pub.'

The landlord winked at her. 'Yes, and they like our women too, don't they?'

She followed his lead and laughed, then lowered her voice. 'We heard there was some nasty business regarding a couple of American soldiers who were working on a farm not far from here.'

'No one's said much about it,' said Walton. 'The police have no idea who did what, and they've more or less left it to the Yanks. They came in here and asked a few questions, but I had nothing for them. Can't keep tabs on everyone who rolls in for a pint or two.'

Maisie nodded. 'They probably think publicans know everything and everyone.' She opened her purse. 'May I have a packet of crisps, please?'

Walton turned away, took a packet of crisps from a box underneath the counter behind him and set it on the bar in front of Maisie. She paid, but lingered. 'I'm curious, do you see many Americans in here?'

'A few. The pubs nearer their bases will see more, and they're a good few miles away. We saw more of them at harvesttime, when they were helping out on the farms around here.'

'Hmm. We heard that a couple of my husband's old friends were in the area, though we don't quite know where they might be living or working – my husband reckons his pals would always manage to find a friendly bar at home, so here we are!'

The landlord nodded and scratched his head as he looked towards the table where Mark Scott was sitting alone. 'Now I come to think of it, a couple of them Yankee blokes – civilians – have been in a few times. Always when it's busy though, so I suppose they like a crowd – or they don't want to be seen, eh? Are they famous film stars?' He laughed. 'If that table where you're sitting wasn't already taken, that's where they'd sit. Nice and quiet in the corner.'

'I'll tell my husband.'

'Hmm, yes – yes, they must know some locals, because I reckon the other bloke those Americans were with came from one of the aerodromes. Like I said, the Yanks I'm talking about weren't in uniform.'

'Was the other bloke a pilot?'

He shook his head. 'Nah, they always congregate together, those boys.' He nodded towards the pilots, who were now making their way towards the door. 'This one wasn't in uniform, like I said, so I reckon he was a civvy working up there. Funny how things come back, when you start thinking about it. I suppose I thought he had something to do with the RAF because a few of the lads said hello to him. Seemed to know him, and he looked a bit familiar.' He paused and frowned. 'And now I'm giving it some thought, I might have seen him in uniform, though if it were RAF I would have remembered.'

One of the farmworkers seated at the end of the bar

raised his glass. 'Stop chatting up the women, Wally – there's men needing a pint here.'

'You'd better look after those hardworking boys,' said Maisie. 'And I should move along too – my husband will be wondering where I got to with the crisps.'

'Sorry I couldn't be more help about his mates.'

'Oh, that's all right,' said Maisie. 'We'll find them.' She returned to the table.

'A guy could get lonely back here,' said Scott.

'Sorry.' She opened the packet of crisps, reached in for the blue paper twist of salt, and shook it over the crisps. 'Here, have one,' she said, offering first pick to Scott.

Scott reached into the bag. 'No good trying to stop my heart with all that salt, Maisie – it's yours forever!' He leaned towards her. 'Any luck?'

'Yes. Yes, I think I might have something.' She took a sip of her sherry and set down the glass. 'Ready?'

'You're not going to finish that?' asked Scott.

She shook her head. 'Don't want to be late for supper, do we?'

They stood up and began to walk towards the door, stopping when the landlord called out, 'Hope you manage to find your American friends, sir!'

Scott nodded and smiled as he waved to the landlord. 'Thank you – so do I!'

He leaned towards Maisie as they stepped outside the public house. 'What was all that about?'

'Sometimes you have to lie to find a path to the truth, Mark – you know that.'

CHAPTER SEVEN

'Can I do anything to help?' said Patty Hayden, lingering by the door that led from the hall into the kitchen.

Brenda looked up from the table, where she had rolled out pastry to make apple pie. Maisie was basting a chicken and turning potatoes in the roasting pan.

'You're doing a wonderful job keeping Anna occupied,' said Maisie.

'She's usually got her fingers all over my mixing bowls,' said Brenda. 'But thank you for asking, my dear.'

'Is she outside?' asked Maisie, lifting the roasting pan and returning it to the hot oven.

'Playing with Little Emma – who is a really big dog! Those paws!' said Patty, adding, 'I can set the dining table if you like. I know how to do it the English way.'

'Excellent idea!' Maisie wiped her hands on a towel. 'I'll show you where to find the table linens and cutlery – and we'll use the best china today too.'

When Maisie returned to the kitchen, Brenda was finishing the apple pie, making decorative pastry leaves for the top. 'Nice girl, I must say. Always ready to help – no side to her.'

'I know. I hope she will consider this her home from home for the duration – her parents were very good to me.'

'Priscilla won't thank you for it,' added Brenda, using a brush to coat the pastry with milk. 'I think I'll sprinkle just a little sugar on the top – it doesn't look right without it.'

'What?'

'I said I'll sprinkle—'

'No – what do you mean about Priscilla?'

Brenda turned to her stepdaughter. 'Maisie, you are dense sometimes! Look at that girl – she's personable, from a good family and very well turned out into the bargain. A beauty, if you ask me. Priscilla is going to take one look at her and tie up those boys.'

'Oh, I hadn't thought of that.' Maisie reached towards a colander containing carrots, and took up a knife. 'Anyway, they're men now – even Tarquin is seeing a girl from the village, apparently, and Tim is walking out with another university student.' She began to peel the carrots. 'Thankfully Priscilla hasn't been quite so fretful about Tom since he began training other pilots. He's not exactly in the firing line any longer.' She shook her head. 'Imagine being considered an old hand at his age.'

'I just hope it doesn't end in tears, that's all I can say,' said Brenda, opening the oven door. 'It'll be down to you if it does.'

Maisie sighed. 'Brenda, any young people in uniform today deserve all the joy they can get – look at what's happened to Billy's eldest, captured by the Japanese.' She sighed as she picked up another carrot. 'It's a shame Billy and Doreen couldn't come today. It would have done them good to have some respite from their worries.'

'You know what I think?' said Brenda, putting the kettle on the hot plate. 'I think they'll go back to their own house in Eltham soon. There's comfort in being in your own home when worry strikes – and what with losing their little girl years ago, I don't know what they must be thinking. And Eltham isn't right in the middle of London, so they'll be a bit safer there now. The bombs are still dropping every night, but the German aeroplanes aren't coming over in the hundreds all at once, not like they did in the Blitz.'

Maisie nodded. 'You could be right, Brenda, though it's still safer living in the village. Let's wait and see. Mind you, I know you'll be glad to get your bungalow back.'

'Hmm,' replied Brenda. 'Oh, I don't know – this is home for both of us too. And since we adopted Anna, it's lovely to be family, together.' Maisie reached towards her stepmother and put her arms around her.

'What's all this nonsense, Maisie? What's all this?'

'What you just said. About us adopting Anna – that she's ours. We. Together. She belongs to all of us.'

Brenda came into the dining room bearing a large serving plate with roast chicken, brown and crisp on the top and fragrant with rosemary and thyme. Maisie followed with serving dishes filled with roast potatoes and fresh steamed vegetables, picked earlier from the kitchen garden. As she set down the dishes, she looked around the table where thirteen people were now seated close together, all of whom were happy to be in company, to have laughter and a chance for some light-hearted banter. Large though it was, the chicken would offer only a paltry amount of meat for each person, but they could fill up on vegetables from the garden, and there was bread. Brenda baked her own bread, so they would not have to queue up for a single loaf. Country living – and an American husband who had access to a few treats not available to the ordinary British family – meant that while the table was never filled, there was enough, and enough in wartime was more than plenty.

'Frank, you do the honours – you're the man in the hot seat,' said Mark Scott, pulling out a chair at the end of the table for Maisie's father.

'Watch what he said, Dad,' said Maisie.

'I'd agree with that,' offered Lord Julian, his eyes red-rimmed with age, though his bearing revealed only a hint of the arthritis pain he suffered.

'You've lost me there,' said Frankie Dobbs.

'The electric chair,' said Patty Hayden. 'That's what criminals call the electric chair – the "hot seat". I guess it became a description for anyone in a tricky position.'

'What's an electric chair?' asked Anna.

'Can we get the dinner on the table without talking about electric chairs?' said Brenda.

'Hear, hear,' added Lady Rowan, lifting her glass. 'And I don't think these should be empty, young man!' She winked at Mark Scott.

'Uh oh, failing in my duties!'

'I'll say,' said Priscilla. 'I thought the wine boat bound for Kent had gone down in the Channel.'

As she took her seat, watching plates being passed back and forth while Frankie carved the chicken, adding stuffing to each portion as he placed the meat on the plate, Maisie noticed that Tom was indeed paying attention to Patty Hayden, who laughed at his jokes and blushed when their hands touched while reaching for a serving dish. Priscilla was seated next to Anna, and as she leaned forward to cut up chicken on the child's plate, Maisie saw that Priscilla would require at least one more round of skin grafts on the facial burn she had sustained while rescuing two children from a bombed- out building during the Blitz. Priscilla's husband was deep in conversation with Lord Julian, and Tarquin, on Anna's other side, was teasing her, assuring her he was going to marry her when she grew up.

She wished Billy and his family were there, or Sandra and her husband and son. She had begun making the Sunday meal a bigger affair before the war because she had spent so much time alone in her life. It was a feeling of desolation that had grown since the loss of her first husband and unborn child. She had realised she wanted to gather family around her while she could, because she felt the chance slipping through her fingers. And then life had changed. Life and love had lifted her, so even at the worst of times – a time of war – the meal delighted Maisie, for it heralded the first such gathering in many months.

'Time for a toast!' Mark Scott came to his feet. 'Ladies and gentlemen – Tom, pay attention, that means you. Patty's stuck over here with us for a while now, so you won't miss your chance.' Scott waited until the laughter died down and began again. 'Ladies and gentlemen—'

'That's the telephone!' Maisie came to her feet. 'Do carry on without me, darling. I really should answer that. If the telephone rings on a Sunday, it's usually important.'

Maisie departed the dining room as more laughter filled the air, doubtless following another of her husband's jokes. She entered the library, reached for the telephone receiver and, before she had a chance to greet the caller, was interrupted.

'Maisie!'

'Jo – is that you?'

'Yes, it's me.'

'Is everything all right?'

'Yes – yes, it is. But Maisie, I just had to telephone you because I've been doing some of my own digging – I managed to talk to a man who came to Erica's aid when she crashed. His name is Dan Littlecombe. I know Dan because he lives not far from Westerham and owns the garage just outside the town. He told me he was walking his dog at the time – you know, when he saw Erica come down. There's not been much business for the garage since the war started, so he only goes in two or three days each week, unless he's asked to do more – and he walks a lot, thank goodness for us.'

'What did he say?'

'She was killed instantly when she crashed – he said there was no doubt about that – but he told me that after he'd raised the alarm and before anyone came to take her away or inspect the Spit, he had a chance to go over the aircraft.

Carefully. He wasn't asked any questions by the authorities investigating – not that they have time to do much of that. He said it was obviously a mess, but he thought something had caught the tail – some sort of unidentifiable object, perhaps even a bullet. Clearly he didn't want to commit to too much speculation, hence "unidentifiable".'

'Jo – look, I don't know anything about aircraft, but can't they fly with some damage? I've seen newsreels and read about pilots bringing in an aeroplane on fire after being peppered with bullets everywhere.'

'It depends how low you are. But even a handgun can bring down an aircraft. It's more than possible.'

'All right, yes, I understand that.'

'And there's something else.'

'Yes?'

'Dan was first on the scene, as I said. Erica was killed instantly when the Spit crashed, but he said she might have been out already.'

'Out? Explain, Jo – do you mean unconscious? Concussed? And how would it have happened? I can make guesses, but you're the pilot.'

'Her face wasn't too messed up, and he said there was a wound that looked to him as if it had been made by something grazing the skin.'

'How would he know that?'

'He's not a young fellow, Maisie. He might be a motor mechanic now, but he's been around aircraft for a long time – he was a mechanic with the Royal Flying Corps in the last war, and then for a short while after it became the RAF. I know Dan Littlecombe because he used to help out with the flying circus I was with before the war. He loves aircraft – and it goes without saying that he has seen bullet wounds.' She sighed. 'I'm not saying it was definitely a bullet wound, because I suppose something else could have caught her upon impact. Believe it or not, I'm fighting to keep an open mind.'

Maisie was thoughtful.

'Maisie – are you still there?'

'Sorry – I was thinking. Look, first things first – are you down at Hamble now?'

'Yes. I'm flying all this week. Since we found that man, I've been swapping with other women so I can sneak short leaves here and there, but the piper must be paid and I will be airborne for most of the next several weeks – unless I can get someone to spot for me.'

'Jo, I want to talk to Mr Littlecombe. How can I find him?' Maisie pulled a notepad and pencil towards her, writing down the details as Jo Hardy provided them. 'Now, here's what mystifies me.' She paused. 'If it was a bullet that brought down Erica, how does a man on the ground with an ordinary gun – an ordinary weapon – injure a pilot and render an aircraft inoperable when that aircraft is flying pretty fast and the gun has a limited range? I am still trying to understand this, Jo.'

'Apart from sheer luck, several things, Maisie. One, the aircraft is going at a fair speed when it's that low, but not the four hundred miles per hour it can reach at altitude. Admittedly, we shouldn't be doing that sort of thing as ferry pilots, but we've all put a Spit through her paces – it's a super aircraft to have at your fingertips. And like any aircraft, the wrong thing happening at the wrong time can kill you. One of our girls died when the propeller on her kite just dropped off. She was up there and suddenly the bloody propeller vanished.' She gave an audible sigh. 'In the case of Erica, perhaps it wasn't an ordinary gun. It doesn't have to be an anti-aircraft gun to damage the aeroplane or the pilot. I'm not a ballistics expert, but if you're that low and the gun is in the right hands at the right time – as I said – you can be hit and it can all come to an end very quickly. Just think of the aviators in the last war – the first aeroplanes didn't have weapons fitted, and the pilots had to lean out holding a revolver to try to hit the enemy in his Fokker.'

'All right, I can appreciate what you're saying. However, there's another thing, I would imagine,' said Maisie. 'What if the gun were fairly ordinary but caused enough of a shock to distract the pilot? Can that happen?'

'We're experienced aviators, Maisie, and we know how to get out of a lot of trouble, though you are right to suggest that distraction can be a killer. I was distracted too, but that's when airmanship saves you every time – it's rote.'

'But what if it isn't?'

'Then yes, you could buy it.'

'Is there anything else about the aircraft? Anything?'

'I suppose if you aren't used to it, there's the carburettor. It had a flaw that has been sorted out on most of the Spits now. That's why a good number have been in for maintenance and we have to ferry them back into service.'

'I'm not a mechanic – you're going to have to explain, Jo.'

'Well, the Spit has a carburettor – not any sort of injected fuel line, like the Messerschmitt for example. That means when you execute a sudden climb, your fuel line can cut out, and then when you get to level flight again, it floods. Not such a problem for us, because we're not usually darting about in a dogfight, but if you're up there and Jerry is looking for you in the clouds, he'll see your exhaust as the fuel hits the line again, and he'll know you're losing some manoeuvrability.' Hardy sighed, adding, 'It occurred to me that perhaps Erica started a sudden steep climb to get out of the way of a nutcase with a gun, but her engine cut and she was knocked out so couldn't get it going again.'

'First of all, I'm glad you telephoned to let me know about the mechanic – that information could be crucial. I'm not so sure about the carburettor, but at least I'm a little the wiser now. I've also uncovered some more information, which has led to questions you might be able to help me with.'

'Fire away.'

'What do you know about civilian workers at Biggin Hill – or at any airfield?'

'Mostly it's uniformed staff, but there are a few. Some kitchen help, that sort of thing. Various building workers, maintenance bods. That's true of most of the aerodromes, though security is tight too. Fifth columnists and all that.'

'Jo, can you give me a list of all other airfields to the south and southeast of London – no matter what size?'

'Got a pen? I can do that off the cuff right now. I've flown in and out of all of them.'

'Go on.'

Three minutes later Maisie ended the telephone call

with Jo Hardy, who within the hour would be ferrying a Wellington to another airfield. She opened the desk drawer and took out the two sheets of paper she had found at the barn where Jo Hardy discovered Matthias Crittenden. She studied the papers and sighed, setting them on the desk next to the notes she had taken during the conversation. Something was beginning to nag her.

She picked up the receiver and dialled.

'Hallo!' The greeting was more of a shout rather than a welcome.

'Billy?'

'Miss – you all right?'

'Yes, thank you. Look, I've only a moment, but I wanted to let you know that I might be a bit late coming to the office for our usual Monday morning catching up. I've got to see the headmistress at Chelstone Primary School, and—'

'Funny you should say that, miss. Since that new headmistress came to the school, Margaret Rose hasn't been herself. We've even wondered if it might be time for us to leave your Dad's bungalow and take our chances back at our own house so Margaret Rose can go to the local school where she won't be made fun of because of the way she speaks.'

'Oh—'

'Is that why you're calling, miss?'

'No – not really. I just wanted to make sure you'll be at the office and not out seeing a new client or something.'

'I'll be there, miss.' There was silence for a few seconds. 'It's the aeroplane case, isn't it? And the business with that Crittenden bloke – the American.'

'Yes, it is.'

'Will he be all right, miss? I know they do things a bit different over there in America.'

'From everything I know so far – which, granted, isn't as much as I would like at this point – I have reason to believe Crittenden is an innocent man, Billy. An innocent bystander, so to speak, though he is being held on suspicion of involvement in a more serious crime. This is becoming a bigger case than I had at first imagined, but if we do our jobs, then we might be able to save him from . . . well, I don't want to even speculate.'

'I know what you're hinting at, miss. I've read about it, you know, what they do to people over there. It's not hanging, and if it were me in his shoes, I reckon I'd prefer the noose, like we have – not a few thousand volts going through me. You know what they call it, don't you?'

'I'm afraid I do, Billy – in fact, I found out just a little while ago. Someone made a joke about it at the dinner table.' She drew a deep breath. 'And to be honest, we should remember that innocent men have gone to the gallows here, at times when the police and the public have wanted to see a swift end to an enquiry.'

Lord Julian and Lady Rowan were the first to depart following a luncheon that went on almost until teatime. Anna asked to leave the table because she wanted to play with Little Emma, and soon Priscilla and her family were gathered at the door as thanks were expressed for the lovely time had by all. There was much talk about doing it again very soon. Brenda declared that she needed to lie down for a short nap, which was followed by Patty Hayden offering to 'do the dishes,' at which point Tom said he would lend a hand. When Priscilla lingered, saying she wanted to 'have a little chat,' Frankie announced he was going into the conservatory to listen to the news on the wireless.

'That's my signal,' said Mark Scott. 'I'll leave you ladies to your "chatting".' He kissed Maisie on the cheek. 'I've got to check in with the embassy – I'll be in the library, OK?'

'Yes, of course, darling,' said Maisie. 'We'll be in the drawing room.'

'I can't stay too long, Maisie,' said Priscilla, as she sat down at one end of the sofa.

Maisie stooped to light a spill and set it against newspaper, kindling and wood laid ready in the fireplace, then joined her friend, the woman who was more like a sister to her. She sat down at the opposite end of the sofa.

'I love these Sunday lunches, but am always ready to sink into an armchair afterwards,' said Maisie.

'That's exactly why I don't do it. I have my help in London, and of course I found that lovely girl from the village who comes in every day and does what I know I cannot do – which is cook.' Priscilla sighed. 'I am a great believer in working to one's strengths, and mine is the ability to give someone instructions and then execute a brisk sit!'

Maisie laughed and was about to speak when Priscilla began again.

'My eldest Lothario is having another love-at-first-sight moment, Maisie – thanks to you!'

'I am sure he will survive, Pris. He's not a child or an

adolescent. Two young people finding some joy in wartime isn't a bad thing.'

'Be that as it may, but I don't want to lose anyone else to an American.'

Maisie reached for her friend's hand. 'I am hardly lost, Pris. Think how I felt when you went off to live in France! And Tom has only just met Patty – he's hardly leaping onto a ship bound for Boston.'

'I know, I know . . . it's this war. And this.' She pointed to the skin just above her ear. 'I thought the operation in December would be my last, but now I'm told there has to be one more, perhaps two.'

'You have the very best surgeon in Mr McIndoe,' said Maisie. 'I am confident all will be well.'

'Yes, but—' Priscilla stopped speaking as Mark Scott entered the room, clutching two sheets of paper in his hand. 'Mark – you look like you've seen Lincoln's ghost lurking somewhere.'

Maisie came to her feet. 'What is it, Mark?'

'Maisie, I have to talk to you – it's urgent.'

'Time for me to take my leave,' said Priscilla as she, too, stood up. 'I'll just go into the kitchen to make sure that the dishes have indeed been done!'

Mark Scott looked around as the door closed behind them, then turned back to Maisie.

'Where did you get these?' He waved the papers in his hand.

'Mark, those are private. It's part of my investigation. I shouldn't have left them on the desk, but . . . but you know better. We've always agreed that—'

'I don't have time to run the issue of privacy up the family flagpole, Maisie. Tell me – where the hell did you get these papers?'

Maisie felt her throat constrict. She placed her hand against her belt buckle, her trusted method of calming herself: a reminder that the power to overcome unforeseen trouble lay in her ability to remain true to herself, to maintain balance even when the winds of the unknown were whistling around her.

'I found them while searching the barn where Matthias Crittenden was discovered bound and gagged. I – I was going to take them to someone who might be able to interpret the meaning, as it seemed to be in code, though I thought the numbers might allude to dates.'

'Oh, I can interpret it for you, my love. Why didn't you show this to me?'

'Because it's to do with a case! We've agreed that—' She shook her head. 'Just tell me what it is. I mean, for all I know it could be about a dog! Or a motor car.'

'What?'

'The word Rover – it's a motor car. Or a dog's name.' She reached to take the papers, but her husband shook his head. 'Mark, for heaven's sake – tell me what all those . . . those words mean.'

'Well, you're right, it is in a code our people have been using to refer to a specific person.' He held up the papers. 'This is the proposed schedule for the tour of Britain by Mrs Roosevelt. By the wife of the President of the United States. Her code name for the purposes of her visit to Great Britain is "Rover".'

'Oh—' Maisie put her hand to her mouth.

'This isn't just your case any more, Maisie – and let's be fair, from the moment an American serviceman was part of the equation, this was no one person's case.' He held up the sheets of paper. 'This is a serious breach of security and it concerns a woman who is hard enough to keep safe at the best of times, because you never know when she's going to march into a whole battalion of soldiers to talk to one boy in the middle who misses his mum.' He held his hand to his forehead. 'As if I haven't got enough going on to worry about the minute she starts diving into crowds to talk to people.'

Maisie nodded, feeling lightheaded as she raced to imagine a connection between Mrs Eleanor Roosevelt's visit to Britain, the American Private Matthias Crittenden and the death of a British aviatrix. However, she had made one swift decision.

'Mark . . . Mark, I must continue with my work. I have a client to whom I have made a promise – and when I accept an enquiry, it becomes my promise, and I keep my promises.'

Scott opened his mouth to interject, but Maisie shook her head.

'I will do everything I can to get to the bottom of what is happening here, and I will take most seriously the fact that there could be a threat to your Mrs Roosevelt. Mark, I . . . I must continue to conduct the investigation Jo Hardy has retained me to complete. And I promise I will keep you apprised of anything I discover that is pertinent to keeping the visitor safe – would that do?'

Maisie watched as the muscles along her husband's jaw flexed. It was a situation they had feared but hoped never to encounter – a conflict of interest that had the potential to cause devastating personal damage.

'Maisie, whether information you discover seems pertinent or not, I want to know about it.'

She thought for just a few seconds and then nodded. 'Then I have something else for you. Wait here.'

When she returned minutes later, she was bearing the dog tags issued to one Private First Class Charles Stone. Scott closed his eyes, then opened them again. 'Oh Maisie. How long have you—' He stopped talking, took the chain and pulled her to him. 'It doesn't matter. We'll work it all out, and we'll do it so you can do what you have to do. But I am one of the people who has a big job on their hands right now, and that is to keep a very important lady safe.'

'I know.' She felt the warmth of her husband's arms around her.

'Oh dear, everywhere I go, I find two people in a clinch!' Priscilla had half entered the drawing room. 'So sorry, darlings.'

'Oh, it's OK, Priscilla – come on in. I'm just thanking my bride for a wonderful Sunday lunch.' Scott turned to Priscilla. 'It was great to see you and Douglas and those boys of yours. Don't be strangers.' He laughed. 'I don't think there's much of a chance of that with your Tom, because Patty's going to be a regular visitor to Chelstone – it's her English home away from home for the duration.'

'Oh, I know about Tom's plans only too well. It's written all over his face. Anyway – I'm off now. By the way, your daughter apparently decided against playing with her dog and instead both of them went to have a nap with Brenda, who I am sure was not able to nap at all with a wriggling child beside her and a snoring mound of a dog on the floor. Anna, having napped for about a minute, is now "helping" in the kitchen, which has at least put a temporary damper on another Anglo-American affair!'

'I'll walk you to the gate, Pris,' offered Maisie.

'It's all right – Tom is ready to leave and Patty said she'd walk with us.' Priscilla kissed both Maisie and Mark Scott on the cheek, and left the room with a singsong 'Goodbye-eee!'

Before the door closed again, Brenda could be heard talking to Anna, and Priscilla calling to Tom as she walked towards the kitchen to let him know that it was time to leave. Scott turned to his wife. 'OK, Maisie. Take it from the top. I have to report the finding of dog tags, so I want you to tell me everything. Now.'

Maisie nodded. Pulling away from her husband, she reached towards the coal scuttle and fed the fire now smouldering in the grate.

'Let's sit down. I'll tell you what I've been doing, and what I've discovered so far.'

It was after her husband, daughter and father had taken Little Emma for a late afternoon walk that Maisie returned to the library where Brenda had lit the fire in anticipation of Maisie working as she did every Sunday evening, going over her notes and plans for the coming week. She took her customary seat alongside the fireplace and for a moment stared at the burning coals, allowing the warmth to envelop her as she sat in the low light of table lamps. She held all the notes she had taken since meeting Jo Hardy, but did not study them. Instead she looked up and stared at the empty chair opposite.

'I know, Maurice, I should be ashamed,' she whispered. 'I should have handed over those dog tags as soon as possible after I found them.' She felt tears well up. 'I had plenty of time to sit with them, to grasp them in my hand as you would have instructed me – and I did. I know what they hold and I believe . . .' She shook her head. 'Oh, Maurice, there are times I wish you were here to ask me the next important question.'

She continued to sit in silence for a while, then began to speak again in a low voice, making enquiry after enquiry of herself. Hadn't Maurice taught her that the power of a question was in the question itself and not in the answer? Maurice was dead, so she had to ask those questions aloud, one after the other, and when the answers began to make themselves clear in return, she turned them over in her mind while keeping the path open so she might better understand her motives.

'What am I afraid of losing, that I would cling to evidence I know should have been handed over?' And as a realisation came to her, she felt a chill. 'It's the same with Anna, isn't it?' Her heart began beating faster. 'Even Billy – I don't think I've been fast enough to give him cases that reflect his strengths or expand his knowledge without me. But I'm trying – I'm doing my best to provide him with the chance to build a reputation in a field of enquiry that suits him.' As more questions formed in her mind, she felt the weight of an insidious threat that had crept into her psyche, an interloper who moved in silence and with stealth. Were her actions a symptom of the same sickness? And was that sickness a belief rooted deep inside that she could so easily lose all that defined who she was in the world if she did not hold on to it with a tight grasp: her daughter, the business she had worked so hard to grow, and another new case that challenged her? If all that were so, how would she put it right? How would she let go?

With each thought, an image that had at first appeared as only an outline in her mind's eye became more defined. She was standing on a beach looking out to sea, waving to small boats. Mark was on one, Anna on a vessel close by. Billy was at the helm of another, and there, overhead, aircraft were flying out across the water, away from her. It was the constant nightmare of losing everything – all that she loved was leaving her.

Maisie knew she had committed a dreadful error, if not a crime in keeping back evidence. Now she had to rectify the situation, and handing over the tags to Mark Scott wasn't enough. She had to redeem herself in her own eyes, or everything she had achieved would be rendered null and void in her life's account.

If Maurice Blanche had been with her, she knew he would have told her to make amends and to do the work with all speed – then there would be no need to punish herself. But as she looked towards the chair where Maurice would sit in days gone by, it was empty, and the man who had been her mentor since girlhood was long gone, the true sound of his voice silenced.

CHAPTER EIGHT

'At least with only one plait, you will only lose one ribbon,' said Maisie, brushing a tendril of hair away from her daughter's eyes.

'Doesn't she look smart, Daddy?' She turned to her husband, who was looking at other parents as they waved their children into the playground. Only a few accompanied their offspring to the school; others were already at work, which for many meant an early start at one of the local farms or perhaps a journey by bus or train to Paddock Wood or Tonbridge, to work in a shop or an office.

Mark Scott knelt down and looked into Anna's eyes. 'She's beautiful – the best little girl in the school.'

Anna glanced around at the other children running to greet their friends on the chilly Monday morning.

'Grandpa will be here with Little Emma to meet you this afternoon. Mummy and Daddy will be back from London soon.'

'How soon? One sleep or two? Last week you stayed in London for more days.'

'I'll be here for supper on Wednesday, so two sleeps, my darling. Daddy will be home on Friday.' Maisie watched as Scott came to his feet again, and resumed observing the coming and going in the playground. 'Won't you, Daddy?'

'Oh yes – and I'll have a surprise for my girl!'

'Sweets?'

'Perhaps. Let's wait and see – if you know now, it won't be a surprise!'

Anna drew her attention back to Maisie, looking up into her eyes as she reached back and began turning the unfamiliar single braid of black hair around and around her fingers. 'Can't I come to London with you? Can't I go to school there, like Margaret Rose?'

'Oh, she's only gone for a day – she'll be here at school tomorrow.'

'But she said she's going forever and I'll never see her again.'

Maisie kissed Anna on the cheek. 'Oh, yes, you will, I know that for a fact, sweetheart. Can you see any of your friends? There's Jane over there. Isn't she your friend?'

Anna looked down at her feet and kicked a stone. She shrugged, and seemed about to say something when a teacher came into the playground and began ringing the handbell, a signal for the children to assemble in two lines: boys on one side and girls on the other.

'That's the bell,' said Maisie. 'You'd better run along.'

Anna nodded and reached to put her arms around the man she now knew as her father.

'Oh, half-pint, what is it, darlin'?' said Scott, bending down to look into her eyes.

'I miss you, Daddy.'

'And I miss you too, sweetie. But guess what – think of everything you can tell me about when I get back on Friday. Aren't you starting a new reading book today? And what about the cob nuts we found for the nature table? Your teacher will be really impressed. We didn't have nature tables where I grew up – or cob nuts!'

Maisie felt tears begin to prick her eyes – tears she did not want her daughter to see, as the child looked from one parent to the other.

'Two sleeps – promise, Mummy?'

'Absolutely. Now, a quick cuddle or the teacher will take me in for a caning!'

Anna began to chuckle as Maisie turned a hug into a tickle before the little girl with the long black plait ran to join the line of girls.

'We should take her out of there. I don't like it, Maisie,' said Scott.

'Nor do I – but removing her from a school could cause more trouble.' She watched as the children filed into the austere Victorian building, boys through one door, and girls through another. 'Mark—' She turned to her husband. 'Let's walk away together now – I don't want to take a chance on her watching us from the window and seeing me turn tail to make a beeline for Miss Patterson's office. You go on to the station – you're late already. I'll see the headmistress and find out if any of the teachers have noticed anything going on that shouldn't be going on.'

Scott nodded, though he seemed reticent to leave. 'I saw one mother give Anna a strange look, and then she went over and spoke to another woman.'

'Mark, let's not start trying to find an errant mother – for all you know, they could be looking at us because you're an American. You're the oddity outside the school gates, my love.'

'And on that note, my oddity of a wife, I am heading for the station right now! Can't wait to find out what Miss Patterson has to say for herself.'

'Mark—'

'OK, OK.'

'Mrs Scott – really, it might have been best to make an appointment. This is a very busy school, you know. We have new evacuees from Margate taking over one of the classrooms, which makes my job even harder. Time is of the essence. Now, what can I do for you?'

Maisie was seated on the opposite side of the tidy desk. Files were in a neat pile, and at the corner of the desk a single African violet in a plain terracotta flowerpot added the only hint of colour to an otherwise spartan room. She had taken the measure of the headmistress the moment she entered the office. Miss Patterson was of average height, dressed in a pale grey jacket with a matching skirt that had kick pleats at back and front. A navy blue blouse buttoned high at the neck appeared restrictive rather than modest, and her hair – nut brown threaded with grey – was pulled back in a bun pinned tight at the nape of her neck. The woman's spectacles were plain, with thin wire frames that made her seem stiff and studious. As she drew breath to speak, Maisie could feel an aura of melancholy surround the woman, who was perhaps only a few years older than herself. It struck Maisie that had Miss Patterson not made such an effort to be plain, she would be deemed a very attractive woman. In her day, dressed in more appealing clothes and with the application of a little rouge and lipstick to set off her clear complexion, she might even have been described as a beauty.

'I have some concerns regarding my daughter, Anna.' Maisie went on to explain the behaviour traits that had become evident of late, and the bruise on Anna's arm. 'Miss Patterson, I thought you might be able to throw some light on what might be at the root of Anna's current unhappiness. She's always been a very happy-go-lucky child.'

'Hmm.' The headmistress swivelled her chair away from Maisie, opened a filing cabinet with a key she wore on a long chain around her neck, and leafed through files until she found what she was looking for.

She opened the selected folder and began to read.

Maisie waited, realising that even when employing the usual methods of feeling balanced in a situation, she was not going to garner any ease in Miss Patterson's company. In fact, she was a little intimidated by the headmistress. She drew a breath, and began, 'Miss—'

'Well, Mrs Scott, I would say it's all here.' Patterson tapped a short, blunt fingernail on the first page of notes. Maisie noticed a ring on the woman's right hand, and it struck her that if it were on her left, it would have been an engagement ring.

'What's all there? Perhaps you would explain, Miss Patterson.'

Patterson looked up over her spectacles, now perched on the end of her nose. She tapped the file again, this time as she closed it. 'Look at the child's background, and let's be honest, shall we? Illegitimate. Father a sailor on a cargo boat – he was some sort of foreign chappie. Probably dead, given what's been happening to merchant shipping, not that we know who he is. Dead real mother. Dead real grandmother. And goodness knows what kind of life and education she enjoyed before she was evacuated and you charitably gave her a home – and you a widow at the time. Now you've married again, and to an American.'

'With respect,' said Maisie, knowing she only ever used that phrase when any chance of respect was evaporating at speed. 'With respect, Anna has weathered her storms in a mature manner and has been given every support at home. She is much loved – she is our daughter, we have concerns about her well-being, and we thought you might be able to assist us with some . . . some perception, perhaps. I hoped you could discuss the situation with her form teacher. At the parents' open evening in July, Mrs Chivers told us that Anna was doing exceptionally well.'

'Mrs Scott—'

'Miss Patterson, I believe my – our – daughter is being bullied by another child. Perhaps more than one. I know children do not like to be seen as snitches and she has not named the perpetrator, so I was reticent to come to see you. However, now that I have asked for your help and your thoughts on the matter, I find that I am disappointed.'

'Mrs Scott, most children have to endure a playground upset at one time or another, and I have always thought it best to let them sort it out themselves. In that way as headmistress I prepare them for adulthood, because they cannot have their parents swooping in to rescue them when they are twenty- five, can they? Where would we be if every young man at Dunkirk had been dragged back by his mother instead of fighting for his country?' Patterson sighed and tapped the file again. 'Be assured we have noticed no bullying, nothing untoward. Except, perhaps, a child whose life at home has been less than stable. I suggest you look there, Mrs Scott.'

Maisie and the headmistress stood at the same time, but as Maisie was about to speak, Patterson cut her off. 'You know, Mrs Scott, I am only a few years older than you, I would imagine. Women of our age who are married and have children are the lucky ones. I am therefore surprised that now, as a recently remarried widow with a daughter, you are not content enough with your lot to remain at home.' The woman paused, but not long enough to allow Maisie to interject. 'Especially a woman with your connections in Chelstone.'

Maisie stared at Patterson, and at first thought she might not find words to counter the headmistress. Having gathered her wits, she responded. 'Thank you for your time and your candour, Miss Patterson. It seems I have caught you on one of your less than stellar days.' She stepped away as if to leave, then turned to face the woman again. 'Be assured of this – I know what has come to pass in your life. I do not need a file to refer to, because you wear your personal history cloaked in anger. When I was a very young woman, my fiancé was lost to me from the moment he was wounded. He died some years later – and yes, I've been fortunate since then to have found companionship again, despite another tragedy. If you had done your homework beyond the few notes in Anna's file, you would know that my child is loved beyond measure, not just by her father and me but by her grandparents, and my late husband's parents too – they adore her. I also know the physical signs of bullying when I see them – and I can tell you now that I will not allow my child to suffer if I can possibly help it. I will be in touch again, Miss Patterson. In the meantime, please ensure you keep tabs on my daughter while you are *in loco parentis* – I believe that is the essence of any teacher's remit.'

Patterson, however, was not a woman to let another have the last word. 'Be that as it may, but might I also suggest that the child would feel happier if she had the same name as her *American* father. On our records she is still listed as Anna Dobbs.'

'I will let you know when the necessary legal papers have been completed, and you can change her name on your records. I will speak to my daughter regarding which name she would like to be known by, and you can adhere to her wishes. I trust I have made myself clear.'

Fighting the urge to walk straight into Anna's classroom and remove her from the school, Maisie made her way to the station. She purchased a return ticket, but instead of taking a seat in the waiting room, she stepped out onto the platform, pulling up her collar against an autumn wind that seemed to whip up her emotions as she considered the conversation with the headmistress of Chelstone Primary School. She looked down at her ticket as the rails began to rattle and vibrate, signalling the approach of the 10:15 to Tonbridge, where she would change for the London service. Her appointment at the embassy was on Wednesday, so in truth there was no reason for her to go to the office. Indeed, there was much she could do and still be home in time to collect Anna from school, then there would be one less 'sleep' away for her child to endure. Yes, she knew exactly what she would do.

'Mr Potter – I'm so sorry, but I've just remembered something I have to do in Chelstone. Can you change my ticket? I think . . . I think I'll go another day. I've forgotten a really important appointment today. Would you mind? I know it's not usual, but—'

'Don't you worry, madam,' said the station master. 'I see you and your husband here enough. I'll change it directly.'

Maisie thanked the man, took her new ticket and began a brisk walk towards Chelstone Manor. She would telephone Mark at work, tell him what had happened with Miss Patterson, and of course, he would agree that she was absolutely right to remain, to meet Anna after school. Then she would have to deal with a nagging thought: that while Anna was without doubt the victim of bullying at school, her headmistress was not completely wrong in her assessment of the root cause of Anna's distress. Patterson might not have hit the nail squarely on the head, but the hammer had come too close for comfort.

At the same time, another seedling of thought was taking root in Maisie's mind, and that was a feeling she had seen Patterson somewhere before, but she could not put her finger on the place or the circumstances.

Instead of travelling to London, Maisie once again claimed the Alvis to continue her investigation. The garage where Dan Littlecombe worked was just outside Westerham, and had once been stabling in the years before the internal combustion engine began to drive horse-drawn carriages off the road. The doors were open, and as she pulled up alongside the garage, she could see a motor car inside with the bonnet open and a man wearing blue overalls bent over the engine. She left the Alvis and walked towards the man, who stood up and began wiping his hands on an old cloth as she approached. He was of lean build, with high cheekbones that made his face appear hollow and thin, as if he had suffered an illness of late. Despite Littlecombe's pallor, the flesh at his temples crinkled when he smiled, so his eyes seemed to reflect a kind and caring soul, thought Maisie, a man who with the passage of time could never quite brush off life's slings and arrows, much as he tried.

'Mr Littlecombe?'

'That's me. How can I help you, madam? Your motor sounded as if it's running all right.'

'Oh, it's driving perfectly, thank you.' She reached into her jacket pocket and pulled out a calling card, which she handed to the man. 'My name is Maisie Dobbs. As you will see, I am a private investigator. My client has a special interest in the death of a woman pilot with the

133

Air Transport Auxiliary, so I am charged with finding out as much as I can. My visit here must be in complete confidence, though I can inform you that I also work closely with the police. I will give you the name of someone at Scotland Yard, if you would like to check my credentials.'

Littlecombe shoved the cloth into a pocket, looked at the card and rubbed his chin, leaving a small smear of oil under his lower lip. Then he nodded.

'I would ask you back to the office, but you'll come out looking like me – covered in grease. We can talk here, if you like.' He pulled the back of his hand across his chin, as if knowing he had left a mark.

'Thank you – and here is perfectly all right.' She smiled, then began. 'I understand you were the first person to reach the aircraft that crashed a couple of miles away. You tried to assist the pilot.'

'I was walking old Jess, my dog. It's a good walk, and I hadn't much work on. What with a lot of people giving up their motor cars for the duration, I don't have as many repairs coming through as I did before the war, though the farmers keep me busy. Some of those new- fangled tractors are more trouble than the horses. Ask old Barney Love what he thinks.'

'Oh, I've heard about him – the aircraft came down not far from his farm.'

'Three fields over. I reckon the pilot tried to pull up; tried to bring the Spitfire in for a rough landing, but she had no chance before she passed out.'

'Tell me what you found, Mr Littlecombe.'

The man rubbed his chin again as he began to recount the story Maisie already knew, but adding the sort of details that are never revealed when the narrative is heard second hand. It was different hearing Littlecombe's account in his own words.

'I was a mechanic with the Royal Flying Corps in the last war, so I have an idea of what I'm looking at – saw a lot, you know.' He closed his eyes tight, as if to banish images that came to him at the mention of the previous war. He shook his head, and continued. 'Of course, the aircraft then weren't like what our boys are going up in now. They were death traps before they even got up there. Anyway, enough of that – just to say I reckon the young woman pilot must have been hit by something before she went down.' He gave a chuckle, though it was an expression without humour. 'I've seen them pilots – the RAF boys and them ferry pilots. They all love the Spitfire. They're only youngsters aren't they, going up there before they've got many miles of life in them? So you can't blame them if they have a bit of fun every now and again.'

'You're right there, Mr Littlecombe. My godson flies Hurricanes, though it seems it was only yesterday he was on the cricket team at school. But please,' she continued, 'tell me more about what you found and what you thought when you inspected the aircraft.'

'I couldn't do anything for the poor girl. Once I knew that, I had a walk around the aeroplane. The tail was off, the propeller bent into the ground. The hood was back, which I thought was odd – made me wonder if she'd had time and the strength to pull on it before she lost consciousness;

a sort of – what do they call it?' He scratched his head. 'Reflex. Doing something to get more air, to stop herself passing out.' Another pause, another closing and opening of his eyes. 'I looked at the tail – it was close, and I saw marks that I don't think could have been made when she crashed. I checked the rest of the Spitfire and saw some dents and chips – the sort of scars that seemed a bit odd – and for all the world, it looked as if the aeroplane had been hit by something.'

Maisie nodded, frowning. 'This is what bothers me. Could she have been hit by a bullet, for example, aimed from the ground?'

Littlecombe nodded. 'If she was low enough.'

'This is something that has just occurred to me – do you think anyone taking a potshot at an aircraft would have an idea that the pilot was a woman?'

He looked at Maisie, his eyes appearing to stare through her. 'She didn't have a helmet on and she had longer hair – she certainly wasn't a bloke with the regulation RAF short back and sides! So I would say that if she were low enough at any point, you could have even imagined the colour of her lipstick. Yes, someone could have guessed it was a woman in the cockpit.'

'Who else arrived at the scene, after you reached the site of the crash and had a look around?'

'One of those land girls came running over, so I told her to go back to the farm and summon the police. I knew they would get in touch with Biggin Hill – and they probably knew anyway, on account of the radar.'

'Then what happened?'

'Wasn't long before everyone seemed to turn up. The RAF bods, an ambulance – oh, and the local bobby was one of the first to reach me. Probably the only occasion he's arrived anywhere on time in his life.'

'Might that be Constable Eames?'

'That's him. Nice lad, but not the sharpest knife in the drawer, if you catch my drift. He said he saw the Spitfire in trouble, so he rushed over. Mud all over his bike and trousers, but he got there.'

Maisie nodded. 'Did he inspect the wreckage?'

'He kept away from the front end – I thought he was going to pass out, to tell you the truth. But he looked over the rest of the aircraft. I reckon he wanted to seem as if he knew what he was doing. Then the cavalry turned up – as I said, the RAF bods, the police. I was asked to give a statement and that was that – sent on my way, and—' He stopped talking mid-sentence and smiled at someone approaching behind Maisie. He waved. 'Hello Ronnie, how are you, my boy?'

A young man in a Home Guard uniform had stopped to look at the Alvis. Maisie judged him to be about twenty-three or twenty-four, perhaps a little older than Tom, her eldest godson.

'Miss Dobbs, this is Ronnie Watkins, my occasional apprentice when he isn't looking for errant invaders or helping out his mum. Ronnie, this is Miss Dobbs, she's – anyway, she's just dropped in because she had a noisy bit of grit in the wheel. Didn't take a minute to find it.'

Ronnie Watkins touched his cap and nodded a greeting. 'Them little bits of grit get on your nerves, don't they? Rattle, rattle, rattle and it's all you can do to find them.'

'I was so grateful to come across this garage – I thought the sound would give me a headache. And you never know whether there's a serious malfunction with the wheel.' She smiled at Watkins, who she could see might be a shy young man, or perhaps not used to greeting strangers, as he avoided her eyes and instead focused on a place above her head, or to the side. 'I see you're with the local Home Guard, Mr Watkins,' continued Maisie. 'I don't know what we would do without you.'

'Poor old Ronnie here couldn't join up with the regulars on account of his leg, could you, Ron?'

Watkins glanced at his feet and shrugged, and when he looked up again, he focused his gaze on the open engine Littlecombe had abandoned to speak to Maisie.

'I'm sorry to hear that, Ronnie. You must have been very disappointed, but as I said, I don't know how we would fare without our Home Guard looking out for us.'

Watkins nodded and thanked Maisie, then drew his attention to Littlecombe. 'Do you want me to come in this week?'

'I've got that tractor due again, if they can get it over here tomorrow, and a motor from the American, though I don't know which day, so I could use your help, Ronnie. You've got a talent with tractors, lad.'

'See you later then.' Watkins touched his cap again. 'Nice to meet you, madam.'

Maisie watched as the young man turned and walked away from the garage.

'He seems all right to me, Mr Littlecombe. What's wrong with his leg?'

'Goes out on him if he moves any faster than a doddle. Been like that since he was a boy. The doctors said it could be a neurological sickness, his brain not able to tell his legs properly what to do. I feel sorry for him – all the blokes he was at school with have gone into the services, and there's him stuck with a load of old duffers in the Home Guard.'

'That must be difficult. One of my godsons was wounded trying to bring men back from Dunkirk – his arm had to be amputated. He's had a very difficult time since then.'

'Ronnie's mother lost her husband before the boy was born. Poor man copped it in 1918, just before the Armistice. He'd only just gone back over there after a couple of days' leave. She said when Ronnie was born, 'No war will ever get my boy.' And look what happened to the lad. But she was right – he won't be going away to fight. Hasn't done much else to ever get hurt either. No climbing trees, no football or running with the other lads.' Dan Littlecombe looked at his watch.

'Oh goodness, you're right to check the time – it's marching on and I've another call to make today.'

'Local?'

'One of the farms not far from here. I want to see Mr Love, so it's a coincidence you should have mentioned him.'

'Good man, that one. Runs a tidy farm.'

'Now that's funny, because I heard it from one quarter that he was . . . that he was a little too parsimonious and that the old barn was filled with nothing but mouldy hay that should never be put out for cattle. I confess, I have been in that barn and it's not how it looked to me.'

'Show me a farmer who hasn't had to do some belt-tightening, and I'll show you a man who doesn't know his crops or his herds and is going out of business. And Barney Love knows better than to use mouldy hay – he wouldn't want to lose a single head of cattle or one sheep.'

'That's what I thought.' Maisie smiled, thanked the man again and turned as if to leave, but instead looked back. 'Oh, there is one thing. You said you had a motor car coming in for repair soon and it was owned by an American. Is the American a serviceman based not far from here? I thought they would undertake all their own vehicular maintenance.'

'Yes, you're right, they do. But you're mistaken – I said the motor car was American, not the bloke who brought it in. It's what they call a Buick. Not sure what he does, the owner, and I don't know where he lives. I've always assumed he was a . . . a . . . well, come to think of it, I have no idea. None of my business. Only business I'm interested in is whether someone can pay for the work, and if they don't, well, I'm the one with the motor car and a lock on my garage door! That soon gets the slow ones to pay up!' He leaned towards the open engine again, but kept his gaze on Maisie. 'Any particular reason you're interested in whether I had an American in here?'

Maisie laughed. 'This is going to sound silly but, well, my husband is an American. I thought it might be nice if he met another fellow from "back home", as he calls it. But there's no guarantee that just because people come from the same country, they'll get on with one another, is there?'

'Never a truer word said, madam. There's plenty of people from round here that I would leave the country never to see again!'

'Anyway,' said Maisie, laughing at the joke, while considering another angle to her enquiry, 'I wonder if it wouldn't be too much trouble to find out the owner's name and where he lives, then I could just ask my husband if he'd like to get in touch and he could make up his mind about it. They're very convivial people, Americans.'

He nodded. 'You're right there, madam, but as I said, the motor car's an American, not the owner. Mind you, if your husband wants to talk about American automobiles—'

'I'm sorry – I must be slow today. Took me a minute to grasp that the owner isn't American! And I can safely say that my husband has little interest in looking at motor cars, wherever they're from!'

Maisie thanked Dan Littlecombe for his time, and turned towards the Alvis. She knew without looking back that the garage owner was watching her as she walked to her motor car.

Consulting the map, Maisie drove in the direction of the Love farm. Had Dan Littlecombe told a half-truth? He might be a proprietor who didn't care for paperwork, but she couldn't imagine he would be so cavalier as to not keep records. On the other hand, it was also fair to say she had never known a blacksmith who kept a ledger. If the farrier had a horse in his charge, the owner would not get his property back until the bill was settled in cash. It appeared Littlecombe applied the same rule to the repair of vehicular horsepower.

CHAPTER NINE

'Mr Love? Oh dear, I seem to have disturbed you in the middle of having a bite to eat.' Maisie stepped back from the open door.

Love shook his head and held up a finger to indicate he was still chewing whatever he was eating when Maisie knocked at the door. He wore old grey corduroy trousers tucked into black Wellington boots, with a tweed jacket, frayed at the cuffs, that he possibly acquired as a younger man, because Maisie could see the buttons would only have fastened across a more slender girth. His collarless shirt was topped with a Fair Isle pullover – Maisie noticed a single blue woollen thread coming loose at the neck, which looked as if it would soon unravel if not attended to.

'I was just having a quick slice of toast when I heard your knock,' said Love. 'Give me a minute.' He walked back into the kitchen, where Maisie could see a woman putting half a loaf into an enamel bread bin. Maisie moved away and waited alongside a wheelbarrow that was leaning against a wall.

Barney Love emerged from the house, closing the door behind him after two collies had come to heel. 'Right you are, miss – what can I do for you?' He nodded at the dogs, who sat on their haunches but continued looking up at their master, waiting for his next command.

'I left my card with the Land Army women I met last week and asked them to pass it on to you, but I know how busy you must be, so I was in the area again today and hoped to see you.'

'Yep – they gave me your card and I was meaning to get in touch, but you know, we don't like to use the blower too much. Not cheap, you know, making them calls, and the wife worries that it would be just our luck that one of our sons tried to get through while we're jawing away on that thing.'

'Of course, I understand. I—'

'Madge said you were interested in one of them American soldiers who came to help with the harvest, the dark one – we called him Mattie. Nice boy. Very good manners – my wife said she wished a lot of youngsters were more like it. We're all very grateful to those RAF lads, but the way they race around the lanes when they get in a motor car – you'd think they'd have enough of dicing with death, up there. Anyway, I've got a bit of time, so let's get on with it – how can I help you?'

'I understand Private Crittenden – Mattie – was good friends with another American soldier, Private Charles Stone.'

143

The farmer nodded, fingering the loose thread on his pullover, then tucking it inside. 'Funny that – young Mattie Crittenden having a name you could have found on the local cricket team. There they were, Americans from the same place who weren't even supposed to talk to one another. All very strange, if you ask me – but I suppose our ways are a bit strange to them, eh? No accounting for folk, as they say.'

'Did you ever see them with anyone else – not a soldier, but other men?'

'No, never. I mean, I kept an eye on all the soldiers working out there, and of course we're all in the fields, come harvest time. We've got to move sharpish while the weather is with us – that's why the American army offered to help. Something about winning the hearts of us British. Well, I don't know about my heart, but they won my respect – hard workers, all. But I didn't hold with their military police turning up, checking on who was talking to who else and getting upset if they saw them even working too close to one another, you know, the colours.' He shook his head. 'No, I told them – this is my land, and you don't come here telling people who they can work alongside when I need my harvest in and no one has the time to be picky about the colour of the next man's skin. Job needs doing and I don't care who's doing it.'

Maisie opened her mouth to ask another question, but the farmer kept talking.

'Of course most of the white soldiers did their best to keep away from the likes of Mattie, though after a bit, all working together, a couple of them mixed a bit, but to

144

be fair, we only had a few like Mattie. I suppose that's what made young Charlie different. I'm a busy man, Miss Dobbs, but a farmer can size up people as fast as he can get the measure of a bull, a herd of sheep or the quality of barley coming through. Charlie's a boy with a good heart and so was Mattie Crittenden. They were drawn across the bridge of friendship and it made their summer easier, because I reckon they were homesick. They were all homesick, those boys, never mind their colour – and they all know that they're not going to be spending the rest of the war working on a farm, though I doubt they know what's in store for them. Young men never do. Mind you, it came as a shock to them, according to one I spoke to, when they saw what was left of a street after a bombing raid.'

Maisie agreed, but was anxious to make progress. 'I believe you know what has subsequently happened to Mr Crittenden.'

''Course I know. Had the MPs here, asking questions and going over my barn.'

'Have you ever seen anyone using that barn?'

'No.' He shook his head. 'Well, I mean the local nippers go in there at times, and I know it's where a courting couple might get up to some mischief, but no one's had permission to use it – though of course I was told that's where Mattie Crittenden was found, and it's had me right worried. Now that the authorities have finished with their looking around, I'm making sure it's repaired. Replace the boards at the back and put new hinges on those doors, and I suppose I should padlock it too, though it's a blimmin' nuisance, because you've never got the blimmin' key when you want it.'

Maisie nodded. 'Tell me, Mr Love, I wonder if you've seen any other Americans coming to the farm.'

Barney Love rubbed his chin. 'Now it's funny you should ask. I had a bloke knock at the door – it was a good number of weeks ago, if memory serves me well. Tell you the truth, I wouldn't have pegged him for an American at first – he sounded like he was English. Then the odd word slipped, and I thought he might be one of those Canadians, but the more he went on, the more he sounded like an American. Some of 'em can sound quite posh, can't they?' He laughed. 'He said he saw an old barn as he was passing and asked about it for his horse. I said I was sorry, I couldn't help him – so off he went.' Love frowned, and shook his head. 'And in truth, I didn't like the look of him – and he didn't strike me as someone who'd have a horse. I must admit, it was only after he went that it crossed my mind that it was a bit odd, him asking about the barn.'

Maisie met Love's eyes. 'Is that because you can't see the barn from the lane when you drive in? You have to know it's there – just like the woman who saved Matthias Crittenden's life knew it was there because she had seen it from the air.'

'A woman saved his life?'

'Were you not told?'

'I was told a pilot had seen something from up there, but – a woman?'

'A ferry pilot. She was delivering a Spitfire to Biggin Hill.'

'A Spitfire? A woman?'

Maisie nodded.

'Well I never.' He paused. 'Mind you, that Madge – the land girl – she can plough a straighter line than any man I've seen working around here, whether she's using the horses, or that blimmin' tractor what broke down and can't be mended.' He shook his head. 'Well I never, a woman up there,' he repeated, before returning to the question of the barn. 'But you were right, Miss Dobbs – that American could never have seen the barn as he drove in along the lane from the road. He must already have known it was there.'

'How do you think he knew – if you had to guess?'

'Either someone told him, or—' Barney Love gave a throaty laugh and pointed to the sky. 'Or he's been up there too!'

Maisie smiled and glanced at her watch. 'I know you have to get on, Mr Love – but I was told Matthias and Charlie liked to go for a walk along by the river and that they sometimes went fishing there. I'd like to wander down in that direction – would you mind? And could you direct me?'

'All right by me.' He lifted his hand and pointed across a field. 'Make your way around that pasture and you'll see to the right there's a stile. Hop over that and you'll come across a footpath through the trees going down to the water – but be careful, the banks are steep in places, and the water is not as shallow as it looks. We get a nice run of trout in that river, you know – well, we always used to, but what with the rationing, there's more people sneaking out there with their rods, even at a time of year they're not supposed to be catching the fish.' He gave a chuckle. 'And I happen to know the best "fisherman" around here is a ten-year-old girl who slips in there and doesn't know I've seen her. I say "good on her" and just turn a blind eye to the trespassing.'

Maisie laughed. 'I'd better set off then. I'm used to walking in the country, Mr Love – I live in Chelstone.'

'You're as good as a local then. Look out for me after you get back, I should be in the milking shed. If I don't hear from you, I'll have to go out and make sure you haven't fallen in and drowned down there. The last thing I want is a herd of coppers running all over the place looking for another dead body!'

Maisie set off towards the pasture as directed by Barney Love, and began walking around the edge of the field, which had been left to lie fallow and regenerate for the next planting. Most farmers adhered to the rotation system of leaving a field untouched and unused for a year before moving in livestock the following year, and in a later year planting a fresh crop in soil well fertilised by a constant supply of manure. It was a means of building resilience in the land, in the same way that a cup of Ovaltine gave the promise of a good night's sleep to a tired human being. Fallow land was rested land, and rested land was hardy. Maisie suspected that Barney Love might have had words with the men from the ministry about that – in wartime fallow land was considered a waste, especially when U-boats were attacking ships bringing supplies of food to Britain, and Adolf Hitler was trying to starve the country into surrender.

The stile at the edge of the wood was old and lichen covered, so Maisie watched her step as she climbed over and set off along an ancient footpath that would take her down to the river. Even before she heard the rushing water, she knew it was close – it might be autumn, but wild garlic underfoot had retained its pungent aroma, though it was without the company of the delicate celandines that, come spring, would open their egg-yellow faces to the promise of warmer days ahead.

She reached the river, which spanned about twelve feet across, though she imagined the flow would diminish in summer. There was a half-moon-shaped sliver of land between woodland and the water's edge. An angler would have chosen that very spot. It was perfect for an overhead cast – there were no hanging branches for the line to catch, and with a flick of the wrist at the end of the cast, the fly would land in just the right place on the water to attract a passing trout. She smiled, remembering fishing with her father when he first departed London for Chelstone, having been offered the job of groom when the younger men left for war – the war everyone believed would end all wars. Lingering on the sandy soil, she remembered the peaceful rhythm of standing alongside her father, casting her line yet feeling a certain guilt to be doing such a thing when not fifty miles away, in France, young men were dying in the tens of thousands on just one day.

Maisie began to look down as she approached the spongy area closer to the flow of the river, giving thanks that she had remembered to bring her Wellington boots. The sound of tree crowns swaying in the breeze and the running water settled her thoughts. Standing in the silence, she closed her eyes. The last leaves of the year rustled in a breeze that seemed to brush against the water, causing ripples to dance in the waning afternoon sunlight. Birdsong echoed, as if to let her know that not all fowl had flown away to warmer climes, that there were those sturdy enough to weather winter's coming.

'There's something here for me,' she whispered. 'There's something for me to discover.'

In her mind's eye, she felt the company of two young men so far from all that was known to them, and in stolen moments finding balm in one another's company. She imagined them fishing with borrowed rods; Matthias perhaps showing his friend how to pull out a measure of line, how to bring back the rod and use the swift back-and-forth flick of his wrist to cast shadows that moved across the water, teasing the trout.

He would play out the line to settle the fly, and then begin tickling the thread to land a fish. She saw Charlie laughing, not dexterous with the rod, catching his fingers in the line. Maisie envisioned them having thrown their jackets on a fallen tree, then . . . she looked behind her, and there it was, the moss-covered trunk of a tree that had come down long ago, perhaps in a storm. She walked towards the felled giant and felt it for dampness – it was dry, so she sat down and looked out at the water again, gathering her thoughts and marshalling what she knew to be anticipation.

She looked down at the soft ground around the tree trunk, at moss that had grown up and around her makeshift seat. She studied the undergrowth behind her, the shadowy glade where bluebells and primroses would bloom in spring.

'Where are you, Charlie Stone? Because I do not believe

you're dead. I don't know whether you are part of something I don't understand or if you are a bystander caught in a maelstrom, but I must find you, because if I don't, Matthias Crittenden's freedom will be compromised. I know you were here and that you came here with your friend, both of you seeking respite from the world into which you were plunged. But I have a feeling you were brought here again, later, by someone else.' She closed her eyes. 'Where are you, Charlie Stone?'

Her words flowed in little more than a whisper, as if she were petitioning the very atmosphere around her for answers to her questions.

A loud screech at once filled the air, causing Maisie to jump up and look around, her hand on her chest. She cast her gaze up to the trees, as another screech caught her attention to the right.

'Oh, it's you! My goodness, are you following me?' A barn owl stared down from a branch. 'And aren't you supposed to be resting in a barn and not out at all hours?'

The owl screeched again.

Maisie stared at the creature. 'I suppose I could call you Athena, couldn't I? I know all about you. A friend taught me years ago – the owl, a protector of armies, beloved by Greek soldiers.' She sighed. 'But you also portend death, don't you? And to see you in daylight, well, that isn't favourable at all.' She felt herself shiver, and clapped her hands. 'Go back to your barn – go back and don't come out until it's dark!'

The owl opened its wings and swooped low over her head, then took flight above the treetops in the direction of the barn, its wingspan sunlit as it moved towards its home. Maisie turned to step around the tree trunk, caught her foot and almost fell. Righting herself, she looked down, and as she lifted her foot away from the creeping vine wrapped around the toe of her boot, she saw something that did not surprise her. In fact, later, she thought she might have been disappointed not to have found an item she deemed important.

Maisie considered all the innocent ways that a button could have come loose from a soldier's jacket. It could have caught on something – but what? Servicemen from any army were required to check their uniforms daily, because woe betide the soldier found with a loose or missing button. She imagined Crittenden and Stone carrying their jackets as they wandered along to the river. Or if they removed them to cast a line, they would have taken care not to tear or damage any part of the uniform. Or . . . or could it have been removed deliberately? Starting at the point where she found the button, she began a search, her eyes focused on the ground. Back and forth, back and forth she moved across a grid in her mind that only she could see. She walked farther along the beach area, to the place where a meander in the river widened the expanse of water, and then she stopped. Another button, half submerged in the soil, caught her eye. And then one more. She looked along the water line at the path she had taken, and wondered. Now she had to find Barney Love.

Once more negotiating the slippery, lichen-covered stile, Maisie glanced at her watch and cursed the passing time. She ran alongside the fallow pasture and gave thanks when she saw Barney Love walking towards her, his two dogs following in his wake, tails low, their eyes searching back and forth, awaiting their master's next command.

'Mr Love!' Maisie waved and called out, catching her breath when she reached the farmer.

'Came to find you – thought you might have fallen in down there.'

'No, I didn't fall in – but you were right about the river. I can see it's deeper in places than you might at first imagine, and it's quite wide as it goes into that meander.'

'There's people who've underestimated the flow, that I can tell you. Serves 'em right, far as I'm concerned.'

'Mr Love – do you think anyone could bring a rowing boat along that stretch?'

The farmer pushed back his cap and scratched his head. 'Saw some children come along on a homemade raft once – little blighters fell in when it all came apart. Had to laugh – but they were lucky I was down there landing a trout for our tea when it happened. But to a rowing boat – never seen it done, but doesn't mean it couldn't be done. It's certainly deep enough for a little flat-bottomed thing.'

'Do you know anyone who has such a craft?'

'No, sorry, Miss Dobbs – but I remember hearing that John Eames had one years ago, though I never saw the thing. He used to work for me – bit of a sly one, was Eames. His boy, Peter, is a local bobby now.' He pushed back his cap and scratched his head. 'Your best bet is to ask Dan Littlecombe at the garage. He's got a good number of tools, so people take all sorts of bits and bobs in there to be mended, or they have a word with him if they want to borrow something or other. But aside from Dan, I don't know.'

Maisie nodded. 'All right.' She looked at her watch. 'I've just enough time before I must dash to collect my daughter from school.'

'Daughter?' He glanced at her finger. 'You a Miss Dobbs, yet you've got a ring and a daughter. I tell you, I can't keep up these days.'

'I'm Miss Dobbs for my work. I'm married, and I have a little girl. And she will be very upset if I'm not at the school gates! Thank you very much, Mr Love. I must dash!'

'Miss Dobbs. I was just about to lock up and go home for the day.'

Dan Littlecombe was securing the doors to his garage with a heavy padlock.

'I've just been to see the farmer, Barney Love. He was very helpful, but he referred me back to you – he thought you could help me with a question.'

'Fire away,' said Littlecombe, slipping a key into the pocket of his overalls. 'I'll do what I can.'

'I was just down at the river, and—'

'Lovely trout in there, you know.'

'Yes, I know. However, I noticed it's quite deep in places, and—'

'Boy almost drowned in that river a few years ago.'

'I'm glad to hear it's an "almost" – but I wondered, are you aware of anyone ever taking a small craft along that river, a rowing boat, for example? And do you know anyone with a rowing boat?'

Littlecombe laughed. 'A boat?'

'I know, it's a strange question.'

He frowned. 'The only person I ever knew to take a boat down there was a good while ago now – got to be, oh, twenty-odd years. Probably more. Time flies, doesn't it?'

'Oh dear.'

'Yes, that was the father of Peter Eames – you know, Constable Eames. His dad. John Eames. Johnny Eames was an only child, you know. His father, Michael – that's Peter's grandfather – was a carpenter, and when John was a lad, he went on and on about getting out on the river, so the old man made a little rowing boat for him from wood left over from his jobs. I remember my father saying that old Michael Eames wasn't always on the up and up, so he'd overorder on the wood for a job, and that's how he made the boat. It's probably rotted away to nothing now. And I might add that Johnny Eames was like his father before him – not exactly above board – so they kept it quiet about having a boat, probably because he used it for something underhand. Don't think even Barney Love knew about it. It's a wonder young Peter is in the police force, given what his father and grandfather were like.'

'Didn't Constable Eames's father used to work on the farm, for Barney Love?'

'That's right – but not any more. They live in one of them new council houses now. John had a bit of a row with Barney Love – or as word went round afterwards, he had a bit of a barney with Barney!'

Maisie smiled. 'That's a good one! Thank you, Mr Littlecombe, for all your help. Now I must rush.'

'You won't have any trouble in that motor car – the Alvis

155

has got a fair few horses under the bonnet, hasn't she?'

'Oh, she has indeed, but I don't want to fall foul of Constable Eames, and have him flagging me down for being too speedy!'

Maisie stood at the school gates and watched as other mothers arrived to collect their children. In the past she had never had sufficient time to strike up conversation or to mingle. On the days she met Anna, she arrived with only a minute or two to spare, having run breathless from the Dower House library, where she had been working, or from the station, the train sometimes pulling in late, leaving only minutes for Maisie to reach the school and greet her daughter as she ran across the playground.

Several of the mothers were gathered in a cluster. Maisie wondered whether to approach them – they seemed to be well acquainted, and were deep in conversation. She looked away and saw another parent approaching the school. Maisie waved to her as she came closer.

'You're Jane's mother, aren't you?'

The woman nodded and gave a half-smile before glancing towards the clutch of women Maisie had thought twice about greeting. The woman was dressed in a lightweight woollen coat with wear showing at the cuffs and around the collar, and one spot on the shoulder where a moth had begun to feast. Her shoes were polished, and Maisie felt a certain defensive pride envelop the woman as she nodded.

'Yes. I'm Mrs Heywood. Jane is my daughter.'

'It's lovely to meet you, Mrs Heywood – my name is . . .' Trying not to reveal a frisson of panic, Maisie fumbled for the right words. 'Mrs Scott. I'm Anna's mother.'

'Anna, yes, Jane's mentioned her. The orphan girl.'

Maisie forced another smile. 'Oh, that's well in the past. I'm her mother, and she is surrounded by her family every day, so all is well for her. Anna is a happy child, and that's all any of us can ask for, isn't it?'

'She certainly landed on her feet, didn't she? She must be very grateful to you.'

'I am not expecting gratitude, Mrs Heywood, not in the way that an adult might wish to express such a thing – but we are incredibly happy that she has adjusted to life with us. It's been over two years now.' Maisie looked away for a second, as she struggled to maintain an expression that belied the despair and anger she was feeling. 'Ah, that's the school bell. They'll all come running out soon. Mrs Heywood, I was wondering – would Jane like to come to our house to play with Anna, perhaps one Saturday morning? I think it's good for the children to have the opportunity for fun with friends outside school. Or you could come to tea. We live with my parents.'

'Well, I don't know. I'll have to see.' Heywood raised her hand. 'Jane – over here!'

'Ah, there's Anna,' said Maisie, watching her daughter begin to run towards her – and then stop. Even from a distance, Maisie could feel her daughter's reticence, as if she had careened into an invisible wall. And she knew very well what had extinguished Anna's joy.

Jane reached her mother, waving to a few children who had joined the other women. 'Let's go, Mum – quick!'

'Oh, all right. You must be hungry, Jane.' Heywood

spoke in a deliberate voice, louder than necessary.

Maisie knew she was meant to hear every word and wondered whether to ask about tea again. Perhaps Jane would prove to be a better friend to Anna if they were alone.

'Would you let me know about tea? We'd very much like to see you – and I know Anna would love to have Jane over to play. Truth be told, I think she finds us grown-ups a bit tedious sometimes.'

Heywood looked back at Maisie as she began to move away. 'Jane's scared of dogs and you've got that great big Alsatian, so . . . so no, I don't think it's a good idea. It might end in tears and Jane does get very sneezy around animals. Sorry about that. Nice to meet you anyway.'

'Mummy?'

Maisie looked down at her daughter and knew straight away that something was very wrong. Not a hair on her head was out of place. She knelt down.

'Hello, my darling – see, I'm here. No sleep away tonight.'

Tears filled her daughter's eyes. 'Can we go home now?'

'That's why I'm here – to take you home.'

'Where's Little Emma?'

'She was with Granddad when I left, down at the stables. I didn't want to be late, so I came without her. Mind you, it's just as well, because according to Jane's mother, she doesn't like dogs and gets a bit snuffly in their company.'

'No, she doesn't,' said Anna, leading her mother away from the school. 'She goes to Beryl's house to play and they have two dogs.'

158

'Oh, perhaps it's because Little Emma isn't so little any more.'

Anna shrugged.

'Guess what – Daddy left me a present for you.'

Anna continued looking down as they walked along the road towards Chelstone Manor, and home.

'Anna, what is it, my darling?' Maisie knelt in front of her daughter.

'I don't feel very well.'

'Does your tummy hurt?'

Anna nodded.

'Then let's get home and you can have a nice bath and go straight to bed. Mummy used to be a nurse, you know.' Anna nodded again.

Maisie ran a warm bath, testing the water with her hand. She called to Anna, who she could see in her room from the open door – of late the child would only undress on her own if she could see her mother or grandmother.

'The water's just right, Anna – let's get you in.'

Maisie helped her daughter into the bathtub, steaming with lavender-scented water. Brenda had suggested a few drops of the fragrant oil to calm the child.

'There we go! Let's get the soap.'

'I can do it,' said Anna, taking the bar of soap from Maisie.

'All right. I'll just go and find your dressing gown and pyjamas. I'll only be in your room – not far. The door's still open – I'll be back in two shakes of a lamb's tail.'

'Hurry, Mummy.'

Maisie stepped into her daughter's bedroom, took a pair of pale peach-coloured pyjamas from underneath the pillow and the red dressing gown from a hook behind the door.

'Here we go, Anna. This dressing gown is getting—' said Maisie as she returned to the bathroom. Then she stopped, and looked at her daughter. 'Anna, whatever are you doing?'

Anna was scouring her body with a nail brush, running the harsh bristles up and down her arms and then around her face.

'Anna, don't do that, darling – sweetheart, you'll break the skin. Anna—'

She knelt at the side of the bathtub and with a gentle grasp removed the brush from her daughter's grip while holding the weeping child to her.

'I was just—' Brenda came into the bathroom, Anna's school cardigan in her hands.

Maisie turned to Brenda and shook her head, then spoke in a low voice. 'Oh Grandma, just in time – could you pass me Anna's favourite big fluffy towel?'

Brenda took the thick bath towel, warm from the radiator, and passed it to Maisie, who wrapped her weeping child and carried her into her own bedroom, where she lay on the bed and enveloped Anna in her arms.

Brenda followed, and without speaking held out the green cardigan Anna had worn to school so that Maisie could see. It was ripped at the shoulder. Maisie nodded.

Taking slow, deliberate, audible breaths, she soon felt Anna's chest rising and falling in concert with her own. Her voice a whisper, she tightened her hold. 'Anna, what were

160

you trying to do with the brush, darling?'

'They said I didn't wash properly, because I look different. If I scrub harder I might get some of the brown off.' She faltered, then added. 'Mummy, what's an eye-tye?'

CHAPTER TEN

With Anna asleep, Maisie placed a telephone call to her husband, recounting the day's events, and adding that she would be keeping Anna at home and not be in London until Wednesday morning.

'That's it then. We'll find another school,' said Mark. 'I'm not having my daughter upset by small-minded people who can't see to the ends of their noses. I know you've been in favour of that village school, but I don't like what I'm hearing.'

'Brenda said the same. So did my father. He said that if he and my mother hadn't been poor, they would have sent me to a different school.'

'Why? What happened to you?'

'Oh, it's nothing – long time ago. But it's crushing, knowing my daughter is being bullied for her appearance because they think she's the enemy – they called her an "eye-tye", for heaven's sake! Anyone would think she was Mussolini's agent. And the headmistress was just awful.'

'Anna should go to one of these international schools.'

'That would mean bringing her back to London, though most of the private schools have left for the country anyway. And she's not going to boarding school, Mark. Absolutely over my dead body.'

'Then what?'

'I don't know. I'll have to think about it.'

'We can't keep her out of school for very long, can we?'

'No. But I have one idea – I'll tell you before I interview Private Crittenden. I've got to go over it in my mind.' She sighed. 'There is something else, though. Could you get some chocolate for Anna? Just a little something.'

'I'll have a truckload sent down, if it cheers her up.'

'Oh, Mark . . . see you on Wednesday, darling.'

'You too, hon. You too.'

Maisie set the telephone receiver in its cradle, then picked it up again. Time was getting on, but there was one man she knew who would often work late – and at this time he would doubtless answer the call himself, having allowed his clerk to go home.

'Klein!' The call was answered after one ring.

'Mr Klein – it's Maisie here.'

'Maisie! To what do I owe this call – is everything all right? How's Anna? And Mark?'

'Everyone's well, thank you. I'm calling because I have been most remiss in not instructing you in the matter of my husband's parental responsibilities with regard to Anna. We have discussed the matter, and it's time for him

to formally adopt Anna, to be her father legally as well as
. . . as well as—'

'As well as the father of her heart? Indeed, it is a
coincidence, because I had made a note to be in touch
regarding this very subject. Shall I consider this my
instruction to draw up the necessary papers to petition the
court? It really is a formality, so shouldn't take long at this end.
Of course, the wheels of legal administration have not been
working at full speed, but we can get the vehicle in motion.'

'Thank you. Yes, consider this telephone call to be your
instruction.'

'I should also advise you, Maisie, that we must soon
sit down and discuss the outstanding matter of your last
will and testament. I had to virtually nail your benefactor
to the desk for the same purpose, but we were able to
draft documents that were absolutely right for him and
all concerned. You have a husband and a daughter, ageing
parents and former in-laws to whom you are devoted, and
they to you – and the fact that this is wartime renders the
task one that should be dealt with as a matter of some
urgency. I believe your husband might say it is just a case of
taking care of business.'

'I'm very busy, Mr Klein – but I will attend to it as soon
as my current case is closed.'

'Which will be when?'

'I really don't know – but there is some urgency at this end
too, so I would imagine within a couple of weeks.'

'Right you are. I will be in touch regarding Anna's
adoption by Mr Scott. I take it her surname will change
accordingly.'

Maisie paused, closing her eyes. 'Yes, indeed. If I'm honest, she's been calling herself Miss Anna Scott since the wedding.'

On Wednesday morning, as Maisie settled back into her seat, she thought she had never welcomed the peace of the first-class carriage more. The easy rhythm of the train and the clackety-clack of wheels on rails tempered her mood, allowing her to reflect. Yes, if she were honest, Anna had assumed the family name even before Maisie had become accustomed to it. She had scribbled it in every book, crossing out 'Dobbs' and writing 'Scott.' On one page, she had written 'Miss Anna Dobbs Scott' but had erased it, as if she had spoken the name aloud and found it wanting. But what on earth were they to do about her schooling? Maisie was sure her one idea would fall on hard ground, and never take root, though she had to try it. In the absence of anything better, she knew she had to look into moving Anna to another school.

Once again Maisie's thoughts turned to her mentor, Maurice Blanche. Now, as the train rocked from side to side and she was soothed by the view of Kent's soft, undulating countryside from her seat alongside the carriage window, she remembered his counsel during her apprenticeship, when he noted that she should not be surprised when a new case followed the template of a previous investigation or a personal challenge. He suggested she should consider the phenomenon as she would a teacher, that it was a means of looking at a similar problem from another vantage point, and that there was always a lesson for her in the process.

'Always look to the teaching in the moment, Maisie – only when you see a lesson for what it is can you reach into the knowledge you've accrued and incorporate what you have learned. That is the way to mastery, Maisie, and mastery means being open to that which is new. Even at my age, circumstance challenges me to be vigilant when I encounter a fresh experience, especially when it reflects what has gone before.' He had laughed. 'And beware people who claim to "already know that" – it reveals a closed mind, and in our work, the minute the mind is closed, we might as well tender our resignation.'

Thus this looking-glass moment was not lost on Maisie – the fact that she was now on her way to interview a man who was being held on suspicion of committing a murder, his word doubted because of his colour and origin, was mirrored in her personal life. It was happening at the very same time her daughter faced prejudice at school due to being mistaken for an Italian – for an enemy – due to the colour of her skin. Maisie bit her lip as she stared out of the window, and felt the anger rising again when she recalled Miss Patterson's insinuation that Anna's father being an American was perhaps contributing to her distress.

'Bloody awful woman,' said Maisie.

'Nicely on time, Maisie,' said Robert MacFarlane, as Maisie was shown into his office at 64 Baker Street. He held out his hand towards an unwelcoming hard wooden chair. 'Take a seat for a minute or two. Miss the place, do you?'

Maisie shook her head as she sat down and placed her document case on the floor. 'Sorry, Robbie – approving candidates for clandestine work never suited me, so I think the Special Operations Executive is better off without my reports, don't you?'

MacFarlane raised an eyebrow. 'The SOE would welcome you back with open arms, if you decided to help us out.' He placed two buff-coloured folders on the desk in front of her.

She shook her head again as she pushed the folders away. 'I took on the task because I wanted to do my bit, but my enquiry business is, well, more my line of work – and now Billy is doing very well with greater responsibility, I am able to plan my time a little better.'

'I know, I know.' He stood up and reached for his overcoat and hat, hanging on a stand in the corner. 'You've only just sat down, but we'd better be on our way over to Little America – or as some are calling it, "Eisenhowerplatz". Don't want to be late for the Yanks, do we?'

Mark Scott had been awaiting their arrival in the foyer of the American embassy at One Grosvenor Square. He squeezed Maisie's hand in lieu of a kiss.

'We're going next door to the general's headquarters. Crittenden is there, under guard.'

'He was being held here?'

Scott shook his head. 'No. Somewhere else. They brought him in this morning. Questions were asked, but I gave the right answers to get him here, and so did Mac.' He turned to MacFarlane. 'Thanks, pal – but I've got to tell you, I just want this one over. It's too much of a hot potato, if you want my opinion.'

'Can't disagree with you there,' said MacFarlane.

'Can we get on with it, please? I am anxious to meet Private Crittenden,' said Maisie.

Mark Scott led the way to the adjacent series of offices. Protocols were observed: Maisie and MacFarlane were required to register their names and time of arrival. Maisie relinquished her document case, but kept her notebook and a pencil.

Maisie looked at MacFarlane, her brow creased.

'Don't worry, lass,' said MacFarlane. 'I'll make sure your tête-à-tête with Crittenden is as private as possible – you don't need too many uniforms in there with you.' They stepped into the corridor again.

Two military police approached, Matthias Crittenden between them, his wrists in handcuffs behind his back. Maisie wondered what the exact nature of the charge against him might be. An accessory to a possible crime? Assisting a deserter? She knew of cases where a man had been remanded in custody on suspicion of murder at a time when no body had been found, and wondered whether military authorities needed any legal reason at all to retain a soldier.

MacFarlane stepped towards them, along with Mark Scott, who indicated to Maisie that she should remain where she was. She watched as the men leaned towards one another, with voices that started low, were raised, then lowered again. Another man joined them, also in uniform. He exchanged a few words with the group, nodded, and approached Maisie.

'Miss Dobbs. Good morning. Colonel Theodore Wright.

I'm a lawyer here – a judge advocate general – and I'm afraid I cannot allow you to be alone with the prisoner. However, in light of . . . of the details I've been given by our political attaché and Mr MacFarlane, I understand the importance of your interview to an investigation. I will be in the room, though I will not interject. However, I hope you understand our situation, Miss Dobbs. We cannot allow you to be in the room alone with this man without a US Army legal presence.'

Maisie felt a prickle of disappointment, but understood the implication. 'We are in effect on American soil here, Colonel Wright, so I appreciate that it's a case of "when in Rome".'

Wright nodded. 'Let's get on with it then.' He summoned the MPs, who led Crittenden into the room.

Maisie followed Wright, with a brief glance at her husband and MacFarlane. She turned back in time to see a military policeman attaching one half of Crittenden's handcuff to the chair.

'I don't think that's necessary,' said Maisie. 'If a man's body is restricted and he's uncomfortable, I can't expect his memory to work very well.'

Wright nodded at the men, and the cuffs were removed from Crittenden's wrists. The guards left the room. Instead of taking a seat at the table, Wright pulled a chair into a corner so he would be seated behind Maisie. He looked at Maisie and indicated that she take the chair facing Crittenden.

Matthias Crittenden was a tall man, taller than the military policemen and Colonel Wright. Maisie thought her stepmother might have described him as a "long, tall drink of water" – he was slender, a physical trait emphasised by close-cut hair and a uniform that was just a little too big. A vulnerable demeanour was accentuated by the fact that Crittenden's whole body seemed to be shaking, just as Jo Hardy had described when she discovered him in the old barn. At once Maisie felt as if she wanted to reach out and hold his hand, to have him trust her. So she waited, and for a moment, with eyes closed, she imagined a circle of light around them, encompassing the table but shutting out Colonel Wright. She breathed in deeply for a count of four, and in silence let out her breath to a count of six, a means of restoring calm that she had learned from a Ceylonese man named Khan when she was a girl. She heard Crittenden's breathing fall into rhythm with her own. She opened her eyes. Crittenden was looking at her. His stare seemed to have a colour of its own, almost white against his ebony skin. She noticed he had blue eyes.

'My name is Maisie Dobbs, Private Crittenden. May I call you Matthias?'

'Yes, ma'am.'

'Thank you.' Maisie paused, hearing the man behind her clear his throat. She had overstepped a mark – Private Crittenden should have been addressed as such throughout the interview, but it was too late now, and in any case she thought some informality would help the man to settle. 'Matthias, let me tell you why I am here. I am an investigator, though I have nothing to do with your present circumstances. However, I am looking into the death of a young woman, a pilot, and it seems you may have come by some information that will help me. The lady who found you in the barn, Josephine Hardy, has asked for my assistance because the victim was her friend.'

'Miss Hardy is a good lady, ma'am. She found me and she saved me. Miss Hardy said she'd vouch for me, and I don't know what "vouch" is over here, but I don't think any vouching can help.' He looked towards Wright. Maisie did not follow his gaze. 'I hope them ladies are OK.'

'Matthias, both Miss Hardy and Miss Marshall are well. I should add that I have been told what happened when Miss Hardy found you, and I know you worked on the farm for Mr Love during the summer harvest.' She smiled. 'The women of the Land Army stationed there asked to be remembered to you – you made some friends, didn't you?'

He nodded, the hint of a smile creasing the corners of his mouth. 'Ma'am, they were good to me. I'd never had that from white folks before. And I could talk to them and not be afraid of what might happen to me.'

'Tell me about the summer and bringing in the harvest.'

Maisie knew that remembering summer's warmth would settle Crittenden even more. The images that came into his mind's eye as he recounted his days on the farm would help to open his memory, bringing to the fore events he might otherwise have forgotten – or that were too painful to recall.

'We was volunteered, ma'am. I was happy to do it – happy to be on a farm. It was like home. The land is kinda like it is where I'm from.' His smile broadened. 'And you know, it feels good – feels good to have that sort of ache in your bones. The farmer was fair with us. Mr Love is a hardworking man, and you could see he put his all into that farm. Took a pride, he did. My daddy would have liked that.' He became silent. 'Last words my daddy said before I left home when I got my papers. "Make us proud, son. Never forget your good name".'

Matthias Crittenden looked down at his hands, then lifted one to wipe tears from his cheeks.

Maisie was anxious to move on, but wanted to settle Crittenden again. 'Do you write to your people, Matthias?'

'I did. Wrote to them about the farm.' He looked up at Maisie. 'Can't write to them now, on account of . . . of my situation.'

'Well, when you do, tell them that you're really a local.'

Crittenden frowned. 'I don't understand, ma'am.'

'Didn't anyone tell you? Crittenden is a name firmly rooted in the area around where you were working. It's from that part of our county – Kent.'

'Daddy reckons our name came from his own grandpa's owner.' He rested his hands on the table, and sat forward, curious. 'The man who had the land. My folks was sharecroppers.'

'I know, Matthias. But that name means you're one of us.' She smiled, and – now without thinking – reached out and laid her hand upon his for a second. 'Tell me about Charlie. What happened, Matthias? What happened to Charlie, your friend?'

Crittenden's eyes widened as they filled with tears again. 'There was white boys – Americans – on the farm working. They kept away, because the MPs came checking on us. You don't have no signs here, tellin' us to keep a distance from whites and places we shouldn't go. They would come to the farm lookin' for trouble, so we kept apart when we saw them. But we kinda mixed – not much, but kinda – and me and Charlie talked. It was good. We came from the same place, the same town, only my folks lived on a different side. We could talk about home, about what we missed. Charlie's a good person. His daddy is a pastor, and he said his daddy don't like what was happening to folks like me. But that's not what we talked about. We went fishing in that creek on the farm – farmer called it a river, but to us it was a creek.' He laughed, but the smile was short-lived. 'Then it all kinda changed.'

'What changed?' said Maisie. She withdrew her hand, taking up her pencil.

'Ma'am, you gonna write all this down?'

'I think it might be important, don't you?'

Crittenden nodded, glanced across at Theodore Wright, and drew his attention back to Maisie. 'Them other boys, you know, white boys, well, they started going to the bar after a day's work – that place they call the pub. They got the truck, the one that takes the white soldiers back to their base, to come by the pub – it was called the Eight Bells. There's another truck comes for black soldiers. Anyway, the truck picked up the white soldiers right there, instead of at the farm. Charlie, he said to me, "You should come with me – there's mixing there. You don't have to go in another door. We can walk over there." I was scared. My daddy never liked us to drink alcohol, said it was a man's ruin, but them days were hot and the nights – the nights in summer go on stayin' light right up until late here, don't they? So a few boys went over there one day, and our truck came by the pub. It was good, ma'am, but I gotta confess, I was a bit, you know, uneasy about it.'

'Yes, I can imagine you were. But go on, Matthias.'

'Me and Charlie, we had a fine time, sitting outside on an old wooden seat, bein' able to talk holdin' a beer in our hands, and them men and women from the village coming by and sayin' hello and then just leavin' us alone.' He laughed. 'One old guy told us not to take all their young womenfolk, because they were needed for when your boys come home!'

Maisie could see the memories working, opening a channel for Matthias to speak without fear.

'Then one day, after work, we were outside.' He closed his eyes, and frowned. 'It's startin' to come back now.' He looked at Maisie. 'Sometimes I remember things, and then they go. It's like a flash; I see a picture and then it's gone. But I remember Charlie sayin' there was time for another beer, and I said, I don't know about that, my friend. One's enough for me.' Crittenden closed his eyes, pausing before going on with his story. 'He took my glass and went inside. Was there for a while – mind, it was busy, with guys buying drinks and them girls – land girls, you call them – they were around. Then Charlie came back, looking even whiter than he was going in.'

'What had happened?'

Crittenden opened his eyes, his hands shaking as if the memory had caused shock to rise again. 'Charlie said he was standin', waitin' his turn, but he was pushed back as some other guys came in. Then someone said the MPs were on the way, so he stepped to the side, leanin' against one

174

of them wooden beams. He said that's when he overheard three guys talking at a table. They were keeping it low, like they didn't want anyone to hear, but Charlie said that he could hear them, and they were up to no good.'

'What sort of no good?'

Crittenden inspected his hands, his voice unsteady.

'You sure you're gonna believe me, ma'am? Because ain't no one around here believin' me.'

'If you speak your truth, I will know. And I will know if you lie, Matthias.'

He nodded. 'I figured that, ma'am.'

'Go on.'

'He said they were talking of killin' someone, and it was an important someone.'

'Did he know who?'

'Charlie wasn't sure. He only heard them say "he", and he wasn't sure if it was "E", like they really meant someone called Edward.'

'What else?'

'He said one of the guys was American, and one was like you – British. He said he couldn't be sure about the other guy.'

'Then what happened – according to Charlie?'

'He said he thought he was leaning too hard in their direction, because the one who wasn't doing the talking looked up at him, so he held up the glasses towards the landlord and asked for two more beers.' He glanced at Maisie, leaning forward, his hands now clenched into fists. 'Your beer's strong, so he made sure he looked like he was already gone, and rolled out of the bar with the beers. I said

"Whoa, Charlie, what're you doin'?" and he said "Acting, Mattie. Let's get outta here."'

'Go on, Matthias, close your eyes again and tell me what happened next.'

The man's breath quickened. Maisie countered with her own measured breathing.

'We put down our beers and we started walking away – we moved fast, through the garden and onto the road, then we started to hightail it back to the farm, figuring we'd see one of the trucks on the way, though we didn't know which one but it didn't matter if one of us had to walk instead of catching a ride. Charlie was scared, ma'am, and so was I. I was scared of gettin' in a truck with white guys, and he was just wantin' to get right away from that bar.' He swallowed. 'We were heading back to the farm when we heard an automobile coming – a big automobile. It braked right beside us, and . . . and, ma'am, I don't know what happened next because I was hit. Knocked clean out.' He opened his eyes once again and turned his head to Maisie, pointing to the place where a cut had been stitched. 'Doc said he wasn't dressin' it so it would heal better. Said it needed air.'

'Please continue, Matthias – when did you come round again?'

'I reckon that was when I was in that old barn. Hog-tied and with a scarf tight around my mouth. They'd put cotton right on my tongue before they'd tied me, so when I tried to make a sound, I choked. Thought I was a goner, ma'am. And Charlie wasn't there – but I reckon he was alive.'

'Why?'

'I heard them men talking – and it sounded to me like two Americans, and there was an English guy there.' He choked on his words, settled, then went on. 'I heard them saying that if both of us were missing, there would be an investigation, but if the white boy was missing, and the black boy left, then the . . . the black boy would be blamed, would stand accused of murder, even if there wasn't a body, and I would be . . .'

'Matthias?'

'The man, he said, "If that black boy don't die in here, he'll be lynched good and proper when they send him home, no matter how we leave him."'

'Do you remember anything else, anything at all?'

'Ma'am, I've torn my mind into little pieces tryin' to remember, but I don't know how long I was out. I'd wake up, then it'd go dark again. I couldn't hear Charlie, but maybe he was dead. Maybe he was out cold. Maybe . . . maybe he won't ever go home.' He began to weep.

Maisie waited a moment for the man to settle, then pressed on. She knew she was at the very edge of her time allowance – and the patience demonstrated by Colonel Wright.

'Matthias, I have just a couple more questions. Did you ever hear the men talking about weapons? Do you know if they were armed?'

Crittenden rubbed his eyes with both knuckles, reminding Maisie of a small child, tired before bed.

'They argued about guns, that's what I heard. I reckon they had a lot of guns. One of them called the other one "trigger-happy", and . . .'

'What is it, Matthias?'

'I'm remembering now. I'd come round, but didn't move because I didn't want them to know or they'd knock me out again and my head hurt real bad. One guy called the other a "trigger-happy limey".' Crittenden choked on his words and held his hands to his face. 'Oh, Lord Jesus. Oh, no. Maybe he shot Charlie.' He moved his hands to his chest, as if to still a heart out of rhythm. 'I reckon I must have passed out again, because I don't remember them saying anything else like that.'

'Was there any mention of pilots?'

'Pilots?' Crittenden paused, then shook his head. 'No, ma'am, I don't recall hearing anything about pilots. Just about a guy who liked to shoot a gun. There was shouting about a gun and him picking it up when he shouldn't.'

Theodore Wright cleared his throat once more. Maisie turned and nodded. She brought her attention back to Matthias Crittenden. 'Private Crittenden – Matthias – listen to me.' She waited until he raised his head, his skin shimmering with shed tears. 'I know truth when I hear it, and I know lies – I told you that. And I know you've told me your truth.' She stopped for a few seconds, framing her words. 'But Matthias, I think there could be more and you just cannot remember because you are still in a state of shock. Yet the gates have been opened, and I have a feeling you may have fresh recollections in the coming days. Talking has allowed some of your grief to come out, and it's made room for those memories to rise up in your mind. If that happens, make sure you let someone know, and tell them to get in touch with me.' She turned to Wright. 'Can you arrange a means of communication, if necessary?'

Wright nodded.

'Ask for Colonel Wright.' She smiled as Matthias met her eyes with his own. 'It's an easy one to remember, isn't it? You only have to do what is right.'

'You're different, ma'am. You ask different questions.'

'That's what my husband says – he's an American too.' Maisie reached forward and pressed the man's hand. 'But between you and me, I don't think it's always a compliment when he says it!' She became serious again. 'Thank you, Matthias. Thank you for opening your heart and mind.'

'Can you find my friend? Can you find Charlie?'

'I don't know. I can't promise anything. But you have helped me enormously, and I think finding Charlie – or what happened to Charlie – is a key to helping the young lady who came to your rescue.'

He nodded. 'She called herself Jo, and her friend was Dizzy. She was tiny, Miss Dizzy, drivin' that automobile like she was made of steel. They were good to me, those English ladies.'

Maisie nodded and came to her feet.

'Thank you, Matthias. Thank you very much.'

She was about to step away, but stopped to ask one more question. 'Matthias, while you were a prisoner, did you hear your captors discussing anything else? A plan of any sort?'

The soldier shook his head. 'I was out a lot of the time, ma'am. My head was spinning whenever I came to, and if they saw me, they knocked me out again. I didn't even have to look up, they just sort of knew.' He rubbed his forehead.

'I thought I remembered something then, but it went away.'

'Not to worry – just let Colonel Wright know if you recall anything.'

Wright opened the door and Maisie stepped out as two military policemen entered, the handcuffs rattling as they approached Crittenden and pulled him out of the chair.

'This way, Miss Dobbs. I'll escort you to meet Mr MacFarlane and Mr Scott,' said Wright. He pressed his lips together and waited a second, as if having difficulty framing what he wanted to say. 'Not exactly how we do things.' He held out his hand, and they continued to walk along the corridor.

'And it's not exactly how they do things at Scotland Yard or at our military prisons either, Colonel,' said Maisie. 'But I believe Private Crittenden, and I know you must be wondering how to continue with an accusation against a man who could not have tied his own hands and feet after placing cotton wadding on his tongue and securing it so he was unable to call out – though I understand there are special knots known to sailors and magicians. I'm not sure what the precise charge against him is, but I believe there is much room for doubt in this case.'

'He said more today than he's told our guys.'

'He was tired, likely concussed, during the early interviews. I've interviewed people in equally troubling situations, and often, once the memories begin to emerge, it's rather like a tide coming in. I daresay Private Crittenden was fearful of the outcome when first questioned, and with an ingrained belief that his truth would be received as a lie.' She stopped walking and met Wright's eyes. 'There is every reason to believe Private Matthias Crittenden is an unwitting pawn in a much bigger game, Colonel Wright. Protect him – for goodness' sake protect him, not least because his testimony could be valuable to our authorities as well as yours.' Turning, she saw MacFarlane beckon to her from the foyer. She brought her attention back to Wright. 'But thank you for allowing me to interview the man in my own way without interruption. I had not expected you to accord me that privilege, so you have my gratitude.'

'I did some enquiring of my own, and it seems you have a fine reputation, Miss Dobbs. I thought I could learn something.' Wright smiled. 'By the way – Mr Scott has given me the dog tags you found. I'll have to get people down there to comb the area again.'

Maisie shook her head. 'I doubt you'll find anything else, Colonel. However, I believe I am getting closer, and the interview with Private Crittenden helped.' She paused, using the hiatus to ensure she had Wright's full attention. 'I realise there are certain protocols you must follow, but remember this is also my investigation and I have other responsibilities, so I wonder if there might be a few days' grace before your prisoner is removed to the United States. For you time has elapsed, but for me it is of the essence, and I have a feeling I can kill two birds with one stone, as the saying goes.'

'This is really—' Wright stopped himself, shook his head as if clearing his thoughts. 'OK, I'll see what I can do.'

Maisie inclined her head. 'Thank you, Colonel Wright.'

She paused. 'I will be in touch.'

'I hope so.'

As Maisie walked towards MacFarlane at the entrance to the building, she placed her right hand in her jacket pocket and fingered the buttons she had found alongside the river. She could not say why she had not given them to Colonel Wright, though there was no regret. She knew there was a risk that the discovery could have gone against Crittenden, perhaps misconstrued as a premeditated tactic on his part prior to taking a white man's life.

'Time for a bite to eat and a wee beverage?' asked MacFarlane.

Maisie shook her head as she looked towards the embassy entrance. 'Mark knows the interview is finished and will surely be along in a minute. I want to talk to him. Then I must see Billy at the office, and after that I'll be catching the next train down to Tonbridge or I'll miss the Chelstone connection.' She glanced at her watch. 'Anna's not been well.'

'Right you are.' He paused. 'What do you think? Truth or lies?'

'Truth, Robbie – but thin on details, though Crittenden gave me a couple of nuggets. I'm hoping he will remember more as time goes on – I've been wondering if the effects of a fairly severe concussion have been taken into account during his military interrogation.'

'Whatever happened, it doesn't look good – an American missing on British soil, and a vicar's son at that! At the very least they are looking at Stone's disappearance as a desertion, perhaps kidnapping or murder, and thus far Crittenden is being held on suspicion of being an accessory to a crime, and any one of those is a crime.' He sighed and patted his stomach. 'Time to feed the beast. I'm off back to Baker Street, Maisie. But one thing – if you want to save that man from being sent back across the ocean to his fate, you'd better get on with it. Don't drag your feet.'

Maisie nodded. 'I'm very aware of that, Robbie.'

Mark Scott joined Maisie just as MacFarlane's black motor car was pulling away into traffic. 'How did it go?'

'I'm not sure, but Wright seems to be a fair man.'

'He is. I've known him a few years – we turn up in the same places.' He put his arm around his wife. 'What do you think, now you've spoken to Crittenden?'

'I think there's more locked away in his mind, but he's still suffering from concussion and shock. I've asked him to request an interview with Colonel Wright if he suddenly remembers anything.'

'That's tricky.'

'Why?'

'Someone will say it's a false memory, a lie from a guy acting his heart out to save his life. The longer Stone is missing, the longer it looks like he won't be coming back, whether his body is found or not.'

'But I believe Crittenden is telling the truth. I have no proof, but I usually know when I'm being lied to, and I don't think that man was trying to pull the wool over my eyes.'

'Oh, Maisie – you're not in Kansas any more.'

Maisie looked up at her husband. 'I'm not sure if that's a joke or sarcasm.'

'*The Wizard of Oz*? Dorothy?' Scott pointed to the building that housed American military headquarters in London. 'The world in there is not the same as the world out here.'

'I'm sure you're right, Mark.'

'Do you think you can find Private Stone?'

'As impossible as it sounds, I believe I can – it's just a feeling I have. And when I locate him, I will have something concrete to report to Jo Hardy. She'll be telephoning later to ask me what I've discovered, and so far it's precious little, yet it's all a step towards finding out if there's a connection to the death of Jo's friend Erica. Anyway, Crittenden remembered what might be an important clue – I'll tell you more later, though I still feel as if I'm breaking down a wall to find a door.'

'What?'

'Never mind.' Maisie smiled at her husband, then glanced down at her watch. 'I'd better get on my way – Billy's probably pacing the floor waiting for me. Oh, I asked Crittenden if he heard his captors talking about their plans – I was trying to find out if he'd heard anything about your Rover. I think he started to remember, but then the recollection vanished – which isn't unusual with concussion and his sort of head wound.'

'Thanks for trying – but as I said, we've ramped up security anyway.' Scott reached into his pocket. 'Here, take this.' He handed Maisie a scrap of paper with a name and telephone number.

'What is it?'

'Got it from one of our diplomatic staff, a regular who's in contact with the other embassies. It's the school in Kensington where they all send their kids – and they're a real mix. When war was declared, they evacuated everyone, teachers and all the children who couldn't get home. Took over one of those manor houses that would otherwise have fallen down. You know – the heir was killed in action at Ypres, and the old girl and boy didn't know what to do with the country pile.'

'Where is it? I told you, Mark, I'm not sending her to a boarding school, and—'

'It's only two miles outside Chelstone. Two miles, Maisie. Let's look into it.'

'But then she'll only be with children who are—'

'I know what you're going to say, Maisie – she'll only be with privileged kids. But it's better than being where she is right now. And she will be with children who come from a real mix of places and who have moved around a bit. They're used to it. They're all . . . well, I guess they're habituated to being different. Which means they're accustomed to finding out all the things that make them the same as one another, and yet they take their individuality in their stride. Let's look into it. I'm a bit stuck here right now, but let's do something soon.'

Maisie nodded. 'Yes, you're right. It's something to consider.'

'Anyway, that George needs a job over at the manor house. All he does is polish autos all day, and then maybe take one out for the odd spin to keep it ticking over. His entire focus is on building up his stash of gasoline. He could drive Anna to school and bring her home – get himself out into the world.'

'Mark—'

'And before you say it, you can bet those kids are used to seeing chauffeured cars turn up with their friends in the back. No one is going to tear her sweater apart because she comes to school in a big old automobile.'

CHAPTER ELEVEN

'Sorry I'm late, Billy – the business at the embassy took longer than I expected. Everything all right? Are Doreen and Margaret Rose at the bungalow in Chelstone?'

Billy nodded. 'Margaret Rose went back to school this morning.'

'Have you made a decision, Billy? Are you moving home to Eltham?'

Billy shook his head. 'We had a mind to, as you know, we're still not feeling right about that village school. Makes you wonder where it all went wrong. Margaret Rose used to be happy there, or so we thought. Anyway, we'll have a think about it again, and if need be, we'll move her after Christmas.'

Maisie nodded and described what had happened to Anna. 'At least with Margaret Rose at the same school, I know Anna feels more secure.'

'Calling the poor little mite an eye-tye – accusing her of

being an Italian when they're now the enemy, that's a bit rich. Kids can be very mouthy at times. There again, look what happened to some of the Italian restaurants when Mussolini threw in his lot with old Hitler – one I knew was burned to the ground.'

Maisie nodded, glancing at the clock on the mantelpiece. 'I know . . . anyway, we'd better get on with the case map. Too much time has elapsed on the investigation anyway.'

'I've got the roll of paper out and pinned to the table, so everything's ready for us.'

'Right, here we go.' Taking a dark-blue wax crayon, Maisie wrote three names in large letters, one underneath the other at the centre of the paper, then circled the names with a green crayon.

'Who's the bloke?'

'Jo Hardy's fiancé. He was killed about eighteen months ago, so there's a long time between his demise and Jo believing someone was shooting at her, which was closely followed by Erica's death. And then of course we have this other situation with the Americans – and helping this man, Private Matthias Crittenden, is something Jo is set on, though now the two stories appear to be more entangled than we thought at first.' She rubbed a hand across her forehead as she leaned forward and wrote Crittenden's name next to the encircled names of Charles Stone and Erica Langley, circled it, and then drew a line connecting it to Jo Hardy's name.

Everyone she had met or heard of in connection with the case as presented by Hardy was listed, sometimes in an individual circle and sometimes alongside other names, and always a thread of red crayon to mark the obvious links, or a broken line to signify those that were only tenuous.

'Got a lot of people there, miss, and the pathways between them are clear enough, but where do we go now?'

'Billy, how busy are you here in London at the moment?'

'Nothing that can't wait.'

'Right. Let's both return to Chelstone after we've finished – I'll fold this and take it with us, because I think the Dower House library is going to be our office for a few days. Tomorrow I'm going to get the motor car again, and here's what I'd like to do – apparently a man named John Eames used to have a small rowing boat that he kept along the river that runs parallel to Barney Love's farm.' She tapped Love's name on the case map. 'I want to see if I can find the boat or any evidence of one – and I know roughly where to search.' She looked up. 'Billy, could you reach into that cupboard? Among the maps in there, you'll find one for West Kent. Let's have a look at it.'

Billy pushed back his chair, opened the cupboard and leafed through a selection of road maps until he found the one Maisie needed and removed it, along with a second map. 'Thought the Ordnance Survey map would come in handy too. And I reckon I know what you're thinking – that the American boy, this Charles Stone, could have been taken away in a boat. Minimal evidence, no footprints and less chance of the police stopping them. Or it could have been a better way to take him somewhere to finish him off.'

'That's what worries me – though I have a strong feeling

he isn't dead.' Maisie took the Ordnance Survey map from Billy and spread it across the table. 'And don't ask me why I think that, but I just do.'

'Oh, I never doubt it when you have a feeling about something, miss.'

As Maisie studied the map, she ran her finger along a thread of ink signifying a road. 'That's the farm, and – ah, there it is, the footpath leading down to the river from the far field there.'

'The river eventually feeds into the Medway, far as I can see.'

'And if you had a small enough boat, you could get there without much ado.'

'A little rowing boat wouldn't get far with more than a couple of blokes in it, mind you.' Billy tapped the map. 'I reckon they would only have to take a boat to this point here, and they'd have a motor car waiting. Or maybe even a house along the way.' He shrugged. 'Doesn't even have to be a house – just a place to doss down. An old barn would do.'

'But they had that, didn't they? On Barney Love's land.'

'Then those lads saw them, and that was a spanner in the works, miss.' He shook his head.

'I know what you're thinking, Billy – someone supplied a boat, and it could have been anyone. We can't just jump at the first suspect we come across.' Maisie walked to the window overlooking the small courtyard at the back of the building, where a gate led onto a narrow alleyway.

Ever since she had suspected a German spy to be living in the basement flat, his radio transmitter disguised by a fake climbing plant, Maisie had looked out of the window to remind herself that the enemy could with ease hide in plain sight – as could vital clues. She turned back to the table, the maps and her assistant.

'Tomorrow we'll return to the farm. We'll go back to the barn, and then we're going to walk alongside that river for as long as we can, so bring your Wellingtons. I doubt the men would have gone for more than a mile, so we have to look for a suitable lair.'

'What else?'

'John Eames comes to mind – oh, and there's someone else I'm a little curious about. I'll tell you about him on the train, because I think you're the person to have a word with him.' She looked at her watch. 'Come on, let's be on our way – we've an early start tomorrow morning.'

Billy folded the maps and handed them to Maisie, who slipped them into her document case along with the road map.

'Don't forget your gas mask, miss – it's been hanging up behind that door for over a fortnight.'

Maisie tutted. 'I'm not surprised, because carrying it around is a nuisance – I'll take it now though.'

They had switched off the lights and were just about to leave the office when the telephone began to ring.

'I'd better answer it,' said Maisie, reaching for the receiver on Sandra's desk. 'Good after—'

'Maisie – glad I caught you!'

'Mark, what is it? I was just about to leave to return to Chelstone. Is everything all right?'

'You absolutely cannot tell anyone about this, Maisie. Not a word.'

'If you speak in more than a whisper, I might be able to hear you, otherwise I won't know what I'm supposed to not be saying, my love.'

'Are you alone?'

'No, but . . . hang on, let me take the call in my office, all right?'

Maisie looked at Billy, who nodded and took the telephone receiver from her. She stepped into her private office, closed the doors, and picked up her extension.

'All right, Billy.' She heard the click as Billy replaced the receiver in the outer office. 'Go on, Mark – no one can hear you now.'

'Rover is in Ireland. She managed to get over here with her secretary, Mrs Thompson, and they landed safely. We had to be careful, as there's been a lot of U-boat and Luftwaffe activity, and the Germans would love to see her go down. Anyway, the weather's a bit rough for the next leg of her journey, but we're hoping to get her out on Friday; wheels down at Bristol Airport in the late afternoon most likely, then on the train up to Paddington so she can be briefed by the ambassador on the way before she meets the king and queen at the station.'

'Won't she be recognised?'

'Oh, that happened almost as soon as she landed, even though they were travelling under assumed names – I mean, Maisie, the woman is almost six feet tall, and you can't exactly miss her in a crowd.'

'Mark, why are you telling me all this? I thought it was a secret on pain of death.'

'If you tell anyone I'll have to kill you.' He laughed. 'Just kidding.'

'Mark—'

'Honey, things are so serious around here, a bit of levity helps. But here's why I'm telling you. Assuming the weather is on our side and she's here as planned and on time, on Saturday morning the embassy is hosting a press conference for her. We know she'll want to emphasise women's work and equality. Back home she's even limited her press conferences to women journalists – it means the newspapers have had to hire more women – but she's not made any such restriction for her press conferences here so far.'

Maisie heard her husband clear his throat, as if he were about to make an announcement.

'Anyway, here's the plan, if you're agreeable, and we hope you're agreeable – and "we" means our folks here—'

'Mark, this sounds very suspicious, whatever it is.'

'Can you bring Anna up to the flat on Friday afternoon? We can have a family dinner – you know she loves my spaghetti – and it will be a surprise for her.' He cleared his throat again, and Maisie realised he was nervous – or excited about something. 'You see, I've been asked if Anna would present a bouquet of flowers to Rover when she arrives at the embassy. She represents something, I guess – you know, British mother and now an American father. She signifies an alliance between our two countries.'

Maisie twisted the telephone cord around her fingers. 'That could be construed as over-egging the pudding, my love.' She heard Mark laugh, then added, 'Anna's had a very rough start to the week. We've kept her home, but she was going back to school tomorrow.'

'Then another couple of days won't hurt, will it? I mean, it's not as if she's heading off to college next year and has to keep her grades up. Let's give the kid a break until Monday, and she'll have something to remember when she's an old lady. And something to tell the other kids at school about.'

Maisie was silent for a few seconds before answering. 'All right. Yes, I'll bring her on Friday in time for us to have supper together. I'll pack her velvet dress and her best coat, the navy one with the velvet collar, and her patent shoes and some long white socks. Oh dear, she'll have to practise a curtsy, won't she?'

'No, hon – we don't go in for all that at the embassy. I can't imagine Rover curtsying to the king and queen, so she won't expect a kid to bob around in front of her. We're Americans, remember?'

As soon as they were seated on the train and Maisie was sure that another passenger would not enter the compartment, she leaned towards Billy, who had taken the seat opposite her, close to the window. Knowing voices could carry in the wooden-walled carriage, even with the sound of wheels on tracks muffling conversation, she kept her voice low.

'Billy, there's more to this case than meets the eye. I had to wait before I could tell you, but now it's time. Our investigation is woven into the visit to this country by the wife of America's president – Mrs Eleanor Roosevelt.'

'I had a feeling there was more going on. Blimey, that's a bit of a shocker.'

'I believe Private Matthias Crittenden was abducted

along with his fellow American soldier, Charles Stone. From what Crittenden revealed during my interview, it seems Stone overheard three men discussing their intentions to kidnap someone important, and we think that person is Mrs R.'

'Did this Stone actually hear the details?'

Maisie shook her head. 'According to Crittenden, he had just heard "E" – not enough information to impress the American military. However, there's additional evidence – two pages of notes I discovered hidden at the barn. Mark read them and recognised the code name for Mrs Roosevelt, the name by which she is known to those charged with keeping her safe during her visit to these shores – it's "Rover".'

'They called her by the name of a dog? Or a motor car?'

'Or someone who's always on the move, Billy – a rover.'

'Do they want to kill her?'

Maisie looked towards the door, checking that no one was in the corridor, then drew her attention back to Billy. 'Apparently she's at a huge risk already, as there is intelligence to indicate German agents are in the country and under orders to . . . to assassinate her. Added to that, she has enemies at home, and they would also like to see the back of her.'

Billy blew out his cheeks. 'And I bet you think there's a local connection.'

'I can't put my finger on it, but I believe I've set course in the right direction.'

Billy nodded. 'Pity they can't call it off, eh? You know, tell her to go back to America, keep her a bit safer.'

Maisie shook her head. 'I think Mrs Roosevelt accepting an order to turn tail and go home is very, very unlikely to happen. By all accounts, she is a woman of some mettle who will not be intimidated by threats from any quarter.'

Maisie and her assistant discussed the case for a while before conversation veered once again towards Anna's problem at school – a problem that was never far from Maisie's thoughts.

'It's that new headmistress, I reckon,' said Billy. 'When I was a soldier, they always said the mood of the battalion was set by the commanding officer. If he was fair, then everyone was fair, and if he was the sloppy sort, then standards slipped. I reckon that all this nastiness comes from her, because I don't think she's a very nice woman.'

'I'd hate to cast aspersions on her, Billy. I've studied her, and I believe Patterson has known a lot of disappointment. It's written all over her face.'

'Be that as it may, but I've known disappointment and a lot more besides and so have you, yet we're not nasty with it. She's got her back up against the wall, and I bet everyone is on tenterhooks in that school – I don't think I've ever come across a person who had an effect like that on so many people. Doreen's even heard talk about her in the village – mind you, in a small place, a new broom sweeping hard is a big story. Probably wouldn't have raised an eyebrow back in London. Anyway, I liked the last headmistress – she was a good sort.'

'Yes, she was lovely, wasn't she? But she had stayed on well beyond retirement when the evacuees arrived. She wanted to make sure they settled in with their teachers.'

'Funny old turn of events, though, that they picked Miss Patterson. Apparently she'd been the deputy headmistress at a school on the other side of Westerham. I bet they gave her good references to get rid of her!'

'I don't blame her for jumping at the chance for advancement when it came up.'

'Stiff old whatsit.'

'Billy—'

'Well, she is. Seen that sort before. They pick on one or two kids, and it makes them look bigger than they are. The teachers and half the parents are scared of her, so no one says anything. And if you ask me, it's our two who are in her firing line, and goodness knows who else we don't know about.'

'Hmm, yes.'

Billy gave her a pointed look. 'Your mind's on the case again – I know when your thinking goes off like that.'

'There are a few other elements nagging at me – but in the meantime, I want to tell you about a young man named Ronnie.'

The cancellation of one of the branch line trains along to Chelstone station meant it was late when Maisie entered the Dower House by the back door. Anna was ready for bed, wearing yellow flannel pyjamas and her red dressing gown.

'There she is!' said Frankie Dobbs, as Anna slipped down from his lap and ran to Maisie, along with Little Emma, who with one bound was licking her hand. 'Trouble with the train again, love?'

'I'll put the kettle on,' said Brenda, rising from her chair.

'You must be all in, Maisie.'

'Mummy, Grandma let me stay up until you were home!'

'That's lovely, my darling. Have you had your hot milk?' Anna nodded.

'Let's take you up to bed then.' Maisie placed her shoulder bag, gas mask and document case on a chair. 'Your eyes will fall out of your head if you stay up any longer.'

Anna squealed and laughed, then flung her arms around her dog. 'We're nearly all here, Little Em. Everyone's home except Daddy.'

'Ah, but I've a surprise, Anna – we're going to London on Friday to see Daddy. A special treat. Now then, let's get you to bed!'

'Anna seems to be sleeping a bit better,' said Maisie as she entered the kitchen again. 'She went right off.'

'She's tired, poor lamb,' said Brenda, as she began to pour tea. 'I've made you a round of cheese on toast.'

'Oh Brenda, thank you. I could have had plain toast – we can't really spare the cheese, can we?'

Brenda winked. 'I managed to get a bit extra this week. And the chickens have been generous for us, if you'd like an egg.'

'This is plenty, Brenda – just the ticket.'

'So, what's all this about London?'

'Oh, nothing really. Mark just thought it would be nice for us to spend a little more time together this week – a special treat for Anna – then we'll come back on Saturday evening. We thought we'd take her to see Buckingham Palace later.'

'Later? Later than what?'

'Um, you know – after we've had breakfast and, well, perhaps we'll go for a saunter along to Portobello Road, because she loves the market.'

'London's not very pretty, what with the shops boarded up and sandbags everywhere. I'm surprised you'd think a child would find it entertaining, but I suppose a change will be good for her.' Brenda sighed, then tapped the side of her head. 'Oh, almost forgot – the American nurse telephoned and asked if it would be all right to come down on Saturday.'

'Patty telephoned?'

'Says she's got another week on her special training, and then she doesn't know where they'll send her, but she would love to see you.' Brenda grinned and rolled her eyes. 'And I can see through that, even if you can't.'

'Don't tell me – Priscilla telephoned within about, oh, ten minutes, to let us know Tom is coming for a twenty-four hour leave, after managing to swap with another officer.'

Brenda nodded. 'That's the trouble with young people. They think they invented courting. And he's managed to get forty-eight hours, so the boy is serious. Anyway, at least we'll be doing our bit for the American army. At the last Women's Voluntary Service meeting, we were told there's a new plan to invite American soldiers and the like into our homes for a Sunday dinner to make them feel part of the family while they're here.'

'I'll get in touch and tell Patty we can't wait to see her. And in the meantime, you'd better bake some of those Eccles cakes, Brenda – make sure we do our bit for the American army.' She put an arm around her stepmother.

'And don't worry about entertaining her until we get home – I'm sure Tom will endeavour to keep her busy, though not before he's polished off a few cakes.'

A morning mist hung low over the river as Maisie and Billy reached the gravelly beach. Autumn's chill fingered their necks, and as they stood gazing at the water without speaking, both pulled up their collars and hunched their shoulders.

'Nippier than I thought it would be, miss.'

'I know. But I bet you're glad I made you bring your Wellingtons.'

'That I am. Mind you, old George was a bit particular, making sure he put down newspaper in the boot, so we didn't get mud in there.'

'Can't complain, Billy – he keeps my motor car in tip-top condition, and he makes sure I've enough petrol for the journey.' She rubbed her hands together. 'Let me show you where I found the buttons.'

Leading the way, Maisie pointed out the fallen tree trunk, and then the places where she had discovered buttons that she believed Charles Stone had left for anyone who might have come searching for him.

'That tree came down a good while ago – look at the moss and ivy all over it. Miracle you found anything there.' Billy poked at the rotting wood. 'You'd have to be careful around here – wouldn't surprise me if there weren't a few adders, you know, in summer.'

'Thank heavens we've boots on.' Maisie moved away from the undergrowth. 'There's no defined path, Billy, but you can see where foliage flanking the river has been beaten back at some point, perhaps by children sneaking down to fish or build camps. Let's set off along there anyway.'

'Right you are, miss. I'll go first – I've got a nice walking stick here, so I can push back those nasty looking stinging nettles and brambles.' He smiled and raised his eyebrows. 'And watch out for adders.'

'Billy—'

The walk was slow as they negotiated the tangled ivy and grasses. They stopped a few times to look across fields, and on one occasion, having spotted another old barn, they left the path and climbed through a barbed wire fence, then made their way across the field. They found nothing of note, so returned to the rough path alongside the river.

'According to the map, there's a railway bridge in about another mile,' said Maisie.

'Wouldn't mind sitting down and getting out the flask of tea, miss. We've been going over an hour.'

'I wouldn't mind wetting my whistle either. We'll stop at half past, shall we? Just another fifteen minutes.'

They walked on, with Billy whacking back branches across the path, or stamping down stinging nettles.

'Let's have a sit down over there,' said Maisie, pointing to a beech tree to their right. 'That one's a giant of the woodland.'

'Definitely what my boys would've called a climbing tree, that one. I bet it's had a lot of nippers up in those branches over the years.'

Once settled with their backs to the trunk, Maisie opened her knapsack and took out a flask and two cups.

'It's a strong brew, Billy.' She served him a steaming cup and then poured one for herself. Cup in hand, she opened the Ordnance Survey map. They sat in silence for several minutes.

'You know, miss, I can hear something. Not just water running, but, well, more water.'

'A stream meets the river just along there.' She pointed to the map. 'I bet that's what you can hear.'

'Sounds like more than that to me – mind you, you can hear a lot when everything's quiet out in the country, can't you.'

'Mmm – yes.' She continued to study the map. 'We're not far from the railway bridge either. I wonder if that's the same bridge Jo Hardy told me about – it's tall enough and wide enough to fly a Spitfire under.'

'They're all nutters, them pilots, if you ask me.'

As if on cue, they heard the sound of aircraft approaching. Three Spitfires flew overhead, then were gone.

'Bet they're off to Biggin Hill,' said Billy. He looked at Maisie, who had returned her attention to the map. 'What is it, miss?'

'You know you heard water, more water than the river here? It seems there's a water mill' – she craned her neck and squinted through the trees – 'Over there somewhere. I would imagine with this breeze in the right direction – and it is today – you can hear it.' She threw out the dregs of her tea and put down her cup. Reaching into the knapsack, she took out a pair of binoculars.

'Them trees are in the way, miss.' Billy leaned forward, shading his eyes with his hand. 'But hang on a minute.

When those branches moved in the wind, I thought I saw something.'

'There are some gaps,' said Maisie. 'I can just about see through them.' She adjusted the binoculars. 'Yes, I think I can see a building.'

'Miss – there's one problem.'

'There certainly is.'

'It's on the other side of the river.'

'Yes, Billy. I can see that – but you know what we can do?'

He nodded. 'Yep. We'll walk down to the bridge, climb up the side of the girders underneath, hop onto the railway lines, stagger along to the other side and down again.'

'Exactly.'

'We'll be worn out by the time we get back to the motor car.'

'Are your knees holding up?'

'Better than I thought they would. That tea did me the power of good.'

'Let's get going then.'

'Here we are, miss.' Billy Beale stopped, gazed up the hill at the side of the railway bridge and removed his cloth cap. 'That river got wider, didn't it?'

'The Americans would still call it a creek though.'

'I bet they would.' He replaced his cap. 'Right then, ready for it, are we? There's plenty of places to hold on as we go up.'

'I'm ready. Let's go.'

Billy led the way, at first moving at a fast clip; it occurred to Maisie that anyone watching her assistant might not even register the slight hitch in his step – the legacy of wounds sustained during the Battle of Messines of 1917. Maisie was the nurse who attended to him in the casualty clearing station. He had always said that he would remember her eyes – a prediction that proved correct when their paths crossed again in 1929.

'Almost there, miss.'

'Thank goodness!'

'Here we go,' said Billy, reaching the railway line and extending his hand. 'Just one more push and you're up.'

'Phew!' Maisie stepped out onto a wooden sleeper. 'I think this is a branch line, though not one I know. I'd remember the view from this bridge.'

'Blimmin' risky, flying an aircraft under that span.'

'It is.' Maisie began to walk along the railway line. 'It makes me wonder who might have seen someone like Jo larking around. Anyway, let's press on. I don't want to be here on this line when the rails begin to rattle because a train is approaching.'

Fifteen minutes later, Maisie and Billy were standing at the foot of the bridge on the other side of the river.

'Sliding down is faster than walking up, I reckon.'

Maisie brushed dirt from her Mackintosh. 'I'll say.'

Billy began to walk away, but turned around to look at Maisie, who was studying the ground.

'What is it, miss?'

'Look at these marks, right here.' She pointed to the place where the riverbank extended down to the water. 'And look at these ridges. It seems as if someone dragged something heavy here, and – oh, well I never.' She pointed into the undergrowth, then ran along the riverbank.

'Miss – miss, where are you going?'

Maisie reached towards a clump of reeds, pulling them back to reveal the prow of a rowing boat. 'And there she is.'

'You were right about the boat.'

'I thought it would be farther along, though.'

The rushing water was the only sound as they regarded the small vessel.

'All right, so say they took this boat – and I can see it has a flatter bottom than your usual rowing boat, so it's been made for this kind of river – but say they had the boat . . . why didn't they just use a motor car? From what Miss Hardy said she saw on the ground, they had one.'

'I would imagine—' Maisie looked at the boat and then the river. 'I would imagine it was to avoid the risk of being halted at any point. On the road they could be pulled over – goodness knows, the local bobby here has stopped me, looking at me as if I had just parachuted in from Berlin and taken a motor car for my convenience.' She shook her head. 'And given what I told you about the notes I found in the barn, I think I can guess why they chose Kent.'

'Close enough to Biggin Hill to cause trouble.'

Maisie shook her head. It was some moments before she spoke again, a silence her assistant was used to.

'Let me just reflect upon what we already suspect – that what happened to the two American soldiers could have been secondary. We assume they were just in the wrong place at the wrong time – though we should allow for a margin of error on that score.' Another silence. Billy remained quiet.

'There were three men, one possibly British. Two other men were – we believe – Americans. But there must have been another connection to bring them to this area.'

'Close to London, but not in London. Close enough to the coast, but not on the coast. Plus they chose a place in Kent – you know we're called the frontline county. Seems they wanted to be on the front line for something.' Billy held up his hand to indicate their surroundings. 'And look at it, miss – whatever they were up to, they could hide out around here for a long time and not be found, eh?'

'Let's just allow that thought to steep in its juices for a bit.' She glanced at her watch and took the map from her pocket. 'Fortunately, Anna's at home, so I don't have to rush to the school to meet her today. I want to look at that water mill before we start our journey back.' Once more with Billy leading, they beat a trail towards the fence around another field, where they found a stream that led directly from the water mill.

'Why do you reckon there was a water mill out here in the first place?'

'It's a grist mill, Billy. For grain. You wouldn't build a windmill when you have a ready supply of water running through the field where the grain is grown. But I bet this mill hasn't been used for a long time. One hundred years ago it would have provided flour for the whole area, but now the grain goes direct to the factory bakers and the flour companies.' She pointed towards the mill. 'See, the wheel isn't turning, so there's a brake on it. But that sound was the water rushing through – you can't stop that.' She caught Billy's sleeve. 'Hold on, I just want to have a look.' She took out her binoculars again and studied the water mill and the adjoining land. 'On three sides we're clear, as far as I can see, though I would imagine a farm road meets the water mill at the other side. Let's proceed with care now – we don't want to come face-to-face with company.'

Maisie moved in front of Billy and slowed their pace, each step deliberate as she stopped to listen. 'Go as lightly as you can.'

'If those people – whoever they are who tied up Crittenden – used this mill, all I can say is they really like their old farm buildings! You'd think it would be the last place to hide out, what with the Home Guard keeping an eye out for spies.'

Maisie stopped walking and looked at her assistant. 'Interesting you should say that, because—'

A loud *crack* came from the water mill. They dropped to the ground. 'Old habits die hard, miss – but that wasn't gunshot.'

Maisie looked up, saw the wheel jolt as if it were about to move, then stop.

'It's just the wheel – I can see what happens from here. Water collects on what's left of the water trough, then it moves the wheel just a bit, but it bounces back because the brake is on. It doesn't move a lot, but enough to cause a sound.' She came to her feet. 'Come on, let's get on with it.'

Creeping to the side of the mill, Maisie looked at the rough track leading to the door of the millhouse and nodded to Billy. *All clear.* They stood in silence once again, listening for even the slightest creak that would reveal someone was inside. Nothing.

Maisie stepped out from the lee of the building, towards the track.

'Tyre marks, Billy. And they're not from a cart or a tractor.'

'I can see that.'

'Let's go in.'

There was no padlock on the mill door. Inside the building was dark and musty.

'Got a glim, miss?'

Maisie opened her knapsack and took out a torch, which she handed to Billy, who began casting the beam around the interior.

'Look at that!' Billy pointed to his left, where two round stones, six feet wide, were held on an iron centre post with divots from top to bottom. 'You could come a cropper in here, if that mill was going full tilt.'

'Those stones are why they call this the "stone floor". Think of the poor boy who had to clean the works! They'd put the brake on the sluice gate and ratchet up the topstone from the bedstone – that's the one on the bottom. Then the lad would have to get right inside to brush away debris and old flour after every grinding. If it started to move while he was in there, he could have lost a limb – or his life.'

'I'm not going anywhere near that thing then.'

'Come on, shine that torch into the corners on this floor – I want to have a good look.'

Billy directed the beam as Maisie instructed.

'Oh look, miss, someone's been dossing in here.'

'More than dossing,' said Maisie. 'It's an encampment.'

Taking a closer look, they could see makeshift beds

with rough blankets, a paraffin stove, kettle, saucepan and several empty bottles. Maisie picked up a bottle and looked at the label.

'Bourbon.'

'The Yanks like that.'

'So do a lot of people, Billy – but you're right, it's more of an American tipple.' She sighed. 'I didn't really want a confrontation, but I would have liked to find something more than this.'

'Let's keep looking.' Again Billy directed the beam around the mill.

'Hold on – Billy, pass me the torch.'

Billy handed Maisie the torch, and she directed the beam to the floor behind the wheel. It was thick with dust and mould. She aimed the beam to a far corner.

'I almost missed that,' she said, stepping forward. 'Come closer.' She beckoned to Billy and pointed where thick dust had been dredged by a finger or piece of wood to leave a series of words. 'Oh, miss—'

'Pvt Charles Stone.' She read out the message illuminated by the torch.

'He was here only yesterday – look, there's a date.' She nodded.

'But wouldn't the people who took him see what he'd done?'

'I would imagine they were in a hurry – perhaps his captors had left him here tied up, then came back, grabbed him and went on their way. He did this because it was all he could think of to do.'

'They could have killed him – wouldn't that have made

it easier for them? I mean, it was lucky we found the place, and I reckon they could have hidden his body anywhere.'

Maisie took a moment to respond. 'I'm not sure, Billy – but my feeling is that he's their insurance, their ticket out if they're cornered.'

'Something must have happened to get them on the move.'

Maisie nodded, her mind racing through recent events as if she were viewing a moving picture. 'I think I know what it is.'

'Miss?'

'Our very important American has arrived on this side of the Atlantic.'

'Oh?'

'And they're on the move because . . .' She considered the possibilities, then looked at Billy. 'Because they've a plan, and it's time.'

CHAPTER TWELVE

Clambering over undergrowth, Maisie and Billy moved with as much speed as they could muster along the rough path back to the farm, but as Maisie watched her assistant beat away the foliage once more, she grew concerned. She had no need to mirror his movement to know what caused him to lose balance and to understand what ailed him.

'Billy, I can see your leg is giving you trouble – let's just take another breather. Stop now.'

'We don't have time to lose, miss, and—'

'True enough – but I'd rather have you reach the motor car so we can get on our way, than have to leave you behind languishing in the undergrowth.'

Billy put his hand to his chest and leaned against a tree. Maisie stood alongside him.

'When did your leg start giving you trouble to this degree again, Billy? You were on an even keel for a long time. It

211

was barely noticeable and your pain had diminished – even when we first started walking today, it wasn't as obvious as in the past. I think you've become very good at masking your discomfort.'

Billy nodded. 'It's the time of year, you know, coming into autumn, that sort of thing, what with winter around the corner and the damp.' Maisie met his eyes as he spoke, but he turned away.

'Billy, your leg started up again when you heard that your son had been taken prisoner. I saw it coming on – and I know what the pain means.'

'Just my old war wounds, miss. Just them blimmin' old war wounds.'

Maisie stepped closer to Billy. She placed a hand on his shoulder.

'Wounds like ours run deep, Billy. Priscilla calls it the dragon living inside that you have to keep mollified. Give that dragon half a chance, and he roars back and the flames rush through you, along with all the memories in the dragon's arsenal.' Keeping her hand in place, she stopped speaking for a moment, allowing the soft rustle of leaves and the soothing sound of the rushing river to fill the silence. 'Yes, I'll allow the weather can bring home the aches and pains, but wounds are also like radar – they tell us when something isn't right. They alert us when the enemy of what we hold dear is approaching.' She lifted her hand from his shoulder. 'You've been taking on your son's suffering, Billy. You've allowed it into your bones – just as your wounds became your sons' wounds when they were young. They may have been children, but they understood that you had endured unbelievable terror.'

'I knew you'd say something like that, miss. I just don't know what to do – every morning I wake up and wonder if this is the day we find out he's dead, or if this is the day we'll hear footsteps on the path and he'll open the door and say, "Dad, Mum, I'm home. Where's our Maggie-Ro?" Every morning, I get up knowing we've got to be a normal family until we go to bed at night and I can stop pretending that everything's all right.' He choked back his words. 'And it's not all right, is it, when your son could be beaten into the next world by an army of Japs? I keep thinking that if I imagine it's me, and I'm the one taking a thrashing, he won't feel it when it comes.'

'Oh, Billy – Billy, you can't burden yourself in that way. Even the strongest trees will come down when a gale blows through, so don't try to battle a tornado.' She took a deep breath and allowed the woodland sounds to envelop them once more before continuing. 'We've worked together for a long time now, and you know how I meet every problem we've encountered.'

'It was hard to get used to at first, miss.'

'Indeed – but you understood, and you know it has value. It's not the be-all and end-all, but at times like this, how we sustain ourselves is crucial, for how can you be strong if you don't give yourself nourishment? Your family depends upon your strength, Billy – so I'm reminding you that you can't just rest your leg for five minutes and think the suffering is going to go away. Do you remember the steps you took to counter the pain last time, and how you brought it under control?'

He nodded.

'There was the physical recovery, the emotional rebound and then you had to care for something else.' Maisie placed her hand against her chest. 'You have to care for your spirit, Billy.' She waited for Billy to nod. 'You know what you must do every morning and every evening to retain your physical strength, don't you?'

Another nod. 'What that bloke taught me about making my middle strong. I haven't done all that business for years, because I felt better. Didn't think I needed to.'

'It's time to return to everything he taught you.' She smiled. 'We all need to keep a strong middle, my friend. The centre is where balance resides, and if you're not in balance, you cannot expect to continue moving forward without a fall. It's like driving along with only three wheels. Look after yourself, Billy.'

She knew they didn't have time to spare, but there was more she wanted to say. 'And we've both learned the value of allowing only the very best pictures into our minds – so instead of imagining the terrible alternatives, make sure you see your son walking into the house and calling your name. See him coming home. Always see him coming home. Every time you think of something untoward, banish it straightaway – restrict your mind to the most wonderful thoughts of your boys.'

'I s'pose you're going to tell me to pray as well. I've never been one for all that praying lark, though.'

'Asking for help never hurt anyone, Billy. Trust that you will be heard, that's all I ask.'

'All right, miss. I'll do my best.' He closed his eyes for a moment, and then looked back at Maisie. 'We'd better get going again, eh?'

'Not far to go now.'

'Where to next?'

'We're driving into Tonbridge. I want to pay a visit to a Mr John Eames, the man who, if I am correct, owns that boat. But before we do that, I'd like to pop along to Dan Littlecombe's garage. If we're lucky, a young man called Ronnie Watkins will be there, and if so, I'd like you to have a word with him. I'll keep Dan engaged so you can get him talking.'

'Anything in particular you want me to find out?'

'Oh, have a word about engines to start, and make sure you mention your boy being on Lancasters – see what his reaction is. Ask where he learned about motors, and where he went to school – specifically which school, not just the village or town. See if you can find out about his friends, if he has a special chum, that sort of thing.'

'Got it, I'll get all that.'

'And find out if he likes going to the cinema – get chatty, tease out what sort of films. If he likes the American pictures, and—'

'Yep, I know what you're after, miss.'

'I thought you would. But before we do anything, I'll see if I can use Barney Love's telephone. I must call Mark at the embassy.'

'You're worried about that American boy.'

'I'm worried about both of them – but it's the one who's been kidnapped that's on my mind. After all, he's currency for his captors – and currency has a nasty habit of losing value.'

'Mark?'

'Maisie? This must be important, for you to call me at work. You're lucky to get me here, because—'

'Mark, I'm using someone else's telephone, so I have to be quick – they don't like the line engaged, just in case their son returns from overseas and tries to get in touch. Anyway, here's what's happened and what Billy and I discovered today.' She described finding the water mill and the message scraped into the dust. 'If those men are on the move, then there's a reason – and I think we know why. Once you'd told me about those coded papers I found in the barn, I knew your Rover was due to be in Kent soon, visiting Canterbury Cathedral as well as a local village. And we know she's going to be in London first. If these men are after her – for whatever reason, and we can only assume it's not to welcome her to Britain – this area is a very good place to wait for an opportunity to strike in either the capital or the country.'

'Got it. I'll handle it from here. We've got her security pretty well reviewed and sewn up, but I don't want any gaps for her to fall through. Did you find anything else? Anything to indicate the next stop?'

'The message Private Stone left in the mill gives us reason to believe he was alive as of yesterday, Mark. There is probably little reason to hold Private Crittenden at the same level of imprisonment.'

'I'll get on to Colonel Wright. He won't release Crittenden until he sees Stone in the flesh before him, but he might have the MPs ease up on him.'

Maisie felt her breath catch. *Ease up on what?* Instead of asking the question, she continued. 'Here's where they can find the water mill – but Mark, I know the embassy has to be careful, that there are respectful protocols to be followed, but don't involve the local police in this instance. Instead call a man named Detective Chief Superintendent Caldwell at the Yard. Just give him your name – he knows who you are – and make sure he understands that he is the . . . let me think . . . yes, tell him I suggested that *in the circumstances*, he is your liaison with the British authorities. Tell him that I will be in touch to explain the circumstances, but ask him not to involve the local police – he'll deal with any consequences and also liaison with the Home Office, but frankly, the police are so thin on the ground they won't mind at all if someone else takes the weight.'

'I'll do it all now.' He was silent for a single heartbeat. 'Be careful, Maisie – there's more going on than just the threat at our end. Anyway, on a more positive note, we're all looking forward to seeing you and Anna here – and I can't wait to show off my ladies.'

Maisie closed her eyes, taking in her husband's words, but there was one more thing. 'Mark, I think either you or the colonel or someone in authority should accompany the military police to the water mill.'

There was another beat of silence on the end of the line. 'I understand what you're saying, Maisie. There should be an independent observer who will witness the inscription you've described. I'll make sure it happens – maybe have someone go along with a camera so the words don't unexpectedly vanish.' Another pause. 'Maisie, if you had to guess, where do you think they're headed now?'

'I don't want to make a mistake here, because it could be fatal, but I don't think these men will go far. I doubt they want to spend too much time on the road, so I'm betting they've gone to ground again, though they could have a safe house in London as well as another place to hide in this area.'

'And when we've got them, we'll find out why they targeted those ATA women.'

Maisie was silent.

'Maisie?'

'Mark, I think those men – and we're assuming they're American – had only one target, and they know where she'll be, and when. Yes, this is conjecture, but given Crittenden's account, it seems he and Stone managed to get in the way, hence their outcome. The problem could be that whoever had the pilots in his sights could also now be a liability. You see, I don't think the men Private Stone is with have any interest at all in aviatrices, whether they are on the ground or in the air.'

Dan Littlecombe was once again bent over an engine, a spanner in his hand, when Maisie parked alongside the garage. Ronnie Watkins was polishing an SS Jaguar that had been pulled out onto the forecourt. Cloth in hand, he leaned close to the vehicle, breathed on the coachwork and rubbed hard, inspecting the result as he continued to bring the jet-black motor car to a shine. Maisie nodded to Billy, who stood admiring the gleaming roadster. As she approached the mechanic, she heard Billy say, 'You're doing a good job there, son – it takes a lot of elbow grease, bringing a glow to a motor like that.' She turned for a second, saw Ronnie look up and nod, replying that it certainly did. She smiled. Billy was off and away – he would get the information she wanted. She drew her attention to Littlecombe.

'Hello again, Mr Littlecombe. We were just passing, and I thought I would drop in and say hello. That looks like Mr Love's tractor.'

'Oh, good afternoon to you, Miss Dobbs.' Littlecombe looked up from his work and smiled at Maisie. 'I don't know how they did it, but those land girls managed to bring her in yesterday. They said they couldn't wait any longer, and a couple of them Yankee soldiers found parts they thought would do the trick. I'm just looking to see if we can get her going properly.' He laughed. 'I reckon the Yanks had something else by way of payment on their minds, but those ladies can take care of themselves.'

'I'm sure they can.' Maisie smiled. 'And I hope you can get the tractor mended for them – those young women work hard, and it would help them no end.' Noticing that Littlecombe had looked over towards Billy, she continued. 'I suppose you never saw the American again – the one you told me about with the motor car.'

He shook his head. 'As I said at the time, it was the motor that was American. A Buick. A few of them were imported over here before the war, but they don't do well on our little roads, and if you ask me, they use too much petrol. I reckon the bloke put the motor car away somewhere, locked the door and threw away the key, what with the petrol rationing. Only way to get about these days is either the bus, the train, Shanks's pony or a bicycle!' He glanced over at the Alvis and shrugged.

Maisie didn't rise to the bait. 'And you don't know who the owner is, or where he lives?'

'I don't, and if truth be told, I'd have trouble if I was asked to pick him out of a crowd.'

'Hmm, yes, I know what you mean. There are so many new people around.'

Littlecombe nodded. 'You'd think we're an occupied country, what with all them armies over here and everyone else besides.' The garage owner returned his gaze towards Billy, who was in easy conversation with the younger man.

'I know I asked this before,' said Maisie. 'But I wondered if you'd since had any recollection of seeing a couple of Americans in the town.'

'Only the soldiers, and they pass through.' He shook his head. 'And like I said, we've got the Canadians, the Australians, the Kiwis, then there's them Polish airmen and I've heard they've even got foreign women delivering aeroplanes, not just our ladies. Then the Yanks came over, and now the place is crawling with them – though we've to be grateful that most of them are over in Suffolk or down in the west country. Anyway, I've not had any Americans in here, just that nuisance of a motor car.'

'I think we're all glad to have the overseas soldiers

on our soil, aren't we? After all, they're here to do a job, and as time goes on, it's not going to be a very nice job either.'

'True enough,' agreed Littlecombe, looking Maisie in the eye. 'True enough.'

'They say the aviatrices are particularly brave – I hear the Polish ferry pilots are every bit as lionhearted as their men who have been fighting for us.'

'All a matter of opinion, I would imagine.' He stole another glance at Billy and nodded towards him. 'I reckon I'll have to charge your friend if he keeps jawing away with my apprentice and keeping him from his work. I've got a customer coming to pick up that motor in half an hour, so Ronnie had better look sharp and have it ready.'

'We're leaving now – I just wanted to ask you about the American motor car again. Thank you!'

Maisie smiled and stepped away, nodding towards Billy, who held out his hand to Ronnie. He raised his voice to bid the young man goodbye, his words spoken for the benefit of Dan Littlecombe.

'Nice to have a chat with you, son. Wait until I tell my boy I've talked to someone who knows more about Lancasters than him! I reckon he'll be right over to see you, next time he's on leave. He can tell you all about flying on the big bombers.'

Ronnie blushed, his smile broad. Then he caught his employer's gaze, and his demeanour changed, so it seemed that at once he appeared diminished and sullen. Maisie kept her eyes on him for some moments, long enough for

Littlecombe to realise that the woman observing had seen more than a simple apprentice. She had looked into the eyes of a confused soul.

'That boy – well, man, I suppose—' Billy stopped himself. 'I've got to stop calling these lads "boys", or they'll all be getting the hump about it, like my Billy before he went over there.' He shook his head, then continued. 'I was going to say – that Ronnie is an interesting study.'

'Tell me – what did you find out?' asked Maisie.

'A few things. First, the lad is obsessed with aeroplanes. Loves them. Could tell you everything about any aeroplane from a Lysander to a Spitfire, a Blenheim to a Warwick, and he even talked about a man in the village who flew a Sopwith Camel during the last war.'

'That's interesting. What stopped Ronnie joining the RAF? Oh, wait, yes, according to Littlecombe, I think it was a failed medical – and his mother.'

'Sounds like it. He mentioned his mum was against him joining up, but it didn't matter anyway, because he failed the physical exam. He seemed quite upset about it, but he said he's with the Home Guard now – I reckon you knew that – and he added that at least if he's wearing a uniform he won't get taken for a conchie. Oh, and apparently there's a couple of RAF lads who bring in their motor cars for Ronnie to polish, that's how he knows them. They probably feel sorry for the lad and try to give him a bit of extra money of his own.'

Approaching a junction, Maisie stopped the Alvis, looked from left to right and pulled out onto the road.

'Tonbridge is the other way, miss.'

'No, it's to the right – this takes us to the Capel road, and from there—'

'I'd have gone left, if I were you. I know this area, and it's left.'

Maisie shook her head as she slowed, manoeuvred the Alvis around and continued in the opposite direction. 'This is what happens when they deprive us of direction signs!'

'I've heard people are always getting lost, even when they know a place.'

'Anyway, go on, Billy.'

'Yes. Ronnie. Well, as I said, he seemed very upset about not being able to join up, but he said he likes having a uniform on, even if it's only a couple of nights a week and on Saturdays and Sundays. Makes him feel like one of the boys, I would say. He said he's met some RAF lads, and they're all good to him – I s'pose they like talking about their time in the air and he likes listening.'

'Anything untoward? Anything that made you want to raise a flag?'

'There was one thing.'

'Go on.'

'You'll never guess where he went to school.'

'Surprise me, Billy.'

'Yep, it was that little school just along the road outside Westerham – Saddledene Primary, it's called. He was there until he was twelve, thirteen, something like that, though he said his mum kept him home a fair bit, on account of him having trouble with his legs. And you know who used to be the deputy headmistress there, don't you?'

'I do indeed.'

223

'Turns out she wasn't very nice to Ronnie. Told him he'd amount to nothing. He liked staring out of the window, watching birds. As I said, he's fascinated with anything that flies.'

'Let's be fair, a lot of teachers say things like that to get the pupils paying attention. I don't like it, but it happens.'

'My teacher said I'd never amount to anything, the way I was going as a nipper. I'm not sure she was wrong. But she never killed a baby sparrow I'd saved, right in front of me.'

'What?'

'Yep, that's what she did.'

'You managed to get a lot out of him, Billy.'

'Oh, you know me and youngsters – I can get them talking, 'cept when it comes to my own. Mind you, I don't know about that apprenticeship or whatever he's doing there with Dan what's-his-name. He's scared of him – I reckon you saw that.'

'I did, yes. But is it fear of not working to a certain standard? Or of intimidation? Does Dan take out his own frustrations on Ronnie? Or is it something perhaps more insidious?' She reached another junction, and took a right turn. Billy said nothing. 'And it might be that Ronnie has a secret.'

'About Dan? Or himself? Or something he's seen?'

'Could be any one of those things, Billy,' said Maisie. She changed gears and began to slow the motor car. Pulling over to the verge, she reached into the glove compartment and took out a map. 'Or all three.'

'Looking for the address?'

'I think I know how to find it, Billy.' She studied the

map. 'I was just wondering – if I was Dan Littlecombe, where would I choose to walk my dog? What sort of range would I be limiting myself to?'

'Perhaps he didn't limit himself.' Billy looked at Maisie. 'But I s'pose it's interesting that a bloke who was with the Royal Flying Corps got to a crashed Spitfire before anyone else, isn't it?'

'Yes, it's interesting. No more than that at the moment, but you know what we do with interesting, Billy.'

'We get a lot more interested.'

Maisie parked the motor car outside a small semi-detached house on the outskirts of Tonbridge. The railway line was nearby. Given the frequency of trains coming into the station, where people would change for branch lines that threaded out into various villages, or travelled from those locations to continue up to London, she wondered how desirable such a place might be. On the other hand, during her childhood she had lived close to railway lines as they snaked their way through Lambeth, and remembered being lulled by the rhythmic sounds of locomotives clanking along the tracks, her dreams laced with the pungent smell of coal-infused steam.

But how might Constable Eames and his family feel, having lost their tied cottage in the midst of verdant countryside, only to find themselves in one of the council houses built since the last war as a result of the housing acts? Those acts of law decreed that there would be 'homes for heroes' – only there were never enough for the heroes who came home from war. No matter how much they appeared to have gained – a council house would at least have a flushing indoor lavatory – the loss of a lifetime job could leach light from a man's spirit, leaving a welter of resentment and anger in its place.

And what of their son, who had a respected title now? Police Constable Eames. Given their first conversation, Maisie thought his opinion might mirror his father's. In witnessing John Eames's humiliation at the hands of Barney Love, the farmer who had sacked him, she wondered if Constable Eames had borne a lingering element of damage too.

Maisie and Billy proceeded to the door, and though Maisie twice lifted the knocker and rapped as loud as she could, no one answered.

'There's no telephone wires down this street, miss, so it's not as if you could have given them a bell first.'

'I know.' She reached into her shoulder bag and took out a notebook. 'I'll leave a message and ask if Mr Eames would be in touch with me.'

'Hello,' said Billy. 'Here's a bit of luck coming down the street. Is this who you're after?'

Maisie looked up and smiled. 'Luck indeed.' She lifted her hand as Eames approached, pushing his bicycle along the pavement. 'Good afternoon, Constable Eames!'

'I recognise you – you're that woman who was parked on the side of the road. What're you doing here?'

She held out her hand. 'Just a reminder – my name is Miss Dobbs. Perhaps I should have told you at the time, but I work as a special officer with detectives at Scotland Yard. If you've any doubt about talking to me, you can get in touch with Detective Chief Superintendent Caldwell at the Yard.'

Eames frowned. 'I've heard of him – he was at the farm when there was all the business with them Yanks, so you must be telling the truth because we both know I can check on you. But what're you doing here? This is my house. Well, my mum and dad's house.'

'I expect you live in a police house closer to Westerham.'

'That's right. Easier for us to get out and on the beat. But I come back to see my mum and dad when I've a few hours off duty.'

'Constable Eames, may I ask a few questions? I think you might be the man with the answers I'm looking for. I know I can always trust a policeman and his family.' She smiled and looked towards the front door, as if willing it to open.

'You can talk to me out here. The house is private.' He reached down to remove bicycle clips from the trouser fabric at his ankles. 'Even if you are a special officer.'

'Of course. To tell you the truth, I like to keep my house private too – in our work it's easy to allow the lines to blur, because we're really servants of the public, aren't we?'

Eames nodded, then looked over to Billy. 'Who's he?'

'Ah, sorry – this is Mr Beale. Mr Beale is my partner – though not in crime, I might add!' She smiled.

'Who's the guv'nor, out of you two then?'

'Depends upon the case we're working on, but let's just say we work together. I'm sure it's the same for you when you're out on the beat with another policeman. Sometimes you take the lead and sometimes it's your friend.' Maisie smiled. Eames appeared to soften. 'I wanted to find out about your father's old rowing boat, the one he kept down by the river.'

'That old thing! He used to take me out fishing in it when I was this tall.' He held out his hand just below hip height. 'We always had to bring a bucket with us to throw out the water it took in. Dad went down there and did some repairs last year. Gave him something to do. Mind you, when we were nippers me and my mates loved that boat.'

'I bet you did! My grandfather on my mother's side became a lockkeeper – going to their house was always an adventure, because he had a boat too. Do you ever use the boat now it's mended?'

He shook his head. 'Nah – he lost interest and I don't have the time, so Dad sold it. Not long ago, now you come to ask about it.'

'Really – who to?'

'Couple of Yanks bought it. Mind you, they can afford it – and they weren't even officers. They were ordinary blokes, the ones who normally dig trenches and flatten a farmer's fields so they can land their blimmin' great aeroplanes. They're always flash with their money, Yanks. Look how much they earn, ten times more than our soldiers. And their flyboys are paid even more!'

'They do get a good wage,' agreed Billy. 'My son is getting four shillings a week in the army, and they get over three quid.'

'I've heard the food they throw away at their barracks could feed ten of our families for a week,' said Eames.

Maisie raised an eyebrow. Camaraderie achieved, she

now wanted to move on. 'Did you meet the men who bought the boat?'

Eames nodded. 'Yep. In fact, they asked me about it first. Pair of 'em were working over at Barney Love's farm for the harvest. A dark bloke and a white bloke. They were friends – and you don't see that much, do you, with the Americans?' He paused, looking from Billy to Maisie. 'To tell you the truth – and I wasn't going to say anything about it, but now I know you're a special officer, I reckon it's all right – but it was the pair who caused the trouble over there at Barney's. You on that job?'

Maisie skirted Eames's question with her next enquiry. 'Why did they say they wanted the boat?' asked Maisie. 'Was it for fishing?'

'Yep, that's what they said. Mind you, I didn't think they'd want it to rob a bank! Nah, they seemed good sorts and they ended up buying fishing rods from my dad too. Then they had to get going before their military police saw them in town together, and they had to return to their different bases.'

'Yes, I know,' said Maisie. 'And do you have their names?'

Eames put on a poor imitation of an American accent. 'Yay'se ma'am, Privayte Crittenden and Privayte Stone.' He grinned. 'My dad said that he couldn't care less about the colour of anyone's skin, as long as they got the colour of our money right. They did, so the boat was theirs.'

'Thank you, Constable Eames. I'll let Detective Chief Superintendent Caldwell know how very helpful you've been.' She smiled. 'We'd better be off now – oh, I almost forgot something else. I'm just curious – for a completely different reason – but where did you go to school?'

'Saddledene Primary, not far from Westerham. It was close enough to the farm, when I was growing up, but I still had to walk miles across the fields to get there.'

'Oh, you must know Ronnie Watkins.'

He nodded, rubbing his forehead. 'I know Ronnie. Haven't seen him in a long while though.'

'Yes, that happens.' She turned to Billy. 'I've rather hogged Constable Eames's time, but is there anything else he might be able to help us with?'

Billy shrugged. 'Nothing really. Pity about Ronnie not getting past his medical for the RAF, isn't it? He could have made a good mechanic, I reckon.'

'They're strict, the RAF. My dad says it's down to who you know, especially if you want to be a pilot. I wanted to join, you know, to fly, but Dad said I don't have the right double-barrelled name or lord someone-or-other for a father.'

'That's a shame,' said Billy. 'My son left school when he was fourteen, and he's worked his way up to being on a Lancaster.'

Eames eyes widened, then he looked down. 'I bet he didn't have flat feet though, which is why they didn't want me.'

'The main thing is that you're doing a worthwhile job now, Constable Eames, and it's a vital one,' offered Maisie. 'We're much obliged to you.'

Maisie and Billy both shook hands with the constable and began walking towards the Alvis. As she reached the motor car, Maisie looked back to see PC Eames staring at her. Then he slipped the clips around his ankles, mounted his bicycle and pedalled off in the direction of the station.

'He never waited to see his mum and dad,' said Billy. 'Where do you reckon he's off to?'

'Back to Westerham, I would imagine.'

'Interesting about the boat, and who bought it.'

'The men probably found it in the same place where we saw it, and they didn't know who it belonged to.'

'And you just promoted yourself to special officer. I don't know how I kept a straight face.'

They were silent for a while, as they were settled in the motor car, and there was no conversation until Maisie pulled onto the A21 in the direction of Chelstone, and home.

'Miss, something else you said back there. You told him I was your partner, not your assistant.'

'That's right.'

'Is it?'

CHAPTER THIRTEEN

Maisie lay in bed, casting her gaze towards the needle of moonlight visible through a slit where the blackout curtains met.

She stretched out her right arm to the place where her husband would be if he were home in Kent and not at the London flat. Tomorrow she would take her daughter – she corrected herself – *their daughter* to London, where the little girl would present a bouquet of flowers to the wife of the president of the United States of America. There she would be, Anna, a child with an American father and a British mother. A child who had been left orphaned by circumstance, but who had been gathered up and cherished, and was now at the centre of a family who lavished her with love.

Maisie dozed a little, then opened her eyes, wakeful, staring at the ceiling as thoughts of the case in hand took the place of family considerations – though, Maisie thought, one aspect seemed to be bleeding into the other. Her child had become the victim of prejudice, and though part of her wanted Anna to never set foot in the village school again, at the same time she was sensitive to her feelings. Anna had loved school – it was a joy to meet her by the gates and watch her running along with other children, laughing and playing. Then almost overnight it seemed everything changed, and as far as Maisie could see, the change had some connection to the new headmistress. But what of the other mothers who had tried to avoid her as she waited for the school bell to ring and the children to be released from their lesson? What was being said in the homes of Anna's classmates? Perhaps Mark was right. Perhaps Anna might do well among children who were used to being a little different, perhaps more at ease among the offspring of foreign diplomats or missionaries; children who reflected the world's colours and creeds, and whose parents just happened to be living in England. Yet the alternative he had suggested smacked of privilege, and wasn't privilege always bolstered by a discrimination of sorts?

Her thoughts drifted back to the case, to her frustration with how slowly it was progressing, and yet she realised she had to step with care, given the need for a sensitive approach. It seemed the war had impeded so many aspects of life, while speeding up others. Intermittent access to the motor car and an insufficient petrol supply had not helped matters, nor did trains that took longer than usual due to bomb-damaged stations or troop movements taking priority over civilian transportation. It was a wonder so many trains and buses managed to keep to a timetable at all.

Despite her impatience with the pace of the investigation, she retained a strong feeling that soon enough Private Stone would be found – though whether he would still be alive was another matter. If Stone's body was discovered, then the situation for Private Matthias Crittenden would become even more critical, and the clock was ticking for the soldier because thus far there were no other suspects in the disappearance of his friend.

Jo Hardy had not been in touch for a few days. Such an absence of contact was not surprising, because as a first officer with the ATA, she could be ferrying any one of over one hundred different aeroplanes to RAF and Fleet Air Arm bases across Britain. Jo had told her that if one of their number was killed – and it was either an aircraft malfunction or inclement weather that posed the most risk – the aviators 'just had to get on with it' because Britain's air defences were dependent on the availability of aircraft. As Maisie imagined the last moments of pilots who had perished in terrifying circumstances, her chances of sleep diminished. She switched on the lamp at her bedside table, but at once turned it off, mindful of the gap in the curtains.

Slipping out of bed, she took her dressing gown from a hook behind the door and, setting off along the landing on tiptoe, made her way to the library. She checked the blackout curtains and turned on the light.

Twenty minutes later, having consulted a series of maps, she picked up the telephone receiver and placed a call to her flat in Holland Park. It was answered on the second ring.

'Hello?'

'Mark—'

'Hon, it's . . . it's just gone three in the morning. What's wrong – is everything OK?'

'Mark, I had to talk to you – it's about the case.'

'Um, OK – what is it? I'll be seeing you tomorrow anyway – well, I guess later today.'

'I'm really sorry to do this – but I've been thinking about your Rover, turning it all over in my mind, and I believe the men who have her in their sights are still in Kent. Which means that Private Stone is still in Kent, and though I've considered the opposite outcome, I'm convinced he's alive.'

'Yes, I know what you think, Maisie, but that might be wishful thinking keeping you awake in the small hours. We had people going over the mill today, and the colonel made sure there was a photograph of that message in the dust for the record. It was apparently very hard to get because it was so darn dark in there. Look – is there anything else?'

Maisie held her breath.

'Maisie?'

'Given where I think they are – I've a rough idea of their range – they will either make their move while Rover is at one of her stops in London or in Kent, and I think it could be as soon as tomorrow – even at the embassy.'

'OK, yeah, I've already got that. You're worrying, but I'll take care of it. I'll talk to the security guys again, but believe me, Maisie, it's watertight already.' Maisie heard her husband yawn. 'Sorry, hon, I didn't hit the hay until an hour ago. Late night, lots going on. Have you got anything else for me?'

Maisie paused before answering. 'No, darling, nothing else. I just wanted to talk to you about the case and . . .

Mark, shouldn't you be down in the cellar? To be honest, I'm surprised you were there to answer the call.'

'I was so darn tired, all I wanted to do was put my head on the pillow. I can hear the bombers going over, and there was one hell of a bang not far away, but we've still got our windows.'

'Oh, Mark—'

'Don't worry, hon. See you later today – I can't wait to hug my ladies!'

'Anna is very excited. We can't wait to see you too!'

Maisie replaced the receiver and put her hand to her mouth. Jo Hardy had come to her because she was convinced that a deliberate act had brought down her friend Erica, and she also wanted to help an American soldier who, it appeared, had the cards stacked against him. That was not one case, but two. The stakes were raised when she'd discovered that another pilot – Nick, Jo's fiancé – might have been targeted by someone who wanted him to crash. Now the wife of America's most important politician was in the crosshairs – and not for the first time in her life. Mrs Roosevelt had stirred up more than one hornet's nest in her bid to prevent the stings of prejudice against the poor, the workers, women, immigrants and descendants of slavery.

As Maisie lined up the events in her mind, it was as if one case had sprouted shoots that were now growing in every direction, and like wayward vines they were insinuating themselves into realms where she had no influence or standing. This was not like having to deal with Caldwell on a single remit where Scotland Yard was also involved –

that sort of investigation now seemed straightforward by comparison.

She looked at the ticking grandfather clock, the timepiece that Maurice had dutifully wound at the very same time each week, maintaining that any alteration in the schedule would upset the delicate works. Frankie Dobbs had assumed the task, so the grandfather clock was always correct to the second. Maisie watched as the hands moved, ticking away the minutes until she could be on her way, for she had a finite window of time she could dedicate to the case today, before she and Anna were due to catch an afternoon train to London. It was in those moments of planning, sitting in the library waiting until George would be up and about in the manor's garage, that she remembered Mr Avery, the gardener, and his warning that ivy growing along one side of the Dower House might look pretty, but was undermining the brickwork. 'I'd have that out, if I were you, ma'am,' he'd said. 'Get it well out before it causes any more damage. And the only way to get rid of ivy growing all over the place is to destroy the roots, right the way down, so we'd better get to it, get the job finished before that wall is done for.'

She studied the clock again, then made her way back to the bedroom to change into her day clothes. Yes, she'd better get to it – there were dangerous roots to destroy before a whole wall came down.

'Mr Love? I'm sorry to knock at your door at this hour, but—'

'Quarter past seven is never too early for a farmer, Miss

Dobbs, though I daresay it is for you. What can I do for you?'

'Mr Love, as you know, I went for a walk along the path flanking the river, and I came across the water mill over on the other side not far from the railway bridge. I know this is an unusual question, but I wondered if you might direct me to any other old buildings, disused barns or similar structures in the area.'

'Do you mean the sort of old building that someone might keep sheep or cattle in, or hay? Like my barn?'

Maisie paused for a moment. How honest could she be? 'Let's say you were one of those people who leaves London every afternoon before the blackout to get away from the bombing before it starts, and you want to put your head down somewhere far from danger even though it means sleeping rough. Or you might be a travelling worker and you don't have lodgings – we know places to bed down are getting very scarce. Or perhaps you're—'

'Come out and say it, Miss Dobbs. I've got your calling card pinned to the wall. I know your business. I reckon you want to know where someone on the run would hide. No good beating about the bush, is there, 'specially as you must have set off at just after half past six to get here?'

Maisie gave a half laugh. 'Yes, that's exactly what I'd like to know.'

'Well, let me see – if I were on the run or I wanted to lay low, I'd probably go where I could make a sprint for it a bit sharpish, if need be. I might even rest my head in plain sight.'

'Oh yes, the best of hiding places, plain sight. But do you have anywhere in mind?'

'Hmm, now let me have a think. I know you've had a gander over the old mill – and so have them Yanks. All over it like a colony of ants they were, yesterday afternoon.' He rubbed his chin. 'What about a platelayer's hut?'

'Platelayer's hut? I don't know if I've ever come across one, but isn't a platelayer something to do with the railway?'

'That's right. They don't use the huts so much any more, but when the railway was built they put a hut alongside the rails every mile or so. Most of the time, they used the same heavy sleepers to build them as they used to lay down the railway, so the walls are thick and it keeps warm enough inside for the workers who check and mend the lines. The huts are black for two reasons – the wood is creosoted to keep away worm, and the smoke from passing locomotives has covered them in soot for nigh on a hundred years.'

'You know, I've seen them alongside the railway lines when I've been on the train, but never given a thought to what they were used for,' said Maisie. 'Platelayer's huts, you say?'

'You can see the huts along the line that runs through my farm. One every mile or so between here and Paddock Wood. They're just off near the verge, so if the platelayer is brewing up inside when a train goes by, it'll make his kettle rattle. You'll see the huts all the way to London, to the coast and to Canterbury, Dover, and down to Hastings. Them huts have been an important part of keeping the railways running.' Maisie heard a voice in the background, shouting.

'That's the missus,' said Love. 'Got to go in a minute, Miss Dobbs. If you want to look at the huts, there's two within a mile of that bridge where the river cuts through the farm. You're welcome to walk across my land to get there, but there are a couple of spots where they're not far from the main road, where it crosses the line.'

'Aren't they checked by the Home Guard? They sound like the sort of place a German pilot might hide after coming down.'

'They used to check them every now and again, but not now. Too busy running across the fields with their bayonets, practicing taking on Hitler's mob when they get here.'

Maisie laughed. 'Ah, but where would we be without our Home Guard, eh, Mr Love? Anyway, thank you for your advice – I appreciate your time. Please apologise to your wife on my behalf, for disturbing you.'

Maisie walked back to her motor car, mindful of the hour and that she had limited petrol remaining. When she arrived at the manor house garage almost as soon as it was light, George had warned her that not only was there not much fuel in the tank, but she was risking being stopped by the police – she was, after all, a woman driving alone at an early hour. But she was determined. She knew she had missed something, a vital cog in the planning of whoever had taken Charlie Stone.

A *platelayer's hut*. Could that be it? The perfect hiding place for someone who wanted to move quickly and who might well need the direction indicator that a railway line offered. But if indeed they were Americans, it was more than likely that they would not have known a platelayer's hut existed, unless someone who knew had told them.

* * *

Maisie consulted her watch. She had to be on the way back to Chelstone by noon, but she had a few hours on her side. And she felt fortunate today, as if she were close to the fount of information. It was a feeling she was often loath to trust, if only to avoid the pitfall of blind optimism, which she knew only too well could render someone in her line of work clumsy and lacking the crucial advantage of acute observation. Now she hoped it was none of these things, and drove to the nearest point at which the road met the railway.

She parked the Alvis on a verge close to an open level crossing, leaving a note under the windscreen wiper blade to the effect that she was out walking and would be back soon. Then she set off, slipping under the crossing gate and onto the railway line. Within a quarter of a mile, she could see a platelayer's hut ahead. She suspected the nondescript structure situated not far from a road would be deemed perfect by the kidnappers. To bed down in one of these huts seemed as good an idea as any. As she approached the hut with care, she noticed the door was closed.

The railway lines began to buzz, vibration along the iron tracks signalling the approach of a train. She checked her watch and, with the sound masking her footfall, ran to the side of the hut. She held her hands to her ears as the train came closer, the wheels loud as they hit the points, steam punching into the autumn skies. The whistle sounded, and Maisie knew that a signalman must have opened the level crossing gates soon after she had parked, and was in all likelihood right now taking a good look at her motor car. She had no time to waste. Once the locomotive passed, she listened at the door and took a torch from her pocket, switching it on as she pushed her way into the hut.

Upturned orange boxes, a primus stove in the corner, an old kettle and a tin with tea and dried milk – the staples necessary for a worker's well-earned break. She closed the door and set off back towards the level crossing and the motor car. The signalman was closing the gate when she arrived at the Alvis.

'That motor car yours, madam?'

Maisie nodded. 'Yes, and I left a note – I'm so sorry if it worried you.'

'Not me. Funny place to be walking though.'

'It was an amble with a purpose, I'm afraid.' Maisie did not miss a beat. 'My friend has lost her dog and apparently someone said it had been seen down here by the railway line, so I was looking for him.'

'Oh, I am sorry to hear that. What's he like? I'll look out for him.'

'He's a spaniel. Not a big dog, but definitely got a nose on him. His name is Charlie.'

The signalman frowned. 'Charlie, you say? Did she have someone out looking for him early this morning?'

'She's asked a number of friends to help. Was someone calling for him then?'

'I was up in the signal box when I heard someone shout that name. I looked down but couldn't see anyone, so I reckoned it was someone looking for a dog. I don't know what it is about railways, but dogs always like to come down for a sniff around.'

'That's what we feared. But was it a man calling out?'

'Yep. Sounded like he came from Devon, down that way somewhere.'

'Hmm, I'll have to ask my friend – she knows a lot of people, and I believe one of them is from the west country.' She smiled. 'I was actually wondering if Charlie had found his way into one of those black huts and then the door closed on him.'

'I'll keep an eye out, like I said. There's another hut about a mile along in the other direction, but I must warn you, madam, not to trespass on the railway again, though I won't report it this time. I'll have a look for him after I've seen the next train through.'

'Thank you very much, sir. I appreciate it. And if you find Charlie, the best thing is to take him to the police – my friend told them he might be brought in. We just hope he's in one piece.'

'Right you are. The police know me down there at the local station. I had to report a motor car not long ago for being left right where you left yours. Mind you, whoever the driver was, he didn't have the sense to leave a message to let anyone know where he was.'

'Oh dear, how stupid.'

'I doubt if he was a German, though – bit of a dopey one, if he was.'

'Why – was it a big motor car?'

'No, little old Austin. Looked like it had seen better days, not like your nice motor over there. Whoever owned the Austin would have to know what they're doing just to get the thing started. Right old banger it was. Anyway,

243

by the time I'd returned to my post and come back to the crossing, he was gone.' He looked at his watch. 'I'd better be off. Be careful around these little roads, madam. You never know who's coming the other way.'

Maisie breathed a sigh of relief as she settled into the Alvis and started the engine. She checked the petrol gauge. Just enough to get home and perhaps a little more besides. It was just past nine o'clock, so she had plenty of time. And she knew how she was going to use that 'little more besides' amount of petrol.

A Devon accent. She remembered reading something in a women's journal, about a famous American actress who had come to Britain as one of the cast members on a picture being filmed in Devon. The actress had commented that at first she thought the local extras were mimicking her accent, but then she realised their regional way of speaking had many similarities to American intonation – they sounded their *r*'s and pronounced a number of words almost the same. Maisie was convinced the signalman had heard Charlie Stone's kidnappers. Her story about a missing dog was a tale told on the spur of the moment. Perhaps because she wanted so much to find a man called Charlie, his name had been the first on her lips, but it was a fortuitous choice on her part.

Then there was an old Austin, a vehicle that to the signalman appeared to need a fair amount of attention to keep it on the road. Someone who understood engines would know how to deal with problems issuing from an old motor. She was lucky – she had George to keep her vehicle in tip-top condition, so she had never had to go far for a garage with a handy mechanic.

Having stopped alongside a telephone box, Maisie stepped inside and picked up the receiver. She dialled the operator, gave the number and pushed coins into the slot as directed, resting her finger on button A, ready to press it home and begin speaking as soon as the call was answered. It took less than a minute for the line to connect, and for her to be put through.

'This is getting to be a habit, hon,' said Mark Scott. 'But I know you've got a good reason for calling.'

'And I'm a bit short of change, so I have to be quick. I think I might know where those men could be hiding out. That's if they're not on the move and in a London hotel already. But if they're hoping to target Rover tomorrow, they might wait until the last minute to come out of hiding.'

'What do you know, Maisie?'

'A lot more than I used to about platelayer's huts.'

'My British education is about to be broadened, I can feel it.'

'Let me explain.'

Maisie summarised the conversation with Barney Love, the hut exploration, and her chat with the signalman.

'And you say there's a hut every mile or so? That's a lot of huts, Maisie.'

'I think they should all be searched within a reasonable distance of London. Pull your political strings, Mark. It's a start.'

245

'Yes, ma'am,' replied Scott. 'But it's also a start that could get me laughed out of the embassy and sent to work in the Pennsylvania mines. A nice end to the career of an investigator with the US Justice Department, now a political attaché in London! Anyway, leave it to me. I'll see you and Anna at the flat. I have some treats at the ready.'

'Thank you, my love. See you later.'

Without replacing the receiver, Maisie pressed down on the switch bar to disconnect the call, then lifted the bar until she heard the signal to dial again. Connecting with the operator, she slipped several pennies into the slot and waited with her finger on button A.

'Marshall residence.'

Maisie pressed the button home and heard the coins drop. 'Oh, hello – this is Miss Maisie Dobbs. I'm a friend of Jo Hardy. I wonder if I might speak to either Mr or Mrs Marshall.'

The housekeeper seemed to growl accord, allowing the receiver to clatter as she put it to one side. Maisie heard her footfall recede into the distance, followed by a hiatus, then lighter steps coming towards the telephone.

'Miss Dobbs, good morning. You appear to be an early bird – what can I do for you?'

'Mrs Marshall, I wondered if Diana is at home – I think she might be able to help me with an enquiry I'm making. I would usually speak to Jo first, but I know she's flying or she would have been in touch.'

'I know our dear Jo wants you to get to the bottom of this terrible thing, because she's told us all about it, but I'm afraid Diana has been flying nonstop for days now.' There was a pause. 'Look, can I help at all?'

'I'm actually not terribly far away – could I come over? I'll be as quick as I can – it's just a few sort of "local" questions, and I know you've lived in the town for a long time, so if you don't mind you could probably help me out. I would do it now over the telephone, but I'm almost to the end of my stash of pennies.'

'Yes, of course. Do come. We'll have a nice cup of tea for you.'

'Ah, so you're a special sort of person working with Scotland Yard. I would never have thought they do that, have outsiders working with them.'

'You would be surprised, Mrs Marshall.' They were seated in the same room where Maisie had talked with Jo Hardy. She set down her cup and saucer on a side table. 'I'm curious about a few things – and I assure you, I won't take too much of your time. Can you tell me where Diana went to school – was it locally?'

'What an interesting question.'

'It's for personal reasons – something on the periphery of my work.'

'Hmm, yes, of course.' Mrs Marshall took a sip of tea. 'Diana started at the local primary school.' She glanced at her husband. 'To tell you the truth – and my husband won't mind my saying this – we were in awful trouble with the grandparents on both sides. You see, they had rather old-fashioned ideas about girls and education, but we were all for our daughter going to school with the local children – after all, they were playing together anyway. One of our household staff brought her little ones here to the house and they attended the school too, and of course we didn't want a governess and we didn't want to send her away to be a boarder somewhere until she was older. We wanted our children to be well-rounded individuals.'

Diana's father laughed. 'And we didn't know about the flying bug until Diana asked for lessons, so of course we let her so she would get it out of her system. Fortunately, the grandparents were past caring by that time.'

'Our sons had done very well at the local school,' added Mrs Marshall. 'Until, of course, it was time for them to become boarders, which they were ready for, I must say.'

'How did Diana get on at the school?'

The Marshalls exchanged a glance. Again Mr Marshall nodded for his wife to take the lead.

'For a while, all was well, and then it wasn't. She had a circle of lovely little friends, but something went a bit wrong. There was a boy who was a bit slow, if you know what I mean, and naturally Diana took him under her wing. She's always been kind that way. Another boy, his friend, wasn't terribly pleasant, and I'm not sure if he was jealous of Diana or his pal. Now, we weren't overly worried – children sort these things out, don't they? But there was a teacher at the school – I think she later became deputy headmistress – and she made more of it, suggesting that Diana had set the boys against one another, and that she really didn't think our daughter fit in very well in a village school. We were told she wasn't from the right background, being well-to-do, which we thought was a bit of a cheek.'

'Really?' Maisie leaned forward.

'So that was it.' Mr Marshall took up the story. 'I said, "To hell with this, I'm not having my daughter ostracised because she isn't a local yokel," and we brought in a governess for a few months and then sent her to boarding school. Of course, it was difficult for her at first, but she began to bloom, absolutely blossom. We are incredibly proud of her, Miss Dobbs. Immensely proud of her accomplishment with the ATA.'

'Can you tell me the names of the boys in question at the school?'

'Yes, Ronald Watkins, the lame boy, is one. Even now Diana will still stop to talk to him if she sees him. The other boy became one of our local bobbies – Peter Eames.'

'And the deputy headmistress – was it a Miss Patterson?'

'That's the woman. She's moved on now – I think she's in your neck of the woods. I'm sure she is an excellent teacher, but . . . well, she was younger at the time and I would like to give her the benefit of the doubt, so to speak. I don't think I could do the job, so I can't judge.'

Maisie smiled and thanked Diana Marshall's parents for their time as they walked her to the door, waving away the housekeeper, who had scurried forward as soon as they emerged from the drawing room.

Maisie suspected she had listened to every word of the conversation.

'I expect you'll be seeing Jo again soon, even if Diana is flying without a break for a few weeks,' said Maisie, as they stood together on the doorstep.

'Indeed, we're hoping to see Jo on either Saturday or

Sunday – she's like a second daughter to us and looks upon us as if we were her parents. I don't think she gets along with her own, to tell you the truth. Anyway, you never know with these young women,' said Mrs Marshall. 'They're working hard and then they want to play, but we're always ready when they turn up!'

'I'm sure I will hear from her in due course,' said Maisie. 'But in any case, please ask her to be in touch.'

'When we last saw her, she said she would be home soon, because she's a bit anxious to return the motor car to her friend,' said Mr Marshall. 'She borrowed an old Austin, and the thing just about got her to the house before rattling to a stop and refusing to start again. I told her to have a word with Mr Littlecombe, who runs a garage not far from here, so she did, and he came and got it going, but said he'd need more time with the engine, given that parts required for a more permanent repair are scarce. She had to leave it at the garage and go back to Hamble by train.' He shook his head, laughing. 'I told her, "Your friend has done well, hasn't she? Lends out a failing motor car and gets a better runner back!"'

Maisie smiled. 'I shall have to remember that trick!'

Goodbyes were exchanged, and as Maisie drove away she looked into the rear-view mirror and saw Diana Marshall's parents watching her. Then Giles Marshall put his arm around his wife's shoulders, and they stepped back into the house.

As she made her way along the road, Maisie doubted that Jo Hardy would have attempted to take the borrowed motor car out on another excursion following her arrival at the Marshalls' house, given that the vehicle had to be teased coughing and spluttering throughout the journey and would go no farther once it had reached its destination. No farther, that is, until Dan Littlecombe collected it to take to his garage for repair.

CHAPTER FOURTEEN

Maisie glanced at the petrol gauge and drove on – but not yet towards Chelstone. Instead she proceeded in the opposite direction, just a small detour, five minutes out of her way. She knew the street she was looking for, because she had seen Ronnie Watkins walk in that direction on the day she first met him at Littlecombe's garage, and there was only a cluster of four terrace houses on the stretch of road. Now she was trusting that she would see something to suggest which of the four belonged to the Watkins family.

The houses seemed worn and in need of attention. Gutters had worked loose, paint was chipped and peeling, and there was the definite whiff of an absent landlord who had no interest in spending time and money on the property. She knew the hallmarks of such a man; after all, she grew up in a street of damp houses with no indoor plumbing, some almost beyond repair, yet the landlord was only ever seen when he arrived on a Friday evening with his ledger in one hand while he held out the other to collect the rent.

Her attention was drawn to the house in the middle of the row, its curtains still drawn. She wondered if this was where Ronnie Watkins lived with his widowed mother – in fact, she suspected it was. She had known wartime's bereaved women who could not bear to allow light into their homes until years after the accepted twelve months of mourning had passed, long after black garb might have been cast aside in favour of lavender, a promise that brighter days lay ahead. She wondered if Ronnie's mother had slipped into an abyss of chronic grief, and how her way of being in the world might have continued to affect her.

Maisie had parked with care under a willow tree, so it was as good as hidden by foliage. She realised that she was waiting for something to happen, yet all was still. Farmworkers had gone to the fields, housewives had not yet emerged to walk along to the shops, ration books in hand, perhaps to wait for an allowance of two sausages or a loaf of bread. Even in the smallest village a queue would form as shoppers patiently marked time before it was their turn to enquire whether this or that item on their grocery list was available. The terrace houses might have seemed a little down-at-heel, but each postage-stamp front garden was now dedicated to the growing of vegetables. *Woolton Pie*, thought Maisie, reflecting for a moment upon one of the recipes handed down by the Ministry of Food, and named after the minister himself. She could not help a half-smile, remembering how she had described the dish to Mark, adding that the vegetable pie in question was a creation from the chef at no less than The Savoy Hotel. 'I don't care which fancy cook came up with it, I'm not eating that!' her husband had said, having cast a critical eye upon the recipe. 'The thought of it will—' She had laughed and stopped him at that moment, not wanting to hear what might happen if she dished up a helping of the famed Woolton Pie. 'Mind you,' Mark Scott had added, 'if we go along to The Savoy and wash it down with something from the bar, now you're talking!'

Maisie shivered, started the engine and slipped the motor car into gear. As she began to pull away, she saw the front door of the house she had focused upon open. A man and woman stepped out, whereupon the man put an arm around her shoulder as if to comfort her. There was no more for Maisie to see, so she eased away from the curb and drove away at low speed so as not to attract attention. There were no other motor cars on the road, so it was a stroke of luck that a trio of aircraft approached at low altitude at that very moment. Dan Littlecombe looked up and gave a mock salute as they passed overhead, and while his attention was deflected he had not heard the Alvis move from the verge. It was also fortunate that he had been concentrating on whatever the woman was saying, so had leaned in closer to hear as the aircraft thundered away towards the coast.

What was the relationship between Littlecombe, Ronnie Watkins and his mother – if it was his mother? Maisie didn't want to jump to conclusions based upon a kiss on the cheek and an arm around the shoulder. One scenario lingered, which she tucked away to consider later – for now she wanted to make one more stop, and it was en route to Chelstone.

At the small school where Miss Patterson had previously taught, children were out, running back and forth in the playground, the girls at one end and the boys at another, separated during playtimes to protect the girls from the exuberant gambolling of boys. In Maisie's experience, girls could be every bit as boisterous and could hold their own with ease if the children were allowed to mix on the playground. She thought of Mark the first time he came with Maisie to accompany Anna to school, and his confusion regarding the notion of playtime. 'Is that what we call "recess" in the States?' he'd asked, and Maisie shrugged. 'I suppose it could be. I don't know anything about your American schools. But it's a break in the morning, then at dinnertime – lunch, that is – and again in the afternoon. It gives the children a chance to stretch their legs, to run around a bit.'

'That's "recess" in my language,' he'd replied.

As Maisie watched, the teacher on duty walked back and forth, sometimes remaining in one place to observe a particular group of children for a few minutes. When the teacher walked to the fence to stand for a while, Maisie approached, noticing the youth of the woman as she came closer.

'Good morning,' said Maisie.

The woman turned, smiling. 'Good morning, Mrs . . . oh dear, I am sorry, I don't usually forget parents' names, but sometimes—'

'Oh, not to worry. It's Mrs Scott – and my daughter isn't a pupil here, but we are thinking of moving to the area, so I thought I would stop to look at the school.'

'I must apologise, Mrs Scott, but the school is out of bounds to visitors without an appointment.'

'That's all right. I wasn't planning to come in, but I've found you can tell a lot about a school simply by watching the children at play – whether it's a good place or not. Everyone seems very happy here, I must say.'

'Yes, Mrs Scott, it's a lovely little school. It's come along very nicely and we're all very proud.'

'It's always encouraging to hear a teacher express pride in her work, and in the school,' said Maisie. She continued as if reticent to ask an important question. 'I wonder . . . oh, never mind. It was just an idle thought.'

'If it's about the school, I might be able to help,' said the teacher. 'No thoughts from a parent are ever idle, in my estimation. We have your children in our care, after all.'

Maisie leaned forward as if to confide in the teacher.

'Well, this is difficult, but . . . I suppose because it's something I've heard regarding a colleague of yours, another teacher who worked here. And one hates to cast aspersions.'

The woman consulted her watch and reached for the hand bell at her feet, though she put her fingers over the hammer. She looked at Maisie as if to gauge how much to reveal, then stepped closer. 'If I'm not mistaken, you're talking about Miss Patterson.'

Maisie nodded.

'I thought so. You must live in Chelstone. Apparently

that's where she's now headmistress at the village school. Has your daughter had some trouble with her?'

Maisie nodded, the intended connection working in her favour.

The teacher consulted her watch again. 'Let me just say that we've had some catching up to do over the past six months or so.'

'Really?'

The teacher looked around as if to check that no one was listening. 'You can be assured that your daughter will be happy here now. As you may have guessed, we had some . . . some hiccups with Miss Patterson.'

'Hiccups?' asked Maisie.

The teacher nodded, primed to take Maisie into her confidence. 'Very critical she was – I came here straight from teacher training college, and I thought I would run away to join the Wrens instead. It was that bad. She picked on me every day because I was new, but as another teacher told me, it was better that I took the brunt of it rather than the children. It didn't do if you were in any way different. To her, "new" counted as a difference she didn't like.'

'And are you sure it's changed here? Please be honest, as I've my daughter's happiness to consider.' She took a deep breath, for effect. 'You see, my daughter is adopted, and her father was . . . let's say she gets her more olive complexion from the paternal side of the family.'

'Then I'm glad you'll be moving here now, rather than a year or two ago.' The young woman looked at her watch again. 'But I felt sorry for her – I mean, you don't pick on people, especially children, unless you've something nibbling away at you inside, do you? I see it every day on the playground. The children who start a fight, who set on others, or who are just mean – they're like a dog with a thorn in its paw, and sometimes it takes a while to find the thorn and work out how to remove it.' She shrugged. 'Anyway, don't listen to me – the other teachers have told me I think about these things too much and that I'll get over it when I've a few more years under my belt.' She smiled at Maisie. 'Time to ring the bell, I'm afraid. I hope we see your daughter here soon, Mrs Scott.'

The teacher turned away and began ringing the handbell. The children stopped playing and ran to form two lines, girls on one side of the teacher, boys on the other. 'Walk, don't run!' instructed the novice teacher, her voice raised. Maisie lingered to watch until the children had filed back into the small primary school, each line through a different doorway.

Maisie checked the time once more and set off on her return journey to Chelstone. However, despite promising herself that the school would be her last stop, approaching the church tower gave her an idea, so she pulled over one last time. She had learned early in her work with Maurice that a church could be a useful resource during an investigation. Sometimes it didn't take more than a vicar with time on his hands, or the parish record of baptisms, marriages and funerals left in a common area. It was worth a quick look.

'I knew you shouldn't have gone out this morning, Maisie.' Brenda stood, hands on hips, in the kitchen as Maisie scraped a small knob of butter across a slice of toast again and again so it reached the edges. 'You were lucky your motor stopped not far from a telephone box, or you could have been stranded on the road for hours! Anna was beside herself, wondering whether something horrible had happened to her mummy.'

'Brenda, it's not the end of the world. I'm here now, and we're in plenty of time to get to the station. And I managed to eke out the petrol, knowing I could reach the telephone box and it was only a couple of miles away from home. I'll admit, I was lucky George had some petrol put by and it was my good fortune that he could come out to rescue me in the Lanchester, but now I have to get Anna ready and make sure we've gathered everything.'

'It's all there, Maisie. I've packed it, and every single thing she'll need is in that little case. Clean pyjamas, polished shoes, her best dress and coat. There's new ribbons for her hair, and . . . and . . . her hairbrush and . . .' Maisie's stepmother began to weep, holding a tea cloth to her reddened eyes.

'Oh, Brenda, what is it?' said Maisie, putting her arms around the woman she had come to love as if she were her own mother.

'It's just . . . it's just . . . she's gone through so much and she's always just carried on with a happy face and now something's bothering her and we don't know what it is. Yes, there's the school, but it's more than that – and now there she is, that poor little mite we all love, going to meet a very important lady. I'm glad you finally told your father and me what Anna would be doing in London, and I can see why you kept quiet about it until after she'd gone to bed last night, but I'm worried it'll all be too much for her, because it's too much for me.'

Maisie said nothing at first, absorbing the sobs that moved through Brenda's body like waves.

'Brenda, I believe I know the root cause of Anna's distress, and I will put a stop to it.' She chose her words with care. 'Our Anna is beloved by us all, and she knows it – we're like a fortress around her. Now then, let me tell you about my – about a plan Mark and I have. Come on, we've time for a cup of tea before Dad gets back from the stable with Anna, and George comes to take us to the station.'

Brenda pulled a handkerchief from her pinafore. 'Oh, I forgot to tell you, what with one thing and another. Priscilla telephoned – she wanted to know which train you were catching, because she's going up to the Holland Park house, and she said she'll be on the same train.'

Maisie nodded. 'That's good – in fact, that's very good.'

'It'll take Anna's mind off everything, seeing "Auntie Pris".'

'Yes, that's what I was thinking.' Maisie put her hands on Brenda's shoulders, leaning forward to look into her eyes. 'This is a house filled with love for Anna, and she loves us back. We can get through anything, Brenda.'

Later, as she readied her daughter for the journey to London, Maisie reflected on her good fortune that Priscilla had decided to join them on the train. Priscilla's London home was just along the street from Maisie's garden flat; she would ask Priscilla to look after Anna for a couple of hours after they arrived at Charing Cross station, allowing Maisie to run an important errand. She would be back at the flat in plenty of time for a spaghetti dinner with her husband and their daughter.

'Oh, Maisie,' said Brenda, as Maisie and Anna were about to leave the house. 'Just a minute – before you go, I forgot to tell you something else – I don't know what's happened to my memory this week. It's all the excitement.'

Maisie patted her daughter on the head. 'There's George now, Anna – you go on and get into the motor, my darling. I'll catch up when I've spoken to Grandma – and don't put your feet on the seat, or George will have something to say to you.'

Anna skipped ahead. Maisie smiled as Frankie took his granddaughter's hand as if she were a princess to be escorted into her carriage – and she knew that George would say nothing about Anna's feet on the back seat of the prized Lanchester. She turned back to Brenda.

'You must think I've lost my mind, Maisie – I am so sorry, but what with one thing and another, I forgot to tell you that a woman called, name of Miss Jo . . . Jo . . .'

'Jo Hardy? Did she leave a message?'

'She said—' Brenda plunged a hand into her pinafore pocket, extracting a handkerchief, followed by a scrap of paper. 'She said to tell you it was about a friend of hers who is a . . .' She peered over her spectacles. 'A photographic interpreter. She said she has some information that could be useful.'

'All right. I'll telephone her as soon as I get to London.'

'I'm sorry, Maisie. I've never forgotten a message before, ever, even when Dr Blanche was ill, I never forgot—'

Once again, Maisie put her arms around her stepmother. 'Please don't worry, Brenda. We've all got a lot on our minds. I will talk to Miss Hardy soon. Everything will be all right.'

It was later, while Anna chattered away to Priscilla about a story Mummy had been reading before bed every night, that Maisie gazed out of the train window and wondered what information a photographic interpreter might have discovered, and where it came from.

'We are going to have a wonderful time while Mummy is off and away for her meeting,' said Priscilla, putting an arm around Anna as the train rocked from side to side. 'In fact, I know exactly what we are going to do. I need a new hat, and you are going to choose it for me!'

Maisie watched as her daughter giggled, comfortable with her oldest, dearest friend, who had readily agreed to look after Anna while Maisie 'had to meet someone.'

'I think your mother is up to some of her cloak-and-dagger business again, Anna – what do you think?'

'What's "cloak-and-dagger", Auntie Pris?' asked Anna. 'It sounds scary.'

Priscilla shook her head. 'Not scary – just sort of secret. That's what Mummy does, you know – she does secret things.'

'Pris—' Maisie cautioned Priscilla. She brushed a tendril of hair from Anna's eyes. 'Auntie Pris is telling tales – but I am sure she means it about the hat, and that will give you something to giggle about!'

The child began to laugh. 'I remember the one Auntie Pris wore when you married Daddy – it was really funny.'

'Hmm,' said Priscilla. 'My sons let me know that everyone at the wedding thought so too, but it was exciting and colourful, and as you will learn, my girl, the only person you have to please when it comes to being stylish is yourself. I will teach you everything I know!'

'And then you can join the circus!' added Maisie.

The banter continued for a while, until Anna rested her head on Maisie's lap and fell asleep.

'Have you got to the bottom of what's been going on at that school, Maisie?' asked Priscilla, her voice low.

Maisie nodded, whispering, 'I think so. Yes, I think I know what's happened.'

'What will you do?'

Maisie sighed. 'I don't think I can wait for things to change, so we may well be sending Anna to another school.'

'Not as a boarder, I hope!'

'Absolutely not.' Maisie shook her head and motioned to Priscilla to keep her voice down. 'No – definitely not boarding,' she continued. 'But she will be among other children who come from different countries, as well as British children. It's not a perfect situation, though I – we – think it's for the best. For now anyway. I can't have her feeling so . . . so . . . so *unsafe*, I suppose. So out of place. She fitted in incredibly well at first, but I suppose given all she has endured in her short little life, a setback was bound to crop up at some point, and fortunately, I can do something about it.'

'Good, I'm glad to hear it. Now, where is it you're going, when we get to London?'

'Scotland Yard.'

'Nice to see you, Miss Dobbs.' Caldwell pointed to the chair on the opposite side of his desk. As usual, the seat was covered with files and loose papers. Maisie picked them up and put them on the desk. 'You could always hang around for a bit and file them for me,' added Caldwell.

Maisie raised an eyebrow.

'Sorry, didn't mean it,' said the detective. 'Just a bit of a joke. Now then, what can I do for you.'

Caldwell leaned back in his chair, his tie askew, his sleeves rolled up. His round face was reddened, the skin under his eyes appearing bruised. Maisie wondered if he shouldn't be paying attention to his heart, given the nature of his work. Crime in wartime had soared, though the papers would have the citizenry believe otherwise. The pressure on Caldwell was evident in his demeanour.

'If you don't mind my saying, you're looking rather all-in.'

Caldwell shook his head. 'Feeling it too, Miss Dobbs. Feeling it something rotten. I'd like a few of these enquiries off my plate – but perhaps that's why you're here.'

Maisie looked at her hands and ran her wedding ring back and forth along her finger.

'You've got something for me, haven't you?' said Caldwell.

'It's tricky, but I know you've been on the periphery of the case involving the missing American soldier at the farm in Kent, though not in the case of a ferry pilot – a woman – who came down not far from the same farm. I had a word with Constable Eames. I saw him close to his home, so I discovered a few things.' She described the sale of a boat and fishing rods. 'However, I think the young constable might know a little more about the pilot's demise than he's let on to anyone, but he surely won't speak to me about it, and might not reveal anything to you, yet I thought you should know.'

Caldwell tapped a rhythm on the wooden desk as he regarded Maisie, and gave a slow nod. 'That's one I owe you, Miss Dobbs. I'll keep it tucked away for now.'

'Daddy, Daddy, Daddy.' Anna ran into Mark's arms as soon as he stepped into the flat, carrying a large brown-paper-wrapped parcel.

'How's my girl?' said Mark, dropping the bulging briefcase he had managed to carry at the same time as he placed the unwieldy package on the floor with care. He swept Anna into his arms.

'Auntie Pris bought me a hat to wear tomorrow!'

Maisie laughed as her husband turned to her, his eyes wide. 'Tell me this isn't true, please!'

'It's all right,' said Maisie. 'It's quite lovely – navy blue with a velvet band, and it matches Anna's coat.'

'Praise be for that,' said Mark, as Anna slid to the ground. 'Now then, what have we here for my girl?'

'Someone's been to Hamleys,' said Maisie. 'Anna, run

and get your hat to show Daddy, then you can open your present.'

As they made their way into the small drawing room, with blackout curtains now drawn, Mark set down the parcel again and put his arm around Maisie's shoulder.

'Nothing on those railway huts yet – there's channels to go through, but we're going to get every single one checked out.' He kissed her forehead. 'Dare I ask about your day?'

'Waiting for a telephone call – I left a message earlier for Jo Hardy. She's been trying to get in touch with me, but I suppose what with one thing and another, we're both horribly difficult to reach.'

'You can say that again!'

'What can Mummy say again?' Anna's voice piped up as she entered the room wearing a brimmed hat.

'Oh my, what a beauty,' said Mark. 'That is a terrific hat!'

Maisie felt her heart swell. 'Aren't you going to open Daddy's present?'

'It's not my birthday – why have I got a present?'

'It's not for your birthday, sweetie – it's a "just because" present.' Mark knelt down alongside Anna.

'Just because what?'

'Just because you're my girl. And also just because tomorrow you'll be doing a very special job – giving flowers to an important lady.' Anna looked at the wrapped parcel, crestfallen.

'What is it, darling?' asked Maisie, running a hand across her child's head.

266

'The important lady might not like me though.'

'Hey, of course she will! She will love you, honey. Everyone loves you.' Mark reached towards the parcel. 'Come on, let's get this paper off together.'

'Not everyone loves me. That's why I'm not at school. Because my friends don't like me any more.'

Maisie was about to say something to soothe Anna when the telephone rang.

'Oh dear—'

'I'll get it.' Mark came to his feet while Maisie took his place. He picked up the telephone receiver with a brief 'Hello,' then turned to Maisie. 'For you – Jo Hardy.'

Maisie stood up as Mark reached out and took Anna's hand, ready to lead her towards the kitchen. 'Come on, sweetie, let's go get dinner ready – can't do it without you! We can open that present when we've all had some . . .' He looked at Anna to finish the sentence.

'Spaghetti!'

'Ha! No, it's a surprise! Tonight we're having something very special from my country – hot dogs!'

'Those are just your funny sausages, Daddy.'

'Funny sausages? Oh, we'll see about that – let me show you my special recipe!'

Maisie sighed with relief. Mark would lift Anna's spirits. She reached for the receiver.

'Jo, I'm so glad you've called. Tell me about your friend, the photographic interpreter – and I know what they do, by the way.'

In her role with the Special Operations Executive, Maisie had often received reports from women working

267

in photographic intelligence, so she was one of a small number of people aware of the department's work. It was a role for which women were considered to be perfectly suited; a rare joint department where British and American interpreters worked alongside one another, concentrating on images as they came in from Allied aircraft fitted with special equipment.

'It's very interesting, Maisie. Here's what's happened.' Maisie heard Jo catch her breath, as if she had been running to report her story and was winded. 'The Spitfire I was flying that day – you know, when the man held up the gun and aimed it at me – I'd forgotten it wasn't a normal Spit – well, it was, but it was geared up for another role. It had a camera on board for photo reconnaissance. I was ferrying it to Biggin Hill, and then an RAF pilot was taking it somewhere else after that – really, I don't know what happens, because my job is just the deliveries. Anyway, I must have activated the camera, because the whole thing was filmed – the men, the motor car. Unfortunately, so was my little foray under the bridge, but let's hope that passes! However, the terrific thing is that I know the interpreter who had the film – stroke of luck if ever there was one, because she's managed to view a close-up of the man on the ground, and also the motor car. It appears to be an American make. There was another man who is not terribly visible, but I think it might be possible to get some sort of clue to the first man's identity.'

'When can I see these photographs?'

Jo Hardy was uncharacteristically silent on the other end of the line; for a moment Maisie thought they had been disconnected. 'It appears you know it's all very secret, what goes on at photo reconnaissance, and usually even the unusable film is stored, just in case. I mean, they can't have anyone going through the dustbins looking for film, can they? Muriel has had her hands on the copies for a few days now, because she knew I would want to see them, but of course that could mean her job, and it would be down to me if she lost it – though she could say she was protecting me and that we need our fearless flyers, even if they are a bit cavalier when they're in a nice little aeroplane like a Spitfire!'

'I'd like to see the photographs as a matter of urgency, Jo.'

'I'm planning to meet Muriel tomorrow – she said she could put the photographs in my hot little hands while we're having drinks.'

'I'm out at an important . . . an important meeting tomorrow, however, you can telephone me at my house in Kent later in the day.'

'Better still – I can come over first thing on Sunday morning. I've to collect a very unreliable motor car from Dizzy's parents' house. Dan Littlecombe was sorting it out for me – utterly gifted mechanic, I must say. Anyway, I'll be seeing the Marshalls later tomorrow and spending the night at their house. I might need to lay my head down at yours on Sunday night though, but I promise I won't get in the way, as I'll be setting off bright and early on Monday morning because I'm needed at our base in White Waltham.'

'Of course you can stay. It might be a packed house though, but everyone's used to mucking in together.'

'Good. I'll see you on Sunday.'

'Let me give you directions – and I want to ask you about that "little Austin".'

Maisie turned around just as Anna was unwrapping the parcel to reveal a doll's house, with Mark on his hands and knees showing her how each door opened to reveal the furniture within. He looked up at her with a broad smile.

'Good news?'

'Promising.'

He came to his feet, rubbing his back. 'I've some news too.'

Maisie looked into her husband's eyes, as if to read his thoughts. 'It's about Private Crittenden, isn't it?'

He nodded. 'He's being flown back to the States the week after next, on a cargo flight via Gander. He was going to be shipped back next week, but the colonel managed to get a short extension due to the "continuing investigation".'

'But . . . but . . . but surely, as his supposed crime took place on British soil—'

Mark shook his head. 'No dice, Maisie. It doesn't work like that, I'm afraid.'

'Mummy – come and see this!' Anna looked up from the new treasure. 'It's even got a little gramophone!'

'Goodness me – however did they make it that small?' She smiled, turning to her husband. 'It means Private Stone must be found soon,' she whispered. 'And believe it or not, so must a murderer whom I believe is implicated in the abduction.'

'What?'

Maisie nodded as she knelt down beside Anna, and continued in a low voice. 'And if we don't find the driver of a certain American motor car, we may be on the lookout for an assassin.'

'What's an assassin?' Anna was staring at Maisie, tiny gramophone in her hand.

Maisie shook her head and laughed, tickling her daughter under the chin. 'You silly billy, I said 'Where's the dustbin?' I'm sure there must be one, because every house has rubbish to be collected, doesn't it?'

CHAPTER FIFTEEN

'Honey, you're shaking,' said Mark, standing next to Maisie just inside the doors of the American Embassy.

'I'm nervous, Mark. Very nervous.'

'Well, the half-pint is taking it in her stride – look at her, she's beautiful.'

Maisie's eyes welled with tears. 'I know. Yes, she looks so lovely.'

'And I can't complain about the hat either. At least Priscilla didn't send her home with the Stars and Stripes on a bowler!' Mark placed a hand on Anna's shoulder and knelt down beside her. 'Here we go, honey – the lady's motor car is almost here. You wait while she speaks to the big folks first, and when she steps up here to the door, off you go.'

Maisie watched as Anna appeared to square her shoulders, holding the bouquet with the stems in one hand and the blooms resting on the opposite arm, as if she were cradling the head of her favourite china doll. A black motor car came to a halt, followed by another vehicle. With her hand resting on her daughter's shoulder, Maisie drew her attention away from the vehicles, away from Ambassador John Winant, who made ready to approach the esteemed visitor, and cast her gaze across the crowd. Londoners had gathered en masse to greet Eleanor Roosevelt as her motor car made its way through the capital.

The First Lady of the United States of America stepped out of the vehicle and stood tall as she reached for the ambassador's hand, beaming her famous toothy smile as she stooped to accommodate the dignitaries waiting to greet her. She wore a coat in a distinctive style, pleated at the back and topped with a long blue fox stole. Her large, plate-shaped pleated hat embellished with coloured feathers had already become a hallmark of her visit. Mark had told Maisie that the VIP had been subject to the same limited luggage allowance as any other passenger on a dangerous wartime air crossing of the Atlantic, so she would be photographed wearing the same clothing through all her appearances – and she would not be leaving the country for a good number of days.

Watching from a vantage point, Maisie took account of the throng as Mrs Roosevelt moved towards the entrance where Anna would present her bouquet. Maurice had taught Maisie how to search a gathering for the one individual who seemed as if they did not belong. It required a slow, deliberate movement of the head, as if following the second hand on a clock, yet with a slight hesitation at each notch on the dial before moving on. Within that microsecond, Maisie would survey the faces clustered within the cone of space upon which her attention was focused.

'You know when you're doing this properly,' Maurice had instructed. 'Time itself will stand still, as if the world around you were recorded on film and you are slowing the motion to consider every single frame. You are suspended in time, watching all that is before you, but you are paying attention, so anything amiss will be evident to you.'

Move, stop, move, stop. She felt anticipation shiver through her daughter's body and squeezed the child's shoulder. Then, at a forty-five degree angle to the statuesque woman who had turned to wave to the crowd and was now stepping towards Anna, Maisie saw something. She cast her eyes back a notch, just one second on the imaginary dial. It was a face among many, but as Maurice had predicted, 'Do not find it unusual if you see the person you seek as if you were looking at a photographic film in the negative. Not only is there pressure upon your eyes, but your mind will be seeking that which is untoward, so you will be aware of a darkness shadowing them.'

'Mark—' She tugged her husband's sleeve, but retained her gaze in the direction of a single man she had seen just beyond those gathered close to the front of the embassy. 'Mark – Mark, that man. At the back—'

Mark Scott raised his hand, and two men who seemed as if they could pass for bank clerks on their way to work emerged from either side of those waiting for Mrs Eleanor

Roosevelt, and began to circle the crowd in the direction Maisie had indicated to her husband.

'He's moving off, Mark – he knows I've seen him. He'll start running.'

'Don't worry – we'll keep Rover safe. OK, here we go—'

Maisie bent down and kissed her daughter. 'Time to present your bouquet, Anna. You know what to say – look, she's smiling at you. Go on, my sweetheart.'

Mark Scott stood behind Anna as she stepped forward and held out the flowers to Mrs Roosevelt, curtsying as she presented the red-and-white blooms tied with a blue bow.

'Well, thank you, young lady. And may I ask your name?' asked Mrs Roosevelt, bending forward so she could avoid looking down at Anna from too great a height.

'I'm Anna, and my mummy is British and my daddy is American, so I'm both!'

Maisie heard Mark begin to laugh as he reclaimed his daughter, who seemed ready to launch into a fuller conversation with the esteemed guest, now being led into the building by the ambassador.

'Oh, well done, darling,' said Maisie, kneeling to wrap her arms around Anna and kiss her on the cheek.

'You're a star, sweetie, a real star,' added Mark.

'She's a very tall lady!' said Anna. 'I think she's as high up as Daddy.'

Maisie took Anna's hand, and with the other she pointed to the returning agents as she whispered to her husband. 'I think he managed to get away.'

The crowd was beginning to disperse; reporters were now filtering into the embassy.

'I'll find out soon enough,' said Mark. 'Look, I know you want to get Anna home, but I have to ask you to make a statement, describe the guy for our people here. And there's something else. We want you to have a sit-down with Mrs Roosevelt after the press conference. In fact, she asked to be briefed about the supposed threat to her life. We want you to try to persuade her not to go off course and into any crowds. She's already bowled over by the number of people who've come out to see her and wants to make sure no one's disappointed. Then when you're done, I'll get away and we can catch the train back to Chelstone – home in plenty of time for dinner.'

'Shouldn't Scotland Yard be—'

'They will. Anyway, you're on US soil in the embassy, and we need your description.'

Maisie shook her head. 'That's almost impossible, Mark – it was more of a feeling than what I saw, and the only way I can describe the man is that for most people, he wouldn't stand out in a crowd. However—'

'However what?'

'I keep thinking I've seen him somewhere before, but . . . but for the life of me I just cannot put my finger on where it might have been.'

'That's not like you.'

'I know – it's not like me at all.'

Having provided a statement, Maisie was later accompanied by Mark Scott and an agent to a small but grand room. Mark

276

knocked at the door, which was answered by an officer Mark introduced as Colonel Oveta Culp Hobby, the director of the US Women's Army Corps. She led Maisie to meet Mrs Roosevelt, who asked if everyone could leave so she could talk to Maisie 'woman to woman'. Only her secretary, Miss Malvina Thompson – she called her 'Tommy' – would remain, though once introduced to Maisie, she returned to a wing chair in the corner and picked up a clutch of papers and a pen. She reminded Maisie of a teacher preparing to mark her pupils' homework.

Maisie held her hand against the belt of her navy blue jacket. To mark the occasion, she had set off the jacket with a silk scarf of red, white and blue roses at her neckline. Colonel Hobby directed her to a chair set alongside a fireplace, where she would be facing Mrs Roosevelt.

'It's very cold everywhere, isn't it?' Mrs Roosevelt had not removed her coat, and pulled the blue fox stole around her neck. 'I've been informed coal must be used sparingly.'

'We've become used to rationing,' said Maisie. 'And that includes fuel.' She paused. 'Mrs Roosevelt, I—'

Eleanor Roosevelt smiled as she interrupted. 'Mrs Scott, I have been given a briefing on the situation you are here to talk to me about, and I am fully aware that you have been asked to persuade me to . . . to curtail my activities. Now, I am not sure what you think about this, but I believe – from what I know of you, and I confess I have asked a few questions of my own – that you will agree when I say I cannot possibly place limitations on my visit to Great Britain.' She glanced at her secretary, who nodded. 'That is not to suggest I have been without nerves regarding this whole trip, because I am not entirely sure I warrant a red carpet and such high status in your country!'

Maisie smiled, feeling more at ease, and was about to speak when America's First Lady continued.

'Before I left home, I had seen photographs of your bombed cities, but I can tell you I was not prepared to see such great areas of destruction, and I have not yet been in London for twenty-four hours.' Mrs Roosevelt fixed her gaze on Maisie. 'Yet even in a short time, I am struck by the crowds and that people who have lost so much are still able to smile and give me a marvellous welcome. I know that every day after a bombing, they pick up and go on, despite great sorrow and loss.'

Mrs Roosevelt came to her feet, a signal that the meeting was nearing its end.

'I understand your stepmother is a member of the Women's Voluntary Service. Lady Reading – who as you know is the force behind that marvellous institution – has been telling me all about the sterling work of the WVS. I'm looking forward to meeting so many of your British women engaged in war work – especially the ferry pilots.' She smiled, and later Maisie would describe a 'sparkle' in the woman's eyes, though in that moment she knew she had witnessed a resolve as strong as steel. 'Before I agreed to this visit, I was assured that I would be given full freedom to see what I wanted to see in the way that would be most useful to me. Given that promise, how could I not continue with my visit as planned when the women of Britain have shown their mettle in the face of a far greater enemy? In the meantime, I will let Ambassador Winant know that you did your very best to persuade me to be careful.'

'Thank you, ma'am,' said Maisie, extending her hand. 'Your response is exactly as I anticipated. You are a most welcome visitor. God speed.'

'A visitor with freezing cold feet already!' said Eleanor Roosevelt, taking Maisie's hand, at the same time as Colonel Hobby returned to the room following a single, soft knock at the door. 'You know, I could only bring two pairs of shoes with me, one pair for day and one pair for evening. I'm sure I will be putting newspaper inside worn soles before I go home – and that *is* a security concern, considering the miles I will be walking!'

Excitement was high at Chelstone that afternoon. Patty Hayden had arrived at the Dower House, having been met in London by Tom Partridge, who was driving a borrowed motor car for his forty-eight-hour leave. Accompanied by her two spaniels, Lady Rowan had walked over from the manor house to hear all about Anna's day, though there was almost an upset when the spaniels began playing with Little Emma, at which point Brenda declared she would fall head over heels and face certain death if the dogs weren't dispatched to the garden.

'I heard Mrs Roosevelt was given a ration card directly she arrived in England, so she can't eat any better than the rest of us,' said Brenda.

'That's right,' said Mark. 'She wouldn't have done that anyway – she doesn't like preferential treatment. She told us that inside Buckingham Palace it's as cold as ice, and a black line has been painted inside the bathtub so that guests don't use more than five inches of hot water. According to her secretary, the wind whistled through the boards where the windows used to be before the palace was bombed. And from the description of the food, I can definitely confirm the First Lady is not eating any better than the rest of us.'

'Absolutely right too,' said Lady Rowan.

'Most Americans don't know what it's like here, that's for sure,' added Patty. 'It's a dreadful shock when you see the destruction for the first time.'

'And that's why we're doing all we can to cheer you up, darling,' said Tom, who blushed when he realised it was the first time those gathered had heard him express affection for the American nurse.

Maisie raised an eyebrow, wondering what Priscilla might say if she had heard the comment – Priscilla would not be returning to Chelstone until the following day. The continuing family chatter seemed to offer an opportune moment for Maisie to slip away to the library. As she left the room, she heard Mark add something to the effect that Tom was clearly doing a good job of cheering Patty, who looked pretty happy as far as he could see, before an immediate segue regarding Anna's presentation of flowers to Eleanor Roosevelt. 'I almost collapsed when I saw my sweet girl curtsy in front of the First Lady – I bet that was your doing, Bren!'

The sound of voices tapered off as Maisie entered the quiet library, where she turned on a desk lamp and closed the blackout curtains. Dusk was falling. Soon the rumble of bombers would be heard approaching, unless tonight was a rare night without an attack that would drive them into the cellar. From this direction, London would be in their sights, though it could be a night when other conurbations around Britain would suffer the onslaught – perhaps Southampton, or Liverpool, Glasgow, or Belfast. She thought of Bobby Beale in a Lancaster bomber, navigating the lumbering aircraft towards Berlin or Hamburg to inflict similar destruction, and closed her eyes, sickened by what might have come to pass by morning.

It was a tower of boxes in the corner of the library that claimed her attention. She had brought them up from the cellar some months ago, when a publisher she had met during her work on a previous case discovered that she had inherited the papers – diaries and case records – of her former mentor, Maurice Blanche. She had already received two letters enquiring about 'the Blanche papers' in which the publisher underscored his interest in the documents and extended an offer of publication. The publisher had encouraged her to consider the papers' importance and interest to a wider audience; she wasn't sure about that, though she knew there was a veritable archive of knowledge for her to draw upon, in particular during those times when she found herself stuck on a case. But what she was searching for now was personal in nature.

Unstacking the boxes one by one, she came to a certain box labelled with a date and list of contents. She opened the lid and thumbed through folders and ledgers until she found what she wanted: a worn clothbound book. She opened it and sat on the floor to read.

'Maisie is developing her skills at a rate that is more than satisfactory. It has been necessary to take due care not to burden her natural intellectual and other innate faculties too soon. To do so would risk the fire of enthusiasm on her part gathering pace and leaving her burned, unable to engage in the depth of enquiry required for the work and for her personal development. I cannot allow her to be scalded by her own curiosity and hunger for learning. Today we discussed what I have termed the 'phenomenon of three,' when it becomes evident that quite different case scenarios demonstrate similarities so acute as to become startling, which can in turn throw off the enquiry if doubt is allowed the upper hand. There is much to teach my apprentice about the role and threat of doubt.'

Maisie turned the pages to the light to better read Maurice's precise yet small handwriting, and read on.

'We have a case in progress that has the qualities of a mirror, and it has unsettled Maisie, who at first thought she was "seeing shadows" from the previous two cases; however, I assured her that this is all part of her education and that I am not her only teacher. There are also lessons from life itself, as if the nature of our work were testing her, showing her the same case time and again so that she might fully learn the lesson. My example was of a mathematical equation repeated in schooldays. One does not only learn a formula once. Instead one has to tackle the problem repeatedly until it becomes easier. Repetition in our work allows us to see the subtle differences that bring a swift conclusion to a case.'

Maisie nodded, remembering many conversations on the subject. But she was looking for more.

'Then there is the phenomenon of the personal mirroring the professional. I have instructed my apprentice that this happens when we see elements of the case reflected in our private lives.'

She had found it.

'I have counselled Maisie that this will also happen time and again, as if providence were choosing a given moment to draw attention to something emerging at home that is currently evident in the case at hand. This lesson is troubling for both teacher and pupil; how can I tell Maisie about such things without revealing elements of my life that might be best shielded from her? I will write again of this – but as her teacher, I have made it clear that when it happens, when the personal and professional collide, then compassion must be brought to bear upon the personal situation in particular. *Compassion.*' Maisie noted dots of ink on the page, as if at this point Maurice had been considering how best to go on and had repeatedly tapped his pen on the page while mulling the problem. 'If there is pain, then it must be noted that anger, petulance, cruelty and despair are leaves falling from that particular tree. I have instructed Maisie to go to the root of such trauma, whether it is identified in herself or another, for the personal challenge has emerged for solution just as the case has been brought to her attention.'

'Phew.' Maisie puffed out her cheeks and leaned back against the wall, shaking her head as she set down the ledger. 'You're asking too much of me, Maurice.' She reflected upon the last paragraph again. 'I don't know if I can bring compassion to the woman who has brought so much pain to my daughter because she is darker than the other children.'

She thought again of Matthias Crittenden, of their first encounter, when he was brought to the stark, unwelcoming room to be questioned by her. There was a moment, just before his handcuffs were removed, the guards rough as they dragged the metal across his skin, when she saw him pull back his shoulders, his chest high and his neck unbowed. He closed his eyes, almost as if he were remembering the counsel of someone dear – indeed, she remembered thinking that she could almost hear his mother or father reminding him, 'Stand tall, my son.' She knew little of life in America for people like the Crittendens, but from what she had gleaned in recent days, they would have known what it was to remain standing tall when the world was bearing down. She wished she had been given leave to speak to Crittenden for longer or even had a second opportunity to draw him out. Maisie felt hampered – more than anything by not being able to truly get to the heart of Matthias Crittenden, for in that one interview she knew she was in the presence of a good, proud young man. But he was exhausted by the weight of worry and fear, which was not to his advantage.

She closed her eyes, and because she was already seated on the floor, she crossed her legs and brought her hands together in her lap, her thumbs one rice grain apart as she had been instructed decades earlier. Motherhood had claimed so much of her time, the opportunity to find moments for silent meditation seemed to have evaporated, though she had been teaching her daughter, hoping it would strengthen her spirit and provide a self-awareness that would serve her well.

Five minutes passed, then she gasped and opened her eyes. Unbidden, it had come to her – the face she had seen in the crowd outside the American embassy. She was right in her assumption at the time – she had never seen the man before. She had only ever imagined him.

Maisie wanted to mull over the demanding week. Her concerns about her daughter and the case had merged. She knew she had to find a path through the undergrowth of information and evidence, and she must do so with all speed given the anticipated departure of Private Matthias Crittenden. Taking into account the circumstances in which he was found, and the suspicion that he had played a nefarious role in the disappearance of a white soldier, Maisie feared his detention might not follow protocols for the fair treatment of prisoners.

Sunday brought with it another addition to the already full house, so a bed had been made ready in the conservatory to accommodate Jo Hardy.

'Mrs R. would love this, Maisie,' said Mark. 'A chance to talk to women in uniform from both sides of the Atlantic in an informal setting. You know she's heading off to visit those ferry pilots next week – I guess that's why Jo Hardy has to rush off to their base at White Waltham on Monday – and she's talking about putting pressure where it counts to get more women in uniform back home.'

Maisie nodded, smiling. 'The way Anna chatted away

to her, I thought our daughter would issue an invitation to supper!'

'Wasn't she just great? With that little blue hat and those patent shoes – she looked like a princess.' Mark put his arm around Maisie. 'Everything OK, hon? The First Lady said you did your best to persuade her to pull back on some of the visits, and the ambassador is happy you tried. But you've been kinda preoccupied since we came home yesterday.'

Maisie looked out of the conservatory window, down towards the Groom's Cottage that was once her father's home. She was about to comment but thought better of it when she heard a motor car approaching along the gravel driveway. A door slammed, followed by the words 'Bloody Austin.'

'That'll be your Jo Hardy,' said Mark. 'I think she needs a stiff drink, not a cup of tea. That woman sure has a head of steam.'

'I'd better go to the kitchen and save Brenda.' Maisie stepped towards the door, but turned back. 'Mark, did you hear anything about the search of the platelayers' huts?'

'Nothing yet, though as of yesterday evening, there's been no sign of anyone sleeping rough. Anyone we'd be interested in anyway. I'll call my people again later to find out if there's much to report.'

Maisie nodded at the same time as Brenda could be heard calling for her. 'You might want to wait before you come back to the kitchen,' she advised her husband.

'Oh, I'm heading straight down to the stables, Maisie. I'll look for your dad and Anna – safest people to be around in this house.'

'All told, Maisie, there are a number for us to look at.' Jo set out a series of photographs on the dining room table, with others pushed to one side.

'Hmm, they're not quite as clear as I'd hoped, so it's hard to see what's what, Jo,' Maisie looked from one photograph to the next. 'You were the one up in the air, so you're going to have to show me.'

'All right, here we go. Here's the farmhouse, right here. And there, Maisie, is the old barn. Then we come in closer on this one – see, there's a vehicle and a man by the door – he's in the shadow. And there's the fellow who tried to kill me.'

'I can't see a weapon, Jo.'

'But look at this one. This is where I came in lower – see?' Maisie leaned over the table.

'Are you sure you don't need spectacles, Maisie?'

'No, I'm not sure at all – in fact, I have some somewhere. But never mind – I can see now – he's holding up something in his hand.'

'That's the weapon.'

'Apart from the fact that it might be a stick, if it were a weapon, could something like this have adversely affected Erica's aircraft?'

'If he'd hit her and she was concussed, yes – any distraction at a lower altitude can mess you up.'

'But there's a hood on the Spitfire.'

'Yes. It's called the "Malcom hood". And a bullet could go through it.'

'Oh.' Maisie tapped the photographs Jo had pushed to one side. 'And what about these?'

'Oh, nothing there – just recording my high jinks under the bridge.'

Maisie reached for the photographs, and began to flick through them. 'Oh my goodness, Jo – you're either brave, highly skilled or completely insane.'

'All three, Maisie – you have to be, in my job.' She reached for the photographs.

'Hold on a minute.' Maisie shook her head. 'Where were these taken?'

Jo Hardy leaned in to look at the photographs Maisie was placing one by one on the table.

'This was where I was sort of gearing up to go under the bridge. I was a little way off by this point – you can see the river below, and—'

'What's this?'

'What's what?'

'Here – you can see something between the trees, here.'

Jo Hardy squinted as she leaned in for a closer look.

'Never mind me, I think you need specs – and you're a pilot.'

'They've got a one-armed pilot flying with the ATA, lost his arm in the last war – so even if I were short-sighted, they'd still need me up there. Anyway, it's just the quality of the image.' The aviatrix picked up the photograph. 'It looks like an old boathouse. Not a big one – probably just large enough to drag in a rowing boat, and—'

'Could you find it again?'

'Let me see.' She picked up the other photographs, then placed them in a specific order. 'I think I could. Yes, definitely. But Maisie, I cannot take passengers, and civilian aircraft are illegal – even if I could get hold of one, we'd be shot down, and—'

Maisie stared at the woman in the navy blue uniform, the wings on her lapel signifying her seniority and accomplishments. 'Good Lord, Jo – I wasn't thinking of going up in an aeroplane, and especially not with a pilot who probably needs spectacles! I was thinking of a motor car.'

'Then I hope you've got one we can use, because that Austin has just about had it. And to think I put my trust in Saint Dan.'

'Saint Dan?'

'The Marshalls swear by Dan Littlecombe for all things mechanical.'

'I've got someone who's probably more saintly – come on, let's take the Austin over to George and collect my motor car. I think he's put some petrol in the tank by now.'

Brenda stood with hands on hips as Maisie and Jo rushed past her. 'If you're planning to be out all day, don't forget supper's at seven, and Priscilla, Douglas, Tim and Tarquin are coming at half past six.'

'Not to worry, Brenda, I will be back in plenty of time to help in the kitchen. Tell Mark we'll be home by about four.'

'Oh, and do you know Patty and Tom have gone for a long walk over to the lake.'

'How lovely for them – see you later, Brenda.'

'But—'

'So, let me get this straight, you've an American nurse visiting, and she's walking out with your friend's son, who's in the RAF?'

Maisie nodded, slipped the Alvis into a higher gear and increased her speed. 'Patty's parents are friends of mine. I'd met her father in France during the last war, though I didn't get to know her mother until I stayed with them in Boston. Dr Hayden was the friend of a friend – he's a very nice man. A brain surgeon, actually.'

'And the happy couple met at your house?'

'Yes.'

'I hope she knows what she's let herself in for. Her best boy's days are probably numbered.'

Maisie frowned, glancing sideways at her passenger. 'Jo, that's a dark way to view the situation.'

'We're in a dark situation, and that's exactly what the poor American soldier is in too. And I know what a dark situation is when I'm in it.' She sighed. 'Remember, Nick was in the RAF.'

Maisie nodded. 'I remember, Jo.' She was silent for a moment. 'But you're here now. Tom is here now, and so is Patty. I learned the hard way that at times like this we must immerse ourselves in the here and now – only the here and now.'

'I bet you find it hard, though.'

Maisie maintained attention on the road. 'Of course I do. Now then, I need some directions – and I'm hoping I can find somewhere to park the motor car so the police aren't waiting for me when I come back to it.'

'Sounds like you've come across the inimitable Constable Eames – oh, turn left here, then an immediate right.'

Maisie followed Hardy's instructions, then picked up the conversation. 'You know PC Eames?'

'Sort of. Apparently he had a silly crush on Dizzy when

she was in his class at the local primary school, before her parents moved her to another school. Stupid boy.'

'He's about your age, Jo.'

'Still a silly boy. And I never liked the look of him myself. Dizzy said he had something of a nasty streak at school and could be rather mean to the boy who was supposed to be his best friend – a slow lad she'd taken under her wing. Apparently – oops, hold on, I wanted you to go left again back there. Sorry!'

Maisie braked, reversed the motor car and turned where Hardy pointed.

'We should reach a gate up here, by some woods. According to this map—' Hardy studied the map and the photograph. 'According to this map, there's a stile along here with a path down to the river – yes, and at that point the boathouse should be just a few yards to the left.'

'Let me see the map, Jo,' said Maisie, stopping the motor car.

She passed the map to Maisie, who ran her finger along the path. 'It's only about a quarter of a mile from the railway bridge – goodness, if only we'd carried on that day, we might have seen it.'

'What?'

'Oh, I walked along the path with my assistant—' Maisie corrected herself. 'My partner in the business, Mr Beale. But we went no further than the railway bridge – though we found evidence of Private Stone's presence in a water mill on the other side of the river.'

'And what do you think we will find in the old boathouse – if that's what it turns out to be?'

Maisie sat back against the driver's seat and looked out of the window into the distance, across fields and woodland in the afternoon light. 'I don't know, Jo. At best I'm hoping to see some evidence that Private Stone and other men have been in the boathouse.'

'And at worst?'

'If it's a case of "at worst" I would say that they are in situ when we get there, because if they are, we'll have to do something about it.'

'All . . . righty. And how many other men do you think there are – a couple?'

Maisie shook her head. 'There could be up to five, counting Private Stone.'

'Well, that's one on our side.'

'Perhaps.'

'Perhaps?'

'Intimidation . . . exhaustion . . . hunger . . . Jo, people can be changed by fear and fatigue.'

CHAPTER SIXTEEN

Seeing an open five-bar gate, Maisie pulled onto a rough farm track and parked the motor car behind a tall hedge. Both women were wearing stout walking shoes and trousers, giving them freedom of movement to forge their way along a narrow wooded thoroughfare – or to run.

'This footpath leads down into the woods, and from there we turn left. The boathouse should be about an eighth of a mile along, with that bridge another quarter of a mile beyond.' Maisie began rolling up the hem of each trouser leg. 'I recognise the landscape, though I must say it's probably so much easier to identify landmarks from the air.'

'Let's get going then,' said Hardy.

Maisie opened the motor car boot, and took out two wooden walking sticks, each with a brass handle and tip.

'Oh, that's all right, my balance is pretty good, Maisie.'

Maisie gave a half smile. 'So is mine, Jo. I wasn't thinking of it assisting my ability to walk in a straight line or get down a hill without slipping. These might come in handy in other ways.'

'Oh yes, indeed,' said Hardy. 'Silly me. And I thought losing a propeller would be the worst thing that could happen.'

'In my estimation, it is. Come on, we don't have much time.'

The two women set out along a footpath flanking the field, before entering the woodland and clambering down an incline to meet a more challenging path alongside the river.

'This looks like it flooded last night,' said Hardy. 'Heck, my trousers are getting drenched. Hang on a minute – I should have copied you.' She rolled up the hems of her trouser legs.

Ten minutes later they were just yards away from the tumbledown riverside shed they had identified as a boathouse.

'I think this structure might have originally been built by Constable Eames's grandfather to shelter his rowing boat. So it's pretty old.'

'The water has got the better of the wood, hasn't it?' observed Hardy.

'It could still offer shelter though, or a hiding place.' Maisie held out her hand to prevent Jo Hardy from approaching the shed. 'You remain here – I'll go ahead on my own.'

'Not likely, I want to—'

'Jo – you are my client. I have a duty to protect you, so don't make me regret bringing you.'

Maisie set off at a slow pace towards the boathouse. Kneeling down by the worn wooden boards, she cupped her ear to block out the sound of rushing water and listened for any sign of life within. There was nothing. She moved to the back, stepping over brambles, and listened again. It was at that very moment she heard footsteps behind her. Standing up, she raised her walking stick.

'For goodness' sake, Maisie – it's me! Quick, I heard someone coming, in the distance along the path.'

Maisie looked back into the woods. 'This way – pull the brambles back as you come through.'

Negotiating the undergrowth, the two women escaped into the darkened woodland behind the boathouse and crouched behind the broad trunk of an ancient beech.

'Can you see anything?' whispered Hardy.

'Yes – but shhh, Jo.'

Three men approached the boathouse in single file. Maisie thought one of the men looked to be in his fifties, another a little younger, perhaps thirty-five. Between the two men was a young man of about twenty years of age. She could just see his expression, and was reminded of her godson, Tim. There was that same blend of confusion and anger, as if he were a boy in a man's world – a world he had wanted, but having reached it, now felt lost.

When they spoke, Maisie could hear that all three were American. She noticed that the youngest man was not constrained in any way, though there was little opportunity to escape, if that had been his plan.

'What are we going to do?' whispered Hardy.

'We're going to wait here until they're inside the boathouse, then we're going to walk back into the woods to the path – but with as much care as we can muster. We cannot have them hear us.' Knowing there was a certain hot-headedness about Jo Hardy – despite her ability to remain calm under pressure – Maisie added another warning. 'Jo, they are likely armed to the teeth, and I believe they would not hesitate to leave us for dead in the undergrowth. These men are here on a mission, and I think they are willing to die before they give up on it.'

Hardy nodded.

Thirty minutes passed before Maisie tugged Hardy's sleeve and inclined her head towards the dark interior of the woods. Treading with care, they made their way through brambles and undergrowth until they reached the forest floor, a carpet of fallen leaves muffling sound as they picked up the pace.

'Maisie—'

'Not yet. Wait.'

Fifteen minutes later they were running across the field towards the Alvis. With shaking hands, Maisie unlocked the door, and they almost fell into their seats.

'Bloody hell,' said Jo. 'Let's get away from this place.'

Maisie nodded, starting the engine.

'And I'm really sorry – I've put a bucket load of mud on your floor here.'

Again, Maisie said nothing. She reversed the Alvis and pulled out onto the road, but instead of driving back along the route of their original approach, she proceeded in the opposite direction.

'Where are we going now?' asked Hardy.

'They've got a motor car, and I want to know where they've left it. It must be somewhere along here.'

A mile passed with no sign of a vehicle at the side of the road, or in a field.

'They can't have fallen from the sky,' said Hardy.

Maisie nodded. 'No, but they could have another hideout in plain sight.'

'Such as?'

Maisie slowed the Alvis and pointed to a rooftop along a narrow lane to the right. 'Such as that.'

'Maisie, are you saying that the cottage could be where we'll find the motor car, or that it will be a similar sort of dwelling?'

'It might be.' Maisie turned to the right. 'I wish I knew the name of this lane.'

Hardy took the map from her pocket, unfolded it and ran a finger along coloured lines indicating different roads in the area. 'Wishbone Lane.'

Slowing as they approached, Maisie and Jo looked to the right at the very moment a woman emerged from the property.

'Give me my hat, Jo.'

Hardy passed a maroon felt hat to Maisie, who drew to a halt as she pulled on the hat.

Winding down the window, she looked across at the woman and smiled, grateful for a certain distance between them. 'Excuse me – I'm ever so sorry to bother you.'

The woman turned her attention to Maisie, but did not speak.

'I'm afraid we're terribly lost – am I going in the right direction for Westerham?'

The woman nodded, rubbed her hands on her pinafore and pointed along the lane.

'Thank you! Very kind of you.' Maisie waved, slipped the Alvis into gear and drove away at low speed.

'Wishbone Cottage – the name is on a cement plaque just under the roof.'

'Thank you, Jo.'

'I don't think we've found out anything useful there – we still don't know who those men were.'

Maisie pressed her lips together, deep in thought as she drove on.

'Jo, look at your map and get us back on the road to Chelstone.'

'All righty.'

Giving Maisie directions, they were soon on the main road.

'You know your way from here, don't you?' asked Hardy.

Maisie nodded. 'Thanks, Jo. We'll be back in time for me to place some telephone calls and then get stuck into helping Brenda with supper.'

Another few minutes passed without comment.

'You're quiet, Maisie.'

'I'm thinking.'

'I hate to say this, but as your client, it would be helpful to know your thoughts.'

'Yes, of course.' Maisie glanced into the rear-view

mirror and pulled off the road. She turned to Jo Hardy. 'Your photographs were more than useful. We found the boathouse, and we know who's using it.'

'Do we?'

Maisie nodded. 'I'm afraid this is where I must be circumspect, because the reason for your visit to me in the first place has intersected with another investigation which is more . . .' Maisie heard her words taper off as she searched for the best way to describe what was happening. 'Which is more political . . . so I've not been able to divulge much of what's been going on.'

'Good heavens, Maisie!'

'Jo, you came to me because you wanted to discover the truth about the deaths of your fiancé and Erica Langley, and of course the identity of the man who fired at you while you were flying. You also wanted to do all you could to help Private Crittenden.'

'That's right. Yes, of course, but—'

Maisie raised her hand. 'I cannot reveal to you the nature of that coincidence, but I owe it to you to tell you what I believe to be true.' She paused as she re-joined the road. 'The younger of the three men you just saw going into the boathouse is, I believe, Private Stone – the soldier who Crittenden has maintained is his friend. Which may or may not be true – though it is to Crittenden. I do not know the identity of the other two men. But I know the woman we just saw outside the cottage, and I also know it is not her home, so I'm wondering what sort of connection brought her there. And one more thing – there was a large motor car to the left of the house as we drove away, and

299

I do not for a minute believe the woman knows how to drive.'

Jo Hardy shook her head. 'I don't know what to say.'

'Jo, you must say nothing – nothing at all to anyone. I have given you this information because as my client, it is your due.'

'Of course.' Hardy frowned and stared at her map, which she folded and unfolded along one edge. Then she looked up. 'That woman was odd – anyone would think she'd been struck dumb.'

'Yes, I know,' said Maisie, changing gear as she approached a corner. 'The thing is, it never occurred to me before, but I think that's exactly what might have happened to her.'

'You're not going to tell me any more, are you?'

'No, not yet, I'm afraid.'

'But at least tell me who you think those men were, the Americans, the older men.'

'I think they're in this country on a mission.'

'Goodness – Americans on a sort of spying mission, and we're all supposed to be allies?'

Maisie did not reply but began to slow the motor car.

'What now?' said Jo.

'There's a telephone box along here. I'm going to make a brief stop – there's someone I must speak to as a matter of urgency.'

'But we're only a couple of miles from Chelstone – it won't take long to get there.'

'I don't have much time.'

'Time for what?'

Maisie looked at Jo, gauging how much to divulge. 'Jo, those Americans are not on a sort of spying mission. I'm afraid there are indications that it's actually a "sort of killing someone" mission. Americans are most certainly our allies, Jo, but they're not necessarily allied to one another. And if you tell anyone at all what I have told you here, there will be consequences.'

Jo Hardy stared at Maisie. 'But . . . but what about Nick, and Erica – and me? Do you know the identity of the gunman?'

Maisie nodded. 'I believe so. But Jo – this is so convoluted, I can't even begin to explain it, nor should I. Be patient. Please be patient.'

'Am I safe, Maisie? Are any of us safe, when we come into Biggin Hill? I mean, it's a crucial aerodrome for the country's defence. Our ferry pilots are in and out of there all the time.'

'Yes, you're safe – I believe you're safe. Trust that everyone who should be behind bars will be locked away soon.'

Hardy shook her head. 'I don't know how you do your job, Maisie.'

'And to be fair, I don't know how you do yours, Jo.'

Holding Jo Hardy's map in one hand, Maisie dialled the number with the other, and pressed button A when the call was answered.

'Brenda – hello. Is Mark there? Can I have a word with him? Oh, and don't worry, we'll be home very soon.'

'He's just walked into the kitchen with Anna and your father. Hold on a minute, Maisie. And Priscilla telephoned

– I thought I'd mention it by way of warning because she's like a kettle on the boil.'

'Not to worry – but could you get Mark before I run out of change?'

Maisie heard her stepmother calling out along the passageway, then a heavier footfall as Mark approached the telephone.

'Maisie, what's up? Will you be home soon?'

'Not too long, but I wanted to talk to you now – we don't have much time.'

'Sounds bad.'

'First of all, we are definitely going to need Private Crittenden's help in the coming days, so could you ensure your colleagues over at Eisenhowerplatz don't change their minds and put him on an aircraft tomorrow?'

'How the heck—'

'I'll explain everything when I'm home, Mark, and I think you will have some answers by the time I arrive, but not one of the bigger ones – that's going to take longer.'

'Go on.'

'Can you ask your friend the colonel to find out everything he can about Private Stone – his family, his father's ministry? Everything.'

'What on earth has happened?'

'I'm pretty sure I've found him, Mark – but at this point I don't know if he is friend or foe. Listen – here's a map reference.' She held out the map, squinting at the lines and Jo's notation in pencil along the margin. 'There's a boathouse – really old – where two men who

302

I could not identify, plus one I believe to be Private Stone, have been hiding. Or it's one of the places – I still think they're moving between those platelayers' huts. There's also a cottage in the mix – I've another reference for you, because the roads aren't signposted, as you know.'

'From bitter experience, Maisie, I know only too well – fire away, I'm writing this down.'

'I suspect the two men – and goodness knows who they are – are the ones who have your Rover in their sights. Stone is either with them or he is being forced to work for them. Some sort of blackmail might be involved. Talk to Caldwell – he'll guide you, Mark, because this involves local people, and for your sake, we don't need some sort of problem with our allies.'

'That's my street, not yours, Maisie. Though we've crossed it enough times. I'll see you when you get home, but Maisie—'

Maisie heard multiple beeps, and pressed more coins into the slot.

'Mark?'

'Maisie? Are you still there?'

'Yes – sorry – what did you say?'

'I was about to ask how you know it's Private Stone you've seen – and what makes you think he might be involved with the other guys?'

'Because he was the man I saw outside the embassy. I remembered later where I had seen him, and of course it was because he had been described to me.'

'So it might not be him at all.'

'But it is, Mark. It is him. And I think even if he is innocent, he might still be dangerous, if only to protect himself and . . . and perhaps someone else, possibly even his family.'

'Mark, what's happening – have you made any progress?'

Having settled Jo Hardy in the kitchen with Brenda, who had set about the task of providing their guest with tea and Eccles cakes, Maisie had rushed to the library to join her husband.

Mark Scott held up both hands, as if offering a benediction. 'Slow down, slow down. We're going as fast as we can.' He walked to the sideboard and poured single malt whiskey into two glasses. 'Now I know why your Maurice kept his poison stocked up – if this is how it goes, I bet he hit the bottle every day!'

'Mark, please—'

'Private Crittenden is not going anywhere yet, and as soon as we have Stone – if we get him – and after he's been identified and debriefed, then the colonel will order Crittenden's release, but not back to his outfit. Not yet. If he comes up clean, he'll probably be transferred to another unit.'

Maisie nodded.

'I couldn't reach Caldwell, and I know how long it takes to get all the authorisations lined up – right down to your home secretary, if necessary – so a couple of my security guys are heading down there now, just to have a look-see and report back to me. It's only surveillance – we want to make sure the men you saw weren't just a happy trio of guys going fishing.'

'But—'

'Not finished yet, Maisie.' Mark Scott took a sip of whiskey. 'The colonel instructed the MPs to pull in a couple of our soldiers who come from the same county in Virginia as Stone, just to see if there's anything they can tell us, but you know, small-town America isn't like small towns here – there can be a big old distance between one place and another, and that goes for information too.'

'All right. I can't think of anything else to do at this particular moment.'

'There is something really important you can do, before you scurry off to rescue your guest from a pile of Eccles cakes – you can bring me up to the minute with what you think has happened, especially after what you've seen today.' He drained his whiskey glass. 'You have a feeling about these things, and I'd like to know everything you suspect might be going on, beyond the Stone and Crittenden problem.'

Maisie closed her eyes and rubbed her forehead. 'There's so much more to this, Mark. Caldwell knows some of my suspicions, but I had to wait until there was information to support the others – and it's all connected. Connected by circumstance, not by original intent.'

'You're losing me, Maisie.'

They both looked up at the sound of Brenda calling from the kitchen.

'I must telephone Billy – could you tell Brenda I'll be along in a minute? We can talk later.'

Mark nodded towards the telephone as he made his way to the door. 'Don't be on too long – calls could be coming in from my guys, and I'm expecting to hear from the colonel.'

Maisie opened her document bag and removed the case

map, which she spread across the desk, using books to flatten down the edges. With several coloured crayons brought from the office in a paper bag, she began to make notes and draw lines between the names and places on the map.

'How can these people who never even knew one another have crossed paths so quickly?' She put down the red crayon and ran her fingers through her hair. 'It's as if they're different grasses caught up in a single turn of the threshing machine.'

She lifted the telephone receiver and dialled a local number. Billy Beale answered on the first ring.

'Yes—'

'Billy, it's me – Maisie.'

'Oh, miss, sorry about that, but I was waiting to hear back about . . . about . . .'

'Billy, what is it? Have you news of young Billy?'

She heard him choke. 'No, it's Bobby. Our Bobby.'

'Oh no – oh my goodness, no, Billy.'

'It's all right. Sort of. They got back from a raid on Germany – engines were on fire, but they landed. The tail gunner copped it – didn't stand a chance, poor blighter – and the rest of the crew are all wounded, one way or another. One of Bobby's mates got in touch, otherwise we wouldn't have known. He says Bobby's been burned, but we don't know how serious it is. We're just waiting. We don't even know where to go, where he is.'

'Right. Let me know as soon as you hear. If you and Doreen need to go to a hospital, I can get George to take you. I know he has a stash of petrol.'

'Much obliged, miss.'

'I'd better get off the line in case someone's trying to reach you.'

'What was it you wanted?'

'Nothing. Nothing. Just . . . just nothing really. Let us know how Bobby fares. He's a strong young man, Billy.'

'Both my boys are. They're both mouthy and bloody-minded, but no two ways about it, they're cloth that's been woven heavy.'

Once again there was a full complement of guests at a supper that was more subdued than usual. Tom Partridge had bagged a seat next to Patty Hayden, which everyone expected, while Tim – home from university for a few days – was in deep conversation with Jo Hardy. Billy and Doreen Beale had elected to remain at home by the telephone, so Maisie had offered to take Margaret Rose for the night – the two girls would sleep 'top and tail' in Anna's bed, and the adults were resigned to the fact that giggles and laughter from that room might keep everyone awake for some hours – unless an air raid drove them all to the cellar. Priscilla and Douglas chatted with Lady Rowan – her husband, Lord Julian Compton, had sent apologies, with a message explaining that as much as he would love to come, especially to hear all about Anna's debut in the spotlight, he didn't 'feel quite up to it.' Such news was a concern to all, given Lord Julian's advanced years.

After supper, everyone repaired to the drawing room, with Lady Rowan exclaiming that it was wonderful that Maisie had jettisoned the practice of the women 'withdrawing' to leave the men to talk at table over cigars and brandy. For Maisie's part, though there was much to concern her, there was little to do except pretend that all was well.

Priscilla nudged Maisie and nodded towards the door, whispering, 'Let's have a chat.'

In the library, Maisie poured a cream sherry for herself and a gin and tonic for Priscilla.

'How does Brenda know I would come in here with you for a chinwag? She's left ice for my G and T.'

'She likes to do it, Pris. Remember she was once housekeeper here, and she still rather enjoys ruling the roost.' Maisie touched her glass against Priscilla's. 'Cheers.'

'Well, my friend, here we are,' said Priscilla, settling into the wing chair Maurice had favoured. 'I suppose I've you to thank for the fact that I have one son absolutely besotted with an American nurse – mind you, she is quite lovely, isn't she? Fortunately Patty's no pushover, which I quite like. It's certainly keeping Tom on the hook – he's had it his way with the opposite sex for far too long, and I didn't like it at all. I told him I found it most unattractive in a man. In my estimation, some of these girls needed a bit of gumption to put him in his place.' She shook her head. 'The RAF gave him wings and he became an incorrigible flirt!'

'Pris – how often do I have to remind you? They assigned you an ambulance in the last war, and you were a flirt too. I remember you telling me, "There's nothing like walking out with a man in uniform".'

Priscilla laughed. 'They put me in uniform again, and now I'm facing another operation! Anyway, did you see Tim in there – on the make with an older woman?'

'Jo Hardy is an accomplished aviatrix. And you should have heard Mrs Roosevelt talk about women and war duty during her press conference. She was incredibly impressed with our women in the services – in fact, I think the reason Jo has to rush off tomorrow morning is to be at White Waltham when Mrs Roosevelt meets the women flying with the Air Transport Auxiliary.'

Priscilla drew from her cigarette, then tapped the lighted end onto the ashtray. 'That's all very well, and good for her ... another reason for my son to be bowled over! Anyway, I suppose that as mothers we do the best we can, and then we have to say "what will be will be".'

'One thing to remember, my friend – Tim is a brave man, older than his years, given what happened to him, and I think Jo can handle him and let him down gently.'

The women were silent for a while, then Priscilla leaned towards Maisie.

'I've been thinking about Anna and that school ever since we chatted about it on the train. Tell me, have you had any more ideas? I mean – what are you going to do?'

Maisie took a sip of her sherry. 'We've had a new opportunity presented to us, which is good news. Through the Women's Voluntary Service, Lady Rowan and Brenda met a lovely retired teacher who lives in Plaxtol. A Mrs Milward. All the arrangements have been made for Anna and Margaret Rose to go over to Mrs Milward every morning, Monday to Friday – Doreen will see them onto the bus, and Mrs Milward will meet them at the stop outside her house. George will collect the girls in the motor car in the afternoon. It's only for a short while, until I sort things out with the headmistress.'

'Don't you mean "sort out" the headmistress!'

'I wouldn't go that far.' Maisie laughed. 'I can't quite see myself getting into fisticuffs with her.'

'Personally, I wouldn't give that school another chance, it's just small-minded and—'

Priscilla was interrupted by the telephone ringing. Maisie stood up, stepped across to the desk and picked up the black Bakelite receiver. The caller began speaking before Maisie was able to recite the number.

'Is that Miss Dobbs? Miss Dobbs who's the investigator woman?'

'Hello—' Maisie recognised the voice. 'Hello, is this Mr Love calling?'

'I'm glad I've got hold of you, Miss Dobbs. I rang the wrong number twice – shaking I was, and couldn't get my finger in the right hole on the dial.'

'What's wrong, Mr Love? What's happened?'

'It's one of our land girls. Madge. Been hit over the head with something heavy, probably a bit of old piping. Knocked out and left for dead, she was. She's in hospital now, in Pembury. Concussion, they say, and it's bad.' Maisie heard a harsh, phlegmy cough and the sound of Love thumping his chest. 'Sorry, miss – had a bonfire going today, and the smoke got down right into me.' He coughed again. 'The other girls said you should know. They said she's been frightened lately. Scared of someone. They reckon she knew something about that pilot, the woman who crashed a Spitfire not far from here.'

Maisie placed the receiver in the crook of her neck as she reached for a notebook and pencil.

'May I have Madge's surname?'

'Starling. Madge Starling. You know – the bird. Mind you, you won't get in to see her until tomorrow morning, I reckon.'

'All right. I've got it. And might you have the name of whoever is investigating at the police station? It would probably be a Detective Inspector something or other.'

'Oh, don't know that sort of thing, Miss Dobbs. I just know she's hanging on. Hanging on for dear life.'

CHAPTER SEVENTEEN

'I wish I could come in with you, but – in fact, I can call ops and say I'm indisposed. Yes, perhaps I should. After all, this is about Erica.'

'Jo – no, it's not a good idea at all,' said Maisie. 'You've got much better things to do today, and this is my work, my place. I'm anticipating enough trouble getting in to see Madge Starling without two of us to account for. I'm grateful to you for dropping me here at the hospital, but you're late already – you'll be lucky to get to Hampshire by lunchtime. If you're able to telephone this evening, I'll let you know what's happened then – you know how best to be in touch over the next several days.'

'I'll probably be flying nonstop for a good while now. I daresay I will find out what's going on by reading the newspapers.'

Maisie looked at Jo Hardy, at the concern creasing her forehead. 'Jo, I know I've said this before, but I must remind you that my work on this case has taken on a complexion I had not anticipated on the day you came to see me, and it's involving not only Scotland Yard, but the American authorities.'

'Which authorities? Their police? Army?'

'I can't say.' Maisie looked at her watch. 'I should go into the hospital now – visiting time doesn't start yet, and I have to sweeten a few people so I'm not prevented from seeing Miss Starling.'

'I bet she saw something – I bet she knows who took down Erica's Spit.'

'Soon, Jo – soon. Be patient. Think of this as bringing a very large bomber in for a difficult landing.'

As Maisie moved to step out of the motor car, she felt the young woman's hand on her arm.

'This has been awful,' said Hardy. 'I mean . . . I mean I wonder if we've all become sort of used to death. Used to just absorbing shock. Someone gets killed flying into a hill, or in an aircraft coming down on fire – like your friend's son – or they're bombed out of their home, or they're just in the wrong place at the wrong time and we all just take it in our stride. That's what we're expected to do. We're all told we can take it, but I'm not sure we can.' She took a handkerchief from her pocket and wiped her eyes. 'Phew, that's enough of that, Hardy. Pull your socks up, woman.'

'Jo, you have every right to weep. Give yourself time to do just that and then gather strength for your work, because it demands every ounce of your attention.'

'Do you know who killed Erica? Or even Nick?'

Maisie sighed, and nodded. 'Yes, I believe I do. Look, I

should have some news in a day or two, Jo. Try to telephone me midweek – I expect to be at Chelstone. You have the number.'

Maisie waved to Jo Hardy as she drove off, the Austin backfiring several times before the engine responded and the motor car picked up speed. Then she turned and walked at a clip past the hospital chapel and on towards the main entrance of the Victorian building, its somewhat overbearing, almost gothic red-brick architecture testament to the fact that it was originally the town workhouse, a brutal shelter for the destitute. Now it was a place of medical busyness, where nurses scurried back and forth, where babies were born and lives were saved – though a sign indicating the direction of the mortuary would give those still conscious pause, along with the tall, looming chimney where anything unwanted, discarded, used or beyond repair, including human limbs, was incinerated.

Stopping at the porter's desk, Maisie enquired as to the ward a young woman named Madge Starling had been taken to following her admittance to the casualty department the previous day.

'Right you are.' The man ran his finger down a column of names. 'There we go. Starling, Margaret. Head wound.' He looked up. 'She's in Women's Medical.' He lifted a pen and pointed it along a corridor. 'Now you go down there, then when you get to the stairs, just follow the signs – you'll be going up the staircase and mind your step, because it was only mopped a little while ago.'

'Thank you, sir.' Maisie turned to leave.

'Oh, and miss – visiting time doesn't start for another hour yet. I doubt Staff Nurse will let you in there.'

'Miss Starling is a dear friend, so she might . . . thank you again.'

Maisie followed the signs as instructed. She stopped at a small office just inside the women's medical ward to enquire the location of patient Margaret Starling, and was again given directions and received another reminder regarding visiting hours.

'Well, well, well, if it isn't Miss Dobbs. Can't say I'm surprised to see you here.'

Maisie knew the voice, so she thanked the nurse at the desk before turning around.

'Detective Chief Superintendent – I'm glad you're in charge of this case.'

'Are you?' Caldwell rolled his eyes. 'I wish I was half as pleased, because I could do without it, to tell you the truth – I've been dragged out of London because they're a bit short on staff at Tunbridge Wells nick. Mind you, as we both know, Scotland Yard and murder, attempted or well executed, go together like a horse and carriage. I must say, though, it's a bit of a nuisance that these country matters always end up on my docket.' He looked up at the large wall-mounted clock. 'We've got a little while yet – let's you and me go over there by the window, have a little chat.'

Maisie again took note of Caldwell's hollow cheeks and the bluish-grey smudges under his eyes. Not for the first time, she felt a welter of compassion for the policeman who had once been a thorn in her side.

'You're either smoking too much, or you haven't had a

day off in weeks, Superintendent,' observed Maisie.

'One gives rise to the other. Can't say you look like a film star yourself.'

She smiled. 'And as usual, we're off to a great start. But let's talk about Madge Starling.'

'I'm the one who's supposed to say that, Miss Dobbs.' He raised his hands in frustration. 'I wish I could hand the whole blimmin' lot over to you. I've got enough on my plate with the black marketeers and some very nasty pieces of work operating south of the river – one of the old gangs is now printing ration coupons, and very good they are too. They've a widespread distribution and they've got previously law-abiding citizens happily acting as receivers. I tell you, this war is making criminals of a lot of what used to be very nice people – everyone is after something they can't get, and they don't care where it's come from.'

Maisie looked out of the window, down towards the hospital entrance. She watched as two nurses ran towards the main door, holding onto white caps while their navy blue cloaks flapped in the wind. She turned back to Caldwell, who seemed poised to add more examples to a litany of occupational grievances.

'I received a telephone call from the farmer, Mr Love,' said Maisie. 'He told me what had happened to Madge Starling. I've met her before, by the way. Love was obviously upset, and—'

'I've talked to him. He's not entirely off the hook.'

'Superintendent, Barney Love didn't have any good reason to attack Madge.'

'But who would whack a land girl over the head? Perhaps

316

old Barney made an improper advance and she didn't like it. I daresay it wouldn't be the first time a land girl has had to put up with a randy farmer.'

Maisie raised an eyebrow, a gesture she hoped would strike down further rush-headed theories. 'Look, I think I know who did it – and I believe I know why. It was to protect someone else.'

'I think we're going to have to sit down for a longer chat, you and me.'

'There's tea in the canteen, straight from the urn.'

'Come on. My shout. It's the ultimate truth drug, as far as I'm concerned. You can get a full confession based upon the threat of a second cup, and I want to know who tried to kill that poor girl.'

Caldwell set down two cups of tea on a stained but clean wooden table. 'There we go. Two cups of char fit for a docker, complete with spoons welded into the brew.'

'Thank you, Superintendent.' Maisie took a sip of tea and winced.She waited until Caldwell was settled.

Caldwell grimaced as he tasted the tea. 'Don't they know tea's rationed and they should go easy on how much they put in that urn? Either that or they brewed it last night and let it sit there stewing ever since then.'

'Superintendent Caldwell, there's more to this business with Madge Starling than meets the eye. I'm sure that once the cards start falling, there will be what Mark would call "collateral damage", and you're going to have to act at speed. There will be two more arrests at our end, and you will have to be light on your feet, because I'm confident the

Americans will have caught up and will be doing the same.'

Caldwell rubbed his forehead. 'I can see it now – this case is like the Jack and Jill nursery rhyme. You know, "Atishoo, atishoo, we all fall down.".' He shook his head. 'Right then, all the cards on the table, because it might see me out of this fog.'

Maisie nodded. 'Truth be told, it all began in the last war when a woman lost her husband. Oh, and that's just the part of the story on this side of the Atlantic.'

'What about the other side?'

'We should discuss the boathouse along the river – in fact, we should have started with that.'

'What boathouse?'

Maisie put down her cup. 'The surveillance – you should have received a message by now to telephone my husband?'

'All right, all right. I've been out and about, feet not touching the ground, so no time like the present – what's going on?'

Maisie was deep in conversation with Caldwell, describing what had happened alongside the river, when the detective was interrupted by his driver, who approached Caldwell and whispered in his ear. Caldwell sighed and nodded.

'Get the engine running, Joe. I'll be out in a second.'

'Trouble?' asked Maisie, pushing back her chair.

'Joe just got a message on the radio. Body found in the rubble of a bombed-out building. Not surprising they want Scotland Yard on it, because the ligature around the neck suggests someone got there before Adolf. And to make things even messier, they've found a stash of counterfeit ration cards not far from the body, so it's a case of "Let's drag in old Caldwell, he's already over that way".'

'Good luck – and thank you for the tea.'

Caldwell nodded. 'I'll be in touch.'

'I know,' said Maisie. 'You know where to reach me.'

'Even if I didn't, it wouldn't take me long to find out.'

Maisie smiled, but felt weary, battered by a feeling of resignation that sometimes assailed her at the most crucial point in a case, rooted in an understanding that there could have been a different outcome. If even one of the steps on a person's journey could have been changed, yes, the future would have followed another path.

'Madge. Madge, it's me – Maisie Dobbs. Can you hear me?'

As the young woman turned her bandaged head towards Maisie, a single tear emerged from each eye and ran down her cheeks. Maisie took a fresh linen handkerchief from her bag and with a gentle touch dabbed the tears away.

'It's all right. You're safe now. No one is going to come in here and hurt you.'

Madge Starling nodded.

'Are you able to speak, Madge?' asked Maisie.

Another nod, and a whispered reply. 'Yes.'

'I had a word with the ward sister, and she said you're coming along surprisingly well – you're a very strong young woman. If you continue to improve, you'll be discharged in a day or two, but you're going to have to be careful. No work on the farm for a while.'

Maisie could see Madge's bottom lip tremble.

'What is it, Madge?' She leaned closer to the patient.

'I don't have anywhere to go – only to the farm.'

'Don't you have family in London?'

Madge shook her head. 'Bombed out.' She swallowed as if trying to digest her own words. 'We don't get on anyway. I don't want to go home. I want to go back to the farm.'

'I'll talk to Mr Love. I'm sure arrangements could be made for you to convalesce there. Easily sorted out.' Maisie reached out and took the young woman's hand. 'Madge, I must ask you some questions. Are you up to it?'

Madge nodded.

'Madge, you saw what happened when that aircraft came down, didn't you?'

Another nod.

'Was it just one man on his own, or were there several?'

'One man.'

Maisie looked around. The patient in the next bed and her visitor had fallen silent. Maisie lifted the flap of her bag and took out her notebook and pencil. She opened the book to a clean page and wrote a name in bold capital letters, then showed it to Madge. 'Is this the man?'

The young woman nodded.

'But he's not the man who attacked you, is he?' A shake of the head.

Maisie wrote another name on a fresh page.

'Him?'

'Yes,' whispered Madge, and began to cry.

Maisie returned the notebook to her bag and leaned forward, once more taking the woman's hand. 'Madge, this is a difficult question, but I have been thinking over the circumstances of the attack. You had gone for a walk, I

320

understand – is that right?' Madge Starling nodded.

'And you met the man, didn't you?' Madge bit her lip as if to stem her tears.

'What he did was foolish and wrong,' said Maisie. 'But I think you were rather foolish too.'

Another nod. Maisie looked around. The neighbouring patient and her visitor had resumed their conversation.

She kept her voice low. 'Why did you do it? Why did you try to blackmail him, Madge?'

'How . . . how did you know?'

Maisie sighed. 'Oh, Madge – how else would he have found out what you'd seen if you had not told him? And there's only one reason to reveal something so . . . so explosive – you wanted something in return. But a person who already has their back against the wall can be volatile. Look what happened to you.'

'I needed the money. I want to stay in the country, and I've been saving up so that when the war's over, I've got a nest egg. But I thought I could get a bigger nest egg, so I can look after myself. I don't have anyone, and I don't want to go back to London.' She fought back tears. 'When the men come home, after the war, there won't be work for the likes of me down here, and I want to stay on the farm. I don't want to spend my life in a rotten factory, going home to a soot-covered old house on a derelict London street.'

Maisie nodded. 'There are other ways to live on a farm, Madge.' She patted her hand and looked around. 'I can see the staff nurse on her way to let me know it's time for you to rest now. You've helped me today – you've confirmed something I suspected but, to be honest, I wasn't completely sure.'

'Will I go to prison?' asked Madge. 'I should have gone straight to the police, when I knew what had happened. That poor woman pilot. I can't get over it.'

Maisie shook her head. 'You won't go to prison, Madge. You'll probably have to give a statement, but I suspect the worst that will happen is that you continue working for Barney Love for a good while yet.' She smiled. 'But that won't be the most dreadful outcome, will it?'

'Thank you, Miss Dobbs.'

'Oh, it's me who should be thanking you.' She pushed back her chair and stood up. 'Madge Starling. It's a lovely name.'

'One for the birds, my granddad used to say.'

'Rest and get well. Madge. I'll talk to Mr Love for you.'

Maisie squeezed the young woman's hand and left the ward, glad to be on her way out of the hospital. All being well, she would be in time to catch the next bus on the Chelstone route; she could walk to the Dower House from there. The journey would offer a time to think, to plan the order of things – better to have a plan than no plan at all, even if events ran awry. Not for the first time in her life, she felt as if she were caught in the lull before the storm.

Alighting from the bus outside the village pub, Maisie had just begun to walk towards Chelstone Manor when three black motor cars approached at speed. She stood back from the road, but the lead vehicle screeched to a halt alongside her. Mark Scott opened the passenger door and stepped out, reaching for the rear door handle.

'Get in, Maisie. We've got them.'

Maisie said nothing until the motor car was under way again, the convoy behind almost bumper to bumper.

'Who are they? Where are they – and is Private Stone with them?'

Mark turned back to face her. 'First of all, location – just like you predicted, it's one of those darn platelayers' huts. They'd moved on from the boathouse. We've got them surrounded – and we've reached your Caldwell on the radio, so he's meeting us. Seems we interrupted him while he was on his way to deal with a murder. Anyway, our MPs are there too, waiting. Caldwell said he'd left you at the hospital just a little earlier, by the way.'

'Mark, who are "they" – do you know?'

'We think we do.'

'You think?'

Mark nodded. 'We've been back and forth with our Bureau of Investigation boys in the States, and it seems the two main suspects are guys from a splinter group of Nazi supporters who've had Rover in their sights for some time, and they've been tagging her from San Francisco across the country. We lost track of them a while ago, and – if they're who we think they are – they've managed to get themselves across the pond, though we're not sure how, but as we know, it can be done. Where there's a will, there's a way; there have been a few hundred Americans working in essential war jobs in Ireland, picking up the slack due to men enlisting – that could have been a route in for them. Anyway, the bottom line is that the group doesn't like the way Mrs R has come out for the workers, for the likes of Matthias Crittenden – she's a supporter of the NAACP – and for women. This splinter group wanted to make a stand.'

'Mark, is Private Stone one of them?'

Maisie stared at her husband, waiting for his reply.

'Mark?'

'He could be. We don't know yet. Or he could be another pawn in the game, just like Crittenden. In fact, our two suspects are not big players in the group we've had an eye on, and it's likely they wanted to make their mark to move up the hierarchy with a massive gesture of criminal activity – apparently they were at the Charles Lindbergh rally last year, and when he capitulated after Pearl Harbour, they were pretty darn angry. Anyway, I think they're what you might call "tea-boys" over here, but as we know, the smallest predators can be the most dangerous.'

'They've used a vulnerable young man to aid them, though.'

'Like I said, we don't know if Private Stone—'

'Mark, I'm not talking about Stone or Matthias Crittenden. They've used someone very impressionable to run their errands, to keep an eye out for them – they found their own local dogsbody. And they've also used his mother. The trouble is, I believe the mother doesn't realise the danger – but they armed her son, and with the most tragic results. You see, the men who recruited him – the men who are targeting Mrs Roosevelt – they didn't realise he was emotionally unbalanced, and in providing him with a weapon, they gave him a power he has never had. Their biggest shock has been that they couldn't control him.'

324

'What? Who the heck are you talking about?'

'A young man called Ronnie Watkins.'

'The kid with the limp you told me about?'

Maisie reached for the leather grab strap above the window as the vehicle swung around a tight corner. She shook her head. 'I don't think there's anything wrong with him at all.' She turned her head to look out of the window, then drew her attention back to Mark Scott. 'I believe he has been brainwashed from childhood, and he is now detached from the outcome of his actions – and I bet he's given those men a headache, but it's a headache that has probably led to us finding them. If he hadn't taken a potshot at Jo, she would never have found Crittenden, never have been like a terrier with a bone and she would never have had the photographic evidence which helped us locate them.'

Mark Scott gave a low whistle. 'This is a big pack of cards coming down, that's for sure.' He checked his watch, spoke to the driver and turned back to Maisie. 'You say he was detached from his actions – what does that mean?'

'It means murder, Mark. I don't think Watkins saw the connection between what he was doing and the death of another human being.'

'Jeez, what the hell are we dealing with here? And what if he isn't with the others when we go in?'

'I doubt he will be. In any case, I'll deal with it, Mark. But I'll need Caldwell – when this is done I will have to move quickly.'

'One step at a time then, I guess.'

Maisie took a deep breath as the driver slowed the motor car. On a verge ahead she could see Colonel Theodore Wright and a group of American military policemen, along with Caldwell and two other men, who she knew to be Scotland Yard detectives. They would all be armed.

'Yes,' she whispered. 'One step at a time.'

CHAPTER EIGHTEEN

The driver decelerated as the motor car approached a makeshift police checkpoint. Taking an identity card from the inside pocket of his jacket, Mark Scott wound down the front passenger window, ready to speak to the policeman who approached the vehicle.

'We're here to meet Detective Chief Superintendent Caldwell.' Scott handed his identity card to the policeman. 'He's cleared us to approach.'

The policeman studied the card before handing it back to Scott. 'All correct, sir – we were told to expect you.' He turned his attention to Maisie, who opened her window and handed over the card issued by Robert MacFarlane a year earlier. It identified her as a special consultant to the Metropolitan Police.

'Oh yes, Miss Dobbs. Of course.' He returned the card and tapped on the roof of the motor car, indicating the driver was free to proceed.

As they drew closer to the cluster of men, one of Caldwell's detectives walked into the centre of the tarmacadam and took a few paces towards their vehicle. He pointed to a spot at the side of the road, guiding the driver to a halt. Taking account of two people silhouetted inside, he opened both passenger doors at the same time.

'Mr Scott and Miss Dobbs. Follow me.'

Colonel Wright and Caldwell stood side by side, deep in conversation with the detectives and four American military policemen. Mark Scott and Maisie approached the colonel and Caldwell; both men stepped away from the group to meet them. Greetings were exchanged, after which Colonel Wright deferred to Caldwell to describe the situation.

'Right, we've got three of them in there. Two we believe to be armed, and probably to the teeth, so we don't know if there is a risk to the life of number three—' Caldwell cast a glance towards the colonel, who nodded. 'Or if number three, one Private Charles Stone of the United States Army, is part of our problem or a victim of kidnap.' He cleared his throat and gestured towards the detectives and MPs. 'The gentlemen here have all been briefed, and I have suggested to the colonel, who agrees, that we should lose no time in going in. Trains have been halted in both directions, as has traffic on this road.' He looked at Scott. 'Yours was the last vehicle through here until we've sorted out this mess.'

Maisie looked around and saw a Black Maria at the ready to escort the alleged criminals away from the scene – breathing or not. The driver was leaning against the van, smoking a cigarette and sharing a joke with his partner. She brought her attention back to Caldwell, who continued to detail the plan.

'This is a civil matter with military implications for our colonial friends here, so my armed detectives will go first, with support from the American military police. Everyone's clear on tactics, and I've made the point that we want to get this done with a minimum of fuss and no one getting silly with a gun in their hand. The colonel has informed his men that we don't want to turn a little railway branch line in Kent into the OK Corral.'

His words were met with nervous laughter. Caldwell and the colonel led the way to the waiting detectives and American military police. The latter had handed out cigarettes, which resulted in a promising level of jovial comradeship among the men.

'Right then, time to sort out that lot in the hut. Follow me.' Caldwell motioned to his detectives and began walking forward towards the platelayer's hut. In his left hand he carried a loudhailer and in his right, a Webley revolver. He motioned the detectives to proceed to either side of the hut entrance and the military police to make their way to the rear and sides of the structure. There were no windows in a platelayer's hut, and the railway sleepers used in construction were thick. Over the years any gaps between the planks had filled with soot from passing trains, so there was little chance of anyone within the hut being able to see the gathering of men outside.

'Gentlemen, do I have your attention?' Caldwell shouted into the loudhailer. 'You are surrounded by armed United States military police and detectives from Scotland Yard, who are also handy with their weapons. Please come out of the hut now, unarmed and with your hands up.'

There was no reply.

'We know you're in there, so do the right thing, lads, and you will be given a fair hearing.'

'Fat chance,' Maisie heard Mark Scott whisper. They were standing back from the hut, but close enough to follow Caldwell's words.

Caldwell made one more request.

'This is your last chance, boys. My men aren't going to stand here all day waiting for you to come to your senses. It's now or never.'

The knot in Maisie's stomach twisted. She had been in similar situations in the past and had the same biting anticipation in her gut – a feeling of just wanting everything to be over and without loss of life. She had seen too much, too many deaths over the years, in wartime and peace. 'This is ridiculous,' said Maisie. 'They won't come out in these circumstances. They'll take their own lives before they do that.'

'Maisie, leave it to—'

She felt Mark touch her elbow, as if to catch her by the arm. But she did not stop. Tapping Caldwell on the shoulder as she came alongside him, she held out her hand. 'May I?' He shook his head, but then appeared to change his mind and gave her the loudhailer.

Caldwell met Maisie's gaze. 'Do you know what you're doing?'

Maisie nodded. 'I hope so. We want this over and done with, don't we? So let's allow an unexpected voice – a woman's voice – to take them unawares.'

Grasping the loudhailer, the tool that would amplify her message, she lifted it to her mouth as she stepped towards the hut, one deliberate pace at a time. She cleared her throat and felt a bead of perspiration run down the side of her face.

'Gentlemen – my name is Maisie Dobbs.' Her heartbeat raced, and her voice seemed to echo in her ears, yet she knew it was coming forth strong and resolute. 'We know all about your intentions, and we know who you have in your sights.' She paused to gather her thoughts. 'Conspiracy to commit a crime is treated differently under English law. You will be given a fair hearing – as long as you render yourselves unarmed and demonstrate no intent to harm anyone waiting for you when you come out of the hut.'

She looked back at Caldwell, who gave his customary eye roll, adding, sotto voce, 'Making up the law as you go along, Miss Dobbs? Justice should be deaf, never mind blind.' He nodded for her to proceed.

Maisie felt her husband now standing next to her, his hand on her shoulder as she continued. 'I know you want to go home. We have information to prove that you have been set up by your people in America.' She stopped, catching her breath. 'Yes, they've set you up, which is why you will be treated with leniency in this country. The people who encouraged your actions and who sent you on your way thousands of miles across an ocean far from home have left you to take responsibility for something you did not plan. You thought they had your backs, but they don't.' She offered a few seconds' silence to allow the trapped men to absorb her message. 'You're on your own in a strange country.'

'Get back to the kitchen, woman – we know who's with

us and who's not. Any of you come in here, and soldier boy dies.'

Maisie pressed her lips together upon hearing the voice. She felt failure looming, and wondered if her feelings mirrored those of the men inside the hut. 'You must feel as if there is no way out,' she continued. 'You must feel as if you've been caught in a web and you're stuck. But you're not. We will ensure your side of the story is heard.'

Caldwell put his hand on Maisie's shoulder. 'You've done well, Miss Dobbs,' he whispered. 'They won't budge. The boys here should go in now.'

'Please . . .' whispered Maisie, before raising the loudhailer to her mouth again. 'Come out now so we don't have to send you home in death shrouds, to be met by your heartbroken mothers, wives or sweethearts.'

Maisie felt Caldwell remain close as Mark squeezed her shoulder, a signal for her to step away. She was searching for the words that might bring a peaceful end to the standoff when the sound of raised voices came from the hut, followed by the thud of bolts being drawn back and one man screaming at another. Maisie heard the clicking of firearms as the three detectives raised their weapons. One of their number took a step towards the door, and the military police readied themselves.

'We're coming out.'

Maisie thought the voice might belong to the older of the three men she had seen at the boathouse.

'Keep your hands raised, gentlemen,' said Caldwell. 'No funny business, no guns, and we can all be home in time for tea.' He looked at Scott. 'Or coffee.'

A man stepped out, his hands held high. He dropped a revolver to the ground from one hand and a semi-automatic rifle from the other as he continued to move forward. A detective reached down for the weapons as another took the man by the collar and directed him towards the path. An MP restrained him while he was handcuffed, then began to lead him away. But the man stopped and turned his head.

'Ricky – Ricky, you'd better get out of there now, pal. We're done. There's no way out for us. Leave him now.' His voice caught as he began to sob. 'The lady's right, Rick – we've been taken for fools. We've been had.'

There was silence, then another voice called from the hut.

'No, I ain't coming! You may be done, you yellow-bellied old man – but I came here to finish a job and I'm going to do it, so help me god. This cry baby army rat knows too much anyway, and so he's going and so is that Roosevelt woman – if I have to run out of here and shoot you all to finish what's been started. She's a traitor to us, a traitor to our country and to our kind, that's what she is – and we know it. I'm gonna see her dead before I go down.'

No sooner had the man finished his declaration than a shot rang out and a guttural scream filled the air. Before Maisie could determine which way to look, a detective had kicked the hut's door back on its hinges and fired several times into the darkness, towards the direction of the voice. Mark Scott pulled Maisie away, but she, too, felt a scream rise in her throat, for at once she was not witness to death on a rural railway line in England but she was at war, the barriers of time crashing down so that even now she could once more feel her woollen uniform dress becoming heavier as blood from the sodden floor leached into the hem. Instead of a single firearm, she heard cannon fire and shelling as every one of her senses was enveloped by the past. Yet she knew she had to go forward, because in war it had been her job to save a life, even if she had to risk her own.

Mark Scott tried to catch her sleeve when she started towards the hut, pushing aside Caldwell to gain entry. A detective was leaning over a man's body, the scene illuminated in a shaft of light from the open door, while a deep moaning came from the filthy corner just visible in the darkness beyond. She called to the military police to help her and to another detective to bring a first aid kit from the police vehicle. Soon the emaciated frame of a tall young man barely out of boyhood was brought out and laid down alongside the hut, his face, hands and clothing soiled by black coal dust and hair that was once blond now streaked with grey. Maisie lost no time and went to work, pressing her fingers into a stomach wound from which blood was pumping, rendering him closer to death with every second. The life of Charles Stone was now in the hands of a soldiers' nurse.

'The doctor says that the bullet is out, but the next twenty-four hours will be critical. Stone is all skin and bone, and there's not a lot of him to bring to the fight, but if he can pull through the night, he stands a chance of making it home.' Colonel Wright cleared his throat as an orderly passed in the narrow hospital corridor. 'If all goes well, he'll be transferred to one of our military hospitals as soon as he's stable enough for the ride in an ambulance.' He drew his attention to Maisie. 'That was a brave move, Mrs Scott. A very brave move. It did the trick though.'

She nodded, pushing hair back from her face. She was tired and had no need of a mirror to inform her that her eyes were red-rimmed, her cheeks streaked with the wounded man's blood. 'What about Private Crittenden – what will happen to him?'

'We now have the confirmation we need that Stone isn't dead and Crittenden is as much of a victim – and yes, I'm aware that's what you've said from the beginning. I'll be working on a transfer for Crittenden. It'll make it easier all around for everyone concerned at our end, but in the meantime, we're looking after him.'

'Transfer?' asked Mark. 'He deserves a good one, maybe even a promotion, after what he's been put through.'

'He won't be disappointed. And I can tell you that in a brief moment of consciousness, Stone asked if his friend was still alive, though I don't think we can exactly arrange a happy reunion with his buddy, not in the circumstances. We have certain—' He looked at Mark, then drew his attention back to Maisie. 'As you understand, we have certain protocols that aren't required under British law, and when the soldiers are on a base, we have to adhere to our US norms and laws.' He adjusted his cap, stepping to the side as another patient was wheeled past on a stretcher. 'This has been a difficult situation from the start,' he continued. 'Yes, I know the evidence against Crittenden was, I suppose, flimsy, but it wouldn't be the first time a man – or woman – was held under suspicion of being implicated in a murder without the proof of a body.' Wright adjusted his cap once again, and looked at Maisie. 'I want you to know that Crittenden was held as much for his own safety as anything else – he was, after all, the last man to see a white soldier alive before his disappearance. I hope you understand my position.' He sighed. 'Anyway, Scott, I take it you'll see me about the man you have in custody, as you're the one with the intelligence on him and his deceased collaborator.'

'We now know exactly who we've been dealing with.'

The colonel looked at his watch. 'Then a briefing in my office in a couple of days. I'll be in touch.' He shook his head, and stared at the ground for several seconds. 'I can't believe this is what I've been doing today. At least the dead American is a civilian, so that one's over to you, Scott. I suppose you could call it practise for what's to come. I'm going to be facing the reality of many dead and wounded American sons before this war is over.' The colonel turned to Maisie again. 'Mrs Scott – that was as fine an example of battlefield medical care as I've seen in my career. Stone has a lot to thank you for. Where did you serve?'

Maisie met the colonel's gaze. 'France, in the last war – and later on in Spain, actually.' She gave a half laugh. 'I was once told that a nurse never forgets how to do her job. I can't work with the same speed as I could when I was seventeen or eighteen and my response isn't quite as rote – but I can get the work done.'

* * *

Seated together in the back of the motor car, Maisie and Mark Scott were silent for the first part of the journey home to Chelstone, then Mark took her hand.

'Maisie, don't ever do that again.'

'Do what?'

'That guy could have come out of there, all guns blazing, and you could have been killed – we were standing back, where we were safe, where we had a chance, and you didn't even think before you moved forward.'

'But that's it, Mark – I did think. I thought a woman's voice would make a difference, would get one or both of them to come out. I had a feeling that if their resolve wasn't broken within seconds, in short order there would be three deaths.'

'Did you consider me? Or Anna? I mean, she could have been motherless for the second time – no, the third time, counting her grandmother – if that move of yours had gone wrong.'

Maisie looked at her hands, at the scars still evident from the time she had dragged her best friend from a blazing, bombed-out building. Of course she had thought of Anna. She never stopped thinking of Anna, and in that moment, at the hut, she wanted one thing, and that was to get the job done and go home. To Anna. Yes, she had taken a chance – a risk based upon experience – and it had worked. To a point it had worked. She sighed.

'Of course. Yes, you're right, Mark – I took a chance. But I also had a feeling here.' She put her hand on her heart. 'I knew that something would happen to bring the standoff to an end, and I knew those men would not shoot me. I felt that if Caldwell went in, then all three people in that hut would die.'

'Maisie, they were planning to take the life of the president's wife – and now we know that if they failed to take her life when she visited the embassy in London, their intention was to assassinate her when she visited Canterbury Cathedral. Can you imagine it – the wife of the president of the United States of America killed in one of your country's most famous ancient places of worship? So being a woman wouldn't have saved you, any more than it saved that poor girl in the Spitfire. What made you think you would be different?'

'It was a bit of a gamble, Mark, and it proved to be a fair one: a wager with myself based upon experience. There was a moment when I thought I'd failed, that I'd made things worse, and I was terrified. But then words came to me that broke the spell, challenging one man's belief that they could prevail – and all because I mentioned his mother, or his wife, or sweetheart. I reminded him that he was a long way from home. It was as simple as that.' She squeezed his hand. 'But I promise, I won't do anything like that again.'

'I'll have that in writing when we get back to the house.' Scott pulled her to him, and changed the subject. 'And speaking of home, what are we going to do about Anna and school?'

'The tutoring with Mrs Milward starts tomorrow, so she'll go on the bus with Margaret Rose. Billy is coming over in the morning and then we're going to Westerham. When these cases are complete, I'll see the headmistress.'

'No showdowns, Maisie.'

'No showdowns . . . well, no big ones anyway.'

'And the headmistress is one of these not-big showdowns?'

'Yes, I think so. And if nothing changes, we'll visit that school you told me about.'

They were silent for a while, exhaustion getting the better of them. Mark began to doze as Maisie stared out of the window, taking account of fields with cattle or sheep grazing, and in others the lines of stubble following a second harvest. A farmer was out ploughing a field, and as the soil was turned, birds – seagulls, crows, sparrows and starlings – swooped down in search of a tasty worm or another of nature's delicacies. Maisie cast her eyes to leaves of red and gold weather-whipped from trees, zigzagging to the ground and across the road as the wind increased and dark clouds lumbered across the sky. Rain began to fall so the driver turned on the windscreen wipers, then brought the back of his leather-gloved hand to the glass to wipe away condensation.

'We might be spared the air raids tonight,' said Scott, awake now and peering out of the window. He turned to Maisie. 'By the way, even before I told you, I think you guessed that the guys in the hut belonged to a subversive outfit back in the States?'

Maisie shrugged. 'I suppose I was thinking of that case a couple of years ago, with those America First people. There seemed to be so many pawns littering this case – people who appeared to be manipulated, either by outsiders or one another. And those men made so many mistakes, I thought they must be amateurs brainwashed by rhetoric. I've seen it before – in fact, my first case, after Maurice retired . . .' Her words trailed away as she gazed out of the window again, as if staring into the past. 'It seems such a long time ago now.' She looked at her husband. 'Anyway, I just thought those men were following orders of some sort. By the way, are you going to tell me the whole story – the precise details of who they are, where they were from and what sort of pressure they were applying on Private Stone? Something doesn't seem to fit.'

Scott nodded. 'You'll have a seat at the table when I talk to Colonel Wright. In normal circumstances it would be irregular – as you Brits might say – but you have some credit in the account over at Eisenhowerplatz, and you've been involved in the chain of events. There's still some pieces missing in the puzzle, but at least we know Rover is safe.'

'Do you?'

'Safe from one source of dissent anyway.' He shrugged. 'And you have the answers for your fly girl, don't you?'

Maisie shook her head. 'Yes. Almost.'

'Look, Maisie, our professional paths crossed on this one. Neither of us saw it coming, but I don't ever want to do it again.' Maisie felt her husband's arm tighten around her. 'And your part hasn't finished.'

'Don't worry. No one will be armed. I'll be safe.' She placed her hand on Mark Scott's wrist. 'And Mark – remember, this is what I do. This is my work – but I have my family, and I won't take chances. You all come first, before everything else.'

'I'd like that in writing too.'

'If you do the same for me.'

The motor car pulled into the carriage sweep at Chelstone Manor, then turned left towards the Dower House. The kitchen door was opened with such energy, it seemed as if it would bounce from its hinges.

'Mummy! Daddy! Mummy! Daddy! Mummy! Daddy! I made a cake for you! Auntie Patty from America helped me, then Tom came to take her back to London. It's a special cake that Grandma Brenda said came from Lord Woolton!'

'Heaven help my taste buds,' whispered Mark, before kneeling down to take Anna in his arms.

Even in this moment of joy, as she walked with her husband and daughter into their home, Maisie felt a deep weight across her heart. She had told what amounted to a lie, because she knew very well that one of the men she would encounter the following day might indeed be armed. And like so many disenfranchised souls she had met over the years, he could be volatile.

CHAPTER NINETEEN

A nna held Maisie's hand as she skipped along to the bus stop, unable to contain her excitement at attending 'special lessons with a special lady,' which meant travelling on the bus with Margaret Rose, the friend she looked up to. The child chattered away as they walked and Maisie was pleased to see little evidence of fear or trepidation on Anna's part.

There was no means of avoiding walking past the school, though it was a good fifteen minutes too early for children to begin arriving, for which Maisie was thankful. However, she could not fail to notice how Anna seemed to speed past the building, tugging her hand so she would walk faster. It was a tactic usually employed when they neared the dentist.

Billy and Doreen were already waiting at the bus stop with Margaret Rose. Maisie waved as Anna pulled away and ran to her friend.

'We thought it would be a good idea if I went with the

girls all the way to meet Mrs Milward for their first couple of days,' said Doreen.

'That's good of you, Doreen. I'm sure they would be perfectly all right on their own, but it doesn't hurt to ease them in. Thank you.'

'Well, I know you've got a lot on,' added Doreen, with a strained smile.

Maisie looked from Doreen to Billy. Both seemed tense, and appeared exhausted. 'Any news of Bobby?'

'He's in an air force hospital in Wiltshire,' said Billy. 'It's hard to keep up with it all, but he managed to get through to us on the blower last night. We're glad you put in a telephone for your dad at the bungalow, miss. Since we've been staying there, it's been a godsend for us, what with all the worry.'

'Bobby was treated for burns to his hands, but apparently there was an injury to his back when the aeroplane came down,' added Doreen. 'So he's in a special unit at the hospital, which is in a place called Wroughton – in Wiltshire, like Billy said. Bobby reckons it won't be long before he's up there again, on the bombers. They need him on an aeroplane, not lingering in a bed.'

'I should go down there and kick him in the knees. Keep him on the ground for a while longer,' said Billy. 'Give the lad a hard enough wallop to make sure he stays out of it all.'

Maisie noticed the look exchanged between the couple. 'It might be a while if he's sustained a spinal injury. You can't put those back into service before the patient is ready, what with the hard seats on a bomber.'

'From your lips to God's ears, miss, though I don't think the RAF is worried about a bit of back pain.' Billy nodded towards the road in the distance. 'Here comes the bus. Right then, you two – be good girls, won't you? Do your lessons and make your mums proud of you!'

Billy kissed his daughter and wife, while Maisie knelt down to check the ribbon securing Anna's single plait.

'I'll see you when you get home, my darling – Grandpa and Little Emma will be waiting here at the bus stop for you.'

'Won't you meet me too?' asked Anna.

'If I can, of course I will – but it'll be Grandpa if I'm not quite home.'

'Come on, ladies.' Billy chivvied both girls and his wife onto the bus, and seconds later they were on their way, waving from the back window.

'Still a bit clingy, is she?' asked Billy, as they turned to walk towards Chelstone Manor.

Maisie nodded. 'Not as much – better, I think, because it's just her and Margaret Rose.' She consulted her watch. 'Come on, Billy, we'd better get a move on. We're meeting Caldwell in Westerham at a quarter past ten.'

'Got enough petrol?'

'George came to the rescue once again – I don't even ask where he gets it any more. And Caldwell has provided some extra coupons for us.'

'The ice has definitely thawed between you two.'

Maisie laughed. 'As Caldwell so eloquently says, "You scratch my back, Miss Dobbs, and I'll scratch yours". I'm not sure I approve of the analogy though.'

Despite Billy's short burst of laughter, he remained drawn.

'I don't need to ask, do I? You've heard nothing from young Billy.'

He pressed his lips together, as if fighting the welter of emotion that came with thoughts of his son.

'We were sort of . . . sort of getting used to it; you know, that our boy is in a terrible place that we just can't even imagine. No, not really getting used to it – it's hard to explain, but we've been sort of existing with it, going along and doing what we always do.' He frowned, as if frustrated by an inability to describe his feelings. 'It's a bit like living in a house with a ghost, something you know is there but you've just got to do what you always do every single day, because there's no other choice, whether you've got this dark shadow following you around or not. So that's what you do – you go on. But our son is the first thing we think about in the morning and the last thing we think about at night. He's become the ghost in the house, and then getting the news that we might have lost Bobby made it even worse – that's when you have to fight the darkness because it's sucking you in and taking you under.'

Maisie said nothing, knowing her presence was all Billy needed from her as he continued talking about his sons.

'Bobby told me a crew of New Zealanders – "Kiwis" he called them, his "Kiwi mates" – had gone out on the same run. Before they left, all the lads had a bet on a drinking competition when they came back in. Bobby said they were full of it before they set off, you know, over there – joshing about who would win and putting the money in a hat so there was quite a kitty to be won. But the Kiwis were shot down over Germany. Now my boy is even more determined to get back on a bomber and give the Germans what for. Before the war, I thought Bobby being good with engines was really something, miss. Then when it started, I even thought that perhaps it would get him into a reserved profession. But look where it's got us. And there was me being proud that he had it in him to really go places, being a qualified mechanic. We told him that one day he could have his own garage, build up a business.'

Again, Maisie said nothing.

'My Doreen – what a brick she's been. Solid, you know. Solid. And I was scared, thinking she'd have another breakdown, lose herself, just like she did when our Lizzie died of diphtheria, and it was years ago now.' He put his hand to his chest. 'You know, miss, I was never one for church and all that, but I pray to Lizzie up there. Every single night, I tell her, "You watch over your brothers, Lizzie, my angel. You're up there, my lovely girl and if God's listening, you tell him – you just tell him your brothers need looking after".'

'She will, Billy,' said Maisie. 'Your Lizzie loved her big brothers, and I know in my heart she will watch over them through thick and thin. She will never leave them.'

Maisie briefed Billy on the journey to Westerham, describing what she thought might have come to pass in the tangled relationship between Ronnie Watkins and his mother, along with Dan Littlecombe.

'What does Mr Scott say?'

Maisie kept her eyes on the road as she framed her reply. 'He's had to be careful, because there's a thread between the men who came to this country with the intention of harming Mrs Roosevelt, and the deaths of our pilots. Interrogation of the man now in custody begins today, and Mark expects to discover the connection between one of them and the Watkins family, though it's fair to say that we could make that discovery first, because I think Mrs Watkins might break down faster.'

'I don't know about that, miss. From what you've told me about her manipulation of her son, I reckon she's a hard woman, deep down.'

'If so, then she's been rendered so by circumstance, Billy – let's not forget that.'

'Sort of like that headmistress – and I don't think you're ready to give her any quarter.'

'Someone told me that becoming a mother turns you into a lioness. I think they could be right.' She moved on to their next task. 'Approaching Dan Littlecombe first will start the ball rolling, and I am hoping his presence when we see Mrs Watkins and Ronnie will smooth the way for the confessions we need.'

'You'll have to press him though, won't you? You have to let him know what happened. Or what you think has happened.'

'That's true. I just hope I'm correct. But I think I am. I've read through some of Maurice's old case notes pertaining to the subtle coercions that can change both the emotional and physical health of a child. As a young doctor he had one case that continued on into adulthood and it mirrored

347

Ronnie Watkins's situation – where a parent persuaded the child of a quite serious fictitious ailment.'

'Is there a name for this . . . this sort of coercion stuff?'

'Not as far as I know. According to Maurice, it has a profound impact on the spirit, yet it can also lead to anger, violence and other manifestations later in life. It can also result in complete acquiescence along with a misplaced depth of love for the parent – not ordinary love, like your sons for you and Doreen, but a love that is almost obsessive.'

'And you really reckon this Ronnie's mum is that controlling, and the son just accepted it?'

'I haven't been able to do as much delving as I would have liked, but yes, I think it could well be the case.'

'What do you think started it all?'

Maisie felt a wave of apprehension begin to envelop her. It was a familiar feeling at this point in a case, when all that remained on the journey to conclusion was the revealing of truth – and when lies had caused so much damage, truth could result in even more pain.

'I think grief started it all, Billy.'

Seconds passed as Billy stared out of the window, then turned to look at the road ahead. 'Yeah,' he said. 'I can see that.'

Caldwell was waiting at the top of a hill about a quarter of a mile from Dan Littlecombe's garage. Maisie parked behind a black Wolseley motor car, and she and Billy joined the detective and two constables.

'Morning, Miss Dobbs. Got a bit of news for you. That young Yank soldier pulled through, and according to what I heard first thing, he's going to be transferred by ambulance to an American military hospital later on today. I daresay they will be questioning him as soon as he's strong enough to hold a conversation. Wouldn't mind having a word with him myself, but I've heard from echelons far higher than my exalted position that I'll be lucky. So it's all down to you and me to sort this one out – though the powers that be at our end don't know about you being part of this song and dance. Not yet anyway.'

Maisie was about to speak, but Caldwell held up a hand. 'Miss Dobbs, taking into account our situation here, I am more than willing to defer to your approach, because you know the Littlecombe bloke, and judging by yesterday's outcome, I reckon he might be more . . . let's say more amenable to telling you the truth than he might with me.'

'Thank you, Superintendent,' said Maisie. 'I have a feeling Littlecombe wants the weight off his shoulders. He strikes me as a tired man, one with a great desire to escape this situation. I believe he's worn out with taking responsibility for his sister and her son.'

'How did you find out about Mrs Watkins being his sister?'

'The church. It was something I learned very early on in my apprenticeship with Dr Blanche. You can spend hours at the registrar of births, marriages and deaths or at Somerset House, or any one of those places where records are kept, or you can go to the local church and look through the book where baptisms, marriages and funerals have been recorded. The book is usually out somewhere, or you find a friendly verger to let you into the vestry. It's harder in

London, I must confess, but here in the country where people tend to stay for generations, the church can be a mine of information.'

'Right, now I've had my lesson on how to find out someone's familial relationships – shall we?'

'I'll second that,' said Billy, smiling. 'I thought we were going to be standing here jawing about birth records all day!'

Caldwell raised his eyebrows. 'We'll go along in my motor car, park just around the corner from the garage, and then you and I will go in. My boys have already checked – he's in there, working away on an engine.'

'Good morning, Mr Littlecombe,' Maisie called out as they approached the garage.

Littlecombe looked up from the open engine of a Morris Cowley. He put down a spanner, grabbed an oil-stained cloth and wiped his hands as he walked towards them. 'Morning, Miss Dobbs. Looks like you've brought some official with you – police, is it?'

Maisie smiled, attempting to keep the situation on an even keel. 'Yes indeed – this is my colleague, Detective Chief Superintendent Caldwell. I thought I would do the introductions because you and I have met before. Can we go into your office?'

'You know what it's like in there – bit of a pigsty.'

'Don't worry about that,' said Caldwell. 'Probably palatial compared to mine.'

Maisie studied Dan Littlecombe's gait as he led the way. Tension in his shoulders and spine shortened his step, and she could almost feel an invisible weight bearing down upon the man. She turned back to Caldwell, who nodded an understanding of Littlecombe's state of mind.

Inside the office – which was as Littlecombe had warned – there was only one oil-stained chair set behind a small wooden desk, so all three remained on their feet.

'Go on, Miss Dobbs,' said Littlecombe. 'Tell me why you're here.'

Maisie took a deep breath. She had practised the order of her every word as she made an accusation tempered by acknowledgment of the man's difficult circumstances. She wanted to meet guilt with compassion because she needed Littlecombe's help.

'Mr Littlecombe, we find ourselves at a troubling point, don't we?' She paused, but Littlecombe was silent. 'It is my belief that you have been protecting your nephew – Ronnie Watkins – to the extent that you attacked a young woman who could have identified him as the gunman who succeeded in bringing down two aircraft, and very nearly a third, from the field near Barney Love's farm.'

Without looking away, Littlecombe reached for the chair, pulled it towards him and sat down. He had placed himself in a vulnerable position, Maisie noted; now he had to look up to them. It reminded her of a weakened dog showing his throat to the pack leader.

'I know there has been much sadness and much fear involved,' said Maisie. 'Ronnie has had a great deal to bear since childhood, and I believe the feeling of unworthiness in him grew into an anger so deep that he struck out and attacked the very people he not only revered but, in the

case of two women, envied. All were strangers to him.'
Littlecombe studied his hands in silence.

Maisie felt Caldwell shift in place alongside her, and
knew he was feeling the same anticipation. If Littlecombe's
emotional dam broke, would it be with violence or collapse?
She suspected the latter, so she went on, taking even more
care with her words.

'I have had to speculate upon where it all started, and
I think it was with your sister – Ronnie's mother – and it
began even when the boy was so small, he would never
have known that there is no real medical reason for his
physical limitations. I believe his lameness is – and I hate
to use this term – "all in his head". It was put there by his
mother and substantiated by her when she reminded him
time and again of all the things that were beyond him, so
Ronnie assumed the demeanour of a crippled boy – to the
extent that he is now a man disabled in body and in his
state of mind. His anger at not being able – or allowed – to
engage in so many activities and pursuits intensified as he
grew to manhood, didn't it?'

Littlecombe stumbled on his words as he began to tell
his story. 'You don't know what it was like, seeing that
boy. I – I always thought something wasn't right, because
he seemed well enough as a little baby, kicking his legs in
his cot. And he loved anything that flew, would reach out
to a bird, because Beattie, my sister, had him lying down so
much all he could see was the sky. She was always going
on at him, telling him he had trouble walking because
something was wrong with his body. He got used to being
told that he wouldn't be able to run with the other boys, or

play on the swings or the merry-go-round, or climb trees – and because she went on about his limp and his twisted spine, he never walked without that limp. He didn't know whether he was in pain or not. And you couldn't talk to her about it, because it would have made everything worse – she would have kept him home more than she did. That little scrap of a lad would hold out his arms and pretend he was a bird, because he thought it would make him fly.' The words began to come faster, as if the truth, now unbound, was in full flood. 'And I saw the meanness start to grow as he got older, then of course he was a man, and you should have seen the look on his face when he saw a couple of those women ferry pilots in the pub. He couldn't understand why they could get a job flying and yet the RAF laughed at him. Because of his lameness, he couldn't even pass a medical to work in the air force kitchens. Then that long-lost bloody cousin of Beattie's husband came over, and that was it – the boy seemed to lose his head, and the cousin helped him do it. He was evil, you know. Rotten to the core. Ronnie believed every word that came out of his mouth, just like he believed his mum.'

'Tell us about the cousin,' said Caldwell.

Maisie turned to Caldwell and nodded, acknowledging his tone, which was softer than usual.

Littlecombe avoided their eyes as he continued. 'He was the son of Brian's uncle, so his cousin – though they'd never met. Brian was my sister's husband; got himself killed in 1918. He went back over to France after a few days' leave, not knowing he'd left his wife with a baby on the way, and he was shot in the head a week later. Anyway, this uncle of his had been sent to Canada as a lad. I'm told he was sixteen years of age at the time and in trouble, so he was shipped out there to work on a farm. That's what they did then – shipped the rotten young felons overseas. He was a bad egg, but he sorted himself out and ended up across the border in America. He found himself a wife, got married and had a couple of nippers – Brian's cousins, a boy and girl. They were all ordinary people, working people by all accounts. The boy grew up in hard times and got in with a mob who were blaming everyone else for the fact they couldn't find work – I mean, you should hear the bloke when he gets going. I only met him a few times, but he went on and on about everyone who had a job bar him, and I told him, "It's not much different over here, mate – the slump went around the world and a lot of people lost their jobs and a place to live".'

Littlecombe drew his hands down his face, from forehead to chin. When Maisie and Caldwell said nothing, he went on. 'Anyway, from what I can make out, the cousin joined in with people who took things a bit further, and they had it in for immigrants and black people. I told him, "As far as I can make out, you're all immigrants over there, unless you're Indians." Then he started on about them too. He seemed a bit mad, to tell you the truth. But Ronnie thought these Americans walked on water, which might have been on account of the younger one who came over with Brian's cousin. He was a mouthy whatsit – about thirty-five years old. Didn't like him at all.' Littlecombe raised his head and looked from Maisie to Caldwell, then back to Maisie again. 'I can't say as I understand it all, but it seemed to me they couldn't abide that president and his wife, and it was all to do with the people who were coloured, and them getting jobs . . . I don't know, like I said, they wanted to blame everyone else for what they didn't have. They said it was all wrong, that the wife in particular – the American woman who's over here now – was really the one to watch, because of how she was standing up for people who shouldn't be stood up for.'

'And so they became more active with this political group in America, and then they came over here,' said Maisie.

Littlecombe nodded. 'Tell you the truth, I didn't even want to know about it, what they did and how they got here. This lot back there in America paid for it, and Brian's cousin and the bloke with him came to my sister because it was a connection, someone local who could help them hide out. As far as Ronnie and his mum were concerned, you'd have thought a couple of gods had turned up to change their lives, but I could see they were up to no good. All I wanted to do was protect Beattie and Ronnie.'

'How did Ronnie get involved?'

'Like I said, they became his heroes, promising him a better life over in America if he helped them. They had him running errands and finding out things for them. But then it all got out of hand, because they had guns and let Ronnie try them out to have some fun. It started with hitting a few old tins, then he was shooting at birds, and soon he was looking for something bigger.' Littlecombe sighed. 'It was as if he didn't understand what he was doing – as if he couldn't see that shooting at something could have a bad ending. I saw the same thing happen to lads in the last war – they'd had their training, shooting, bayonet practice, but the biggest shock was seeing the bodies when they were shot through. But Ronnie wasn't shocked – it was as if he had no feelings inside him.' Littlecombe shifted in the chair. 'I thought about it and I reckon it was to do with them giving him a gun and how he felt when he had it in his hands. It was as if for the first time in his life he was strong – the guns made him feel as if he was important and he'd never felt like that before. Anyway, after a while the American cousin and his mate realised they had a serious problem on their hands with Ronnie – it's a wonder they didn't finish him off.'

'And that ultimately led to you attacking Madge Starling,' said Maisie, watching for Littlecombe's reaction.

Littlecombe pressed his fingers to his closed eyes for a moment, as if trying to erase the events from his mind.

'She saw Ronnie trying to shoot down that Spitfire. When you came to see me that day, Miss Dobbs, and I said I didn't think it was an accident, her being killed in that field, it was because . . . I suppose I wanted it to stop. I felt terrible for that poor girl, terrible. But I couldn't finger my own nephew. Then that Madge Starling tried to get money off me, and I don't have the kind of money she wanted – this garage is it. And since my wife died, I've only got my sister and Ronnie. The missus had gone to visit her old mum in Hackney and timed it right to get herself done for by a bomb dropping in the street – terrible thing, it was.' Littlecombe pinched the bridge of his nose. 'But I lost my mind with that Starling woman, Miss Dobbs. Lost my mind and just went for her. Really, the one I should have gone for is that bloody American cousin instead of working on his rotten American motor car. They must have had a fair bit of cash with them, because he came over here and said, "I want a good American automobile." That's how stupid the man was – dangerous and stupid.'

Caldwell ran both hands through his hair. Maisie looked at him and stepped back so he could face Littlecombe.

'It's not a lot of help, but I would say you feel better now, getting all that off your chest,' said Caldwell.

Littlecombe shrugged. 'I suppose you're going to read me my rights.'

'Not quite yet, sir. First, we want a favour from you.'

'Me?'

Caldwell met Maisie's eyes.

'Mr Littlecombe,' said Maisie. 'We must go to Ronnie's house because your nephew is a killer. His mother is also an accessory to a crime, so Superintendent Caldwell will be placing them both under arrest. We believe we will require your assistance to render the proceedings as calm as possible because it is clear they are both of unbalanced mind. You seem to have some sort of influence over your nephew, and of course you can communicate with your sister, who I believe has difficulties with speech.'

Littlecombe shook his head. 'I'm the rigid old uncle now, and I'm not a man with a film-star American mouth on him, but I'll do what I can.' He looked up at a grease-stained clock on the wall. 'They won't be at home for another twenty minutes. Beattie has a cleaning job, and Ronnie goes with her when he's not here with either me, the Yank cousin, or the Home Guard. The lad doesn't do much with the latter, but they let him wear the uniform. And these lads do like a uniform, don't they?'

'Speaking of uniforms, Mr Littlecombe,' said Caldwell, 'and seeing as we have a few moments, I wonder if you could tell us about the friendship between Constable Eames and your nephew.'

Littlecombe rested his forehead on his hands, his elbows on the dust-covered desk before him. 'Evil meeting opportunity, I suppose. Eames was another one – not the brightest star when they were at school, and that blimmin' teacher let him and Ronnie know it. Pushed together, I suppose, because they didn't have much in common, except for the fact that the Eames boy was turned down by the RAF and every other service on account of his medical not being up to snuff. What didn't help Ronnie was Peter Eames getting him going with his moaning and groaning about everything that was bad in his life. You should have heard him when the Land Army women started working on Barney Love's farm, especially because Eames's father had lost his job there – not that it came as a surprise to anyone. Johnny Eames liked getting down the pub more than he liked ploughing a field, and it got to the point where Barney had had enough and sent him packing. All Eames's ranting rubbed off on his boy – especially about the Women's Land Army working on the farm, and then the American soldiers – so the chip on the boy's shoulder grew into a tree trunk. I reckon whenever he passed Ronnie in the street, Peter Eames complained about this and that, and of course it unsettled Ronnie's mind even more.'

'Yes, I see,' said Maisie. She looked at her watch. 'It's

time for us to go to your sister's house, Mr Littlecombe. Ready?'

Dan Littlecombe stood up. 'Yes. More than ready. Let's just get it finished. I'm all but done with everything. Prison will be a lot calmer than this sort of life. Nothing's been right since my Meg died. Too much war, that's what I've seen. Too much war.' He steadied himself against the desk. 'Too much hatred. Too many lies told. And too much bloody pain.'

CHAPTER TWENTY

Maisie stood back against the hedge and watched as a woman police constable left the run-down terrace house with a handcuffed Beattie Watkins, followed by two police constables flanking her son, also handcuffed, who began screaming out to his mother. Maisie shuddered, the sound reminding her of a foal taken from the mare when the weaning was done.

Two Black Marias stood ready to receive the prisoners. Dan Littlecombe, his head down, emerged from the terrace house in handcuffs, led by a constable to the waiting black Wolseley. Billy followed with Caldwell, who locked the door behind them. The two men walked towards Maisie.

'You were right, Miss Dobbs – it was best you weren't in there. Got pretty nasty. Beattie Watkins went for her brother with a carving knife, and it was all we could do to get her under control. Ronnie Watkins struggled, but like you said, Mr Beale is good with young men and knew how to calm him down enough to get his confession. With a little encouragement from him, the lad told us all about aiming his gun at aircraft bound for Biggin Hill and said he didn't know which ones had women pilots, but he bet the aeroplanes that came in on their own and at an odd time with no air raid going on were more likely to have a ferry pilot at the controls, and it just wasn't fair that he couldn't fly too because he thought they weren't proper pilots, not like the RAF. And it turns out that even before the American relatives got here, Ronnie "borrowed" a rifle from one of the houses where his mum worked and took a shot at a Spitfire, so he was already a bit unhinged. I've an idea he might have been the cause of your client's fiancé coming down, but we'll never know.' Caldwell put a hand on Billy's shoulder. 'Anyway, if he wasn't already your right-hand man, I'd have Mr Beale working for me any day.'

Billy blushed and looked away.

'I don't know what I would do without him.' She caught Billy's eye and smiled, then drew her attention back to Caldwell. 'Will Watkins get any help? I believe his is a case for Broadmoor, where he should undergo a thorough psychiatric evaluation and orthopaedic therapy.'

'You really think that gammy leg can be dealt with?'

Maisie nodded. 'It'll take time – the indoctrination started so early there is muscle atrophy – but I think it can be reversed.'

'I can't get over it, how a woman could do that to her son.'

'You should tell him what Dr Blanche said about it,' offered Billy.

'Well?' prompted Caldwell. 'What did old Blanche say?'

Maisie rubbed her forehead, gauging how to relay the details in the nutshell of a response preferred by Caldwell. 'Beattie Watkins would have discovered her pregnancy after receiving news of her husband's death in 1918 – the shock of both had a terrible impact on her speech, and she lost the ability to communicate verbally with ease. I suspect Ronnie became her entire focus even before he was born – as one might expect. However, it seems the depth of her grief had a profound effect on how she brought up her son – it had clearly sent her to the brink of madness. Her intense need for him to remain close to her was damaging in the extreme, for both of them. In short, she didn't want to lose him, whether to an accident, an illness, or to any life he might forge on his own, and she certainly didn't want to see him march off to war. This desire on her part became pathological, so she used any means to keep him at her side from babyhood onward, and without conscious consideration of the outcome. I suspect his medical history might reveal a turned ankle as a very small boy, or something similar that a child might recover from quickly, but she kept him in a state of . . . of disability. If you tell someone they are in pain often enough, they will feel pain. Maurice wrote extensively about the sort of psychological—'

'All right, all right, that's the magic no-no word for me – soon as I hear "psychological" my brain shuts off and I get all psychological myself. But I've followed you, Miss

Dobbs – poor old Ronnie was brainwashed. He was the bird who was never allowed to find his wings – so he went after anyone who had wings when they got close enough to the ground.'

'Yes, that's just about it.'

'And then we throw in the Yanks, those two coming over and controlling him to get what they wanted – which was someone who could look out for them and run their errands,' said Billy. 'I reckon we'll find out that Ronnie was bright enough to get them all sorts of information, what with him being in the Home Guard.' He turned to Maisie. 'And you were right about his mum keeping an eye on the gaff where the Yanks were living – they'd got themselves a little cottage down a road that didn't see much traffic.'

'That's where I saw her with their motor car.'

'It's one for the books, make no mistake about that, Miss Dobbs,' said Caldwell. 'Now then, want me to run you back to your motor car?'

'I think Billy and I will walk, it's not that far. But thank you for the offer.'

Caldwell touched his forehead by way of marking his departure. 'Tomorrow in my office nice and early to get your statements?'

'Early-*ish*, Superintendent. About eleven o'clock?' said Maisie.

'Suits me. Right then, I'm off. Got to get this little trio registered at one of His Majesty's fine accommodations.'

Maisie and Billy watched Caldwell depart.

'Accommodations?' said Billy. 'That's a new one –

Holloway prison for her, and I reckon Brixton nick for the other pair.'

Maisie nodded. 'That's about the measure of it – I hope mother and son are both transferred to secure institutions where they will get help. Come on, Billy – let's go home. If I put my foot down, we might be able to meet the girls at the bus stop.'

'Darling.' Mark Scott took Maisie by the arm as he met her just outside the embassy. 'Are you OK? Your call left my head spinning yesterday – our intelligence guys are kicking themselves for not picking up the connection between Beattie Watkins and the guy we have in our custody.'

Maisie's head was spinning as well. The past twenty-four hours had passed in a whirlwind: supper and a troubled sleep at the Dower House, followed by an early morning train to London with Billy for interviews and the signing of sworn statements at Scotland Yard. She was relieved to see her husband.

'I guess someone changed a name somewhere along the line,' continued Scott. 'Turns out he's a Watkinson, according to our records. We're tracking the movements of him and his sidekick – his name is Richard Robbins – from the time they left the USA and put their feet on British soil. And we're rounding up their connections Stateside. They've been here a while, so we don't know whether they were dispatched on some sort of other nefarious business and were redirected to the Roosevelt job, or whether that was their intention from the outset.'

'What you might call the grand unravelling,' said Maisie. 'When do we meet the colonel?'

'We'll go over to military headquarters now – just next door, same place where you met Crittenden. Shouldn't take long. It'll be the usual let's-lay-it-all-out-on-the-table talk, and he'll give us the latest on Stone and Crittenden.'

Maisie nodded. 'Good. I've to prepare a report for my client – she telephoned the house early this morning and is due at the office at—' she checked her watch '—half past four.'

'I'll bring home a nice bottle of wine tonight, hon. I'm looking forward to an evening alone, just the two of us at the flat, relaxing. I've forgotten what that feels like.'

'Me too, Mark. Me too. It'll be lovely.' She nodded towards the door. 'Come on, let's get the job finished, shall we?'

'Mrs Scott.' Colonel Wright held out his hand towards Maisie as they entered his personal office, escorted by a military policeman. 'Though I've been corrected again by my secretary and reminded that you should be referred to as "Miss Dobbs" when acting in your professional capacity – I'm sorry.'

Maisie inclined her head. 'I try to keep something of a barrier between my working and home life, though sometimes that division crumbles.'

'It sure does,' added Mark Scott.

The colonel smiled and gestured towards two chairs positioned in front of his desk, which was as plain as his office. An American flag hanging behind the desk offered the only splash of colour. He gave a single nod towards the military policeman, who left the room. Resting his arms on the desk, he drew his attention to Mark Scott.

'Scott, I've received your briefing paper this morning – only had a chance to cast my eyes over it, but let's hear the basic details on who those guys were and how the heck Privates Stone and Crittenden got themselves mixed up with them.'

Mark Scott cleared his throat. 'As you know, Colonel, the two men, Watkinson and Robbins – the latter now deceased – were members of a splinter group allied with the America First organisation. We know they supported the Nazi regime before the war, and we know they continued their sympathies following Pearl Harbour, though with not so much visibility. No more big jamborees in New York with the swastika flying. The Justice Department had been keeping an eye on them, but – let's be honest within these four walls – it can't have eyes everywhere, because there's just not the manpower. Now, there's evidence to indicate that the organisation circled Stone because his father – a pastor – has become outspoken in support of an end to segregation. They've had their eye on him. To be honest, so have our people back home, and—'

'Just a minute,' said Maisie. 'Why have you had your eye on Stone's father for speaking out on something so . . . so . . .'

'Maisie—' said Mark.

The colonel interjected. 'We're not here to debate what's right or wrong with how things are done in parts of the United States, Miss Dobbs. Over here you have all these different classes that people don't seem to marry out of and places where your "lower orders" can't get into; and we have a more formal segregation – it's just how it is. At the moment.'

Maisie felt her cheeks redden. 'I'm sorry. It's just . . . anyway, yes please go on.'

'Scott?' said the colonel.

'Right, yes. As I was saying, the group to which Watkinson and Robbins belonged had the Reverend Stone in their sights, but instead of burning down his church or threatening his safety, they discovered his son had shipped out with the United States Army. Anticipating the presence of a high-level visitor from the States on British soil at some point following our declaration of war on the Axis powers, they sent over a couple of agitators. It was a fortuitous crossing of paths that led them to Private Stone, that's for sure. Those agitators thought they could manipulate the man by threatening to take the life of his father, telling him that they had Stone senior and the mother under surveillance and unless he helped them, the entire family could expect to meet their maker.'

The colonel shook his head. 'As if a war isn't enough, we have these killers on the loose.'

'OK, winding it up. There was the unexpected friendship with Matthias Crittenden, and when things started to unravel – Watkinson and his pal had begun to realise that their plan had holes everywhere – the conspirators made one mistake after another. As we know, they kidnapped Stone after he'd heard them in the local pub, though we believe they would have found him anyway. When Stone didn't immediately do as he was told, they left Crittenden to take the fall for Stone's disappearance, and he could have died in that barn in any case. They believed Stone could be of use, because their next idea was for him to be part of an assassination attempt on Rover – they used a threat against his family, but the kid just couldn't kill. You saw him outside the embassy, Maisie.'

Maisie saw the fatigue evident in her husband's eyes as he took a breath before continuing his account.

'Then there's the Watkins family, Ronnie Watkins and his mother. They were just a couple of locals swept along for the ride because they could be useful. It's evident that *Watkinson* was chosen for the job by the splinter group because there was a local connection he could put to work and a place to hide out easily procured – and that place was convenient for London and Canterbury, both on Rover's itinerary. But the Ronnie they thought they'd use as a gopher turned out to be a lot to handle, because the kid had a short fuse – and he sure took a shine to the firearms stockpiled by the American side of the family. We've found a lot of weaponry hidden along those railroad tracks.' He paused. 'The biggest problem was that we were dealing with inconsistent bunglers, and that made them even more dangerous than a professional hit man.'

The colonel nodded and looked at Maisie. 'I've received a report from Detective Chief Superintendent Caldwell and have been in touch with the commissioner over at Scotland Yard. There's transparency at the highest level, as appropriate with regard to our responsibilities here as allies of the United Kingdom.'

'Thank you,' said Maisie. 'Mr Beale and I provided our official statements this morning.'

'I guess that's about it.' The colonel stood up. 'Though we'll be talking to the general later, Scott.'

Mark Scott nodded, and pushed back his chair.

'Colonel, I don't think we've quite finished,' said Maisie, who remained seated. 'I'm very interested in the future plans for Private Crittenden, if that's something you can tell me.'

Colonel Wright looked at Maisie, and for a moment she thought he might decline to respond, but he took his seat again and looked down at the files on the desk. He selected one, opened it and removed a sheet of paper.

'Miss Dobbs, the situation regarding Private Matthias Crittenden was brought to the attention of the First Lady. Now, though you've met her, I don't know what you might know about our military or Mrs Roosevelt, but she has been a supporter of bringing . . . how can I put this?' He tapped the desk with his forefinger, as if planning a careful response. 'She supports bringing greater opportunities to black enlistees in our military. She has been particularly vocal after experiencing a flight piloted by a black aviator, who she deemed excellent at his job. Mrs Roosevelt has therefore suggested that Private Crittenden should be transferred to the Tuskegee air base in Alabama. He has shown a flair for mechanics, and we have concluded that he might well be suited to training as an aircraft technician, which would also afford him opportunity after the war.' He paused to offer a wry smile. 'And the bottom line is that if Mrs Roosevelt wants something, she can be very, very persuasive.'

'I'm glad she is. My colleague, Mr Beale, has a son doing a similar job with the RAF.'

The colonel nodded. 'I think we're making the best of a bad situation, given our limitations, Miss Dobbs. Crittenden will be returning to the United States shortly, though given the way the war is developing, I believe it's entirely likely he will see these shores again soon enough.'

'And Private Stone?'

'Honourable discharge. Though he is showing great improvement, our doctors have told us he will no longer be fit for service. He can go home, I would imagine, in about three weeks, maybe a month. I understand he will follow in his father's footsteps and intends a path in the ministry. Maybe he'll join us again, become a military padre.'

'I'm glad to hear he's improving,' said Maisie, as she came to her feet and extended her hand to the colonel.

'A pleasure, Miss Dobbs.'

Maisie turned to leave, but stopped. 'Oh, one thing, Colonel – a request, if I may?'

'Try me – I can only say no.'

'My stepmother is a member of the Women's Voluntary Service – you may have read about the sterling work women across the nation are doing in bombed-out areas especially, and Mrs Roosevelt is very taken with their work – she's a friend of the founder, Lady Stella Reading. Anyway, my stepmother told me they are encouraging British people to invite young American GIs to their homes, a gesture of friendship to help assuage their feelings of homesickness. The same has been done for troops over here from the Empire, though many of those men already have relatives in Britain. I would therefore like to invite Private Stone, if he's well enough, and Private Crittenden to our house in Kent for a Sunday lunch before they depart for the United States. We call it "Sunday dinner", but we usually sit down at around one or two in the afternoon and we sometimes have quite a nice crowd, though the quality and variety of food might not be what your men are used to.'

'Yes, you're right about us welcoming the invitations to join a family meal, Miss Dobbs, but they're restricted to white military personnel only.' The colonel held up his hand as he saw Maisie move to speak. 'But given the circumstances, I guess I might be able to push it along the line and make an exception.'

'Do try,' said Maisie. 'Yes, please do try to push it along the line.'

A taxi dropped Maisie in Fitzroy Square, but she decided not to go into the office straightaway. She had half an hour before Jo Hardy was due to arrive. Taking a key from her document case, she unlocked the gate to the square's garden, walked across the grass and seated herself on a bench. An earlier shower seemed to have brought out the loamy fragrance of turned soil and fallen leaves, a respite from the ever-present odour of cordite from the previous night's bombing. Now the sun filtered through cloud and she felt the day's conversations and revelations seeping from her body and spirit into the earth.

She heard the clang of the gate open and shut, but kept

her eyes closed, even as she felt the bench shift under the weight of someone joining her.

'Miss?'

'Just taking a moment, Billy.'

'Been a rough old time, eh?'

She shrugged. 'I think it's harder getting to the bottom of crimes committed by complete incompetents than it is when the killer has a grain or two of common sense.'

'Easier to follow the clever bloke than the idiot, because the idiot is all over the place.'

Maisie opened her eyes and studied the man who had been working alongside her for years now.

'How do you fare, Billy?'

'Head above water, miss. Head above water.' He met her gaze. 'I try not to think about it, but it's terrible having to go through this war business a second time, eh?'

She nodded, consulted her watch and turned to Billy once more.

'The girls seemed to get on very well with the teacher in Plaxtol.'

'Oh, Margaret Rose was full of it. But what do you reckon will happen about the school? Something's got to change, because my girl's not going back to that nonsense, teasing about the way she talks and her being a Londoner.'

'It'll change, Billy.' Maisie came to her feet. 'Mark my words, it'll change. It might not happen fast enough for us, though I'm going to try to do something about it this week.' She looked through the trees towards the office. 'Come on – I can see Jo Hardy walking towards the front door now. One more meeting, and this case is finished.'

'You mean the *cases* are finished. And then you'll do your final accounting and move on to the next thing.'

'The next thing, Billy?'

'You should see the pile of post upstairs. And I bet old Caldwell will have something for you soon – let's hope it's only the British we have to deal with. I like the Americans and all that, but, well, you know, they're over here from over there.'

'Billy—'

'Sorry miss. Forgot myself.' He grinned. 'And we're very happy to have them with us, no two ways about it.'

As Maisie concluded her recounting of events leading to the closure of the case, Jo Hardy stood up from the chair in front of the floor-to-ceiling window and stared out across the square. Maisie remained seated while Billy came to his feet and left the room, stopping to take the tea tray with him.

'I can't believe it. Erica and possibly even Nick were brought down by a damaged boy with a gun. And he almost got me too. Let's face it, however old he was, he was still a boy due to his selfish mother. Stupid woman turned him into a killer with a chip on his shoulder because he couldn't bloody fly! It beggars all belief.'

Maisie watched the anger rise in her client. 'The manipulated mind can be dangerous, Jo. And do try to remember – grief was at the heart of her coercion.'

'Manipulated mind? The chain of events you've described is full of manipulated minds. Those lunatics who came here thinking they could do what they liked, and while they were about it they demonstrated what a manipulated mind can do to a poor man who just happens to be a different colour.' She paused. 'Mind you, I must admit it's made me wonder about my grandfather.' She turned to Maisie. 'When I think about it, my flying lessons were paid for out of my father's cheque book, but in truth they were financed by the success of the old man's tea plantations in India. I never considered it before, but I'm thinking about it now.'

Maisie did not reply, but came to her feet ready to absorb the tumult of Jo Hardy's bottled-up sorrow as it replaced her anger. She held on to Hardy until the racking sobs subsided, supporting the still-shaking woman until she took her seat once more.

'I didn't know what I was asking when I came to you, Maisie,' whispered the aviatrix. 'I had no idea I was opening a can of worms on this scale, that the heartbreak of losing Nick that I'd replaced with work would come home to roost like this. When I saw that man, Matthias Crittenden, I was already so angry, I just had to do something. It was the helplessness in his eyes – and look where it's taken us. And where it's taken you.' She stopped speaking to draw breath. 'If you'd have known, would you have turned me down?'

Maisie shook her head while handing Jo Hardy a fresh linen handkerchief. 'No,' she replied. 'No, I wouldn't have turned you down, because this is not the first case that came in like an iceberg.'

'An iceberg?' Jo frowned, wiping her eyes.

'Only seven percent of it visible above the surface.'

Hardy laughed. 'We women take on the hardest jobs, don't we?'

Maisie nodded. 'I couldn't do your job though, Jo.'

'And as I told you before, Maisie – I couldn't do yours.'

Maisie was thoughtful. 'You know, Jo, I have a young daughter, Anna. I can only hope she grows up with your strength and fortitude. I'm not sure how I would feel if she told me she intended to become a pilot when she grows up, but I very much want Anna to set her sights high, so whatever she does in life, she can fly.'

CHAPTER TWENTY-ONE

'What do you actually do, you know, when you go about your final accounting, miss?' asked Billy. 'I mean, I have an idea, but I reckon I don't quite understand it all.'

They were seated in Maisie's office at the long table set perpendicular to her desk, a pile of opened letters and plain postcards bearing handwritten messages before them. 'Do you just sort of see people, have a chat, say goodbye and that's it – job done?'

Maisie laughed and pushed a letter towards Billy. 'This is one for you – a household security case,' she said, sitting back in her chair. 'It's more than that, Billy. I've always thought it's a bit like washing the laundry, hanging it out to dry and then folding it before putting it away in the linen cupboard. It tidies up the whole case in our minds. And we learn from it.'

'Not sure I follow, miss, and I've worked with you for years.'

She leaned forward, pulling up the sleeves of her cream silk shirt lest they catch on the wood, then rested her arms on the table. 'As you know, at some point after we've completed our work on a case, when all reports are done and hopefully we've received payment for the account, I visit people and places pertinent to the investigation. When I have the opportunity to speak to someone whose path I've crossed in the execution of my work, perhaps an individual who has had a distinct impact on how I see each problem, of course I welcome the opportunity to acknowledge them, even if it's only to say a simple "thank you" before moving on.'

'But what about places?'

'Place is a crucial factor in our work – and places leave their mark in the same way that a human being can touch us.' She held her hand to her chest. 'We have to make our peace with place, with the locations where we have spent time. We consider how we've been affected by being present in a certain spot – and how the place itself is changed by what has come to pass. You only have to visit a battlefield long after a war has ended, to know that places are never quite the same following a tragedy.'

'I think I get it, miss.'

Maisie smiled, adding, 'Sometimes you'll be looking for a clue, an indication of what might be your next step in the case, and you might not even know what it is, but in that place, wherever it is, you know something is there for you to view, to hear or understand. And then perhaps a sudden breeze blows through, causing a tree to bend, which in turn allows you to see the unexpected, and you realise you've been given the gift of another building block in your understanding of the investigation.'

'Yeah, I see what you mean – the wind blows, the tree moves and then you can see a water mill on the other side of a river that you didn't see before,' said Billy. 'What do you do – thank the wind?'

'A quick sign of gratitude to the wind wouldn't go amiss. Or you could look up and thank the barn owl who screeches at you because you're about to touch something that makes a noise she hates, and that thing under your fingertips turns out to be something very important, a vital clue.'

'You thank a barn owl?'

'Don't put it past me, Billy – I've done stranger things.'

'Hmm, I've noticed that when you've put cases to bed, something changes around here. Like emptying a bucket of dirty water down the drain after washing the floor. Everything's fresh again.'

'That's a good way of looking at it, Billy. Now then, we've got some work to get through here and then we can catch the train back to Chelstone. We'll make some more progress on this lot in Maurice's library tomorrow.'

'You still call it "Maurice's library" sometimes, don't you, miss?'

'It's a reminder of all I have to be thankful for, and perhaps something more important.'

'What's that?'

'The basics, I suppose. It reminds me that we can never forget our earliest lessons. If we think we know it all, we become complacent.' She was thoughtful for a moment, then continued. 'There was something I read in Maurice's notes, when I was fumbling around, trying to get to grips with what had happened in the case of Ronnie Watkins and his mother. I came across a page or two that Maurice had written about the roots of a crime, what he called the "provenance of human behaviour".'

Maisie closed her eyes for a second, summoning the exact words. 'He said it was almost like meeting a patient with a debilitating illness that manifests in what at first seems like a series of unrelated symptoms. With further investigation, there is the realisation that one untreated ailment has led to another, which has led to another, so now the physician becomes a detective, because at this point every one of those layered conditions must be treated separately, yet with care because they have adhered together.'

'Just like this case. Started with one death, and all them roots got caught up in a tangle.'

'That's the measure of it,' said Maisie.

'So when will you see that blimmin' headmistress? She's a bit of a tangled old root, if ever I saw one.'

'You have a way with words, Billy, I'll give you that! I'm returning to Chelstone as soon as we're finished here, so I'll see her after I've taken Anna to the bus stop tomorrow morning. I've made an appointment.'

'I hope you tell her off good and proper. I reckon we should've gone straight to the school board about her, because I don't think a woman with that sort of chip on her shoulder can change how she does her job.'

'I want to give her a chance.'

'A chance for what?'

Maisie shrugged. 'I suppose a chance to relinquish her attachment to a life bound by the rage she keeps locked inside. I want to give her a chance to be free of her past.'

The following morning, Maisie waved to the two girls, who had taken their usual seats at the back of the bus so they could indulge in their new game of pulling monster faces at their parents, who waited until the bus rounded the corner at the end of the high street before going on their way.

'I've got to get back to the bungalow,' said Doreen Beale. 'We had a letter from Bobby yesterday. He might be discharged in a week or two and able to convalesce at home, and he said he would try to give us a bell this morning. Now Billy's waiting by the telephone, willing it to ring.' She shook her head. 'He keeps lifting the receiver to make sure the line's still connected.'

'We're all anxious to hear good news, Doreen, so let us know how Bobby fares.'

'I will – must dash now. Good luck with that old ratbag over at the school!'

Maisie dressed with care that morning, thankful for Priscilla's determination to find a 'good little seamstress' upon moving to a cottage in the village. Priscilla's handy needlewoman, Mrs Drury, had come to Maisie's aid, tailoring a matching navy blue coat and dress ensemble purchased years earlier and rendering it somewhat more stylish and fitted to Maisie's frame than the drape fashionable when she bought the costume. Maisie complemented her choice with navy blue shoes and carried her document case. On this occasion she decided to forgo a hat, instead using silver combs to draw her hair from her face, given that all efforts to tame it into an up-to-the-minute pageboy style had failed.

The children were in their classrooms when Maisie walked along the empty corridor and knocked on a wooden door with a frosted glass window marked with the single word 'Secretary'. An older woman, perhaps in her mid-fifties, opened the door. Maisie noticed she was shaking.

'My name is Miss Maisie – sorry, my name is Mrs Scott. I'm here to see the headmistress.'

'Right you are, Mrs Scott.' The secretary smiled, as if attempting to lighten the atmosphere. 'I'm from the village, Mrs Scott, so I know you're not twelve months married. I'm hardly surprised you'd forget yourself every now and again. All new brides do it. I'll let—'

'Mrs Wood! Mrs Wood, this letter to the inspector—' a voice bellowed from beyond an open door to the right. 'Come into my office now so we can sort this out immediately. It's utterly appalling, and it must be corrected before that foreign child's mother gets here, hopefully not with the dreadful American in tow. You've caused an inexcusable waste of my time!'

Maisie raised an eyebrow and looked at the secretary, who whispered, 'I'm so sorry – she's very busy. I'll tell her you're here.'

Maisie put a hand on the woman's arm and winked. 'Not to worry, Mrs Wood. You should make yourself a nice cup of tea and sit back for five minutes. I'll see myself in, and I might well be a while.'

'Oh dear, she'll—'

'No,' said Maisie. 'She won't.'

'Mrs Wood – come here at once!' The voice grew more insistent.

Maisie smiled as she stepped towards the door leading to the headmistress's office. 'Good morning, Miss Patterson. I'm glad you remembered my appointment.' She closed the door behind her and without receiving an invitation to do so, took a seat.

The woman before her, clothed in an austere grey jacket atop a black skirt, said nothing, her rounded lips forming an O.

'Now then, let's get started, shall we?' said Maisie.

The headmistress took her seat on the other side of the desk and cleared her throat to speak, but Maisie did not allow an interjection.

'I am here on several counts. Number one, on a personal level I would like to discuss your treatment of my daughter. Second, I will broach the subject of two pupils, now grown, who were in your care and who, as a result of bullying tactics on your part not befitting a teacher, have been wounded to a damaging extent. Admittedly your negative contribution to their lives is not the prime reason one of them went on to commit crimes, but it was without doubt a factor. The issue of the cause of your conduct is of some concern.'

'I don't know what you're talking about, but regarding Anna—'

'Yes, let's start with Anna. Since the day you assumed the position of headmistress at this school, my daughter has gone from being a happy child, confident in her lessons

382

and her ability to form friendships with other children, to a child who has shown the hallmarks of being physically and verbally attacked.'

'You can't blame that on me – blame the Italians! Children know what's going on in the world, and they hear their parents talking, so they understand why we in Britain do not trust Italians.'

'Quite apart from your misguided interpretation of the situation, you have been woefully misinformed regarding my child's background, though that is no excuse for allowing other children – and their parents – to demonstrate such prejudice towards Anna. There is blame on the side of those parents, but this is a sensitive time for everyone, and you took advantage of it in an act of extreme spite. Let me say it again. *Spite.* Please do not deny it. In any case, Anna was perfectly happy and nothing untoward was ever suggested regarding her background until you decided to make something of it.'

'Mrs Scott, this is what I have learned over the years and what I bring to my position here – children must be prepared for adult life. They must be made hard enough to withstand the knocks and disappointments that come when they leave school – most of them will be working at fourteen, and that demands a thick skin. They cannot be soft. When I discover a child has an Achilles' heel, I believe it is better for them to be prepared for the slings and arrows of circumstance sooner rather than later. I create a strong childhood backbone.'

'Two things,' countered Maisie, feeling her temper rising. 'It is your job to see that my child receives a well-rounded academic education appropriate to her age, and that she is both enthusiastic and disciplined in her schoolwork.'

'Mrs Scott—'

'I haven't finished yet, headmistress! It is my job and that of Anna's father and her extended family to ensure she has emotional balance, that she has strength of spirit and she has love. Anna has known more tragedy than most of her age, and she has weathered her storms. She is confident and has all the support she needs as a growing child. She is very tightly held.'

'Exactly my point. It never did anyone good to have that confidence, as I have made clear. When she goes out into the world, life will try to knock it out of her, and—'

'Your inability to regain your balance after a terrible loss is not a good enough reason for you to manipulate the lives of the young – very young – people in your charge.'

'I – I . . . I don't know what you're talking about. Mrs Scott, in the circumstances, I must ask you to leave—'

'Captain Robert Bridges was wounded in the early summer of 1915. He was brought to the London hospital under cover of darkness – the injured were transported home at night, so people wouldn't know the terrible cost of the Spring Offensive. He died a few days later. His shattered fiancée sat by his bedside every single hour, refusing to move because he was screaming in intense pain, despite the great amount of morphia injected into him. He knew a terror beyond all description, and the woman who thought she would be his bride was crushed because she could not help him. In truth, he should have perished on the battlefield, so terrible was the trauma to his body.'

'How—?'

'Your grief was intense. You did not know how to go on. Yet there were so many women in your position. Some bore their anguish; they wore black for a full twelve months, then they dressed in lavender to let all know they were ready to enter the world again. Yet you remained in that terrible abyss, screaming because you could barely endure your loss, and when you could scream aloud no longer, I believe you screamed inside because the well of your misery was so deep. You returned to the role of teacher, but your mind had become poisoned to a point where you even harboured an envy of children for being born, for existing, for being happy little souls, and you began to torment those around you because if you could not attain a state of personal equilibrium, then no one else would.'

Patterson stared at Maisie. 'And how would you think you know anything about me?'

'You have Anna's details in a file here. My profession is listed – I am a mother with a job, after all. My role requires me to find things out. I investigate. That's what I do. And I solve problems. You are a very big problem in my daughter's life, and I had to solve it with the skills I have to hand.'

'I stand by my methods. I – I believe that people must . . . people must . . .'

Maisie came to her feet.

'There are two ways out of this dilemma, Miss Patterson. You could change your ways, to the extent that you are able. Or you will resign your position. If neither of those things happen, I have strings I can pull. Please do not underestimate me, because I can pull very, very hard on those strings. I hope you might apply for a leave of absence

385

to reconsider your position, make your peace with the past and then return with a renewed sense of what in loco parentis means.'

'Your daughter won't have an easy life, Miss Dobbs.'

'My daughter is a beautiful, adored child, so do not worry about her life ahead because she has a veritable army of people who will be there to catch her if she falls. And to correct you – because obviously you've made a terrible error somewhere along the way – her lovely olive complexion, black hair and deep brown eyes are due to her Maltese heritage. Oh, and one more thing.' Maisie pointed to the newspaper on the desk in front of Patterson. 'You've obviously not had an opportunity to cast your eyes over the news much lately, but do find the column about the little girl who represented her country while Mrs Eleanor Roosevelt was in London. That child is Anna. She is a credit to us all.' Maisie turned to leave, but Patterson called to her.

'Mrs Scott – how did you know . . . about Captain Bridges?'

'I think you would agree, Miss Patterson, that in our busy lives women like you and I – women who work for a living – cross paths with people in the course of our daily round who are unforgettable. That said, do you remember the young nurse who stood beside you and did not return to her lodgings at the end of her long shift, because she was fearful for your wellbeing? She was still in training – and yes, sometimes incredibly inept, given her youth. But she knew a broken heart when she saw it.'

'Vaguely. Yes, I think so. She had silly hair that kept

slipping out of her veil, that sort of cap they wore. It made nurses look like nuns. Yes, I remember her now. Clumsy thing.'

'That nurse was me. Within a few months I was doing my job in a casualty clearing station close to the front, thankfully with more dexterity than was evident when I was a probationer.' Maisie paused. 'I know what a terrible death looks like because I saw it hundreds of times.' She watched the headmistress absorb her words. 'Do your best for my daughter and for Margaret Rose Beale, with her cheeky London accent that you have found it necessary to criticise, and make amends for any other child you have verbally assaulted in this school. And think hard about how you treated a boy named Ronnie Watkins at your last school. You are far from the only reason he is now in prison, but the fact that you tried to toughen him up for what you perceived to be the wicked world outside the school contributed to his pathology.' She looked at the woman before her. 'Anna will return to her class only if I hear sterling reports of Chelstone Primary School. In the meantime, other arrangements have been made for her education.' She paused as she reached for the door handle. 'You could start by apologising to your secretary.'

Walking away from the school in the direction of the Dower House, Maisie felt a knot in her stomach, as if the fire at her core was still smouldering. While she had said what she wanted to say to Patterson, it had not diminished the anger that had taken root when she realised her daughter was being bullied, and the fact that she blamed herself for her ignorance of its insidious source. Now there was only one way she could extinguish the flame, and that was by immersing herself in her family and the task of her final accounting. She would do as much as she could to douse the embers of the angry blaze, the sickness she had felt from the moment Jo Hardy told her about an American soldier named Matthias Crittenden, a man with bright blue eyes that seemed to speak his truth before he even opened his mouth.

Instead of returning to her home, she took the path around the side of the manor house and entered the garage.

'George, I promise I won't need the Alvis for a while after today, but I wondered . . . how much petrol do we have in the tank, and do you think I could have the motor, just for the afternoon?'

George pointed to the Alvis. 'Been doing a full engine overhaul on her, Mrs Scott. Big engine like that, you've got to look after it.'

'Oh dear—' said Maisie.

'But I tell you what I have got.' He inclined his head for Maisie to follow him. 'Your secretary brought in the MG and asked if I would give the old girl an oil change. She didn't really need it, but the lady likes to keep up maintenance on the motor car, especially as you gave it to her.'

'Oh George – that's wonderful.'

'The MG is outside because she had a good wash and polish first thing. I gave the tyres a once-over. And there's petrol in the tank.'

'Thank you, George.'

'Be nice to her – that little motor is no spring chicken.' He grinned. 'Mind you, I reckon she could do with having you put your toe down a bit, because she was meant to blow away the cobwebs every now and again.'

'I'm off now, George,' said Maisie. 'Back by four.'

CHAPTER TWENTY-TWO

B ehind the wheel of the MG, Maisie felt as if time itself had melted away and she was just starting out again. She had purchased the motor car from Lady Rowan years before, when the older woman declared that due to an old hunting injury, driving had become somewhat difficult for her. The MG had given Maisie freedom, not only from the inconvenience of trying to work while using public transport, but because she felt as if she were truly her own woman, able to go where she wanted at the drop of a hat. On 'top down' days, when she rolled back the roof and felt the wind in her hair, it was as if she were leaving all cares in her wake.

The Alvis was a fast vehicle, much admired by those who saw Maisie behind the wheel, but the MG had been her first motor car – her first ticket to the open road. As she slipped the MG into gear and drove through the Chelstone Manor gates, she thought she might know how Jo Hardy and those other ferry pilots felt as they lifted their aircraft into the skies above. It was the thrill of freedom.

Maisie visited Dan Littlecombe's now boarded-up garage and moved on to the Watkins' run-down terrace house. Having made her peace with what had come to pass in those places, she drove along the narrow road taking her past the cottage where the Americans had found refuge, aided by Beattie Watkins. From there she made her way to Barney Love's farm. She parked the motor car and walked to the front door, rapping her knuckles against the paint-chipped wood.

'Miss Dobbs,' said Love, as he opened the door. 'Didn't expect to see you again, not now it's all out about what happened on my farm! I tell you, I've had everyone stomping across my fields – reporters, police, a few more Yanks here and there. It's been like a blimmin' circus out there.'

'They'll leave you alone soon enough, and I believe you will be due compensation for any losses to your crops. But I wondered, is Madge Starling out of hospital?'

'Coming home to the farm later today. She telephoned from the hospital yesterday and asked if she could recuperate here and the missus told me to get in the van this afternoon to fetch the girl home. I'll be bringing her back here because it wouldn't do her any good being sent up there to the Smoke, what with all them bombs and the sort of people she comes from. She'll have a room upstairs until she's all better – and she deserves it, when you think of what she's gone through.'

'I'm glad you'll be looking after her.'

'The other ladies said they'll be in to help, and Madge says she'll be back at work as soon as she's up and about. I reckon it'll do her the power of good, getting out there into the fresh air. She likes it here.' The farmer rubbed his chin. 'I'll be sorry to see those women go at the end of the war. I wasn't sure about them at first, to tell you the truth – I thought I'd have shirkers wasting time all day, but those young ladies know how to graft. They roll up their sleeves and they get the jobs done – and mark my words, they do them well.'

Maisie agreed, and asked Love if she could walk across the field and down by the river.

'You can go anywhere you'd like, Miss Dobbs. I wouldn't venture near that barn though – it's cordoned off by the police, and there's an owl in there who gets a bit nasty when anyone goes near her.'

'Thank you, Mr Love – and I'll keep away from the barn.'

Maisie walked alongside the field, then to the stile that led into woodland flanking the river. She felt a deep autumn stillness envelop her as she moved farther into the wood, the ground underfoot thick with fallen leaves, a low afternoon sunlight fingering the fragmented canopy above. Water in the distance rushed by, as if the flow were in a hurry to become wider and stronger on its way to meet the sea. Soon she was alongside the river, her steps becoming heavier in the mud as she approached the fallen log ahead. She sat down facing the river to breathe in the chilled air and the thick vaporous aroma of wood, fertile loam and moss.

The faces of those she had met and questioned came to mind, as if to force her to look into their souls. How had she treated each human being? Had she considered their past with enough depth of insight and clarity of thought? What would be their reckoning, and what part had she played in the outcome of their lives as time went on? All these elements came to mind, not least her tone with Miss Patterson, the headmistress. Maisie had been disturbed by her cold response to the woman, though now she was even more taken aback by a lack of regret. Sometimes a shock was required to change a pattern of behaviour, and she hoped she had at least inspired self-reflection in the woman. Indeed, when recognition of their connection finally came to her, she had experienced a surprise of her own.

A screech from above disturbed Maisie's thoughts as a barn owl swooped low from the branches, over her head then up into another tree.

Maisie looked up at the owl. 'All right, all right. I know what you're telling me. It's time to leave. Time to go home.'

Maisie was putting finishing touches to a report when Billy called out from the main office.

'Miss – your godson, Tom, is on the blower. Wants a word with you. He says it's urgent.'

'Tom? Goodness, I wonder what he wants. I'll answer it in here, Billy.'

She reached for the telephone and heard a click as Billy replaced his receiver. She looked up as he began to close the inner door.

'Better close this, miss. There's a bloke working outside and making a right old racket with a hammer and I don't know what else. You can hear the banging coming up the stairs.'

Maisie nodded and brought her attention to the caller. 'Tom – what is it? Is something wrong with your mother? Is she all right?'

'Nothing's wrong with Maman,' said Tom. 'I wanted to speak to you, Tante Maisie. I need your help – well, I need help, and you're the only person I know who has the sort of contacts who could give me a hand.'

'Gosh, Tom, that sounds a bit suspicious. What can I do?'

'It's to do with making telephone calls overseas, and – well, you know, ordinary mortals can't do that sort of thing because of the war.'

'Hmm, yes, I think I'm with you. Go on.'

'Do you know anyone who can help me? Someone in power.'

'Could you be a bit more, well, specific, Tom?' Maisie twisted the receiver coil around her fingers as her godson explained his dilemma. 'I take it your mother—'

'Good Lord, no, Tante Maisie. Are you kidding?'

'You sound like an American.'

Tom laughed. 'Hardly surprising. You have your moments too now, Tante Maisie.'

'I'm sure I do. But Tom, regarding your mother – you realise there is a thin line between a surprise and a shock.'

'Tante Maisie—'

'All right, Tom. There's someone who may be able to

help, though I will now be in hock to him. He's not a man to let a debt go unpaid.'

'I can pay, Tante Maisie.'

Maisie laughed. 'Oh no, you can't afford this kind of arrears – it's never about money with Robert MacFarlane. Anyway, I will draw his attention to the debt the country owes you and your RAF pals. Telephone me again in about ten minutes, and with luck I'll have a contact for you.'

'Thank you, Tante Maisie. I knew you could help me.'

Maisie replaced the telephone receiver, waited a second, then picked it up again and began to dial.

'MacFarlane!'

'Good morning, Robbie. Maisie Dobbs here.'

'I knew who it was as soon as I heard your dulcet tones. What can I do for you? I can detect an "I want something" voice.'

'It's actually a favour for my eldest godson, Tom Partridge. Actually, he's now Flight Lieutenant Tom Partridge.' Maisie explained the situation, adding, 'I think we owe him this, don't you, Robbie?'

'One of the Few and all that? Yes, you're right. We do. Tell the boy to get in touch on this number and I'll pull some strings.'

'Thank you, Robbie – I won't forget it.'

'Neither will I, lass. Neither will I – you can depend on that!'

Billy was standing by the window when Maisie joined him in the outer office, having completed her telephone calls.

'I reckon whoever he is has finished doing whatever

he was doing down there. I just saw him walking along towards Warren Street, carrying his tool bag.'

'Let's go and look, shall we?'

'Look at what?'

'Just come with me, Billy!'

Billy frowned. 'All right. Better have a gander at what he's done to the front door. He could have been anyone fiddling with the locks. You never know what that landlord's been up to. I should've gone down there and asked the bloke what he was about.'

Outside, Maisie beckoned to Billy and gestured towards the front door. 'See anything different?'

Billy shrugged. 'Can't say as I can, miss. What am I supposed to be looking for?'

'This, Billy.' Maisie pointed to a brand-new brass plaque on the wall to the left of the door.

Billy was silent for some seconds as he stared at the plaque. 'Oh, miss. Miss—'

Maisie rested her hand on his shoulder. 'I told you, Billy. It's overdue. This is your specialty, after all.'

Maisie watched as Billy shook his head in disbelief, then walked towards the plaque and ran his fingers across the words engraved onto the brass.

M. DOBBS, PSYCHOLOGIST AND INVESTIGATOR

W. BEALE, SECURITY ADVISOR

FIRST FLOOR

* * *

As the date for the planned Sunday dinner attended by Private Matthias Crittenden approached, the number of guests had grown to the point where Maisie could see Brenda on the verge of panic.

'Everything will go off perfectly well, Brenda,' she assured her stepmother. 'Our guests will be delighted to be in company, so they will hardly notice any menu shortfalls.'

'And our boys always help out when they visit British people at home – that's why American soldiers get invitations to dinner,' said Mark Scott, entering the kitchen with Anna holding his hand and Little Emma following. 'We Americans always come bearing comestibles.'

'Yes, but what sort of comestibles? That's what I want to know,' said Brenda, hands on hips. 'We can't all eat chocolate and tinned peaches until they come out of our ears, and we can't digest nylon stockings either.'

'I'm sure the boys would like to try, especially if—'

'Mark . . . careful!' warned Maisie, smiling.

He laughed and put an arm around his wife. 'Coming for a walk with Anna, the hound and me? Get you out of Brenda's hair?'

'Yes, you can all get out of my hair now!' said Brenda. 'I've the ration book situation to consider. All I can say is, thank heavens everyone's chipping in and the butcher is helping us out too.'

Mark put a free arm around Brenda. 'You are my shining star, Brenda.'

Brenda blushed, pushing him aside. 'Go away now, you silly American man!'

Anna squealed, reaching for Maisie's hand and pulling

her mother and father along towards the door.

'Brenda's really in her element, isn't she?' said Mark as they walked along the path towards the stables.

'Loving every minute of it.'

With Mark at the carving end of the table, Maisie took her seat opposite. An old table had been brought from the shed so everyone could be seated, though two unlucky souls were required to put up with a bump where the two tables had been pushed together. Priscilla and Douglas were at lunch, plus Tom and Tim; Tarquin was working that Sunday. Jo Hardy had managed to get a day's leave – much to Tim's delight, as he claimed the seat next to her before Maisie was able to direct everyone to their places. Patty Hayden arrived with Tom, and Lady Rowan and Lord Julian were both present, as were Billy, Doreen, Margaret Rose and Bobby, his head bandaged and wearing a metal brace from his neck to his waist. He was seated next to Matthias Crittenden, who seemed to take it upon himself to aid him, plumping up the cushion at the back of his chair and heaping his plate with vegetables and Yorkshire pudding. Private Charles Stone was not in attendance after all, due to the onset of an infection that delayed his departure from the military hospital. Frankie and Brenda sat on either side of Anna, who was opposite Matthias. Two military policemen had brought Private Crittenden to the house and awaited to return him to his unit; Mark had warned Brenda against inviting them to the dining table, as they were on duty and would be happy with something to eat in the kitchen, and when done they would resume waiting outside in the motor car.

Tim had just started telling everyone that Brenda had made his favourite apple and blackberry pie for the pudding course when Maisie noticed Anna staring at Matthias Crittenden. She tried to attract her father's attention in the hope that he might distract his granddaughter from saying something that would embarrass them all, but her efforts failed and she held her breath when it became clear Anna could not be stopped.

'Mr Matthias – Mr Matthias!' Anna waved at the visitor.

Matthias Crittenden turned his attention from Bobby, who had been describing his job on the Lancaster.

'Yes, Miss Anna?'

'Mr Matthias, have you ever been called an "eye-tye"?'

Voices were lowered around the table. Maisie put a hand to her heart; she should have said something to Anna before they sat down, anything to circumvent the faux pas.

'Well no, no one has called me that name before, though I've been called some other names.'

'That's what they called me, at school. They said I looked like a rotten eye-tye.'

'Matthias, I am so sorry, I—' offered Maisie.

'No, ma'am, it's OK.' He smiled, and turned back to Anna. 'You know what my mama says to me, when people call me names?'

Anna stared at Crittenden, her eyes wide.

'My mama says people call us names because they don't have minds big enough to see inside at the size of our hearts. That's what she says.'

'Can you see my heart?'

'I sure can, young lady.'

'Do I have a big enough heart?'

Maisie looked at Priscilla, who had pulled a handkerchief from her sleeve and was dabbing her eyes so as not to smudge her make-up.

'You have a very big heart, Miss Anna,' said Crittenden. He looked around the table. 'Just like your people here.'

'Well, I'll drink to that,' said Priscilla, raising her glass. 'In fact, my poor old heart could do with a thumper of a gin and tonic at this very moment.'

Mark Scott looked across at Maisie and raised his eyebrows as if in relief, while Frankie Dobbs pushed back his chair and said that if Priscilla wanted a gin and tonic, she should have one.

Lord Julian cleared his throat. 'Now, I do hope someone has told you, Private Crittenden, that your name is very much a Kentish name. I'm interested to know what you might know about it.'

Lady Rowan began embellishing her husband's explanation with more details, adding that many of the earliest settlers in America came from the county. Soon the hubbub of voices around the table became louder, and from the odd word here and there, Maisie was aware of all manner of topics being discussed, from the plight of Americans of Japanese descent to the harvest this year, the sugar situation, the push into North Africa, and whether London would ever be herself again. Much was made of the fact that on the day after Mrs Roosevelt visited Canterbury Cathedral and the nearby village of Barham, the cathedral had been subject to intense bombing, the Germans having acted on faulty intelligence in a quest to take the life of the president's wife.

'They were a day late and a dollar short,' quipped Mark Scott, now in conversation with Douglas Partridge and two of the Canadian officers billeted at the manor.

Following the pudding course, Mark stood up to thank everyone for coming to Sunday dinner, adding that it was a fine thing to have a couple more Yanks at the table for a change, to even up representation from the British Empire. Glasses were raised to toast Crittenden's return to the USA and his new posting to Tuskegee in Alabama, and to Bobby and his recovery. There was another toast to honour Mark officially becoming Anna's father. As Mark took his seat, Tom Partridge stood up, tapping his glass with a spoon.

Priscilla looked at Maisie, a frown forming. She mouthed the word, 'What?'

Maisie shrugged, feigning ignorance.

'Ladies and gentlemen. Please charge your glasses – Mark, I'm sure you'll do the honours and get everyone topped up. I have an announcement to make. Well, *First Lieutenant* – let's not forget the title – First Lieutenant Patty Hayden and I have an announcement to make.' There was some muffled laughter around the table in anticipation of what might come next. 'I have asked Patty to be my wife, a proposal she has graciously accepted. Her father, Dr Charles Hayden, gave his permission when I requested her hand in marriage – Tante Maisie helped with that part.' He looked down at a blushing Patty Hayden. 'We're engaged – though before you ask, we must wait to be married until the war is over due to Patty's position with the American Army Nursing Corps here in England – I don't want her sent home for marrying a limey!'

Applause erupted. Maisie watched as Priscilla and Douglas made their way around the table and embraced their son and his bride-to-be, before Priscilla left them and approached Maisie, who had come to her feet and was holding out her arms to her friend.

'How could you not tell me?' said Priscilla, pulling back from Maisie's embrace.

'Pris, I knew only that Tom wanted to make a telephone call to the United States. Nothing more.'

'And that's a fib!' countered Priscilla. 'Oh, it doesn't matter, for goodness' sake,' she added, overcome with emotion. 'I fear for them, Maisie – it's so fast and they're so very young. And it looks as if I'll lose my firstborn to bloody Boston!'.

Maisie reached for her friend's hand. 'Today is a good day, darling Pris. You have three sons doing well and you're gaining a wonderful daughter. Think of Billy and Doreen and what they are enduring even now in the midst of this joy. There's been no word at all from their eldest.'

'Yes, of course. Stupid me. Always thinking of myself. I'm going back to my place, to my husband and my G and T. And I'm also keeping an eye on my second-born and that woman with her wings!'

EPILOGUE

Late November 1942

Jo Hardy studied the chit that had been handed to her as she waited for the day's instructions. She smiled. Her first job was to ferry a Spitfire to Biggin Hill. After landing, she would be collected by the Anson air taxi and taken to another airfield, where she would climb aboard a Wellington. Later she was scheduled to collect a Hurricane for delivery, followed by one more job – a flight on a Short Sterling. But first – the Spitfire. She had just enough time to make one telephone call before the air taxi took her to the factory to collect the aircraft. She dialled the number for the Dower House at Chelstone Manor, which was answered on the second ring.

'Maisie!'

'Jo – is that you?'

'Yes – I'm glad I caught you in Kent.'

'Why? Is everything all right?'

'Nothing to worry about – but listen, I've come up

with a brilliant idea. When I saw you in London, you said something about your daughter and how you wanted her to always reach for the skies. Well, I have a plan for a little exercise in inspiration.'

First Officer Jo Hardy of the Air Transport Auxiliary eased the Spitfire low over the fields of Kent and looked down at the barn where weeks before she had seen a man with a gun try to strike her aircraft – and take her life. She gained height, watching the barn become smaller, almost insignificant below, then descended once more, looping around to identify her landmarks and prepare her planned flight path. She checked the time. Her estimate had been bang on target. She was ready. More than ready.

Executing one more circuit of the farm, she set her direction towards the railway bridge. She felt like a bird on the wing, the Merlin engine filling her with confidence as she came in low, ready for the thrill. The woman and child were waiting – she could see them on the bridge, just as she'd instructed this morning. They had come.

Jo manoeuvred the Spitfire into position, then swooped down towards the bridge, screaming with the thrill of the moment, unable to keep the physical sensation bottled inside her body as she flew under the span, pulling up the nose and clearing the treetops on the other side. With the bridge and the past falling away behind her, she felt a boost in power as the carburettor thrust fuel into the engine, propelling the aircraft upward at speed. With dexterity and ease, Jo levelled the Spitfire, then came around and descended again, once more pinpointing the woman and her daughter before passing overhead, dipping her wings as they waved back with furious abandon, the girl using both hands and jumping up and down. Jō laughed. It felt good to laugh, and it was a very good day to fly a Spitfire.

With the skylarking over, she was on her way to deliver her charge in good order and on time, because this aircraft was needed for more serious business. A young RAF pilot would be waiting in anticipation, at the ready to climb into the cockpit to do his bit, risking his life for his country before coming in to land again. And again, God willing. Yet, for now, on her way to the airfield, Jo felt as if she were cruising the firmament, her hands light at the controls of the fastest fighter aircraft in the world, an aeroplane that was surely made for a woman, lifting her high into the sunlit skies.

AUTHOR'S NOTE

'Men take ownership of war and talk endlessly of their duty. I can't imagine why they don't think women feel such things too.'
Mary Ellis, née Wilkins
1917–2018

I love Mary's words, which seem to underline the commitment made by thousands of women during both World Wars – a commitment to duty and to country at a terrible time. Mary joined the Air Transport Auxiliary in 1941, having already learned to fly at age sixteen. During the war she made over one thousand flights in seventy-six different types of aircraft. She was also one of the first women to fly the Gloster Meteor, Britain's first jet aircraft.

I am sure a good number of readers are familiar with the history of Britain's Air Transport Auxiliary, a civilian organisation founded in 1939 under the administration of Gerard 'Pop' d'Erlanger, who was then head of British

Airways, which later became 'BOAC' (and later still, back to being British Airways). Commander Pauline Gower was given the task of organising the women's section of the ATA, with the first eight women pilots starting in January 1940. One of the early 'Atta girls' was American Jacqueline Cochran, who later returned to the USA, and with the support of Eleanor Roosevelt founded a similar organisation known as the Women Airforce Service Pilots – the WASPs. It should be underlined that while the women ferry pilots of the ATA garnered a lot of attention, they were still outnumbered by almost ten to one by male pilots, many of whom were veterans of the First World War or commercial pilots. However, as has been the case for many women throughout the years, they had to be at least as good as the men!

Though most writers of fiction will weave facts into the narrative when facts either inspire or support the story, as a group we're probably more interested in touching upon universal truths – which means we sometimes take a few wide turns with those facts. One wide turn that historians and aeronautical aficionados will recognise in *A Sunlit Weapon* is the mention of a female member of the ATA piloting a Lancaster bomber in 1942. Women were not assigned to ferry that particular aircraft until 1943. I moved the timeline up a bit, not least because I love the Lancaster. One fact I just had to weave in was that women members of the ATA were indeed the first government employees to achieve pay parity with men, again in 1943. Such developments were a far cry from the early experiences of the ATA's aviatrices, when they were assigned the worst ferrying jobs – flying in open cockpit training aircraft on freezing cold days. It was later that they were given Sidcot suits, which kept them a bit more comfortable. However, even as they moved on and up to other aircraft, the job remained one of the most dangerous in aviation, as the aircraft were not fitted with radios or any sort of defensive weaponry. In addition, many aircraft had to be ferried to maintenance depots or to the breakers yard – which meant they were far from airworthy. The weather could be a killer too.

Readers will have noticed references to 'aviatrices' – this is the traditional spelling and pronunciation of the plural of a word ending in 'x' and is a nod to those women of the ATA, who in memoirs referred to themselves collectively as aviatrices, not 'aviatrixes', which is how some readers might have expected the word to appear.

I always have a lump in my throat when I watch a newscast featuring Britain's 'RAF Battle of Britain Memorial Flight' – comprising a Hurricane, a Spitfire and a Lancaster (the three aircraft are part of major national events and State occasions). My curiosity regarding the ATA was piqued many years ago when a girl I worked with introduced me to her mother, who had been a member of the ATA. Later, I worked as assistant to a man who had been a Spitfire pilot during the war when he was eighteen years of age – he told me a few of his stories. Writers tend to squirrel away such meetings and conversations.

I hope I've managed to bring to the page something of the spirit and bravery of those women of the ATA, and indeed all women engaged in 'war work'. One of the documentary excerpts I watched as background research for this book, was an interview with Mary Ellis. She described one day ferrying a Spitfire, and because it was a lovely day, she took some time to herself to 'play in the clouds'. It was a reminder that it is the young, both men and women, who go to war. Nothing has changed in that regard, and so much is expected of them.

ACKNOWLEDGEMENTS

With this, the seventeenth novel in the series featuring Maisie Dobbs, I would like to thank the following for their support, not only with publication of *A Sunlit Weapon*, but in their understanding of what I wanted to create with the series – which was to follow a woman named Maisie Dobbs and her fellow characters as they navigate the many tumultuous events over a period of time encompassing two World Wars. I have always believed the mystery – that archetypal journey through chaos to resolution – to be the perfect vehicle with which to explore the human condition under pressure.

My utmost respect and gratitude goes to Amy Rennert, my long-time literary agent and dear friend. Jennifer Barth, senior vice president and executive editor at Harper, has been my editor for some fifteen years – her counsel is always spot on. Also at Harper, Katherine Beitner, director of publicity, is a brilliant publicist. I'm immensely grateful for the work of president of sales Josh Marwell and his stellar team. Thanks also to Tom Hopke and Sarah Ried.

In the UK I am blessed to have Susie Dunlop and her terrific team at Allison and Busby working to bring the Maisie Dobbs series to readers throughout the UK and Commonwealth – needless to say, I've missed seeing you all over the past couple of years.

Artist and craftsman Andrew Davidson created another stunning cover for the series – when I saw the sketches for *A Sunlit Weapon*, I could not have been more excited. Archie Ferguson's creative direction pulls everything together, and once again, Andrew and Archie – you have outdone yourselves! Thank you.

To my husband, John Morell – dedicating this book to your mum, 'First Loot' Margaret Morell, was one of my best decisions. I loved the twinkle in her eyes as she recounted her stories of being an American in wartime England.

JACQUELINE WINSPEAR is the author of the *New York Times* bestsellers *The Consequences of Fear*, *The American Agent*, and *To Die but Once*, as well as thirteen other bestselling Maisie Dobbs novels and *The Care and Management of Lies*, a Dayton Literary Peace Prize finalist. Jacqueline has also published two nonfiction books, *What Would Maisie Do?* and a memoir, *This Time Next Year We'll Be Laughing*. Originally from the United Kingdom, she divides her time between California and the Pacific Northwest.

jacquelinewinspear.com

THE CONSEQUENCES OF FEAR

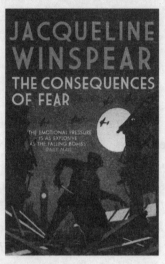

London, October 1941. Freddie Hackett, a message runner for a government office, witnesses an argument that ends in murder. Dismissed by the police when reporting the crime, Freddie turns to private investigator Maisie Dobbs for help. While Maisie believes the boy and wants to help, she must exercise caution given her work with a secret government department spearheading covert operations against the Nazis.

When she stumbles upon the killer in a place she least expects, Maisie soon realises she's been pulled into the orbit of a man who has his own reasons to kill – reasons that go back to another war.

THE AMERICAN AGENT

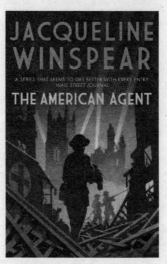

September, 1940. When an American war correspondent's murder is concealed by British authorities, Maisie Dobbs agrees to work alongside an agent of the US Department of Justice to discover the truth.

With German bombs raining down on London, Maisie is torn between the demands of solving this dangerous case and the need to protect a young evacuee. The stakes are raised when she faces the possibility of losing her dearest friend – and that she might be falling in love again.